FREELIGHT

First Edition

August 2018

Should our paths cross in Elysium,
present this page and I will gladly sign.

Savis,

Jon Aspen

FREELIGHT

JON ASPEN

WINTERLEAFE PRESS

MINNEAPOLIS

Winterleafe Press
2751 Hennepin Ave, Suite 704
Minneapolis, MN 55408
https://winterleafe.press

A11B8B95A075F578
D3AE83FC33A210F6
55BEE8A1580D87DD
1FB53E9312647B76

First edition August 2018

ISBN 978-1-948624-00-8
ISBN 978-1-948624-01-5 (ebook)

Printed in the United States of America

For my father, Francis

1948 - 2011

PART ONE

THE THING ABOUT GHOSTS

*First the orange ones hunt you down
oe'r land and sea, city or town.
The violet ones shape your mind like clay
and cut those impure thoughts away.
If you're still not right within the head
the yellow ones will make you dead.*

—The Venator's Rhyme

1

THE SUMMER OF 1889

'Tis a difficult feat to die with a smile on your face. To prevail over the fear, the sorrow, and that instinctual commandment to hold on for just one moment longer. To let go, and to do so without regret. For Raphael and his beloved Elisabeth, the smile was the only thing that mattered now, the only way this injustice might one day be undone.

A smile.

Strange, reflected Raphael, that so much should hinge on such a simple act. And circumstances made that act anything but simple now.

It would be impossible.

"Look at me," called a baritone voice. The words echoed about the dimly lit cavern.

Raphael was afraid to look up. He didn't want to acknowledge the fear, but what difference did it make now? Only the smile mattered, only the acceptance.

They would go together at least.

He was kneeling next to Elisabeth under a veil of soft, violet light. With her hand wrapped tight in his own, Raphael could feel her pulse thumping against his wrist. There they remained, two faces lowered in surrender, two hearts beating fast, ticking down to the end of all things.

It was all his fault.

"*Look* at me," called the voice again.

Raphael sensed the mounting anger. Elisabeth regripped his hand as if trying to soothe him. She was stronger. She knew what had to be done. The smile, the acceptance.

The smiles used to come easy.

Less than a year ago he had married Elisabeth in the Florum way, bare feet touching the earth. With toes turning in warm alabaster sand, he delivered his vows under a late Polynesian sky. Small waves prattled to the beach. Palm trees slipped into feathery black silhouettes. Under the last threads of daylight, Elisabeth's eyes posed a question, and Raphael answered it with a grin and a single whispered word:

Forever.

So they loved and lived and set off to see the world, collecting sunsets like autumn butterflies. They made home in foreign lands and distilled friendships from strangers. But with a single act, everything changed. They became the hunted, and forever became a matter of days.

They fled, getting farther than they'd ever imagined, but Raphael knew it would end here in this cave, just off the shores of Lake Superior on the American side.

Now, a lifetime away from their former bliss they waited in submission like gothic statues before the man who'd soon dispatch them, Supernus Kyzhere. Only he wasn't a man in the usual sense of the word.

He was freelight.

"*LOOK* at me!" roared Supernus, his voice now rippling with anger.

Raphael continued to stare at the rocky floor; part defiance, mostly exhaustion. He watched violet light shimmer off its uneven face. There would be needless pain if he resisted. He wanted it to be quick, for Elisabeth's sake.

This was all his fault.

Raphael arrested his pride. With reluctance, he looked up.

Before him floated Supernus Kyzhere, wreathed in ethereal violet light. He was ascendant as one would conceive a seraph, his presence striking Raphael with awe—beautiful even here in the form of his executioner. Every facet of him was weaved in scintillating light. His penetrating eyes, perched above a triumphant leer; the muscular spread of his neck; even his clothes and the cruel hands that emerged from their vaporous, regal cuffs. Raphael shut his eyes. He tried to remember a time before all of this. A time when his sensibilities were anchored to reason and ghosts were confined to folklore.

Ghost.

That word was the beating heart of the world's most perfectly crafted lie. A ruse so faultless, all humanity had assigned ghosts to the realm of the dead when in fact they were very much alive. They were extraordinary and beautiful and dangerous.

They were freelight.

But with the veil in place, they would never be discovered. The faintlight world would remain blissfully unaware of what was in their midst, right in front of their eyes. Raphael knew their ways. He had dwelled among them in Arbor Florum. And though it had led to this, his unjust demise, he wouldn't have traded a moment of it.

He had *lived.*

Raphael drifted through his memories of Arbor Florum one last time. He saw the city and the great tree of light at its heart. He saw the gardens and the grand thoroughfares, the kaleidoscopic citizenry threading the air above. He shook his head at the impossibility of it all, the freelight-faintlight coexistence.

"You must have known it would come to this," said Supernus, calling his attention back.

Raphael released a wavering exhale. "Yes."

Elisabeth squeezed his hand again, trying to calm him.

"I begged my father for this opportunity, and at last he granted my wish."

Raphael said nothing. He looked past Supernus to the pair of freelight who floated silently at the back of the cavern…the yellow ones. The killers, the *interfectors.* Their light cycled fast and luminous like the morning sun. Raphael had never been able to endure their dead, catatonic stares and was unable to look into their eyes now. So aloof, yet so attuned to the external world, ready to reduce their prey to ashes in the beat of a heart. They'd practice that soon enough.

And then:

For the fifth time in the last hour, a vision flashed into Raphael's field of view. It consumed his senses, washing away the scene of Supernus and his interfectors. This one, from only months ago. He and Elisabeth, clinging to the spire of the Eiffel Tower on a dare, just after it was opened to the public. A cool midnight wind tossed Elisabeth's hair across her cheek. Far below, the faintlight world strolled through the streets of Paris and its *Exposition Universelle.*

Then the vision was gone.

Back to Supernus, smiling and savoring.

"You're seeing the light," said Supernus, gliding up to them. His movement issued a soft melodic hum. The edges of his body rippled like candleflame in a breeze. "What is it like, for one's life to flash before their eyes? I've always wanted to know."

Raphael met his gaze, trying to summon courage. "I trust that even you will know one day."

Supernus bared his teeth and grew radiant like a blacksmith's furnace. Hum became roar, matching his illuminative angst. The cave went bright violet, revealing its walls. Seconds later, both sound and light eased as Supernus reined his temper.

"Perhaps," said Supernus. "But not this day."

Another vision seized Raphael.

He was in a forest in the Russian Empire now. Branches clacked in the winter wind, and the scent of pine laced the air. Elisabeth's breath warmed his cheek as they walked. She clung to his arm and indulged in the local tongue, *"Ne zamyerzni lyubov moya. My pochtee doma!"*

The scene vanished, returning Raphael to the subterranean gloom. The echoes were coming fast now; it wouldn't be long.

"You hunted me down," said Supernus, tracing bright violet fingers through the air. "You exposed me, and now I shall repay the favor."

Raphael felt a bead of sweat fall from his chin. "This isn't revenge."

"But of course it is."

Raphael swallowed, watching tiny points of violet light race up Supernus's neck like shooting stars. This wouldn't end with them. Supernus would hunt Firas next and kill him, and Firas knew *nothing*. The secret would die with them in this cave. No ears remained to hear it. None but its unwitting protector. Raphael felt the weight of it all, knowing he'd find no convert in Supernus. He could only plant a seed of doubt, and perhaps one day…

"Supernus, your father deceives you," said Raphael.

Supernus loosed a derisive grin. "My father keeps no secrets from me."

"I know of at least one, and we are about to die for it." Raphael's antagonism faded. The lines of his face took on desperate contours. "Supernus, please. You don't understand what your father is—"

"He is the DOMINUS STELLARUM!" Supernus blazed into a wrath that rendered the cavern walls bright violet again.

"Supernus!" called Elisabeth through the fury. "Supernus!" Still radiant, his eyes locked onto her. She held his gaze. Her words escaped, reaching him softly, "I forgive you."

Supernus paused.

His expression bled away, leaving one Raphael couldn't quite place, only that her words had struck him deep. Supernus's face flickered toward sorrow. But he suppressed it with vengeance, becoming proud and predatory again. Raphael felt Elisabeth's hand clutch his, trying to reassure him, trying to prepare him. Raphael lowered his chin. From the edge of his vision, he saw Elisabeth do the same.

It was time to let go.

They gazed hard at the ground together, the light of Supernus and his interfectors painting violet-yellow ribbons all the way to their knees. For a moment, there was only silence. Then Supernus spoke a sharp word.

"Nex."

The killing command sent Raphael's heart racing. Elisabeth's hand constricted tight about his own, trying to hold him steady. Raphael looked up, watching the interfectors drift forward from the back of the cavern. With wide eyes and dead expressions they began to flare and grow bright, preparing for the deed.

Trembling, Raphael composed his final thoughts.

If there were to be any justice in this, it *must* begin with the red ghost. It might take a year or ten or a hundred, but one day it would find another. The chosen would be driven mad by the vision of the eyes, just as he was. But if they persisted—*if* they solved its riddle before the freelight world found them, there would be a chance. It was a frail hope, but one Raphael held onto with all his heart. And for any of it to be possible, he had to let go.

His brave, dear Elisabeth already had.

The interfectors began to roar, their presence growing unbearably bright. Raphael drew in a long breath. He closed his eyes for the very last time.

Raphael's life flashed relentlessly before him now. Visions rushed to him like a flood destined to erase its riverbanks. Seasons flew by on five continents. Silhouettes of the world's cities pinned to pastel sunsets. Cosmopolitan marvels of the faintlight world—its music and fashions, its railroads and electric lights stretching across the land like determined vines. He saw Elisabeth for the first time, her amber eyes catching his. A grin broke loose across her face, its sublime curve hinting at a lifetime of adventure and want of a daring accomplice.

Then, further back, deeper into his youth. He saw the soft rolling hills of Tuscany, the land veiled in voluptuous green; he felt the trickle of crushed grapes between his toes during the autumn harvest; he saw the white sails of merchant ships recede into the chronic blue sky over Venice.

Then at last it came.

The vision that didn't belong to him. It was a gift from the red ghost. A pair of eyes looking at him—a woman's. He didn't know who she was or what it meant but wanted to believe the new speculations more than ever. He wanted to believe the eyes represented a person whose time was yet to come. A time when another would carry this vision and continue its story; a time when the world might learn what had happened here and why they had died.

The shearing wail of the interfectors passed beyond physical limits, rendering the last sound Raphael ever heard as a fierce, whistling ring. Deaf now, he squeezed Elisabeth's hand, signaling to her from the rim of oblivion. A single pulse, marking farewell and a lifetime of love. She responded in kind. And with that, they were ready. Together, they pushed through the pain, willing their bodies toward one final act, an immutable declaration to Supernus that he would not win:

They smiled.

Raphael and Elisabeth fell from the bonds of the present and drowned in remembrance of their past. So extraordinary, this life they had lived together. So wrapped in elation, they never recognized the killing stroke when it came.

2

THE MODERN DAY

The Renslit Artists' Cooperative was a block of nineteenth-century brickwork that housed a mercurial band of young tenants. Wielding pencils and paintbrushes, computers, cameras, and clay, their creative fires ran hot through the stubborn cold of the Minnesota winter and diminished as summer approached. Though it was the end of May, the enthusiasm in Loft 303 still burned supernova. At twenty-five years of age, Jordan Wakefield had gone quite mad—that's what his colleagues would say of it. But he didn't give a damn what they thought. Not anymore. He was getting closer.

He knew what she looked like now.

Jordan's weary eyes drifted across the room, his head turning like a weather vane in a just-capable breeze. The walls of his loft were covered in sketches. Women's faces, all composed by his expert hand, nearly photographic in detail. From floor to ceiling, from one side of his loft to the other. At first glance, they were all unique, differing by hairstyle, ethnicity, or facial expression. Upon closer inspection, they were eerily similar in nose, mouth, or the distance between features. In one way they were all the same.

The eyes.

Those eyes stared back at him now in clinical silence. Like members of a cult, they waited with rapt attention before their creator, wanting to know why he had brought them into existence. Like all proper creators, Jordan ignored them. They were unworthy now; they were his lessers.

With the remnant stub of a charcoal pencil in his hand, he stood before his masterpiece. His sketching hand pulsed pain with every beat of his heart. On a vellum board, taller than a door and twice as wide, he had rendered the image of a woman weeping. A stunning work of artistry, created over a five-day marathon. A product of sheer revelation. With hands hanging limp at his sides, he whispered to the colossal image.

"I'm going to find you."

The charcoal stub fell from his grasp, hitting the floor with a tiny pat. He backed away slowly, studying the image with zeal: the long dark hair that poured down the sides of her oval face, strands of it cast across her cheek at the want of the wind; her skin tone, a touch lighter than his own; her eyebrows, expressive arcs, gently rounded, not sharp in the path they took above her eyes; her mouth, beautiful and supple, but trembling with emotion. And her eyes...those eyes...

They were his life's purpose. Striking and beautiful, but this time with tears streaming from them. In the background coursed a violent darkness, which he did not yet understand. It moved like a storm, the clouds pitch-black in constitution like plumes of soot. But they were too far away to discern with any clarity, too out of focus. The scene was a perfect replication of the vision inside his head. He discovered it in full only days ago. It appeared to him in four-second exhibitions, whenever he called upon it.

A knock at the door broke Jordan's trance.

"Just brought your ladies back," said his hall-mate Maggie, shoving the door open with her backside and pushing her way in. She dragged in two framed sketches. "I shot these and loaded them to the co-op's website—HOLY FUCK you look like shit! What happened to you—were you trapped in a coal mine?"

"Oh good, you're here." Jordan rubbed his face, smearing sweat-glazed charcoal across his cheek. He marched up to Maggie and took her hands with a grand smile. "Maggie, get your camera. I need a shot of this." Jordan gestured with his chin to his masterpiece. "I want it on the co-op's website. Tonight."

Maggie's eyes were already all over it. She swallowed hard. "It's incredible, but…but…" Her face was more distressed than the one in his creation. "You're not feeling well, are you?"

"Never better." Jordan released her hands.

"You don't look it," said Maggie. Her blue eyes scrutinized him from under a disheveled nest of strawberry blonde hair.

Jordan marched over to a plank swing that hung at the edge of his loft's work area, an inventive transplant from his hometown. He dropped into it, wrapping his arms around the ropes.

"How about we get a beer and talk." Maggie approached him cautiously. "And I'll shoot it tomorrow…or maybe you could get some sleep?"

"No. Tonight—and we'll still do beers." Jordan lurched out of the swing. "We have to celebrate—listen, it doesn't have to be perfect with the lights and umbrellas. Just shoot it hand-held and get it online right away—oh, and I need the digital afterward. There's something else I want to do."

"What do you want me to call it?" said Maggie, trying to digest Jordan's rapid requests. "They need a title for each piece on the website."

Jordan stared into the giant image. After a series of blinks, he returned with an answer: "Have You Seen This Person?—that's what I want to call it."

"Um, alright…okay." Maggie stared at him with unease. "I'll shoot it. Go take a damn shower."

* * *

An hour later, Jordan sat down with Maggie at a table in the Pilgrim Cat, a local dive attached to the backside of their cooperative. With daylight fading, the bar's neon lights were taking over the heavy lifting. A shower and a shave had marched his appearance back toward acceptable, but he drooped with regularity while eating a plate of quesadillas like a wolf. All the while, he spied an unsettling gravity in Maggie.

"So, we're celebrating tonight, are we?" asked Maggie.

Still chewing, Jordan nodded and waved his fork like a conductor's baton.

"Nobody's seen you in days." Maggie leaned forward, folding her hands. "You had *WORKING* on your chalkboard, but we couldn't hear a thing in there. We thought you were dead. I volunteered to check."

"I was working at night." Jordan chewed ferociously. "Mostly."

Maggie's fingers drummed the tabletop nervously. "They're going to kick you out, Jordan. You have 'til the end of June."

Jordan stopped chewing. He sighed through his nostrils and felt his body go lax. *Here it comes.*

"You came in six years ago with the most talented hand in three hundred miles, but they don't see you like that anymore. You're a mad scientist. You didn't even respond to their request to make your case. They won't take you seriously when you're skipping exhibitions and relying on a day job."

"Well, it shouldn't be a problem anymore. I lost the day job."

Maggie grimaced. "How are you getting by?"

"On rice, mostly…"

"This is not a joke!"

"…and the money I borrowed from Steks."

"The drug dealer?" Maggie jolted up from her stool. She burned a stare into him before sinking back down.

Jordan chewed and shrugged. "Remember when we all did New Year's resolutions and vowed to stick to them? Well, this was mine. I had to let some things slide, like paying gigs. I guess I dug a hole."

"And Steks is going to bury you in it." Maggie slapped her palms on the table, nearly toppling her bottle. "Jesus leper-loving-mother-fucking Christ, Jordan! How could you do this?"

"I was broke, but it doesn't matter now. I had a breakthrough."

"You mean a breakdown?"

Jordan tossed her a cross look and took a swig of beer.

"You want your teeth knocked out with a wrench?" Maggie's anxiety nearly levitated her off her stool. "That's Steks's thing you know—how bad is this?"

Jordan picked at his bottle's label like a scab. "Two thousand, plus…whatever. And my watch."

"Fuck, man!"

"I'll buy the next round."

"You're not buying shit!" Maggie pinned his hands to the table like she was trying to prevent him from falling overboard. After a heavy second, she let go and stomped off to the bar. She returned a minute later and slid a beer over to him. "So what are we celebrating? Do I really want to know?"

"You ready for it?" asked Jordan, his attention flicking up to her.

Maggie shrugged. "Why the hell not."

"Remember a few years back, when you came out to your parents—how they already knew, and you knew they knew, but it was still difficult to say it?"

"Yeah, you were there, remember?" Maggie's taut posture sunk, her frustration faded. "Couldn't have done it without you. My dad would've ended me and buried me in the back yard had you not been there as a potential witness." Maggie half-giggled and went silent.

Jordan gave her a reassuring smile. "Well, now it's my turn. This is me coming out."

Maggie scrunched her expression. "You tellin' me you like dudes now?"

"No—"

"Didn't think so."

Jordan shifted uneasily in his seat, forcing himself to meet her eyes. "But I do have a secret."

"Yeah?" Maggie tented her fingers as if unable to find a more suitable gesture.

"I have a vision," said Jordan.

Maggie winced. "Like…Steve Jobs. Or Zuckerberg?"

"No, more like Joan of Arc."

Maggie closed her eyes and took a stuttered breath.

"When I was eleven," Jordan slid his beer bottle from one hand to the other, "I went on this camping trip near my hometown. Remote cabin, secluded lake. I saw a ghost there—a red one. I was—"

"RED?" Maggie sounded like a car revving its engine.

"Yes, red." Jordan scratched at his neck. "I was in a rowboat stargazing, and this tiny wisp of red light floated by. Then it came back and hovered in front of me. It grew into this…thing. But it didn't have a face. That's all I really remember."

"Ok-aaaay." Maggie looked ready to run out of the bar.

"The adults had the cabin, the kids had tents. I don't know why, but I wanted to see the stars. So I snuck out. I saw the red ghost and blacked out. When I came to, it was gone. I've tried to find the thing for years. I'm not sure it's really out there—"

"You don't say—"

"—but here's the thing. It gave me a vision. And I still have that vision."

Maggie paused and resumed reluctantly. "A woman's eyes?"

"Yup." Jordan stole a slug of beer. "But it was only a flicker; a pair of eyes that appear in my field of vision as if real. Looking right at me. Thirty-one inches away, but they vanish in under a second. Just like *that*." Jordan snapped his fingers for effect, startling her. "It's always the same. I can make it happen whenever I want."

"Like right now?

"If I want to."

 Maggie examined the open air between them nervously.

"It's like a lighter that only sparks no matter how many times you spin the wheel. There's never a flame. That's what all my previous sketches were about, just a flash of those eyes. For fourteen years I've been trying to guess at the rest."

"And when you said you had a breakdown—"

"Breakthrough. Two weeks ago, happened entirely by accident. I was on the bluffs sketching, and these kids were playing soccer and their words triggered it."

"Triggered what?" Maggie pulled at the coils of her hair.

"A bigger vision—the sketch you just photographed. But that one is different. It takes over all my senses. For four seconds, it's like I am somewhere else."

"This also happens whenever you want it to?"

"Yeah, like this." Jordan placed his arms on the tabletop to steady himself. His expression went freeze-frame. Eyes wide, glassy and petrified like a mannequin, as if time itself had stopped. Four seconds later he was back.

"Fuck, man, don't do that!" Maggie jerked her head back as if retreating to a quarantine space. "That's creepy as shit. Is this real or are you fucking with me?"

"It's real." Jordan dropped his hands into his lap. "What can I say, Maggs? I'm a man with a vision."

"This is so much worse than I thought." Maggie struggled to look at him. "Jordan, as artists we have social license to act like *that*, but there are still limits. You need to see someone. You can't go around talking like this."

"Why not?"

"Because it's fucked up—it's fantasy."

"Everyone gets by on fantasy, Maggs. Think about it." Jordan tapped the sides of his bottle with busy fingers. "We constantly fantasize about a better tomorrow. We do horoscopes, we wish on shooting stars, we pray into the void. And we do it because people taught us to do it. It's all herd mentality."

"So what are you getting out of *your* fantasy?"

"That's my point." Jordan leaned forward and Maggie leaned away, seesaw-fashion. "It's not fantasy. It really happened to me, and I'm not afraid to say it anymore." Jordan watched her throat move like she was swallowing a brick. "I'm going to find her. I have to find her."

Maggie took a shaky breath. "You tell your dad about this?"

Jordan's expression fell flat. "Not yet. But I will. I wanted to start with someone open-minded, like you."

Maggie released pressure from her stare.

"I nearly have this figured out," said Jordan. "I'm getting closer."

"To the loony bin?" muttered Maggie to the floor.

Jordan glared at her.

"I'm sorry." Maggie grasped his fingertips. "I'm having trouble adjusting to this new you."

Jordan pulled his fingers free.

"So how are you going to find her?"

"With the photograph you took. The co-op's website is just a start. I have to spread it around, like the police or the FBI. It's the social media age, Maggs. Someone out there knows who she is." Maggie delivered a pallid nod to the logic, though Jordan continued to detect despair in her eyes.

With averted gazes, they remained silent for some time, letting a jazz tune carry the conversation. The few remaining patrons of the Wednesday night crowd filtered out, leaving a bearded bartender slumped in his stool, watching a muted television.

Jordan felt cooled now, his body less agitated. "There's something you need to understand. I put my life into this. It has to mean something. I've done nothing else."

"What do you want from it?" asked Maggie, her voice also gentler. "Your life, that is."

"Something that means something." Jordan shrugged, tilting his head to the side. "I don't want to collect shiny consumer shit. I don't want forty hours and a mortgage. I don't want to fade into the polite American void."

"Jordan, listen, you're just having your quarterlife—I mean we all live ordinary lives in the end. We might not matter in the greater scheme of things, but—"

"I don't need to be anyone that matters." Jordan's eyes found hers again. "I just want to be part of something that matters."

"Mystery woman gets you there?"

"Maybe." Jordan knew it was a weak claim.

"You're all over the map, Jordan," said Maggie gently. "You need some sleep."

"I know." Jordan stared into the table.

The moment softened Maggie. Her shoulders sunk, and her tight-jaw appraisal faded. Her expression became a safe harbor again, allowing the conversation to slip into pleasant reminiscence. A few beers later, they wandered back to the Renslit. Parting ways, Jordan walked the quiet hall to his door alone.

Once inside, he flipped on a lamp and went to the swing. He surveyed its worn plank where his name was cut crudely, recalling the summer day when his fourteen-year-old self carved it with a pocket knife. Sitting down, he wrapped his arms around the ropes to prevent himself from falling. He imagined the magic words, the ones that conjured the vision. They had issued from a boy's lips, responding to his mother:

I don't know what you want me to do.

A cracking sound blasted through Jordan's head like a point-blank lightning strike. The world in front of his eyes buckled and vanished as if sucked into a jet engine. Jordan was standing now. It was pitch black. She was there with him—directly in front of him. Her eyes were unmistakable. Tears were streaming down her cheeks. Her mouth quivered while she stared at him, her face lit by flashes of distant lightning. His body was tense, prepared to fight or run. His right hand felt distended, as though his fingers were floating away. He tried to look at them, but his head would not obey. When he tried to speak, his mouth would not open; when he tried to move, his body refused. They just stood there, looking at each other while an icy wind whipped them.

And then, a second thundering crack.

Jordan was back in the real world again, still sitting on the swing. Leaning forward, with the ropes holding him at the elbows, his jaw juddered and his eyes blurred up with tears. He blinked them away, listening to tiny wet pecks hit the floor. Words escaped his lips in a frightened whisper, "What the hell is happening to me?"

Then he paused. His mind went into reverse.

A realization shot through him, something he'd missed until now. Securing himself, he called upon the vision again. Four seconds later he returned with something new. He saw it during the moments of darkness, between the flashes of lightning: the underside of her face was lit by a faint crimson glow.

The red ghost.

It was there with them in the darkness.

3

BROAD STROKES
AND ROUGH EDGES

Jordan slept in late and woke rested. Five seconds into his day he sprung to his feet, horrified at his confession to Maggie. He paced and cringed, and cursed at the bathroom mirror until he thought it might break. Ill-conceived words from the night prior pelted his conscience, adding to a swamp of problems that already mired his quest for the mystery woman.

It got worse.

He sat down at his drafting table and thumbed through a stack of tri-folded papers, ones he'd been trying to forget. A credit card bill with a big positive number, a bank statement with a negative, and a repo notice on his car to claim the triple crown of fiscal fuckups.

Next was their co-op's website. It targeted locals and wouldn't reach a Jack-shit's percentage of the world. Since he wasn't law enforcement, he couldn't marshal a nationwide hunt based on the sketch of a crying woman. He'd have to go it alone, concoct some sort of clever, viral social media play. That would take time, which also meant it would take money. Getting tossed out at the end of June left him a month to get his shit together and find a new place. And then there was Steks and his guerilla dentistry, which already had Jordan counting teeth with his tongue.

The unpleasant truth coasted in like a sick fog. His fate rested in the hands of the urban professionals who'd descend on the scene in two days, looking to decorate their upscale pads. He had no idea what these damn people wanted but would have to create a lot of it fast.

Mystery woman might have to wait.

He needed a plan, but a more pressing need for caffeine sent his anxious feet out the door to the local coffee shop. He returned, ready and renewed, marching the Renslit's halls with such deep focus that he failed to hear steps catching up behind him. A hand seized him by the shoulder and spun him around. It slammed him into the wall. Out of reflex, Jordan knocked the grip loose and shoved his assailant back.

Steks.

The grip returned in a flash, grabbing Jordan's chin and pushing it skyward. A metallic click later, he felt a knife tip at his throat.

"Dumb fuckin' move, Wakefield." Steks released the chin-grip but maintained the knife. "Now look at me. Tell me where my money is."

Jordan lowered his chin slowly, feeling the cold metal point under it. Steks's coal-black eyes panned into view, along with a facial tattoo and a riled sneer. Jordan assessed his muscular arm and shoulder. They both had a physique shy of athletic, suggesting an even match. But Jordan hadn't thrown a punch since high school, and guys like this were practiced in this shit. Plus, the knife.

Steks raised his wrist in front of Jordan's face, dangling a fancy watch on it. "Have to say, Wakefield, I'm really liking the timepiece. Gonna be mine forever if you don't pay up."

Jordan caught his own pissed-off reflection in the watchface.

"Shoulda asked your old man for help." Steks lowered the watch hand and used his palm to hold Jordan to the wall. "If he bought you this, he must have money. Or else he's as stupid with it as you are."

Jordan struggled to prune his rage before he spoke. "The art crawl's in two days. That's when we sell the most. I'll have it all by Monday."

"Yeah?" Steks retracted the knife. "Better be true for your sake." Steks smiled at him for a moment. Then he drew a fast throaty inhale and spit a stringy gob square into Jordan's eye.

Jordan cursed through clenched teeth and started to retaliate. The knife flicked back to his neck.

"Fucking leave it, or it'll be your blood next." Steks loitered with an epic smile, waiting for Jordan to settle. Then he folded and pocketed the knife. "By Monday…and it's two-seven now."

Jordan bit his lower lip. Road-flare wrath burned inside his skull. He tried to blink away the runny-egg assault.

"You wanna keep that nice white smile, right?" Steks put his hand on Jordan's shoulder and pulled him close.

Jordan took in the smell of garlic-sodden something.

"Make me happy again, Wakefield."

Jordan granted him a tiny nod and Steks's hand came off his shoulder. Like a rat trap, it whipped back fast, cracking Jordan hard across the face. Steks laughed as he swaggered off. Jordan caged his tongue and wiped his face clean with a trembling hand. As he listened to Steks's boot heels clang down the metal stairwell, he splurged on a quick fantasy. He imagined landing his own heel square in the back of that piece of shit, sending him to the ground floor like a diver. With that satisfying visual out of the way, Jordan got back to work.

Mystery woman would definitely have to wait.

Back inside, Jordan locked his door, washed up, and cleared his drafting table. He swallowed down white-hot frustration. It came back up through his hand. First was a panoramic party scene—no time for minutiae, only broad strokes, edge detail, and motion. Arms and exuberant profiles raising drinks high in the air, bodies swaying in dance. It was good charcoal scrape, but its attitude demanded release from monochrome, so he slashed in some reds and blues. This gave it a patriotic vibe, and he imagined some young, conservative-banker type snapping it up. With a smirk, Jordan sketched Che Guevara into the background, beret and all. It would pass notice until up on the wall.

Bankers blow.

Next came some Frankenstein cityscapes. He hammered out Saint Paul's skyline from memory, replacing the State Capitol with the

Eiffel Tower. Then Minneapolis, where he swapped the IDS Center for the Empire State Building. After leftover Chinese takeout for dinner, he did Chicago, planting Saint Basil's Cathedral on Navy Pier. The final piece, which wrapped up shy of Friday morning, was Godzilla hugging the Statue of Liberty with Manhattan in the background—why the hell not?

Jordan crashed on the couch and woke late in the afternoon. Through the home stretch, he dashed out still lifes; bottles of wine, fruit, and other mundane artifacts. He finished these late into the evening and priced them all under a hundred. Moving into the preparation phase, he found his masterpiece too big for the hallway, so he positioned it line-of-sight from his door. He tagged the earlier works in the high-hundreds and easeled them into the hall with the cheap ones at their feet. The crowds were just starting to filter in. Across the way, Jordan spied Maggie. She pinned her stare to his every move like he was a rabid dog. Jordan gave her a thumbs-up and smiled. After a flat moment, she returned the gesture, and with that they were underway.

A lively banter, sweetened with compliments, laughter, and veiled sales pitches, filled the air while music issued through the halls. Out of the gate, Jordan's enthusiasm flared like a tumbler of whiskey pitched into a fire. Yet fatigue dragged him down fast. After half an hour, he set a folding chair in his doorway and sat down. He smiled at the passersby, which worked for a few minutes. Then he faded into terminal slouching.

Then his eyes slid shut.

He took in the sounds around him, creeping closer to slumber. Voices came closer, then receded. Footsteps escalated, then faded. Everything had a distinct cadence. Most pleasing was a pendulum pattern, clacking out slower than the span of an actual second, as though time itself were slowing down. Jordan locked onto it with the intent of riding it to sleep. Then it vanished. Jordan's consciousness prepared to depart the wakeful world nonetheless. But it was arrested by a voice:

"What inspired this?"

Jordan's faculties reengaged. Sound took focus. He processed the words that had floated into his ears. He opened his eyes to find a man standing before him, hands crossed over the top of a cane. They were well-manicured hands—Jordan noticed this first. Jordan's eyes drifted up. A dark navy blue suit, impeccable and pressed, fit the man's frame perfectly. Reaching the apex of his study, Jordan found an olive complexion, dark brown eyes, and a face wrapped in a trimmed white beard. The man presented a pleasant countenance, which did seem to be waiting, quite patiently, for his response.

"I was wondering what inspired your work. The one inside." He pointed past Jordan to the masterpiece, while his other hand remained fixed on the cane. "Do you know this woman?"

Jordan suppressed a grin; the man had clearly not seen the sketch's title on the website. "No, I made her up. Mostly." The man lifted his chin as if performing the first motion of a nod, a strange flicker of skepticism in his eye.

Jordan got to his feet.

"Are you from around here?" asked the man.

"Yes—well, not originally. I'm from a small town in Michigan. Ironwood, it's nowhere—"

"A Yooper then?"

"I'm impressed." Jordan paused. "Not many people know that word."

"I'm well-traveled, and my name's Christopher Johnson." He offered his hand.

"Nice to meet you," said Jordan, shaking it. "Jordan Wakefield."

"A pleasure." Christopher's gaze lingered on him a bit long. "May I take a closer look?"

Jordan moved aside and waved him into his loft. "Of course."

Christopher ambled inside and up to the sketch, the colossal image staring down at him like a deity. Jordan moved in next to him to catch the reaction. Christopher's eyes narrowed and darted about in sharp movements. All the while, he gripped and re-gripped his cane.

"When did you do this?" asked Christopher, his eyes still locked on the work.

"Finished it a few days ago."

"It's extraordinary." Christopher blinked his gaze loose. He looked to Jordan. "I'd like to buy it. How much is the piece?"

Jordan paused. He didn't actually intend or expect to sell it. Having never considered a price, he fired off a number: "Twenty thousand."

Christopher turned away. He cane-tapped toward the door with haste. The name *Steks* pounded at Jordan's head; everything could be fixed with a single sale, at even half that price. Jordan's nervous feet stammered while his mind kicked into a repricing debate. Jordan turned around with five thousand on his lips. Christopher's cane caught the backside of the door and whipped it closed. He turned to face Jordan.

"Agreed," said Christopher, his eyes running a fast semi-circle about the room, noting the other sketches. "But with a few conditions."

Jordan struggled to secure his open-mouth stare.

"I have a gallery in San Francisco, and I have particular tastes. I'd like you to pay a visit and see if you fit. I'll pay three thousand now, and the rest when you come out west." Christopher's gaze slipped back to the masterpiece. "I will trust the piece to your care until then. Do we have a deal?"

Trying not to over-smile, Jordan marched up to him and shook his hand. "It's yours."

Christopher went to the kitchenette and snapped down a business card. He began to write out a check. "I'll leave my assistant's information with you. Call him with your itinerary." Christopher tore the check loose and made his way back to Jordan, glancing across the wall of sketches on the way. "Oh, and one more thing."

"What is it?"

"I want you to take the image down from that website." Christopher leaned closer to Jordan. "Exclusivity is a critical facet of the art market. I want the piece to make a formal debut at my gallery, which means we don't want record of a prior showing."

Jordan leaked a polite smile. "Consider it done."

With that, the conversation slipped into the smallest of small talk, a sequence of pleasantries so deftly delivered Jordan only recognized a possible choreography long after they'd parted ways. Tired and defocused, he rode the night out with no further sales. During it all, his mind chimed two words at a regular interval:

San Francisco.

After the show, just shy of midnight, Maggie filled Jordan's plastic wine glass with an unsteady hand, sending splashes to the floor. She sauntered over to a painter named Blake who was examining Jordan's grand creation.

"All the way from San Francisco?" asked Blake, pinching his chin between thumb and index finger. His free hand cradled a glass of wine.

"I guess so. It was all business. He came, wrote a check, and ghosted."

Blake turned and walked to Jordan with the gait of a museum curator. "Just as well. You *are* going out there, aren't you?"

"Yeah, I'm going."

Blake raised his glass. "Well then, to a good night. May we all stay ahead of obscurity, or at least poverty."

After the toast, Maggie and Blake returned to their wine-fueled chatter while Jordan's mind worked on a math problem. Between fixing his bank account, staving off credit problems, and buying a flight to San Francisco, he couldn't pay Steks.

He had to cut some corners.

Despite the risk, an optimistic fire prodded Jordan. His new-found benefactor had deep pockets and an established gallery, which bode well for his near-term prospects. Yet something in the way the man absorbed his masterwork suggested more. Christopher Johnson might not be interested in his art at all. It might be those eyes that had his attention the whole time.

And that meant he knew who she was.

4

COMFORTABLE SHOES

Early Saturday morning, Jordan texted Maggie, disclosing his plan to skip town on account of Steks. After wilting under the condescending gaze of a bank teller, he drove to the Minneapolis side of the metro. Waiting for the check to clear, he bounced between twenty-four-hour stores and park-and-rides at night. During the day, he lounged in city parks, reading Dostoyevsky's *The Brothers Karamazov* under shade trees. After his bank account was a go again, he secured a flight and called Christopher Johnson's assistant with the plan. A text came rolling in moments later:

> Thought ur funny giving me a fake cell motherfucker?
> Got the real one off one of your pals. U skip town?
> Answer me u fuck.

Jordan's jaw went tight. His finger hung over the screen. Before he could respond, another message from Steks:

> I know u see this.
> Answer me or I'll smash your fucking watch right now.

Jordan glared at his phone while his index finger stabbed away:

> Please don't I'll have it next week
> Have to travel to get the rest

An immediate response:

> Its three five now. SIX if u want the watch back.
> Gonna hurt you for this.
> U know why they call me the dentist?

Jordan slammed his phone down on the park lawn. He tried to return to his book, but circumstances pushed his thoughts away from Russian literature. Grabbing his phone, he started to stalk his benefactor-to-be online. After an hour, his phone ran red-hot from use. A Gordian knot of panic barged into his stomach, ramming up against the one Steks had already built: there was nothing of an art gallery under the name Christopher Johnson in San Francisco, despite an ocean of unrelated hits to the name itself; nothing for Eli Windali, the name on his assistant's card. There wasn't even a gallery name on the card! No ties or leads from galleries that *did* exist in the Bay Area.

Not a single detail checked out.

But he was locked and loaded. He had to squeeze money out of this gig somehow or he was fucked. This thought plagued him throughout the rollercoaster lifts and dips of his first-ever flight. With forehead pressed to the cool airplane window, he watched the checkerboard farmlands of the Midwest slide away, wondering if it might be a viable move to never return.

At San Francisco International Airport, Jordan shuffled through the crowds while scrolling his phone to Christopher's assistant, Eli. He tapped the name to life. While it rang, Jordan scanned the crowd, looking for the man he thought might match the voice. It was an energetic one, anxious and precise in pronunciation, bearing an accent he pinned to Africa. He spied a man holding a sign that read "Mr. Jordan." The man was lifting a phone to his ear.

"Never mind, Eli. I see you…Bye."

Jordan watched Eli pocket the phone and tip his chin down, searching the crowd over the top of his large-framed glasses. Spotting Jordan, Eli broke into a polite smile, pushing the glasses up the bridge of his nose. Eli was short and thin, clean shaven, and of dark complexion. Like Christopher Johnson, he was very well dressed.

"Welcome to San Francisco," said Eli, extending his hand. "I left without your last name." He held the sign like it was a menu. "I usually don't make mistakes like that."

"No problem."

"This way, then." Eli walked toward the doors but stopped suddenly. Jordan almost bowled him over. "Any luggage?"

"Just my backpack." Jordan jostled it.

"This way, then." Eli adjusted his glasses again and resumed a brisk pace. They weaved the airport grounds, arriving at a jet black Mercedes. Jordan slipped inside, sinking into plush leather. The accommodation boosted his spirits, shifting his perception back toward legitimacy. He let his limbs go slack, allowing the seat to swallow him up as they drove off.

"I'm afraid Christopher Johnson is not available to see you this afternoon." Eli glanced in the rear-view mirror. "But he wished to have dinner this evening. Shall I tell him you'll accept?"

"Sure," said Jordan. "I have nowhere else to be. Are we going to the gallery now?"

Eli paused, his eyes dodging out of the rear-view mirror. "I'm taking you to your hotel. We hadn't planned on…" Eli drifted lanes and yanked the car back, causing Jordan to rap his head off the window. "Sorry for that. Traffic moves fast out here."

"The gallery, are we—"

"Mr. Johnson will show it to you personally, but *not* now." Eli tapped on the radio with an agitated finger, causing Jordan to relent. A few songs later they arrived at the Palace Hotel in the heart of San Francisco, a venue that matched its namesake. A regal accommodation to Jordan's eyes, especially compared to a week of sleeping in his car.

Eli departed, leaving Jordan to seek out a late, street-side lunch, which boosted his spirits. He felt a pinch of bliss, being in an unfamiliar place. New city, new perspective. He wondered if he could call the place home, despite its insane cost of living. Trying the idea on like a new pair of shoes, he felt something of a fit, but a need for wearing in. If his life *was* to be spent plumbing the depths of his vision, what better place to bathe in crazy than San Francisco? Besides, Steks couldn't reach him out here.

New city, new start.

Arriving back in his room around five, Jordan showered and was ready to go by six. He culled humble dinner attire from his backpack: blue jeans, a red t-shirt, and a black hoodie. His phone rang. He plucked it off the bed and took a seat at the window sill.

"Hey Dad," said Jordan.

"Just wanted to see how things were going out there," came his father's voice in diced-up, rural digital. "Heading back from bowling."

"About to go to dinner here. With the gallery owner I told you about."

"So things *are* going well."

Jordan hesitated. "Well, we haven't talked yet. He was unavailable for the day."

"Did you see the gallery?"

"Not yet," Jordan hesitated some more. "It's been a bit disorganized and…odd, but—"

"Are you safe?"

Jordan avoided letting his sigh reach the phone. "Yeah Dad, I'm safe. It's an old man and his assistant. The guy's check cashed. He's legit and there's a bigger check coming, as I said."

"Don't want to be the one to say it seems too good to be true—"

"Then *don't*." Jordan drummed frustrated fingers against the window pane. "Be happy for me. This might be a good thing out here." Jordan listened to the wind hitting the receiver for a while; no words. Not initially.

"Pretty long ways from home, Jordan. Expensive place."

"It's just a possibility, that's all I'm saying." Silence resumed. Jordan listened to his father open the front door and kick off his shoes.

"Listen, I want to ask you something," said his father.

"What is it?"

"Do you *love* your art thing, Jordan?"

Jordan dragged his hand through his hair.

"High school was seven years ago, and you did the art thing—I mean, you're doing the art thing, but is it what you really want? You could be doing something better, like drafting or engineering. It's creative, but realistic. Like a practical pistachio."

"Like what?" Jordan rumpled his brow.

"A practical pecan…pistachio—*who's* that famous painter?"

"Picasso, Dad."

"A practical Picasso," said his father with enthusiasm. "A friend of mine here, his son's going to Tech this fall. The kid's not even close to your talent with a pencil—"

"Dad, that's a different discipline. There's math and computers—"

"Just hear me out, Jordan. I know there's more to it than that, but that's what going to college is about. It's learning those things in addition to your natural talent—and you've got loads of natural talent. I'm just asking you to consider it."

"There's debt, Dad. Lots and lots of debt, and that's not good for me." Jordan went silent for a moment, hoping that would be the end of it. He sensed his father assembling further volleys. "Did I ever tell you what I did at the bank?"

"Not exactly…you type a lot of stuff into computers right?"

"Yes, and—"

"See! There's computers. Now it's just the math part."

Jordan shook his head. "I did data entry for accounts that defaulted. Student loan debts, Dad. A bunch of kids my age who had hopes and dreams, really expensive ones that went to hell because there's not enough of those jobs. Now they can't pay them back."

"Doesn't mean it will happen to you."

"I'd be thirty years old by the time I graduate. Who would want a thirty-year-old beginner when there'd be an army of younger ones?"

"I'd hire you."

"Well, that's nice, Dad, but you're not the one doing the hiring." A pause.

"Wait a minute…what do you mean *did* at the bank?" asked his father. "You're talking like you—"

"I don't work there anymore."

"What happened?" His father's riled breath hit the phone.

"Does it matter?" Jordan rubbed the side of his face so hard it felt like sandpaper.

"Just answer the question—"

"Things fell apart."

"Fell apart—what does that mean? When do you *grow up* Jordan?"

"When—do—I—grow—up?" repeated Jordan in cold, seething monotone. He clenched his fist and dragged it across the window pane, producing a squeegee sound.

"I'm worried about you. You're so distant. I want to know you're okay. It's just the two of us now."

"I know." Jordan opened his fist and tipped his forehead against the window. "I'm okay. I'm just going through some stuff." A double-beep interrupted the conversation. Jordan looked at his phone and saw Eli's call. "Dad, the gallery assistant is calling—I have to go." He tapped over to Eli without saying goodbye.

"Jordan, it's Eli. I'll be out front in a minute. Are you ready?"

"Yeah."

"Good…make sure to bring a jacket. It gets cool around here at night. Wear comfortable shoes too…if you have them."

Jordan crumpled his expression at the request, while Eli's voice stumbled through some unintelligible words. Eli returned with clarity: "I'll be there shortly."

Jordan stared at his phone and bounced it in the palm of his hand before leaving the room. He looked down at his shoes. He rocked back and forth on them. They were comfortable.

5

AWKWARD QUESTIONS

Through a tinted car window, the red-orange cables of the Golden Gate Bridge flitted past as Jordan looked westward into the expanse of the Pacific Ocean. Daylight was fading, leaving a gentler light in its stead that lit rocky formations jutting into the waters at the far end of the bridge. Outside of a mundane inquiry into whether or not he had any food allergies, Eli had said little since picking him up. Though Jordan wanted to probe, he surrendered to the fact that his host was setting the agenda. He wanted to play it cool, but something kept his feet fidgeting and his fingers scraping at the car-seat leather.

As the exterior world's west coast pastels flew by, Jordan kept circling back to a single detail, which stood out like a red flag in a winter-white landscape: the Saint Paul art crawl was attended by locals. Yet here he was, in San Francisco at the behest of a high-rolling benefactor, who emerged out of nowhere on the heels of his work hitting the internet.

Exquisite homes on Pacific hillsides kept racing by. Jordan's mind went to work on a second theory. His mysterious patron wasn't mysterious at all. Christopher had a talented eye and he had a talented hand. That such things would find each other was inevitable. Should the evening go as planned, he'd pole-vault his peers at the co-op, professionally and financially. That would solve the Steks problem and he'd get his watch back. His ambitions took a step further: his career would achieve liftoff. His work would appear in a gallery whose owner fired off five-figure checks and had an assistant driving S-Class.

The car came to a stop.

Jordan's nerves kicked him toward a conservative game plan. The fact that this Christopher Johnson now constituted his entire income stream tamed his desire to venture forth with questionable questions. He would be pleasant, attentive, and try not to say anything particularly stupid.

"We're here," announced Eli.

Jordan disengaged from his thoughts to find an architectural masterpiece outside the car window. An Immaculate cobblestone driveway; perfectly manicured landscaping; meticulous stonework running across the face of the two-story home. Eli opened the door, allowing Jordan to emerge. With his eyes still climbing the estate, Jordan's head issued some last minute advice:

Don't fuck this up.

Quaint stone paths ran in front of the home, split, and curled away to unknown places behind. The colors of the structure and its appointments intermingled with the hillside and a dense growth of redwoods, aesthetically unifying it, making it feel secluded and far-removed from the notion of urban life.

"Shall we go in?" asked Eli.

Jordan realized he was still standing next to the car. "Yeah."

"This way, then." Eli led him to the foyer. "Let me call on Mr. Johnson. He'd like to show you around personally."

Eli departed. After a minute, Jordan heard the tip-tap sound of a cane. He straightened his posture, crossing his hands in front of his waist like a groomsman at a wedding. Finding it awkward, he shifted his hands to his pockets. Now he thought he looked like someone waiting for a bus. Before he could find another pose, Christopher arrived in a casual button-down shirt and a navy blue suit jacket.

"Mr. Wakefield," he said, extending a hand. "A pleasure to see you again."

"Thanks for having me." Jordan yanked his hand out of his pocket so fast he almost ejected his phone with it. He was too enthusiastic on the handshake too.

"I apologize we couldn't tour the gallery this afternoon. I trust dinner and illuminating conversation will be an adequate substitute?" He put his hand on Jordan's shoulder. "Come, now. Let me give you the nickel tour while Eli prepares dinner."

Jordan crouched and began to take his shoes off.

"Please, leave them on. The floors get cold in the evening."

"Just a force of habit. Don't want to track dirt in."

Christopher rapped his cane against the floor. "Leave them on. I insist."

Jordan retied his shoes and stood up. Eli breezed into the room with two glasses of wine and handed them off. Though Jordan lacked experience, he was certain this wine was tiers above any he'd had before. Christopher guided him through the picturesque home, pointing out its architectural highlights, making deep commentary on its many works of art—all of which Jordan found pleasing. After viewing the grounds behind, which comprised a courtyard, a guest cottage, and a thick wall of redwoods, Christopher brought him to a windowless, circular library that occupied a full two floors.

Jordan meandered to the center of the room, which must have spanned forty feet. Grinning wonderment, he turned in a slow circle, hands out to his sides to balance against vertigo. Every surface that wasn't occupied by books or artwork was faced with dark, dramatic woods, harboring complex patterns.

"This is amazing," mumbled Jordan, completing his carousel rotation.

Then he saw the painting.

It hooked him through the eyes. With a silent siren call, it beckoned him to come closer. So he did. It was a stunning work in a faded gold frame, depicting a woman in the throes of dance. Her entire body was consumed by yellow fire. But the flames were peculiar: the purest of yellow, not a trace of orange; coronally brilliant in the way one would imagine the surface of the sun. Everything about the dancer's pose suggested an unbreakable will to perform, while everything about the fire suggested the deliverance of unbearable pain. The dancer was the phoenix in her final moment, locked to her vocation as her body was being rendered to ash. The contradiction paralyzed Jordan, leaving him unable to parse the work in the way one struggles to decipher the Mona Lisa smile.

Christopher moved in, grasping Jordan's shoulder.

Jordan turned to him, still dazed.

"I see you're out of wine."

Jordan blinked at his empty glass.

"Let us have another, and see what Eli has prepared for dinner."

* * *

They sat down at a long dark dining table in a room done in desaturated browns. Its accents—the chandelier, the winding grapevine centerpiece, the small paintings framed on the wall—were all wreathed in bright silver. Place settings were in the middle, across from each other instead of at ends. An intimate configuration; one that made Jordan apprehensive about the approaching conversation.

Yet it was the painting in the library that continued to haunt Jordan after he sat down. The fleeting flash of the fire-dancer swept through his mind like a lighthouse calling across black waters. Jordan tried to tie this unease to the power of the piece. It was stunning, it moved him—a most natural reaction. But something unnatural coursed behind it, if not the veneer of the evening itself.

"Risotto duck confit," announced Eli, arriving with the first course.

The initial bites yanked Jordan away from his lighthouse sophistry. After a week of fast food embalmed with fat, salt, and sugar, Eli's creation dazzled his palette.

"Let us speak of your work." Christopher cradled his wine glass, its stem swinging beneath his fingers like a clock's pendulum. "Tell me how you got started, tell me what inspires you."

"Well, I was good at it as a child, so I kept at it. Tried a lot of mediums. I found pencils and charcoals to be the most expressive, despite the presumed simplicity. It's an art form in itself to work with only black against white, to trick the eye into seeing all those shades of gray that aren't actually there."

"Beautifully said. Were your parents supportive of your efforts?"

"They weren't against it…I should say, my father wasn't against it—it's just the two of us." Jordan thought back to the phone call. He didn't say goodbye. He just bailed and took Eli's call. "Anyway, he wanted me to live a more typical life; wanted me to be into sports, go to college. He didn't see the art *thing*, as he called it, going anywhere. At least until you changed that a week ago."

"Sales were meager?"

"You could say that." Jordan took small bites, trying not to rush through it. "I lacked focus, commercially speaking."

"I recall a lot of sketches of faces on your walls." Christopher's eyes went narrow. "A striking similarity in the eyes. You seem very fond of that subject."

"I guess."

"Might I ask what inspired the work I bought?"

Jordan borrowed time by chewing slow on his duck confetti or whatever the hell it was called. "She's someone I thought I saw once."

"Where?"

Without looking at his plate, Jordan stabbed blindly for something else to plug his mouth with, but came up empty. Loose talk about visions would torpedo that big check. "Perhaps another time. It's a long story—can you tell me about your gallery?"

"My gallery…" Christopher flickered disappointment and leaned back, his chair creaking. His attention drifted to the wall and then returned. "I specialize in stunning works and unique visions."

"What's the name of it?"

Christopher paused, his fork in the air. "The San Francisco Gallery."

"I looked around online. I couldn't seem to find anything. The business card just had your assistant's name."

"It's very small and very exclusive. And I don't advertise."

The words felt final to Jordan's ears, so he resigned himself to scraping up the last morsels of rice. While Eli gathered plates, Jordan glanced at his empty wine glass, then to the bottle parked next to Christopher. The letters "BRION" were visible across the bottle's curve.

"I'd slide this over to you," said Christopher, "if I thought it would pry loose the story of your inspiration."

Jordan responded with a diplomatic nod. "You seem quite interested in that subject."

"I like to know who I'm working with."

Jordan wanted to respond in kind but held his tongue. He didn't divulge. Christopher didn't refill. While they waited for the next course, the conversation drifted to the arts in general. Though Jordan found his host's words enlightening, frustration pecked at him over this strange little game of chess they were playing.

"Miyazaki Wagyu with truffled Madeira sauce," announced Eli, gliding in with the main course, "and smoked potato mousse."

Jordan fixed his eyes on the plump steak. A moment later, and a bite later, his career aspirations took flight; he could get used to this. Fuck the eyes and the stupid red ghost.

The conversation dried up while they ate. Later, Eli strolled in and struck a stout pose, hands behind his back. "Should I open the parlor?"

"Yes, Eli. And another bottle of wine. Surprise us."

Eli nodded and walked off.

After excusing himself to the bathroom, Jordan returned to find a small wedge of chocolate cake on a pristine white dinner plate, laced with a jagged arc of raspberry sauce. Like the steak, they worked through it in near silence.

Jordan finished first. He took a deep breath and decided to roll the dice. "You know who she is, don't you?"

Christopher looked up from his plate. His expression revealed nothing. "A question on both our minds, it seems."

"And since we keep avoiding talk of it, what are we to do?"

With no particular urgency, Christopher finished his last bite. After wiping his mouth, he took the time to fold the napkin almost perfectly in half. He laid it upon the plate and got to his feet, cane in hand. "I imagine you wondered why I invited you all the way out here…" Christopher began to walk around the table. Slow steps, firm clacks from the cane cracking off the floor. "…why I came all the way across the country to your local art show."

"That thought crossed my mind."

"As it should."

From the depths of the home, Jordan heard a dry creaky moan, which he presumed was Eli opening the parlor. Christopher had reached Jordan's side of the table. On final approach, the cane was unbearably loud. Jordan looked up at him, Christopher's proximity forcing his chin into a steep, uncomfortable angle.

"I will keep my end of the bargain," said Christopher. "I will write you a check for seventeen thousand dollars. But I will ask, once again, what is the inspiration for the piece?"

"Why does it matter?"

"Because I…" Christopher closed his eyes for a moment, then opened them. "Because I need to know it's *you*." Christopher studied him with frightening intensity, the act triggering panic in Jordan.

"What the hell does that mean?"

Christopher's hand returned to the cane, gripping it hard. "The inspiration, Jordan."

"She's—" Jordan drew in a long breath and let it go. "She's a vision in my head." Jordan looked away.

Silence took the room.

When Jordan finally dared look back at Christopher, he found a pleased look on the man's face.

"Now that wasn't so hard," said Christopher. "One final question."

Jordan's mind whirled.

"Do you need to use the bathroom again before we continue?"

"Whu-What?" Jordan shanked his attention to the far wall. "This is getting very strange—I should leave." Jordan moved to stand, but Christopher's cane came slapping down across the chair arm, blocking his escape.

"The vision in your head, Jordan. It was given to you by a red ghost, was it not?"

Jordan's muscles went rock-tight. He looked up at Christopher, who lifted the cane and moved away. "How could you know that?"

"A red ghost you encountered somewhere near your hometown," continued Christopher, moving toward the hallway.

"Yes," said Jordan, dumbfounded.

"And all that remains—all that's left of that event is a haunting memory, an echo of a dream that resides just beneath your wakeful thoughts."

"Yes!" Jordan stood up and staggered, his sweaty fingertips clutching the chair for reprieve.

"…and you've never seen it again."

"Do you know where it is?" Jordan staggered and knocked over his chair. It hit the floor hard.

"I do, and I will call upon it." Christopher reached the mouth of the hallway. He paused and turned to Jordan, a strange, almost predatory glint flaring in his eyes when he spoke again. "The first thing to understand about ghosts is that they're not actually dead."

Jordan wobbled on adrenaline-jacked legs. A lifetime of futile efforts, only to discover that this hobbled old man could summon the fucking red ghost in his parlor. Christopher vanished down the hall, calling to him from its depths. "Come now, let us discuss what you really came here for."

The dim dark hallway beckoned to Jordan. His cerebral lighthouse, born of the fire-dancer painting, was in close proximity now, its bright beam revealing treacherous shoals. With it, came a revelation. Lighthouses do not issue invitations. They are warnings to stay away. Yet Christopher's confident departure told Jordan what he only now accepted: they already held him in their sway.

He had to know.

6

THE RED GHOST

Jordan reached the threshold of the parlor to find Christopher and Eli trading sharp whispers. Their friendly demeanors returned with the flip of a switch when he stepped into the room. Christopher appraised him, hands crossed over the top of his cane. Eli filled three glasses, spilling frequently as his attention jumped between the task and Christopher.

"I'd like to show you something." Christopher turned sidelong and extended his hand toward the far wall. "My other gallery, you might call it."

Jordan's distrust only allowed a quick glance beyond Christopher's hand. But it was enough. Jordan froze dead in his steps. The hair on his arms shot up. Beyond Christopher's outstretched hand was a painting depicting a familiar scene: a pair of eyes, piercing and beautiful. The strokes and geometry were unmistakable. Jordan's jaw fell open as he approached. Christopher moved aside while Jordan's eyes consumed the work. It was old, yellowed with age. A century—possibly two. But the subject was the same. Identical to what he'd been creating his entire life, as though he'd done it himself—but he hadn't.

"What is this?" whispered Jordan to the image. A tiny signature painted in at the bottom right grabbed his attention: "R. Foscari – 11644." Jordan looked farther down the wall. There were more. He staggered to the next. Same image, same medium, same artist, but this time with the number "11639." The next was far older. Different artist, but paint again, the strokes exhibiting a dense spider web of cracks. Desaturated and centuries old, like something out of the Renaissance. The one after it was so timeworn Jordan feared it would disintegrate if he merely breathed on it.

At the corner of the room, framed in a glass case were the eyes in monotone. An earthen brown series of strokes on a reddish clay fragment indicative of ancient Greece. More variants of this ran the length of the wall. The last was enormous, protruding like a museum display. It housed a slab of stone, covered with symbols, petroglyphs by some prehistoric person. Within the stream of symbols was an uncluttered space—one that featured the eyes.

Jordan's legs felt like wisps of straw, unable to bear the weight of existence. His head turned side to side, a sluggish exhibition of disbelief. He heard Christopher's cane tap the floor gently behind him, coming closer. It was a magnificent sound, the herald of the man who had all the answers.

With eyes still on the petroglyphs, Jordan stuttered words through his emergent bliss. "I-I've spent my whole life trying to figure this out. There are so many things I need to ask you." With nerves settled, he turned to Christopher.

Jordan's emotional state blasted back into overdrive.

Christopher was aiming a gun at him. Eli had one too. Gone were the kind faces. Only deadly dark stares now. Eli's gun barrel shook, an unstable extension of his nervous persona. Christopher's remained steady. Jordan managed to raise his hands in the air, stickup style.

"Empty your pockets on the table," said Christopher.

"You're robbing me? Why—"

"EMPTY your pockets." Christopher wagged his gun.

Jordan hauled out his possessions with trembling hands, dropping his phone, hotel room card, and pocket change onto the table. He finished the task by slamming his wallet down, startling Eli.

"Why are you doing this?" asked Jordan, his hands back in the air.

Christopher spoke a single word: "Eli."

Eli reached into his pocket and pulled something out. He placed it on the table. A wad of cash secured together with rubber bands, like something out of a mafia movie. Dollars on the outside, foreign currencies peeking out at the edges.

"Put it in your pocket," commanded Christopher.

Jordan hesitated, but a twitch of Christopher's gun brought him to the table. He obeyed, jamming the money into his pocket.

"Now back away."

Again, Jordan obeyed.

"Now we finish this." Christopher's grip on the gun tightened.

"Wait! No!" Jordan waved his hands about frantically. "I did what you asked—don't kill me let me go!" He lurched a step sideways. The gun barrels followed. He imagined trying to make a run for it: Christopher's mobility was limited, Eli was too nervous to aim. He'd have to evade the initial shots, get past them somehow.

"You wanted to see the red ghost?" Christopher cocked the hammer. "This is the price."

Jordan just stood there, tense as a piano string, unable to act. He recalled that life flashed before your eyes at the end—but even that wasn't happening. His mind raced to his father's words and his hopes of higher education, noting how much better *that* option seemed now. He'd talked to him only hours ago.

He didn't say goodbye.

Desperate for some final connection, Jordan looked across the room at the works of art. He drowned in the sick irony that those eyes were what brought him here. Now they'd witness him die. He pondered the mystery woman, wondering who she was, if she was even real; what it would have been like to talk to her, to hear her voice…to kiss her. He clung to that last idea.

It was the best he could do.

His attention snapped back to Christopher, to the hammer of the gun. He saw an impulse flash in Christopher's eyes, and race down to his trigger finger. It was really going to happen. Jordan blared his final word like a foghorn:

"FUUUUUUUUCK!"

The hammer surged forward and a deafening flash erupted. Jordan's last act was to leap away, to jump out of the bullet's path. A second violent crack sounded out a split second after the first. The room lit up neon red. Then, a third blast and a flash from Eli's gun. Jordan waited for the pain to sear through him. He looked to his killers, discovering that they were bathed in crimson light.

Jordan continued to wait for the pain.

Christopher and Eli lowered their guns, a downward arc transpiring in slow motion. Expressions of joy flourished on their faces while Jordan swallowed the scene with hypersensitive awareness. Though it happened in mere seconds, it felt like eternity.

Still no pain.

Christopher and Eli tossed their guns on the table. They began to laugh and then embraced, hands clasping each other's shoulders in celebration. Jordan suddenly realized he was looking down at them as if he'd grown much taller.

He was floating.

Jordan clutched at his chest, searching for bullet holes and blood, but his hands couldn't seem to grasp anything solid. And that's when he realized it:

He was on fire.

A deep red fire wrapped him from head to toe—but it was more than that; he was *made* of fire…every single bit of him. The sight of his blazing-red, transparent self pumped pure disbelief into the churning machinery of his mind. Out came the impossible truth:

I *am* the fucking red ghost.

He was a crimson inferno, like the dancer in the painting. Terror rattled through him as he lifted his hand in front of his face. It was composed of deep, rose-red flame. Yet he could see clean through it. The surface features were still present, right down to the lines in his palm and the permanent scar on his thumb. Blood-red light coursed over his hand like a stream over smooth rocks. His clothes—his jacket, shirt, pants, and even shoes—remained, but were all composed of the same fiery red light.

Jordan screamed.

It came out loud, impossibly loud. Christopher and Eli halted their revelry and covered their ears. Jordan was nearly at the ceiling now. Thrashing his limbs about, he found they provided no alteration to his ascent, leaving him positioned like a skydiver looking down at the floor. He panicked and tried to jerk himself out of the red fire.

A thunder-crack rang out and the red light vanished. He was whole again. Gravity ripped Jordan toward the ground. He thrust his hands forward to break the fall. His outstretched fingers jammed into the tabletop, rendering a series of snaps just before his face hit the same spot. The impact catapulted him backward onto the floor, landing him flat. His vision throbbed in pulses of defocused reality.

Jordan staggered to his feet.

This time there was pain and lots of it. It burned across his right hand and up his arm, forming an unmistakable epicenter in his mouth. With vision that spun in and out of focus, he saw Eli rush to him, his face wrapped in shock.

"Jordan! You're okay." Eli reached out to him. "Just a scratch."

Jordan screamed when he saw the twisted wreck of his hand, his fingers broken in multiple places, jagged bones sticking out through the skin.

"Oh no," said Eli, taking a step back, covering his mouth as if to prevent vomiting.

Pain speared Jordan with every beat of his heart. Seizing his wrist with his good hand, he crushed it with tourniquet force.

"More than a scratch!" howled Jordan. With those words, his front teeth fell out onto the floor.

Christopher spoke in a commanding voice, "Jordan, listen to me!"

Jordan watched a gout of blood spill from his mouth. Cradling his ruined hand against his chest, he backed away.

"Jordan! Do it again—do what you did when facing the guns." Christopher's eyes were locked on his.

Eli retrieved the gun and pointed it at Jordan, its barrel trembling madly. Jordan stared at it with dull awareness, trying to coerce his mind through what had transpired…the flash of the gun, the red light, the floating, the lack of pain…the abundance of pain. Then he had it. The leap, the instinctive act of self-preservation.

Jordan tried to focus, the effort draining his remaining strength. He staggered and stumbled. Then, a loud crack called out. Red light painted the room again. The pain vanished, clarity returned. Floating in the air, Jordan raised his hand in front of his face. Red light rolled over it, flickering in tiny gentle flames this time.

"Now change back," said Christopher. "Veil."

Jordan concentrated. After another crack, the red fire vanished out of existence and he dropped to the ground whole, landing safely on his feet. He lifted his hand in front of his face. No broken fingers, no pain, no blood. He checked his teeth. They were all there—yet two broken ones remained on the floor with a post-modernistic pool of blood islanding them.

Jordan clenched his jaw shut and closed his hand into a fist. He lurched forward at Christopher, who stumbled back, losing his grip on the cane. He went down hard on the floor. Eli backed away, raising both hands as though Jordan had the gun now. Jordan's rage petered out, but his hand remained balled in a fist.

"That thing is *inside* me?" asked Jordan.

Christopher struggled to his feet with a groan. "That thing *is* you, would be a more appropriate way to say it."

"Explain," demanded Jordan, glaring at them.

"That thing *is* you," said Christopher again. "The ghost is you, and you are the ghost, just as ice and steam are both water; different states of being. Only *ghost* is a wholly inadequate word."

"That night I saw it… it's been inside me this whole damn time?"

"Correct."

"Did you kill me?" asked Jordan, checking frantically for bullet holes again. "Am I fucking dead?"

"You're still alive, and that *thing*, as you called it, merged with you."

"Why the HELL did it do that?"

"That's another story." Christopher wiped his brow. "We'll get to it."

"You two…" Jordan pointed back and forth. "You two run around finding people like me? You lure us in and scare the shit out of us with guns to see if we're ghosts?" Jordan made a series of gestures that approximated an epileptic mime. "Is this some kind of fucking government-secret-agency job?"

"No," said Christopher. "I assure you the government has nothing to do with this. Let me explain it this way." Christopher stepped forward and let his cane fall to the floor. Still ruled by nerves, Jordan stepped back.

A deep blue light erupted behind Christopher's shoulders and consumed his whole body. Christopher—or what had been Christopher a moment ago—was now a blue silhouette that exhibited the transparency of a jellyfish.

"I apologize for the guns," said the ghostly Christopher, flying deft loops around Jordan, "but it's the easiest way."

When stationary, Christopher's form settled into a perfect blue-ghost version of his human form, right down to his beard, his fingertips, and the stiff-looking collar on his shirt, albeit in shimmering intensities of blue. Against his suit, Jordan spotted what was unmistakably a cane. It followed the lines of his body, but ran a rumpled course, giving the appearance of a giant spaghetti noodle. When Christopher moved again, his ghost presence hummed. The precise details of his form distorted in the way wind would tease smoke.

Jordan looked at Eli.

Eli raised his hand and blue light burst from his fingertips. It consumed his hand down to the wrist and stopped. He wiggled his sapphire, candle-flame fingers.

"In any case," said Christopher, "this way is safer than throwing you off a cliff or a building—that was the old way, sometimes by accident, sometimes on purpose."

"Are you sure you don't work for the government?" sniped Jordan.

Christopher laughed and continued to glide about.

"What if the bullets got to me first?"

"Blanks," said Eli, his blue fingers flaring out, leaving his hand normal again. "We only needed you to *believe* you were going to die." He picked up the gun, aimed it at the bar and fired a shot. None of the bottles broke.

Christopher drifted back to the table. A rustling sound, like that of a small wave breaking on shore, accompanied Christopher's transformation. His human form poured out of the vibrant blue light, feet first. Another cane materialized, and Christopher caught it before it fell away. A second cane—the one he had abandoned before going blue remained on the floor. Christopher was wearing a different suit now, the one from the night of the art crawl.

Jordan rumpled his brow trying to make sense of it.

"The cane and the change in apparel," said Christopher preemptively. "Good eye. We'll get to that later."

"Deveiling for the first time is the hardest," said Eli. "What's needed is the conviction that one is about to die—a *true* conviction, not merely being scared witless. The natural, final reaction is to escape, to jump out of one's skin."

"What did you call it?"

"Deveiling." Eli took a seat and pulled his wine glass close. He was still shaking, but the rest of him seemed relieved. "The opposite of veiling, which is a term akin to the veil, as in brides and weddings."

Jordan shook his head.

"If we tried to explain what you had to do, you'd have thought we were insane."

"You think I consider you sane now?"

"Probably not," said Eli with a light smile, "but you finally have some answers."

Jordan paced. "I have questions. Lots of them."

"Indeed." Christopher took a seat next to Jordan's wallet and phone, next to the bloody Rorschach pattern of his face-plant.

Jordan's eyes darted about like a barn owl. "I need a drink."

Eli brought him a glass. Jordan raised it in the air, his hand shaking wine over the rim. Christopher and Eli raised theirs too. "Here's to not being fucking crazy after all."

7

A Fire Spectacular

Christopher set two empty wine bottles next to each other at the edge of the table. Sitting next to Eli, he watched Jordan, who stood in front of them with a rogue grin. Jordan thrust his hand forward in a boxer's jab and it burst into red light, emitting tiny sparks. The light stopped short at his wrist, leaving the rest of him whole.

"Kick-asssss," whispered Jordan, veiling his hand and repeating the trick with the other. "I can't believe I never did this by accident."

"You can't until you've rendered—that means deveiling for the first time. What you're doing with your hands now, that's called flaying."

Jordan stared through his hand and waved it as though signaling a ship on the ocean. "Okay, tell me if I have this right. I'll be twenty-five forever. If I don't—" Jordan couldn't find the word. He churned empty air with his solid hand.

"Deveil…" said Christopher.

"So, if I don't deveil for three years, I'd be twenty-eight, physically speaking. But as soon as I do, I'm twenty-five again, even though my mind will remain twenty-eight."

"Correct."

"So I'm immortal?" Jordan sprouted a wry smile.

"Only if you don't die."

"Bad echo, talking like that," said Eli, "but you are correct."

"I'll always be wearing this?" Jordan plucked at his red t-shirt and twirled the cords of his hoodie.

"Correct again," said Christopher. "You'll also feel pleasantly full from dinner, physically alert thanks to the guns. You'll always have comfortable shoes." Christopher took a sip of wine. "And you'll always have pocket change."

"But no phone nor identification." Jordan eyed his personal effects on the table.

"As you now realize, that too was by plan."

Jordan paced again. He took off his hoodie and laid it on the table. He grabbed one of the empty wine bottles and held it close to his chest. He deveiled. The bottle was vaporized in the burst of red fire—gone forever. Jordan examined his empty, glowing hand and then plucked at the ghostly red cords of his newly regenerated hoodie, finding he couldn't grasp them. Any effort to touch his deveiled form resulted in something that looked like smoke trying to grab smoke. His fingers lost their shape, producing a painless but strange sense of dislocation. Jordan veiled, bursting back into physical form with a sharp crack. He was wearing a hoodie once again.

"And now you have two of them," said Christopher pointing to the one that remained on the table. "By way of contemporary example, imagine the process of restoring your phone from a backup. It can be wiped clean, but every piece of data—billions upon billions of bits—can be set right back to how they were. With veiling, it's an unimaginable number of atoms being fabricated into your human body and its immediate perimeter. That's why you kept your clothes, though I'm guessing you're missing a bit of the soles of your shoes."

Jordan's mind whirled, and he came back grinning. "That wad of money in my pocket…I could do the same thing with the hoodie over and over and have millions. Like a printing press."

Christopher frowned. "Theoretically, yes."

"That's fucking crazy," said Jordan, still smirking.

"But don't do it."

"Of course not." Jordan let the grin slide and resumed pacing. Questions surfaced in fragments, and so rapidly he failed to forge coherent questions. "The painting in your library?"

"It's called *Silver in the Wind.*" Christopher's voice lost some of its joy. "A portrait of someone we lost long ago. Painted by your predecessor, incidentally."

Jordan stopped pacing. "I have a predecessor?"

"The one who harbored the red ghost before you. You have many of them—we'll get to that."

"Your suit," said Jordan, jumping topics again. "It was different after you changed back."

"A good observation—"

"Your suit is modern, which means you're new to this too."

"I'm actually quite old to this," said Christopher. "But I have a way to pick new starting points at will. That's called *redrafting.*"

"Like a reset button." Jordan tapped the air with his finger.

"Yes, all of us can do that," said Christopher, "but not you."

"Why not?"

"We don't know. It just is."

"So, it's a good thing I didn't piss my pants when you had those guns aimed at me."

Christopher laughed and slapped the table. "That would have been tragic. As you recall I did suggest using the bathroom before we came in here."

"Makes sense now." Jordan's thoughts skipped ahead. "The different colors…why am I red? Why are you both blue?"

"We could provide a tedious explanation," said Eli while Christopher filled his glass, "but at this juncture, I'll use analogy—have you ever been to the orchestra?"

"Never," said Jordan confidently.

"But you know what one sounds like?"

"Yes." Jordan stared straight ahead. He deveiled, causing bright red light to flash off Eli's wine glass.

"Each instrument in the orchestra sounds unique, even when playing the same note." Eli raised his chin and stared off. "The warm percussive sound of a piano key is distinct from the sharp string of the violin, which is distinct from the whisper of a flute.

Each conveys a certain *texture*, if you will."

"So sound is color?" Jordan had floated halfway up to the ceiling.

"Yes, but the analogy wouldn't be necessary if it were as simple as that. We are not merely different by color. Being able to press that reset button, to use your words, is something that varies in difficulty between *colors*, as you say."

Jordan moved his arms and legs as if swimming.

"You're trying to move?" asked Christopher.

Jordan looked at him and nodded.

"Think of ice skating," said Christopher. "Imagine the sensation of gliding to where you want to go, but don't use your feet to get there. Or think of yourself as pouring toward a specific location."

Jordan worked on it while Eli continued:

"In music, the word *timbre* is used to describe the many unique acoustical characteristics of an instrument with a single word. From this, *Timbrelight* came into use—though the word is French in origin, and thus, *Timbrelumière*. This is an antiquated term, one of many. The word *timbre,* however, remains in use as a term of self-reference."

Jordan began to move about in small, stunted trajectories.

"While we differentiate each other by color," said Eli, watching Jordan's flight path, "it's the least significant of our characteristics."

Jordan progressed to making loops around the room, crude ones involving numerous starts and stops. He pulsed bright with each burst of movement, the fastest ones producing a musical hum.

"There are countless other attributes and talents, and—"

Jordan suddenly grew radiant and shot across the room. He plowed headlong into the shelf of liquor bottles. His body compressed and his vision went dark. Sound became muddled, as if he were underwater. His senses returned in time to witness an avalanche of bottles shattering on the floor below him.

Christopher turned his head, waiting for the sound of breaking glass to cease. "Freelight. That's the contemporary term. It evokes our separation from the frailties of the human condition." He stood up and started to make his way over to Jordan. "Aging, hunger, and so on."

"I wrecked your booze," said Jordan sadly, gliding to the floor. He veiled and started to collect jagged pieces of glass, cringing at the harsh odor.

Christopher arrived next to him. "We'll work on flight mechanics tomorrow. Until then, keep your feet on the ground. Your body will be forever twenty-five, but your mind will tick ever onward, which means it still needs sleep." He tapped Jordan's shoulder with his cane. "Stand up Jordan, there's one more thing."

Jordan stopped gathering glass and stood.

Christopher grasped his shoulder as Eli came in next to them. "Your feet stay on the ground. Got it?"

"Got it," said Jordan, spying a traffic-cop wariness in Christopher's eyes.

* * *

Late into the night in the guest cottage alone, Jordan stared into the hypnotic red light of his deviled hand. He could see right through it, yet this strange new physiology manifested itself as pure surface detail—no bones or veins visible, just skin and clothing. A perfectly continuous exterior, composed of a fire spectacular.

This phenomenon burned away his very understanding of reality, leaving him no confident grasp of its weave. With wide, entranced eyes, minutes piled up into hours. Time and again, he blew air at his hand, watching the perfect red-light silhouette of his fingers ripple and dance like the flames of failing candles.

Two days.

That's all it took to find him.

An epic sketch, a photograph by Maggie, a website for local artists—one of thousands in the country. Yet they found him and found him fast. He wondered if there were others looking for him. He tried fruitlessly to divine the intentions of the two that did, finding the whole affair a wasteland of uncertainty outside of one thought: whatever they wanted him for, they must have wanted him bad.

Just before Jordan crashed, one final thought swept through him, much in the manner of his cerebral lighthouse. They hadn't said a thing about his vision, and about *her*. And that didn't seem accidental.

In fact, it seemed quite intentional.

8

———◆◆◆———

READING WRITING
AND ARITHMETIC

Jordan emerged from the guesthouse the next morning. Squinting under duress of the California sun, he made his way to the main house. The sound of clinking cups lured him through the halls and into the kitchen where he found Eli leaning against the counter drinking coffee. As at the airport, he was wearing a suit, and it was pressed to perfection.

"Did you sleep?" asked Eli.

"What time is it?" asked Jordan, sitting down on a stool.

"About seven."

"Had a solid hour in that case."

"It's like that the first night." Eli set his cup down. "Listen, I'm sorry how we handled things. We're not transitionists, which makes this all out of our comfort zone."

"I noticed," said Jordan. The word *transitionists* conjured images of men in sunglasses and dark suits.

"It's been many years since I was there myself. In my case, it was all by accident. I had to figure things out on my own."

"No helpful guns in your face?"

"None, unfortunately. I fell off Table Mountain. Cape Town, South Africa. Deviled before I hit the ground." Eli sipped his coffee and stared at the cabinetry. "I'd have preferred the gun."

57

"How long ago?"

"Decades. Nineteen forty-two, by faintlight reckoning. I've been around for almost a century in all." Eli raised his cup as if toasting.

"What about Christopher?"

"Let's see." Eli looked up at the ceiling and whispered calculations, returning with an answer. "One thousand, nine hundred and forty-three years, eighteen hundred seventy-nine of them as freelight."

"You're shittin' me."

"I assure you, I'm not," said Eli in a way that suggested he'd answered this before.

Jordan's stomach gurgled, prompting his eyes to scan the kitchen counters.

"If you're hungry, just deveil."

"Forgot about that." Jordan rose from his stool.

"Tiptoes, if you please." Eli lifted his cup. "Don't want to damage the floor."

Concentrating on the leaping sensation, Jordan deveiled with a sharp crack. His hunger was instantly displaced, the pleasant feeling of last night's steak dinner arriving in a flash. "That's a great trick." He floated up and started to fly loops, trying not to ram into the cluster of pots and pans hanging from the ceiling. "If we don't need to eat or drink, why the coffee?"

Eli shrugged. "It's good coffee."

Jordan glided down. He floated in close, his crimson proximity tinting Eli's face and suit jacket. "Who is she? The woman in my vision."

Eli shrunk in Jordan's presence, his gaze shifting to each side, then down into his coffee.

Silent and evasive. Quite intentional, indeed.

Jordan relented, gliding up toward the ceiling again. "Nineteen-hundred years, huh?" He resumed a lackadaisical path around the kitchen. "Christopher's really that old?"

Eli unpinned his eyes from his coffee cup. "He is. Right out of Roman times."

"As in Julius Caesar—did he know him?"

Eli shook his head. "Everyone asks that. No, he didn't. Before his time. He did live in Rome, though, and knew Hadrian. He came and went over the years."

"Because of the not-aging thing?"

"Right," said Eli, watching Jordan's flight carefully.

"What did he do there? Was he a merchant or a senator?"

"An engineer—he's still an engineer."

"Christopher Johnson doesn't sound terribly Roman. I take it name changes are also necessary, from time to time?"

"Right again." Eli winced as Jordan bumped into the hanging pot collection, almost dislodging them.

"It's Crispin," said Christopher, gliding into the room.

Jordan turned and watched Christopher's blue silhouette sail over the kitchen island. He veiled on the other side next to the coffee maker, expensive suit in tow.

"Publius Crispus Fluximous," said Christopher, getting himself a cup. "That's my Roman name. I usually go by Crispin."

Jordan zipped down to the counter with a puzzled expression. "When you flew in here, the most random thought popped into my head. It happened last night too."

Crispin raised his hand in the air. Blue light burst from his fingertips like blowtorches coming to life. "Are you having it now?"

"Yeah. I keep thinking of math class in grade school. Mr. Prates. I barely remember him at all, but now it all seems...recent."

"That's called *surface echo*, or colloquially, *feel*. It's like a signature. Everyone's is unique and each is perceived in a very personal way."

Eli sidled in next to Crispin and deveiled his own fingers.

"Now I'm thinking about folding paper airplanes with my dad when I was a kid." The memories would flicker into Jordan's head with force, but become background noise quickly. Like hearing birds chirp in the forest, and filtering them out seconds later.

"Spatial reasoning, a variant of logic."

"So you blue types are all the same?"

"Look closer," said Crispin.

Jordan veiled and sat down on a stool at the counter, with Crispin and Eli on the other side. He alternated attention between their develed fingers. Then he saw it: Crispin's blue was a touch deeper than Eli's, a difference even his artistically tuned eye struggled to notice.

"Despite our visual similarity," said Crispin, "We do not have equal talents."

"Though we often *feel* quite similar," said Eli. Both zipped their fingers back into solid form and returned to their coffee.

"What about others?" asked Jordan. "People not like us?"

"Faintlights," said Crispin. "Yes, but they have a much weaker feel, hence the term. Still quite easy for you, even from a distance. That particular talent is exclusive to your timbre, and I might add, you're without peer."

Jordan's chin floated up with pride.

"The name of your timbre, incidentally, is Lux Sanguinis." Crispin put his cup down on the counter. "That's Latin for *Blood Light*. The process of being able to detect these signals is called *reading*, and the interpretation of them, as we already said, is called *feel*. You would be right to say Eli *feels* like making paper airplanes with your father, or that I *feel* like math class. Your mind seeks out an analogous association from your memories, almost always the first instance that shares a common abstract foundation. For that reason, most of them will be from your childhood."

"You lost me," said Jordan, shrugging one shoulder.

"Let me try it another way: you could say that my timbre is rationality. Logic. Reason. When you feel me, your mind found a memory that first marked an acute experience of that concept. In your case it was grade school math class."

"What do I feel like to you?" asked Jordan.

"Nothing, and there are two reasons for that. The first is unique to your timbre." Crispin's eyes fixed on him with an air that Jordan interpreted as admiration. "In terms of feel—signal detection, that is—it would be perfectly accurate to say that you are like a living radio receiver. The most powerful in the entire freelight world. But just as you have an unparalleled ability to detect signals, you do not emit one yourself. You are invisible. There is no other timbre like this."

Crispin's attention remained on him, his eyes studying away. Jordan wondered if it was *this* talent they were after, and for what purpose.

"Now," said Crispin resuming, "for the second reason. Even if you weren't invisible—that is, even if you had a signal, I would be unable to detect it, for I am your exact opposite. I have no ability to read."

"Yet, I do," said Eli. "Though it is feeble compared to yours and most other timbres."

"And this is the case," said Crispin, stealing Jordan's attention back, "despite Eli and me *both being blue types*, to use your words."

"I meant no insult by that."

"Of course you didn't." Eli chuckled. "Though a number of freelight will take offense to such talk."

"Got it," said Jordan, tucking away the advice.

"In conjunction with me being your opposite," said Crispin, "and having no ability to read, I do have the opposite skill: writing. This is the ability to print sensory experience on a physical object." Crispin turned and fished a spoon out of a drawer. "Allow me to demonstrate."

With the fat end of the spoon in his fist, stem sticking out between fingers, Crispin raised his hand. A flash of blue light erupted from within, a tiny silent firecracker.

Crispin spoke:

"There are a great number of timbres and capabilities. Reading and writing are but two. Some timbres are notable for the way they affect nature, or nature affects them. Others, for how they influence a person's conscious mind. Some, because they can cut through stone with a fingertip as hot as the sun." Crispin picked up his coffee cup and took a sip. "Each capability tends to reach an extreme peak in one timbre, but decline in another, or go missing, as is the case here. I cannot read, you cannot write." Crispin put down his coffee cup and plucked the spoon from his fist, placing it on the counter in front of Jordan. "Now, deveil your hand and hold it over the spoon."

Jordan flayed his hand, red light flashing down to his wrist. He moved it close to the spoon. When the gap decreased to inches, a blue fire leapt from the spoon's surface. Tiny tendrils stretched toward his hand, while his own red fire reached toward them in turn, like flames trying to tickle each other. A pleasant hum issued from the spoon; a mourning dove's coo. Jordan felt grade school math flicker through his head again. When he dropped his hand onto the spoon, his senses collapsed.

He was standing now, looking at himself sitting on a stool. Yet he wasn't himself. An ache chewed at his right ankle, and he had the taste of coffee in his mouth. In his enclosed fist, he felt a spoon and a faint vibration against his palm. His mouth opened. When he spoke, the voice was Crispin's: "There are a great number of timbres and capabilities. Reading and writing are but two. Some timbres are…"

Jordan got it: he *was* Crispin.

He was reliving Crispin's life from a minute ago, as imprinted on the spoon. It was a movie that engaged all five senses and removed every trace of his own. Like the vision in his head, he could exert no will during playback. Every moment, every act was predetermined. When the words stopped and he took a sip of coffee, Jordan tasted hot bitter liquid. Jordan-as-Crispin resumed speaking. "Each capability tends to reach an extreme peak in one timbre, but decline in another, or go missing, as is the case here. I cannot read, you cannot write."

Jordan-as-Crispin put down the coffee cup. The moment he started to pull at the spoon in his fist, the world twisted and snapped away violently. Jordan was himself again, sitting on a kitchen stool, his solid hand resting on top of the spoon.

"And that's writing," said Crispin with a coy smile.

"Damn." Jordan eyed the spoon. "Can I do home video too?"

"Regrettably not. Every other freelight can, except you."

"You can't read, I can't write, huh?"

"Correct."

Jordan's eyes darted to Crispin, then Eli. "Going into the spoon… it's like the vision in my head."

Without a word, Eli deveiled and zipped out of the room.

"What does it mean?" Jordan stood up. "Who is she?"

"*She* is a discussion for another time." Crispin deveiled and floated toward the hall. "Follow me, if you would. We have much to learn today."

Crispin breezed away.

"Wait—does she exist?" asked Jordan. "As in for real?"

"She does," said Crispin, from the distant depths of the hallway.

9

DISORIENTATION DAY

The book spines in Crispin's library reflected red as Jordan raced around the room at Eli's instruction. He weaved around pillars of the upper floor's balustrade, over and around ornate furniture, and past a marble statue that became more familiar with each lap. He moved with a discreet angst, driven by the acknowledgment that his hosts held the reins. To find her meant he'd have to go along with them, and at the moment it meant performing stupid ghost tricks.

"Faster!" commanded Eli like a ringmaster. He stood in the center of the room in a white button-down shirt, having thrown his jacket aside. The circus's only attendee, Crispin, was parked in a leather chair next to a small crackling fire. He maintained a pleased expression, a docile knuckle pressed to his upper lip.

As Jordan pitched and rolled like a human stunt plane, he plumbed the possible politics of the woman in his vision. Jordan wondered if she was somehow dangerous—or if Crispin was. She was a taboo topic to be certain. Yet it was all shabby conjecture, leaving Jordan to chide his impatient nature. Once he knew what they wanted, he might find leverage to tweak the dynamic in his favor.

"Faster!" shouted Eli, his body rotating like the hands of a clock to keep up with Jordan's pace. "Remember, the adynatos field is truly impenetrable. It is pliable when you're of lax light. Think of waving a flag. But when you are bright, as you are now, you won't distort easily."

After zipping up the stairwell, Jordan shot out to the center of the room and hovered above Eli. "I'm getting reads from everywhere. Are those other…spoons?"

"*Reliquiae.*" Eli set his hands on his hips. "*Relics.* Also known as metallum when imprinted on coin-like objects—often copper for longevity reasons, though we can write to just about any inert object."

"What's on them?" Jordan moved his palm about like a radar dish, pinpointing their locations.

"My personal collection," said Crispin, craning his attention up to Jordan. "Places in the world I wanted to remember. Rome before its failings, Medieval Europe, scenes from dynastic China and so on. Others are events I found interesting, or came across quite accidentally."

"I can't imagine what a historian would give to see them."

"It would be just another object to a faintlight," said Eli, whirling his finger at Jordan to resume his efforts. "Only freelight can read them. It's unfortunate, because it's the ultimate medium."

Jordan resumed his laps, admiring the pleasant drone of freelight flight; a hummingbird to his ears but richer, emitting the tone of a cello. At a slow pace, he was close to silent, the sound of a breeze passing through a window.

His tutelage carried into the evening. After tests of motion, which Jordan passed with flying colors, he was tasked with catching coins thrown by Eli and Crispin, who sat with jars in their laps a few feet away. The confidence he built in flight school was whittled away by the humbling experience of interacting with solid objects while deviled.

"Last night you asked if that *thing* was inside you," said Crispin, tossing a quarter at Jordan's outstretched palm, "and I said that it *merged* with you. That was a simplified explanation. It would be more appropriate to say that it became part of you, but first it had to find you, which wasn't entirely by chance. That red light wouldn't have materialized to just anyone. It sought a soul mate—a perfect match. Same notion as star-crossed lovers, only here there's always marriage and no divorce. In the case of Lux Sanguinis, it's an artist. Every single time."

Jordan caught a nickel from Eli and struggled to maintain his hold, watching it bend the surface of his palm and slip away. He wagged his fingers at Eli to throw another.

"Remember the pliability rule," said Eli ready with a dime. "Blaze a bit more."

Jordan brightened and caught the next one in his palm, managing to hold it in place for a few seconds. Where it touched his hand came a faint sizzling sound, like a tiny frying pan at work.

"Prior to the red light becoming part of you," continued Crispin, fishing in his jar, "you were *faintlight*. To avoid a long thesis on light mechanics, understand that the red light, when you took it in, displaced the faintlight part of you. For lack of a more apt concept, imagine this as a rewiring of the soul."

"We're in Sunday school now?" Jordan discarded the coin.

"Mythology comes later, and we have plenty of it. This is science. Know that unharbored light is provincial, which is to say it lingers about a certain geography, quite invisibly, until a match comes along. The red light was drawn to you, and you to it. Soulmates."

Jordan caught the next coin with ease. He held it for a few seconds, flicked it in the air and caught it again. "I remember wanting to see the stars that night. That's when it found me."

"And after you took it in," said Crispin, "you blacked out. Then, you seemed back to normal, as far as you knew, except for the vision in your head. All that time you were wired with a sort of ignition switch, which we flipped on last night."

Jordan, still fiddling with the coin, tossed it high in the air and veiled in a snap. He landed on his feet just in time to catch it when it came down. After flicking it to the floor, he sat in a chair across from Crispin.

"Who is she?" Jordan leaned forward, watching Crispin like a hawk.

Crispin didn't avert his eyes. "As I said, she's a discussion for a later time."

Jordan drummed his fingers on the chair arm. "Listen, I'm trying to be respectful about this—I owe you for finding me. But what do you want from me?" He surveyed both his hosts. No telltale expressions, just guarded contemplation. "My friend put a photograph of that sketch on our co-op's website. Two days later you found me—*two days*. You've been looking very hard for a very long time."

Crispin leaned back in his chair. "Yes, we have."

"You also had me remove the photograph from the website. That wasn't for business reasons, was it?"

Crispin's eyes regarded him in silence. They narrowed and blinked a number of times, indicating the assembly of a very guarded response. An engineer, indeed.

"Your return to the freelight world—specifically the return of Lux Sanguinis—will not be welcome for a great many people." Crispin's hand moved across the arm of his chair as though brushing dust away. "Many paths must be cleared, which is why I am reluctant to jump so far ahead in our discussions. All of this will take time; these are political things, Jordan—dangerous circumstances I can't possibly expect you to understand."

"Meaning, if I left that image on our website…"

"The wrong people would find you," said Crispin.

"And how do I know you're the right people?"

"Because you're still alive." Firelight from the hearth danced reflections off Crispin's eyes, which held Jordan's gaze without blinking. "The wrong people would use real bullets, and wouldn't hesitate to do so in broad daylight. I have ways to know if they know, and fortunately this has all evaded their notice so far. But they have been watching and waiting."

Jordan's throat went tight. "What do *you* want with me?"

Crispin looked past Jordan, his index finger rubbing the head of his cane. "Necromancy is the closest word from the faintlight vocabulary. We need you to find the dead…among other things. Your timbre's capacity for this is unrivaled. That is why you're so important to us."

"What does *she* have to do with any of this?" asked Jordan.

"She has *nothing* to do with this."

"But you've avoided talking about her." Jordan found himself clenching his hands. "You must know I can see that. I've spent my entire life tormenting myself over those eyes. You have no idea what they've done to me…what *I've* done to me." Jordan looked at the floor, then back to Crispin. "Just tell me anything about her."

"Fair enough." Crispin sunk into another measured silence. "But first, I would like to discuss that vision in your head. Would you like something to eat before we continue?"

"Nope. Got that post-steak-dinner feeling thanks to you."

"Well, in that case, there's never a bad time for a good bottle of wine." Crispin deveiled and glided off.

He returned a minute later, floating a bottle on his shimmering palm. He veiled in his chair and wedged the bottle between his knees. He grasped its mouth and flayed his hand, vaporizing the top of the bottle. He passed it to Eli, who filled the glasses.

"The vision you have is called a birth echo," said Crispin. "Every freelight has one, and there's no way to capture them in reliquiae, so all we can do is describe them to one another. We'll start there, if you please…"

Jordan paused and took a sip of wine. "For many years, all I could see was a flash of the eyes. But a few weeks before you arrived, I saw the whole…birth echo, as you call it. That big sketch you bought."

"Is the crying artistic license?"

"No, that's how I see it. It's dark and cold, and there's some sort of lightning going on behind me. That's why I can see her face in such detail. Also, my right hand is deveiled, but I can't make out much beyond that."

"What color are her eyes?" asked Crispin.

"Gray. I had always thought they were blue."

Eli and Crispin traded glances.

"Are you sure they aren't a pale blue?" asked Crispin.

"I'll check again." Jordan cast a dead stare across the room for four seconds. "They're gray. I'm certain of it."

"Do you *feel* anything? Like math class or paper airplanes."

Jordan's gaze slid to the floor. "It feels like my father crying at my mother's grave."

Crispin granted a respectful silence. "Can you sense anything else?"

"I count fifteen flashes of light, the time between each uneven. Everything behind her face is out of focus, but I can see swirling black clouds."

Both Crispin and Eli swallowed in unison.

"How did you trigger it?" asked Crispin, his words noticeably faster.

"Accidentally. I was thinking about the eyes and a child nearby said, 'I don't know what you want me to do.' Those are the magic words, as I call them."

"Do you remember the child's mood? It works by—"

"Didn't my predecessor explain this already?" asked Jordan, frustrated at not being the one to pose questions.

"No," said Crispin. "Every one of your predecessors would have seen only the surface echo—the flicker as you called it. You're the first to see the whole thing. We have a theory on this but that's for another time."

"Of course it is." Jordan threw himself back in the chair frustrated. "Who is she?"

Crispin exhaled, his mind elsewhere. "Her name is Lila. You will, no doubt, meet her one day."

Jordan mouthed her name silently. "Does she live around here?"

"Sort of."

"What is she like?"

"She's Lux Viridis, which means she's a caretaker of gardens in our world." Crispin pursed the side of his mouth. "That is a poor way to explain it. If my timbre corresponds to an engineer's mind, and yours to an artist's, consider hers to be one of ecology."

"That's interesting," said Jordan, "but what is *she* like?"

Crispin's face suggested he was choosing from a long list of words. "Complicated."

"Her timbre makes her that way?"

"No, history does. But this is all another story—"

"You say that a lot." Jordan clenched the chair's leather.

"I'd rather you know her through her own words, not mine," said Crispin, painting the topic with a stroke of finality. "I suspect she'd be grateful that I grant her that honor. Patience, Jordan. I know it's difficult to wait."

"I don't think you do."

"You'll meet her once we bring you into our world—"

"Our world—you say that a lot too. Where is it?"

Crispin's serious face loosened into something of a grin. "We have a saying about that: 'You wouldn't believe me if I told you, and you still won't believe me when I show you.'"

"Very helpful."

"My apologies for the dodge, but I assure you it's well-intentioned. I'd like to return to birth echoes, if you don't mind."

"Fine," said Jordan, his mind too weary to conduct a battle of wits. He sunk into his chair. Mental exhaustion pulled at him.

"A question you've been plagued with…" Crispin paused to finish his wine. "A question more troubling than the ghost itself is the vision. Why does it lurk? How does it invade consciousness so easily, and why does it remain? I can't possibly imagine the ways in which this question has altered the course of your life, but I am certain it has."

"And you'd be correct," said Jordan, thinking about his loft-made-shrine to the eyes.

"The birth echo is an artifact of memory, carried by every timbre. It resides with whoever harbors it. Should that person die, the timbre and this vision will remain together; the timbre and the birth echo never part. But the timbre and the harborer inevitably do."

Jordan listened, but his eyelids went heavy, a product of limited sleep. His mind drifted to the name *Lila*, letting its syllables resonate in his head like a bell. It was a meager start, but he knew her name now.

"…do you understand the implications of this?" asked Crispin.

"I'm sorry, no."

"Accept that the birth echo is fused to the timbre by its parent, and that timbres can span multiple generations. That is, a timbre may beget others, which means that some have more than one echo. There is always one at the surface, and often others beneath, occurring in perfect sequence like links on a chain. Finally, embrace the fact that at the end of every echo chain is the same vision. This we believed to be true for quite some time. Does this make sense?"

"No, but I understand why you feel like math class now."

"In recent times," continued Crispin with a stern gaze, "we've had to accept our understanding was flawed. There were birth echoes that didn't fit the accepted doctrine. An alternate one emerged, and it is controversial."

"Which one is right?"

"The controversial one, it would seem," said Crispin, "which is unfortunate, since the conventional one was my life's work. Thus, I must recant ideas I once held dear."

"Sorry to hear it."

"I can see you're tired, Jordan. You will rest soon. There's something I want to show you tonight. I promise it won't be another tedious lecture or obstacle course."

Jordan nodded, his attention waning fast while his mind echoed *Li-la, Li-la.*

"Before we stop, I'd like to finish this topic. Birth echoes are memories from a parent timbre—that is, a memory from the past. This part you understand?"

"Yes."

"Yours is of a woman's face."

Jordan nodded.

"In my parlor, you saw, alongside your own work, similar ones by your predecessors, stretching back for thousands of years. They all harbored the same timbre, and thus carried the same vision of the eyes."

"I understand…"

"You have *perfectly* replicated, on that big canvas in your loft, the face you see in your birth echo—the full vision."

"Thanks."

"This person exists in *our* time, and her name is Lila. She was born in 1901 and arrived in our world in 1927. She carried her own birth echo, a vision that lingered with her *and* all of her predecessors. But where they saw a mere flicker, she now sees the full vision."

Jordan's mind rose out of its sleepy decline.

"But even in completeness, what she sees is obscured through her tears. Set against an eddying darkness with the staccato of lightning, she sees a man's face. Hidden in shadow, defined only by shape and outline…"

The implications started to trickle through Jordan's head.

"…of the identity of the face, I am now certain." Crispin lifted his cane and pointed it at Jordan. "It is yours."

10

OVER ELYSIUM

A rapid tapping on Jordan's shoulder woke him. He thought it was Maggie at first, believing he was back home in his loft. When he smelled leather and felt its fine surface pressed to his cheek, he remembered his decision to sleep in Crispin's library.

"Wake up, Jordan," came Eli's voice. "We're heading out."

The word *out* sparked his interest. Then his mind jumped to Crispin's explanation that his so-called birth echo was something from the future. Then it jerked to the so-called wrong people, and gunshots in broad daylight; those who would erase him without hesitation.

Jordan sat up and gathered his bearings. It was nighttime. Eli was walking toward the library's door.

"Eli?" said Jordan.

"What is it?" Eli halted and turned to Jordan in the near darkness, the pale light from beyond the doorway beaming twin trapezoids off his glasses.

"The things Crispin said…the right people, the wrong people. What am I involved in? Are you really the good ones?" The optical reflections vanished as Eli turned away. Jordan deveiled his finger, a red candle in the dark. It drew Eli's attention back.

Eli walked toward him, reluctantly. "I'm no longer certain there is good in any of this." Eli winced and struggled to look at him. "There is a terrible injustice at the heart of our world. But it's too late…We can't do anything…" Eli barreled his fist and pitched his chin to the side as though suppressing his words.

"What does that have to do with me?"

The answer escaped Eli's lips in a whisper: "*Everything.*"

Jordan stood, flaring his finger brighter.

"I can't speak more of it. I serve the Prudentiarum, and what we do is important, more important than these unfortunate circumstances." Eli pushed his glasses up the bridge of his nose. "These words I've said…they belong to us, they're not meant for others."

"I understand."

Eli deveiled, a burst of blue light forcing Jordan's eyes into a Venus-flytrap squint.

Jordan went on tiptoes and did the same. He dimmed and followed Eli, who glided out of the room. Down the hall they went, up through an open skylight, and onto the roof. Crispin was floating nearby, looking into the sky like a stoic ship captain.

"It's a good night," said Crispin.

Jordan saw Eli look him over, his expression confirming he'd said far more than he should have. Jordan gave him a reassuring nod. With that, concern started to drain away, the empty space conquered by a sense of adventure. With all the time spent on obstacle courses and textbook matters, he'd neglected thoughts of real flight.

"Remember, you can feel us, but we can't feel you," said Crispin. "We can only find you with our eyes, so keep up and keep close."

"Are we going to *our world,* as you called it?"

"Not tonight," said Crispin, still looking up.

"Are we going to see Lila?"

"Certainly not."

"Can you at least tell me where she lives?"

"Arbor Florum," said Crispin, the last word rhyming with *vacuum.*

"Never heard of it."

"A monumental effort goes into keeping it that way."

"So where *are* we going?"

"Up, Mr. Wakefield. Up." Crispin's dim blue form floated away into the night.

Jordan, still at the roofline, watched Crispin fade into the darkness, though his math-class feel still read strong. Eli went next, looking back until Jordan followed. Nerves caused him to blaze too bright at first. He relaxed it away, keeping his focus on Crispin and Eli, who checked back like uneasy chaperones.

And just like that, he was flying.

The black buffer of the redwood trees fell away. A glittering amber of residential lights blazed into Jordan's peripheral vision, yet he dared not look. Though he had no reason to fear heights now, a lifetime on the ground had left him unprepared. After a nervous minute, he settled into flight, finding ease in its mechanics again. He encouraged himself by way of doctrine: he was as light as a feather but far more indestructible.

More light slashed into view to the south, cutting a vivid line across the horizon. Jordan afforded himself a quick glance this time. Eli and Crispin blazed brighter and pulled away, climbing fast into the sky.

Jordan responded in kind.

He stole more glances at the world below, spying homes, roads, and structures concentrated in the valleys, larger residences punctuating hillsides. Car headlights flowed through networks of roads like fireflies cruising single file. To the south, an intense, radiant bloom emanated from San Francisco proper. The bay revealed itself by its lack of light; a pool of reflective black paint invading a sea of twinkling candles.

Crispin and Eli pulled away. The mental flickering of math class and paper airplanes remained strong. Jordan accelerated and chased it, hearing his melodic hum, feeling the air rush past him.

They climbed for minutes.

Then the flight path changed, from near-vertical to one with horizontal intent. They would arc over San Francisco. Even at humming speed, his hosts were still leaving him behind. Jordan took it as a challenge. He drew in as though taking a massive breath before diving into an ocean. Red light erupted in volcanic radiance about his body. His hum became wicked. He burst forward, the edges of his human form rippling and stretching out, dragging trails of light like a shooting star. As he closed the gap, still accelerating, his body stretched to twice its length. Intoxicating, exhilarating. The surprised faces of Crispin and Eli went by in a flash. Jordan kept going, kept pushing. Faster and faster, until a strange sensation took him. His shoulders felt like they had stretched to his waist. Then came a loss of hearing. Moments later, a radical distortion of vision. Then his senses blacked out completely.

Jordan panicked.

He stopped.

Sight and sound burst back into operation. Jordan faded himself until his body emitted a dim, undulating glow. Still looking upward, he spotted the deep night sky and its starlight. He sprouted a grin. The stars appeared here as they did in his hometown, an infinite array of distinct points, tinged with celestial purple, unhindered by urban glow. This moment of cosmic reflection was interrupted by math class and paper airplanes from below.

Jordan rolled over, looking earthward.

His mind went numb.

The spectacle drowned him: a silent mass of electric light shimmered below. He had seen photographs of this—the light of cities from space—yet images on a computer screen failed to capture the epic grandeur. The sprawl of electric light stretched outward in every direction, shining and radiant; a universe of human activity, as only gods could witness it. Jordan surrendered to a state of pleasant debilitation.

The twin blue ghosts of Crispin and Eli arrived. Their panic wilted into smiles as they settled in on each side of Jordan. Together, they were a trio of skydivers, suspended in space, looking down at a world that never came any closer.

"It is difficult to resist the lure of flight once you've tasted it," said Crispin speaking in a soft cadence. "And most are so enamored with the power, they miss the splendor. So tonight we indulge. But once you're back on the ground, I need you to stay there. Keeping our world secret is a shared responsibility. If one person sees you deveiled, it's their word against the many, which makes it manageable. But if it's more than one person, we have a problem. Delusion among the many is hard to stamp out."

Jordan's attention remained fastened to the canvas of electricity below.

"Before you return, I will write you a check for two hundred and fifty thousand dollars."

Jordan's whipped his attention to Crispin.

"I am pleased to see you're still listening." Crispin wore a faint grin. "The money is not to be spent beyond necessity, however. It will be a necessary step in your relocation to San Francisco. Same goes for the money in your pocket. To bring you into our world will be a delicate matter, so we will take small steps. Resolve any debts you may have, but do not make a show of it."

A touch of shame coursed through Jordan over his money problems. He'd pay off Steks and get his watch back, but he'd still get booted from the co-op.

None of it mattered anymore.

"The world as you understand it will change," continued Crispin. "What you knew with certainty will erode and break away. You'll be disoriented as you become part of our world." He flourished his blue hand as though offering the scene as a gift. "I envy the innocence of your eyes, and what they must be experiencing at this moment. It was so long ago when I was first over Elysium."

Jordan adopted Crispin's thoughts, imagining what it must have been like to see ancient Rome from the sky. Tunic-garbed citizens, bustling about its famous forum.

"I remember when these lights came into being," said Crispin. "I remember how fast they spread across the world. They gave me a perspective I hadn't considered before. A glimpse at the entirety of life."

Staring down at San Francisco, Jordan tried to discern individual buildings and cars but couldn't from these heights. The scene was only vague motion and contrasting intensities of light.

"Consider the human body for a moment," said Crispin. "It

consists of cooperating organs, which in turn consist of cooperating cells and agents, each of which performs a function. There are over three hundred types of agents in every single human being, and billions upon billions of agents in total. Now, consider what it would be like to be one of them. A blood cell, perhaps. Tasked to respond to events in the environment, reacting by instinct. All the while, you hold the inexorable belief that these tasks were the meaning of existence itself; a continued performance of repetitive functions. You remain unaware you're operating beneath the skin of a greater being. One you are a small part of, one never wholly visible from your vantage point."

Jordan glanced at Crispin, then returned to the scene below.

"Now see what is before you. Do these roads and cars flowing through them not resemble arteries and blood? Does the entire network not resemble a fusion of living organs, built from smaller components and deliberate patterns?"

Jordan's mind slid into Crispin's metaphor. He watched massive arteries pump yellow luminescent blood through the city. He saw San Francisco as a beating heart, pushing life through an enormous grid of electrical tissue.

"I've spent ages above Elysium, looking down on it as we do now. Only recently did I consider the possibility that all our actions, our trifles, our grand sense of purpose may be mere trivialities. The story of human history was always one of survival, and that long struggle blinded us. Civilization birthed a selfish belief: we were destined to conquer the earth, not act in companionship with it."

Jordan's eyes tracked the path of the arteries. They broke into thinner vessels, and then dim capillaries, carrying electric lifeblood to the most remote of places.

"The spectacular truth is that we may be nothing more than the blood of the earth; simple functionaries, working at the behest of a great entity we don't understand, one we fail to see. But now you have seen it. And I wish with all my light that this grants you a new perspective."

Jordan let these words flow through him, allowing them to fuse with the imagery his eyes captured. For a moment, he felt removed from the world, a cosmic spectator. When he rejoined it moments later, he did so with a new humility.

11

LOOSE ENDS

As Saint Paul's lunch hour traffic bustled by in the street outside his loft, Jordan smiled at an old photograph. Cased in a cheap frame, under yellowed glass was a picture of himself at a young age. He was standing next to his father, holding a fishing pole. The sun had nearly set in the background, casting amber reflections off the crests of restless waves that lapped against the breakwater. He could remember this moment, but just barely. He wrapped the photograph in newspaper and placed it in a box.

He picked up another picture frame: his father and mother, years before he was born. They were in a bowling alley wearing comical New Year's hats. Sitting down, his mother's legs were draped over his father's, while one of their friends blew a paper horn at them point-blank. With a grin, Jordan wrapped it and packed it away with the other.

He had remained faithful to Crispin's plea. He'd kept his feet on the ground, despite temptation from all things related to flight; travel advertisements, evening news reports shot from helicopters, birds racing by outside the building.

He had kept busy, stripping his loft bare. All the sketches were down. Only the masterpiece remained. The barren walls struck a nostalgic chord, reminding Jordan of the day he moved in. His first order of business had been to hang the swing, a task he performed with glee while plucking pizza out of a grease-tainted box on the floor.

Years ago. An era that would soon end.

Late into the night, with blinds drawn, Jordan had flayed his fingers and practiced the detection of regular people—faintlights as Crispin called them. Their signals bounced off walls, ceilings, and floors. Much like sound, physical obstruction limited transmission but didn't suppress it entirely. Faintlights lacked a unique feel, like Crispin's math class or Eli's paper airplanes. Jordan conceived it as a pale sensation, unspecific, except that it indicated life.

The sound of Maggie laughing caused Jordan to whip around. She was trying to kick loose an empty box stuck on her foot.

"I'm stumbling over your crap, man!" Maggie shook her foot free of the cardboard trap and sat in the swing. "I took your work down from the website and deleted all the digital copies, just as your master commanded."

"It's not like that."

"It's bullshit," said Blake marching into the room and up to Jordan. "It's cool that he's giving you this shot, but he doesn't *own* you. Whatever he's paying is not enough. He should *not* curtail your presence." He waved his finger at Jordan like he was a miscreant dog.

"It's really not like that," said Jordan, struggling to come up with a more robust justification.

In San Francisco, they'd all slept in the morning after their midnight adventure. Eli rushed Jordan to the airport with no strategy to handle questions beyond the announcement that he was moving to San Francisco.

"I know how it is," continued Blake. "Trust me, this sort of thing always starts with smiles and words, because both are cheap." Blake stomped about the room with one hand behind his back. "When these start to falter, the smiles go away, and then the words turn harsh. Then it's threats. What I am saying is this: be careful. Don't get had." Blake stopped pacing and turned to Jordan. He drew his hand out from behind his back like it was a gun. He shook Jordan's hand. "I wanted to say farewell. I'm flying out in a few hours, and you'll be long gone by the time I'm back. Good luck out there."

Jordan nodded, deciding to keep his response minimal.

"You're a good cat, Jordan Wakefield." Blake invaded his personal space. "Still too innocent, still too healthy. You need some mistakes, some scars, some hurt." Blake pinched the air in front of Jordan's face, as if those things were to be found in it. Then, quite abruptly, he walked away.

Maggie giggled. "The man hates planes. That's why he's so spastic." She jumped to her feet. "Hey, I don't mean to pry, but are you good with Steks?"

"Yeah, we're meeting at the Pilgrim Cat tonight to square up."

"Good." Maggie puffed a breath of relief. "We're going to miss you around here, but you're gonna do great out there."

"I hope so, Maggs." Jordan glanced at his mammoth sketch.

"How are you getting that to San Francisco?"

"Crispin is sending his people here to ship it."

"Who?" asked Maggie, rumpling her brow.

"Christopher!" blurted Jordan, trying to keep his face from going flush. He rambled before Maggie could question it further: "Listen I'm heading up north to see my dad before I go. I promised I'd be there for his birthday and that was before there was any real talk of moving away, but we'll have beers before I leave."

"Slow down, cowboy." Maggie scratched her ear and looked him over, giggling. "Are you still telling people about your vision thing?"

This time Jordan blushed. "I decided to keep that to myself after all. Don't know what I was thinking. It was stupid."

"But funny." Maggie drew zipper fingers across her lips. "I haven't told a soul, so your crazy is safe with me. You still might want to see someone…or get more sleep." Maggie giggled herself into a wide smile and marched forward. Jutting her arm out, she channeled her inner Blake and shook Jordan's hand wildly.

"Thanks, Maggs."

"I'll see you tomorrow," she said, her gaze lingering on the way out.

Jordan returned to the realm of the mundane, which ran uninterrupted until late evening when he heard his door creak open. It slammed shut. Jordan turned to see Steks locking it behind him. The watch was on his wrist.

"I do a lot of business in this place." Steks walked toward him, boots thumping on the floor. "Pretty easy to find my way in if I want to visit artsy-fartsy Wakefield." Steks fanned effeminate hand motions as he approached. His alpha-male poise returned by the time he was face to face with Jordan. "You're *late*, motherfucker."

Jordan took a step back. "I have your money. All of it. Hold on." Jordan walked backward, eyes on Steks, who smiled on recognizing the caution. Jordan returned from his bedroom to find Steks leering at the giant sketch of Lila.

"That's one fine bitch." Steks licked one of his incisors. "But what's with all the crying? Could have drawn me behind her, then she'd be smiling."

"Six thousand," said Jordan, ignoring it. He slapped the wad of cash into Steks's hand. "We're square."

Steks lost his swagger momentarily, surprised by the money. Licking his lips, he counted it before forcing it into his coat pocket. "See you around, Wakefield."

Steks turned and started to walk away.

"The watch," said Jordan. "You said six including the watch."

"It was…" Steks halted. "But you fucked with me. Now I'm fucking with you."

"You're not leaving with that watch."

"Is that so, Wakefield?" Steks still had his back turned. He flipped the clasp on the watch open, letting it dangle loosely about his left hand. "Come get it."

Jordan didn't hesitate. He moved fast, eyes on the watch.

"Gonna cost you…" Steks whirled around, the arc of the wrench already in a downstroke toward Jordan's face.

Jordan deveiled violently, vaporizing the wrench head milliseconds from his jaw. Steks screamed as the decapitated wrench seared into his skin, sending wisps of smoke up between his knuckles. He dropped the tool and backpedaled, smacking against the far wall. Jordan flew to him in a flash, stopping inches short. He saw the reflection of his red fiery self shimmering in Steks's wide, frightened eyes.

Jordan veiled, drawing a panicked yelp from Steks. He snatched the watch from his trembling hand.

"We're square. Got it?" said Jordan, his face inches away.

"Wh-wh-what the fuck are you?"

Jordan smiled. Flaying his index finger, he put it in front of his own lips. "Shhhhhhh…" The long exhale wafted his deveiled red finger ever-closer to Steks, who pressed his head against the wall, trying to escape it. Jordan veiled his finger, seized Steks by the coat, and shoved him face-first into the door. Steks fumbled with the lock, opened the door, and was gone.

Crispin's warnings peppered Jordan's conscience. He shrugged. It was just one person. Nobody would believe that asshole anyway.

Wiping his watch clean, he put it in the bedroom. He tossed the still-warm, severed wrench handle into the trash and returned to packing but couldn't stay on task. His machismo was running too hot, which prodded him into taking a walk. Strolling on autopilot, he found himself advancing on the park that overlooked the city—the one where he had discovered his birth echo weeks ago. On the way, low-hanging rain clouds buttressed his thinking: most people would be indoors. As the sidewalk bent south, on final approach to the park, he finally acknowledged the plan he was already acting on.

He would take a flight.

Just a quick one.

12

JUST A QUICK ONE

Jordan crossed the park lawn and slipped past the tree line at the southern edge. A minute later, he reached a steep drop-off which marked the bluff's rim. From here he had a wide-open view of the river valley: industrial parks, railroad lines, and a small airfield, all divorced from the bluff by the meandering thick of the Mississippi River.

Jordan flayed his hand, feeling out his surroundings. Sensing no one nearby, he leaned forward toward the tipping point. A charge of excitement fired through him…and then:

Phone—wallet—keys!

Thrusting his arms out, he paddled the air like a tightrope walker on the verge of a fatal mistake. He fell backward onto the ground.

Fucking idiot.

Standing, he fished out his personal effects, buried them under leaves, and stepped to the edge again. With a decisive leap this time, he was in the air. The forest below rushed toward him. With a quick snap, he deveiled and floated stationary above the treetops. His red silhouette was not prominent against the evening light, a feature he realized would aid him. He went lax and glided up into the sky, away from the protective harbor of the woods. A hundred feet up, he spotted a portly man on a hiking path, looking right at him.

Jordan froze, trying to determine if the man could see him. The inquisitive gaze remained locked on him until his dog yapped. The moment he looked down, Jordan gunned it. The wide, flat plane of the land fell away as he raced for cover like a rabbit.

Jordan shook it off: just one person and his dumb dog.

He reached the clouds, securing himself within their bountiful sanctuary. Breaks in the cotton-white puffs granted him sight of the land below, a perfect balance between seclusion and voyeurism. He set off, a compounding sense of delight infecting him as he darted through the firmament. He indulged in reaching ever-higher heights, veiling at each peak. He felt the bitter cold air whip him like December as he free fell. The plunge rattled his clothes with violence until he develied again.

He paused and took in the westward view.

The sun was low on the horizon. Night was near. Though the upper skies were still lit deep azure, the surface below was already transforming into the gridded electric life he'd witnessed over San Francisco. He raced toward the sunset, letting his mind drift. He would never know hunger or thirst again, or what it was to be sick. He wouldn't have to live his life at the behest of a job, or by *those* rules anymore. There was no longer a need for money, and should a transient one occur, he had it handled. He wouldn't know death.

Free.

The word materialized with new meaning as he hovered a few thousand feet in the air. It pranced through his mind, making him realize he never truly understood the concept. He never considered his life having been lived under any form of servitude. Yet he had never been exempt from the laws of nature until now.

Free.

Jordan burst skyward, his body stretching into a red rocket trail. One final climb, one final drop before going home. At the apex, he veiled, bending into the arc of a backward dive. Chest up, chin aimed into the cosmos. He plunged through icy-cold air, at peace with the furious descent. He watched clouds rip past as if he were stationary and they were being sucked into the heavens.

He closed his eyes.

There was only the fall and its beautiful, unnatural hold. A dull, rhythmic thumping grew audible. He opened his eyes and saw thick, majestic clouds far, far above.

The ground!

The thumping grew distinct, and in milliseconds, it sharpened into drums, guitars, and a howling human voice. Panic seized Jordan, and he deveiled with a violent crack, coming to a stop.

There was a crowd below him, pumping their fists—not at him—but toward a stage strewn with clusters of colored lights cycling in all directions. A long-haired man was wailing into a microphone, contorting himself into a backward arch. He wrestled with the microphone stand as if it were a deadly serpent that had fallen from the sky. The man's face was aimed at Jordan. His eyes went wide and he fell into a sitting position on the stage. Feedback whistled out as the singer jerked the mic back to his mouth, his other hand pointing at Jordan.

"WHAT THE HELL IS THAT!"

The rest of the musicians looked up. Their performance fell apart, leaving only the electrical hum of the amplifiers. They started to point too.

Jordan's mind blew a fuse. This was more than one person. Petrified, he remained frozen, beaming bright red light toward the crowd below. He imagined a deranged Crispin loading his gun with real bullets this time.

This was a lot of fucking people.

At stage right, a woman shouldering a video camera twisted around and adopted the same look of shock. She trained the camera on him. In less than a second, the crowd's confused chatter escalated into a dissonant roar, hundreds of hands in the air pointing. Twinkling light burst forth from everywhere; flashes from cell phone cameras.

The amplified voice boomed again, "WHAT IS IT?"

Move was the word that boomed through Jordan's head.

At last, Jordan shot straight up into the clouds, hearing the crowd emit a collective yelp at his sudden departure. No grace, no confidence now, just aimless flight paths. He forced himself to stop and gain composure. He recalled how Crispin and Eli had to study patterns of electric light to get home.

Crispin and Eli…

They're going to kill me for real this time.

Jordan sleuthed his way back to Saint Paul. After a careful approach to the park, he descended dimly and veiled. He dug his personal effects out of the leaves like an animal and took off in a run.

When Jordan came up alongside the Renslit, he caught his reflection in a window. He looked guilty of murder. He took the back door and raced upstairs. Emerging from the stairwell, he crept toward his loft. His keys jingled as he sorted through them and lifted the correct one to the lock. A pair of hands grabbed him by the shoulders.

Jordan shouted and dropped his keys.

"Jordan!" yelled Maggie. "You have to see this!" She pulled at him like a police officer taking down a criminal. Jordan broke free and snatched his keys off the floor. He tried to unlock his door for the second time. Maggie resumed the wrestling match, giggling. "Why are you fighting me—come on! I'm serious, you have to see this." His next attempt to get inside turned her giggle into mad laughter. "What the hell are you doing?"

Jordan sighed and surrendered. He turned to find her halfway down the first flight of stairs, expecting him to follow. Her chipper face peeked at him from just above the railing.

"You're not going to believe this!" Maggie waved excited hands.

But Jordan knew he *would* believe it. Every single bit of it. He didn't know what else to do, so he followed her with his head down like a convict on his way to the gallows.

Maggie threw open the doors to the Pilgrim Cat. The place was packed, everyone staring at televisions. Jordan refused to look. He instead watched Maggie's heels mow through peanut-shell carnage toward a table in the back. Jordan's first glance up found Chad, a sculptor who lived a floor below Maggie. He was standing on the support pegs of his stool to see above the crowd. Gripping the sides of the table, his face was wrapped in ecstasy. He was into the supernatural and *weird shit*, as he called it.

"Hey, Jordan," said Chad's girlfriend, Helen. "Heard you got a sweet gig in San Francisco. Congrats."

Jordan offered an awkward smile and a huff. A pair of hands grabbed him, yanking him sideways. Maggie again, her mouth pressing to his ear as though preparing to French kiss it. She whispered violently:

"It's real! Your red ghost—it's actually real! I didn't tell anyone what you said, but holy hot shitcakes, you're not crazy—it's fucking real! What are you going to do? How are you going to find it?" Maggie spun Jordan's bar stool so that they were face to face, her eyes drilling eagerly into his. Jordan felt his face go bone white. Ticks and itches erupted from every square inch of his skin. Just as he was about to force a response, a roar of applause snatched her attention away.

"BREAKING NEWS" flew across the bottom of the television. Chad scolded everyone to shut the fuck up. Maggie locked onto the screen, forgetting Jordan was even there. A local news anchor's face spouted words that couldn't penetrate the noise of the crowd. To the right of her talking head was an inset clip of a red ghost floating in the sky.

Jordan started to hyperventilate. If this was already local news, it might go national and Crispin might see it. Who was he kidding? Crispin found him through a picture on their co-op's website. He *was* going to see this. The whole fucking world was going to see this. Jordan tried to gain composure through a fusion of Zen meditation and raging self-contempt; breathe in, breathe out, drop f-bombs through clenched teeth.

The bartender fumbled with three remote controls, stabbing at buttons with his pudgy fingers, maxing out the volume on every television. The news anchor's voice filled the room. The crowd hushed, hanging on every word. The video clip shrank and the camera zoomed out to reveal the haggard figure Jordan recognized from the rock band.

"With us tonight is the man who spotted the red ghost, Roland

Feasel, lead singer of the band"—the anchor stole a glance at a piece of paper on her desk—"Bacon Church." She rumpled her expression as though she'd just cursed on air.

Roland nodded approvingly.

"Okay…so what happened out there tonight?"

As Roland spoke, the video of the red ghost took over the entire screen. Jordan turned away but continued to listen to the singer's analysis, "…and hundreds of our fans have this footage too. Unfortunately, we can't see it close up, but it *does* look quite human. I don't know what it is, but it seems to be a fan. We hope it comes to our next show in Milwaukee. After that, Chicago, then Cleveland."

After the broadcast broke to commercial, the bar erupted with applause and whistles. Jordan scanned the crowd. Animated faces, happy faces. They paid him no notice but beamed at each other with a peculiar pride, anchored to the possibility that their quiet Midwestern domain would become the center of the world's attention. The tendons in Chad's neck ran taut, and just when he started spouting personal vindications for his unwavering belief in the existence of weird shit, Jordan got up and left.

He ran upstairs, gathered clothes and stuffed them into his backpack. In the parking lot, he fished out his phone, afraid to even look at it. He summoned the courage to peek: no calls, no messages. Nothing at all from Crispin or Eli—not yet.

But fucking Steks would know it was him. Jordan started to tap out a death threat to him. But sanity won out and he deleted it. Would he have to silence Steks another way? He could pay him off.

Fucking stupid, stupid, stupid.

A drop of sweat slapped down onto the phone screen, twisting pixels into cancerous shapes. Jordan powered it down and got into his car. With the radio off and windows up, he drove away into the night.

13

REPRIEVE

The next morning a voice from the television boomed through Jordan's childhood home. Though he couldn't hear it clearly through the bathroom door, the topic wasn't difficult to divine, nor his father's level of interest. Jordan stared into the darkened face of his phone, still lacking the courage to turn it on. He shoved it back in his pocket, opened the door, and took a few steps into the hallway. Stopping short of the living room, he pressed his forehead to the wall, keeping himself upright in this manner, simmering in a pool of regret.

He unglued himself from the hallway and pressed on to the living room. Though standing in the open, his father failed to notice his arrival. With a firm jawline pointed toward the television, his father was perched on the edge of the couch as though ready to be called into a job interview. Jordan studied his stocky build, the further silvering of his hair. With an expanding waistline, Jordan wagered he was only a decade away from being a perfect Santa Claus. He'd only need the beard.

Jordan squinted at the television: cable news.

The story had gone national.

As the analysis unfurled, Jordan's eyes went to his parents' wedding picture above the fireplace. He adored that photograph. Looking at it now gave him a moment of reprieve. In it a much younger version of his father and the mother he never knew. His father was gazing off center, too far from the photographer's lens. His mother's elegant hand clasped his shoulder, smiling at him with the side of her face to the camera.

A strange, slow voice on the television pulled Jordan's attention back: "The ghost is clearly there. Floating. It is red." A painful silence followed before the female broadcaster's voice piped up.

"Yes, Mister *For-ray*. We've established that. As a self-proclaimed expert on ghosts, I am wondering if you might tell me more?"

Jordan jogged his memory, the name sounding familiar.

"Yes," droned the slow voice. "I can tell you more about ghosts."

"What the hell…" muttered his father.

Jordan made the connection: Felix De La Forêt, the editor of *Les Revenants*, the street rag Chad was always waving about during his rants on the supernatural. Jordan knew it front to back but read it discreetly. Felix's mannerisms were uncomfortable and wooden, and though his disheveled hair was a fascinating attribute, the greatest oddity was his eyes. They remained wide-open as though fossilized into a permanent look of surprise. The news anchor, quite bewildered, glanced at the man while struggling to keep her face front and center.

Felix stared straight at the anchor. "Might I trouble you for another glass of water?"

"Mr. Forêt: tell us what you see in this video," begged the anchor, as though sensing a secondary fame on the internet, the segment becoming the gravestone of her career.

A red banner with the words "Red Ghost in the Midwest: Real or Hoax?" scrolled across the screen. Below it: "Mr. Felix Lark De La Forêt, Proprietor, *Les Revenants*: Ghost Expert." As Jordan read the words, a question mark materialized after the word "Expert."

"Jordan!" said his father, startling him.

Jordan stumbled back and knocked a pile of books off an end table. "I wasn't expecting you. Heard you come in late last night. You look terrible—been getting enough sleep?"

"I wanted to get out of town."

"You should have stayed there." His father pointed at the television. "This ghost thing happened *right* by you. Did you hear about this—it's damned crazy."

"I heard something," mumbled Jordan, looking down at the worn, earth-toned carpeting.

"Well, have a seat." His father slapped the cushion next to him. "You gotta see this—it's bizarre—this guy here is a total nutcase. I can't believe they put him on TV. The whole thing is nuts."

With that declaration, Jordan found a possible purpose of Felix and his *Les Revenants*: a decoy. A stage act meant to discredit the notion of ghosts by putting a crazy person at the forefront as an expert. Damage control already underway for his indiscretions. His mind wished it desperately, but then skipped sideways: this also meant the freelight world would know he'd returned…and that included the people who wanted to use real bullets.

"I'd rather not," said Jordan, noticing they were airing the rock concert footage. He cringed as the boomy voice in the video yelled to the crowd: *What the hell is that?*

His father alternated attention between Jordan and the television. Though last night's broadcast stated it impossible to make out a face, apprehension seized Jordan, drowning him in the certainty his father would recognize him.

The camera zoomed in on the red apparition.

The television reclaimed his father's attention.

Jordan panicked. "I'm MOVING to San Francisco!"

Startled by the outburst, his father jittered and sank into the couch, his posture deflating like a punctured life raft. After a few seconds he picked up the remote. He turned the volume down, then turned off the television. Jordan watched him stand and walk past into the kitchen, unable to make eye contact.

"You're probably hungry."

Jordan remained stuck in place, looking at the dark television screen while listening to his father rummage about, pulling pans out from under the stove. Jordan turned and took a few steps toward the kitchen. Leaning against the archway, he observed the defeated hulk of his father swing the freezer door open, his head disappearing behind it.

"I have to get to work," he said, his voice muffled by the metal curtain. "Sausage or Bacon?"

Jordan didn't answer, his father didn't wait. He tossed a pack of each on the countertop. A long silence unfolded. His father remained behind the veil of the freezer door, his grip tight on the handle as if needing support. Jordan found himself longing for the noise of the television to return.

14

WAKEFIELD ROCK

While his father was out, Jordan burned the day away on yard work, fueled by guilt. By late afternoon he found himself on the couch, his shirt hanging sticky on him, body arched forward with elbows propped on knees. His eyes went to the wedding photo over the mantle again, recalling the story that came with it.

Despite the photograph being taken before either was ready, it turned out a better shot than the choreographed ones. His father had always struggled to smile on demand, a shortcoming that generated much humor over the years, and likely much frustration with the wedding photographer. Jordan's mother, as the story went, would peek at him during the shots, always falling into peals of laughter over the manufactured smiles. The photographer caught the moment, and they went with it for eternity. Jordan felt all he really knew about his mother came from this photograph. It was of the few that existed.

The couch cushions shifted suddenly, and Jordan found his father sitting down next to him. He hadn't heard him come in. Jordan's eyes fell from the photograph.

"They rarely lose someone in childbirth anymore," said his father, trying to keep his voice steady. "I was numb when they told me. They brought you in and we cried together."

Jordan tried to face his father but found the best he could manage was a quick glance. His eyes drifted to the dark television screen, which bounced back a dull portrait of the two of them, parked next to each other like strangers.

"I did the best I could raising you, but it wasn't easy. I want to see things turn out right. Sometimes that requires a little prodding in one direction or another. At least that's what I think I'm supposed to do."

"You did great, Dad." Jordan swallowed and stared at the floor. "But there are things I have to go through alone."

Jordan imagined himself from his father's perspective: the man harbored dreams that entailed the good job and the good girl, like any other dad. But what he'd witnessed was a son who disappeared from life, engaged in solitary activities with little apparent direction. A son who played his cards so close to his chest, it was difficult to tell if he was holding a hand at all.

"Because I lost your mother, I've always feared I'd lose you too. I hold on too tight—I know I do."

Jordan waggled his chin, reflecting on the heartless announcement of his departure. "How about we go fishing tonight?"

His father smiled and glanced at the photograph. "Yeah, let's do it."

Hours later they were at an old haunt called Black River Harbor, standing atop a line of boulders that formed a breakwater that jutted into Lake Superior. They cast lures into the lake and reeled them back while a pleasant sunset painted the scene in front of them. The sounds—the gentle plop into the water, the buzz of the reel, and the rhythmic slapping of small waves against the rock line—soothed two turbulent minds.

"I shouldn't have yelled it out like that," said Jordan. "About moving away. And I didn't mean to dismiss the college thing so coldly."

His father shrugged. "Quick, like a Band-Aid, right?" He reeled his line, the tip of his pole bending a soft arc toward the water. "At first I thought my college idea was about employment. I wanted to see you in something steady."

"The practical Picasso…"

"Yeah, that." His father grunted a laugh and went silent, leaving only the faint call of seagulls and lapping water. "But it's really about me trying to keep you around. To not let go."

Jordan's expression sunk. He imagined his father's daily life after he moved away: quiet evenings alone at the dinner table, bar-league softball at the best of times. But then came the long winters, snow piling up outside with only the television to keep him company.

"If San Francisco is the real deal—and it seems it is, then I don't have it in my heart to tell you no." Jordan's father kicked his heel against the rock, a reflex Jordan knew to be rooted in stress. "But I know I'm not ready for the distance. We'd see each other once, maybe twice a year. After a few dozen visits, we'll both have gray hair." His father nudged him with a playful elbow.

Jordan absorbed it while his mind jumped elsewhere: he would *never* be old and gray. How long could he fake it—how long would he be allowed to fake it? How could he—

"Jordan?" asked his father. "You didn't sell it, did you?"

"What?" said Jordan, squinting at light glinting off the water.

"Your watch. The one I gave you for graduation."

"Of course not. I just don't wear it all the time." Jordan fell into another silence, contemplating his altercation with Steks, which led to reflections on his reckless flight. Then came the horrifying memory of his red-ghost, rock star fame. He winced and cringed and fidgeted, feeling the bulk of his phone in his jeans. It was still turned off. He couldn't turn it on, he couldn't face the inevitable torrent of messages from Eli and Crispin. So he hatched a fair compromise: as soon as he was on the road, he'd fire it up and take his lumps.

Jordan cast his line out, affixing Zen focus to the whizzing of the reel. He imagined his troubles fastened to that lure, watching them flash through the sunlight and disappear into the purifying blue water. Gone…until he reeled them back in. "We never seem to catch much here, do we, Dad?"

His father let out a hearty chuckle. "You noticed. It's not a good spot this time of year. Only in the spring. But I like coming here. It's where I proposed to your mother, you know."

Jordan stopped reeling and looked over.

"I never told you that story, did I?" His father smiled, staring into the horizon.

"No, you didn't."

"It was a summer evening, like this. I had planned to do it, rain or shine. As luck would have it, I got shine. There was a beautiful sunset, even nicer than this one."

Jordan looked out over the water. The sky was thick purple now, dashed with oranges and yellows, only the upper edge of the sun peeking past it.

"I think she knew I was going to do it. I kept tripping and cursing these rocks as we made our way out here." His father stomped for effect. "She was all smiles, of course, and pretended not to notice that something was up."

Jordan grinned, imagining his father scolding the boulders as if they were part of a grand conspiracy.

"She said yes, and this is where it happened. This rock we're standing on right now."

Jordan had never noticed his father's sentimentality all the times they'd been here, but it was apparent now.

"I stopped coming after your mom passed. I would never have come again, but you asked to. You were just a kid, but led the way, holding my hand."

"I remember that," said Jordan, locating the event in his most remote of memories. Simpler times, before visions and ghosts.

"So, we made something new out of an old place—or I should say, you did. We took a picture together on the rock. I set the camera over there." His father turned his head and gestured with his chin to a tall boulder behind them.

"I still have that picture," said Jordan.

"Well, how 'bout that."

They watched the upper rim of the sun recede behind the horizon, revisiting Jordan's childhood memories as long as light would allow. At the edge of night, they traversed the breakwater back to land and made their way to the parking lot.

As pleasant as it was, Jordan's thoughts quickly raced back to his problems. They were knotting his stomach with machine-like precision. The situation was a ticking time bomb, one he'd have to disarm. And if he couldn't, he would have to flee somewhere fast.

"Dad?"

"What is it, champ?" said his father, catching Jordan's elbow as he stumbled.

"I have to go back to Saint Paul tomorrow."

"You just got here!"

"I know." Jordan looked away but forced himself to look back. "I have to take care of something. I'll be back for your birthday, and the Fourth of July."

His father put an arm out, stopping their progress. "What's going on with you?" He closed in, squaring himself with Jordan face to face.

"Nothing." Jordan gazed at his father, just able to discern his face in the failing light. "I'll be back, Dad. I promise."

15

BACK INTO HIDING

Jordan ascended the Renslit's stairwell with stealth, taking large-arced steps that made him imagine a cartoon character sneaking up on prey. He'd returned to Saint Paul just after midnight, hoping Friday night had lured everyone out to the bars—success on that front so far. On the drive in, he found his phone in hand no less than four times, finger hovering over the power button. But he failed each time, kicking the task into the future. There were over three million people in the metropolitan area. As long as he didn't deveil, nobody from the freelight world would find him.

But fucking Steks…that he *would* have to deal with.

Jordan lifted the chalkboard that hung on his door, which read "AWAY." He was about to rub it clean but stopped. He put it back. In went the key. With the caution of a thief, he turned the knob and slipped inside, closing and relocking. He kept the lights off, lest someone notice his return.

Jordan stretched out on the couch, immediately betraying his vow to face his phone. He'd rest for just a few minutes first. Turning onto his side, he stared at the giant portrait of Lila. There was just enough ambient light passing in from outside to make out her features: the dark shroud of her hair, her light complexion, and, of course, those eyes.

Jordan closed his own.

He begged sleep to take him, but it refused at first, instead pelting him with hypotheticals. What will you do next? What will you say to Crispin? A few frantic seconds later, he was juggling a pair of propositions: hide out or fly away—to where, he didn't know. His head continued to deal out fragments, the shrapnel of a frazzled mind.

Just before nodding off, he reflected on the events of the last two weeks. He saw himself flying over San Francisco. He saw Crispin's parlor, the guns, the dinner, and the painting of the burning dancer. He imagined the veiling sound—he *heard* it as if it were happening in his loft right now. It seemed so real. Finally, at the edge of consciousness, he pondered his vision of Lila—the precursor to all. He glanced at the epic portrait one more time, glimpsing the dark canopy of her hair just before his eyes fell shut again.

Part of her face was missing.

Jordan's mind accelerated into a violent reversal, sending his eyes wide open. Someone was standing in front of the portrait.

Jordan yelled and kicked backward. He launched himself up over the arm of the couch and on top of an end table, which collapsed, causing a lamp to fall into his lap. The figure leaped toward him, landing in a crouched position. A face arrived point-blank in front of his own.

"Quiet," said the voice, just above a whisper. "You'll wake your neighbors, and I *do* suspect you're trying to avoid them...not to mention others, yes?"

"You're here to kill me." It came out like a declaration of fact.

"If I was, you'd already be dead."

The voice trafficked in a faint accent—possibly French. The stranger's hand erupted into a luminous flare, filling the space between them with a fiery orange light. The burst startled Jordan, the sudden illumination making him squint. The stranger's face was visible now. It was a handsome one, peering down at Jordan through confident blue eyes. The gaze made him recognize his own comparative absurdity, sitting on a broken table, holding a lamp like it was a sack of groceries.

"We have a problem, don't we?" said the stranger. He moved his spectral fingers, making them waver.

"Did Eli send you?" asked Jordan, his nerves rattling the lamp like a paint shaker. "Or Crispin?"

"Is there some particular reason they would?" A smirk emerged on the man's face during the silence. His next words came in soft, syncopated rhythm, as if part of a poem: "What—the—hell—is—that?"

The words catapulted Jordan back to the rock concert where he revealed his freelight self to the whole world. "*That* was an accident."

"I certainly hope so, but I must say it was a grand entrance."

Jordan sidled off the broken table and put the lamp down. He reached under the shade and turned it on. The man veiled his fire fingers. "Who are you?"

"I am Sebastién Saint-Vezina." The stranger returned to a standing position. "But Sebastién will do fine." He strolled to the far side of the room and plucked a metal ventilation grate off the floor. He propped it up against the wall and winked. "Service entrance."

Jordan studied Sebastién as he returned. His dark hair sheened black in the low light. He moved aristocratically, like he'd materialized straight out of Victorian high society, mannerisms elegant in a way not easy to describe. He wore an off-white, collared shirt with the top button undone. Over that, and well-fitted to his form, was a black, collarless suit jacket, its *v*-shaped center plunging low. Custom tailored jeans completed the ensemble. Sebastién was taller, but his build less muscular, which Jordan added to his fight or flight calculation before realizing such things were irrelevant between people of *their* kind.

Sebastién extended his hand.

Jordan paused and then took it. He was yanked to his feet, left standing on quaking legs. Sebastién sat down on the couch and stretched one arm across the back of it.

"Please, sit," he said, pointing at the opposite end of the couch with an outstretched hand. "We should talk."

"I'll stand." Jordan grabbed his backpack off the floor, his eyes locked on Sebastién the whole time. Scrounging inside, Jordan drew out his phone. His index finger ran the edge for the power button.

"Haven't had that on since your big arrival, I see. That would explain a lot." Sebastién leaned back, while Jordan waited for his phone to flash to life. Sebastién's eyes wandered to the microwave in the kitchen and then back. "I need you to come with me."

"Is that what Crispin and Eli want?"

"I suspect your phone is about to confirm that."

Jordan looked at it: Fifteen fucking missed calls; two from Maggie right after he had fled. The other thirteen from Eli, who left a voicemail with each.

"Christ." Tapping the most recent message, Jordan shoved the phone to his ear, only to hear Eli's voice explode from it. He drew it away, realizing he must have hit speakerphone:

"Uh, Jordan…it's Eli again. I'm sorry for yelling at you in those first few messages—I'm really sorry. I hope you're avoiding me because of that. If my colleague hasn't arrived by now you need to get out of there. Go somewhere and call me when you get this. Things aren't going well, and I can't reach Crispin. He's halfway across the world. Jordan…you're in danger."

Jordan felt sick to his stomach. The phone fell from his grasp, thumping off the floor like a giant domino. He went to the swing and dropped into it.

"I'm in danger?" said Jordan, his tone rhetorical, his gaze intense but distant.

"Yes. Just as dear Eli said."

"Why?"

"There are people who don't want you to return—Lux Sanguinis, that is. And that group is rather ambitious." Sebastién drummed soft patters on the couch with his fingers.

"What do we do?"

"We run—and by that, I mean we fly." Sebastién glanced at the microwave again. "And we should be embarking on that noble journey now."

"Where?" asked Jordan, realizing Sebastién was reading its clock.

"To Arbor Florum, the Grey City." Sebastién eyed Jordan while a span of silence owned the room. "By the look on your face, I'd surmise they haven't told you about that."

"Just the name. Pronounced differently."

"Ah yes, Floor-*oom* instead of floor-*um*; the elder way—so un-cosmopolitan."

"Crispin said I wouldn't believe it even if I saw it…"

"Oui, oui. That is the place." Sebastién plucked at the fabric of Jordan's couch.

"Where is it?"

"California, though we were there long before they called it that—we should be going."

"I want to call Eli back first."

Sebastién paused and folded his hands in his lap. "If you must. Only, I'd rather you talk to him when we're in Florum, and not linger here any longer. Dangerous people on the prowl, as you know."

Jordan slouched forward, contemplating Sebastién's words. "Why do people want me to disappear?"

"A fascinating story, but one we don't have time for now."

"Give me the short version."

"Very well." Sebastién betrayed a touch of frustration but swallowed it quickly. "Once upon a time, your predecessor tracked down some war criminals. A few years later, said criminals killed him for it. And now they want to kill you for good measure. The end." Sebastién stood and walked over to the giant portrait of Lila, his polished shoes cracking sharp off the floor. "If they get to you first, it would be easy to believe you self-discovered and died by your own foolish accord. That theory would carry weight, given your recent actions—even if Crispin and Eli vouched for having met you, the claim would stand."

"So they sent you?" asked Jordan, hands clutching the swing's ropes.

"I've got speed and luck, and we need both."

"We're safe if we get to California?"

"Safer, yes. And we'd have a chance to right a wrong." Sebastién's eyes slid down the face of the mammoth sketch. "Let me ask you something." He turned to Jordan with a sly grin on his face. "Would you like to meet her, Miss Lila Harper?"

"You know her?" Jordan perked up from his sunken posture.

"Of course. She's a dear friend, and involved in this too." Sebastién took a step closer to Jordan, his sharp eyes peering at him. "Her predecessor and yours were killed together. Crispin and Eli didn't tell you *that* story, now did they?"

"No. They didn't."

"But I did, because it's fair that you know—in fact, it's essential that you know."

Jordan looked past Sebastién, to the sketch of Lila. Then he glanced at his phone on the floor. He'd already decided.

"Does anyone know you're back in town?" asked Sebastién, as though he'd also detected the decision.

"I came in late to avoid everyone. I parked in a different lot far from here in case I decided to run again."

"C'est magnifique." Sebastién plucked Jordan's phone off the floor. "I need to borrow this for a moment." He tapped deftly at the screen and tossed the phone back to Jordan. He turned back to the portrait of Lila and waited.

Jordan looked at the screen. A text to an unknown number:

We're coming in. Tell Lila.

Jordan's heart skipped a beat. He stared at the words until Sebastién's voice drew him back.

"The crying—is *this* how you actually see her?" Sebastién's poise faltered. "Of course…you are the first to see the whole thing."

"So I'm told."

"Well, it was bound to happen eventually." Sebastién motioned for Jordan to stand. "Kill your phone, it's time to go."

16

CROSS COUNTRY

Sebastién's fiery orange form zipped through the Renslit's generous ventilation ducts. Jordan struggled to keep up, distracted by his signal. Sebastién felt like a poker game. A house party during Jordan's senior year where he'd bluffed his way in too deep; heart thumping, one month's pay from his grocery-store gig on the table. On the rooftop, they veiled and Sebastién looked up into the night sky.

"Anyone like us out there?"

Jordan flayed his hand and panned it around. "Nothing."

"You understand how this works, yes? You can detect everyone but nobody can detect you. They *will*, however, sense me, which means it's up to you to tell me if anyone shows up on your radar. Got it?"

Jordan nodded in jitters. "We're flying to California like this?"

"We are, and it's going to take all night. Are you rested?"

Jordan shook his head.

"Falling asleep out of boredom tends to be of the stranger ways we die. It gets dull up there."

"It's still pretty fascinating to me."

"Well then, stay fascinated. And keep up." Sebastién deveiled with a crack, causing Jordan to turn away. When he looked back,

Sebastién was already a slice of orange fire in the dark sky. Not slow and cautious and dim like Crispin, also not looking back.

Jordan deveiled and shot upward, a strange sense of leaving coming over him. He didn't have time to process it. Chasing Sebastién into the night, he needed nearly a minute to catch him.

"The ones we want to avoid will be coming from the north or the west," said Sebastién. "We'll be going south—the long way 'round."

The dense mass of city light faded out. Upon reaching a higher altitude, Sebastién went fiery bright and shot away, forcing Jordan to accelerate to near-blackout speed. Spotting his struggle, Sebastién slowed until he drew even. Southward and side by side they fled. Tiny tufts of light sprouted into view on the horizon, growing into detailed clusters within minutes. Likely farm towns in Iowa, though he didn't know for sure.

Jordan discovered his hearing would phase out just before his vision. He locked onto this pace like cruise control. Wrapped in a comfortable silence, he moved with the orange streak of Sebastién beside him. With time to think, he started to construct an apology for Crispin. He conjured Sebastién into the scene, imagining him using his suave manner to cool the tension. After an hour of this, his mind wandered to Lila, thrilled at the idea he'd finally meet her.

They changed course from south to west. Before long, flatlands became mountains. Small settlements expressed themselves as tight, electric-yellow knots. Jordan speculated these places could be memorized like stellar constellations, allowing freelight to navigate like sailors in the Age of Discovery.

Hours later, the stars faded out and the non-illuminated features of the world began to emerge. Night rolled toward dawn, revealing a deep blue sky to their right—they must be traveling north now. Mountains dominated the scene in every direction, but there was little sign of civilization. Sunlight breached the horizon within minutes, pouring morning over the land. Mountain peaks lit up like golden pyramids, casting sharp, monstrous shadows westward.

Then grade-school math class fluttered through Jordan's head.

"Stop!" yelled Jordan, halting. Sebastién darted back to him.

"Crispin's just ahead of us." Jordan started rehearsing apologies in his head.

Sebastién smiled. "You *are* quite good at this."

"Can you sense him?" asked Jordan.

"Not yet, but it's not him. It's a beacon; a guidepost for travelers. They're all over the formal flight routes. Crispin created them with that perfect signal of his. You're picking up the southern approach to Arbor Florum. We're almost there."

"Good," said Jordan, his nerves unwinding. "I'm barely awake."

"This next part is going to get tricky." Sebastién pulsed an uneasy glance. "You're going to have to sneak in without me."

"What!" said Jordan, blazing bright. "I have no idea where the hell I'm going."

"Nonetheless." Sebastién looked off into the horizon.

"What kind of shit plan is this?"

"The kind you get when you dive bomb concerts and become the target of a manhunt." Sebastién smirked. "But it's kind of fun isn't it?"

"What!" Jordan's head shook out a definitive *no*.

"This is simple," said Sebastién, the fiery tendrils of his hair swaying in the wind. "On approach, they're going to read me and chase me down. It's protocol. Since the point is to sneak you in, we can't be seen together—that is, you can't be seen at all."

Jordan floated closer to avoid missing the details.

"Tell me when they start moving on us. I'll continue as normal. You go down to the road below. Follow it and stay out of sight. When you get to the tunnel, go over the top but stop short of the other side. You'll find another one of Flux's beacons up there. Veil and wait. Enjoy the view if it suits you."

Sebastién zipped away. Jordan chased after him with a head full of questions. Within seconds, a flood of reads came rattling through his head like cerebral turbulence.

"I'm getting all sorts of stuff here. What do I—"

"All in front of us?" asked Sebastién.

"Yes, roughly."

"When they read me, they'll start moving. You'll feel a *tap*—a crescendo of their signal. Tell me when that happens."

Before Jordan had a chance to say another thing, he felt it. "Here they come!"

"Good luck, and remember what I said. Road. Tunnel. Forest. Beacon. Bindo. Bonne chance, mon ami, you'll do grand." With an explosive, bullwhip crack, Sebastién shot away—

"*Wait*—what the hell is a bindo?" shouted Jordan.

Sebastién was already a flickering orange light in the distance. With no choice but to follow the plan, Jordan descended to the winding, spaghetti-thin road below, cursing the whole way. He moved off to its side, weaving through the trees. More pulses erupted to life in the distance, all moving in on Sebastién, whose poker echo grew ever weaker. Seconds later, Sebastién and whoever else was up there came to a stop.

Jordan spotted the black mouth of the tunnel ahead. He zipped above it and searched for the beacon. Develling short, he finished his hunt on foot with a flayed hand, finding a polished rock that shimmered a familiar blue when he put his develled hand near it.

Now he had to find the fucking bindo.

His mind cycled through possibilities, a consensus forming that it was some sort of gateway—but then what? Knock on the damn thing and ask if he could come in?

The cool morning air swept past Jordan, carrying the scent of fertile pine. It calmed him, if only for a moment. Surveying the woods with his develled hand, he found no one nearby. The congregation in the sky remained stationary, too far up to be spotted by human eyes. Sebastién's plan had worked…so far. He marched toward the sunrise, pushing through the forest. After scaling a small slope, he emerged at an opening on the other side.

The view left him speechless, his lips parting in wordless awe. He'd seen this place before in a photograph, but the picture didn't do it justice. It was big—impossibly big. He struggled to accept it, and with a half-cocked smile imagined Crispin saying he told him so.

17

Like a Soothing Summer Rain

Yosemite National Park.

Jordan recalled the famous Ansel Adams photographs, stoic black and white prints that graced countless walls, magazines, and, fatefully, a coffee table book in Maggie's loft. He placed his hand against the tree next to him. Massaging its coarse bark, he tried to recall the name of the iconic photo: a glacially-carved valley with a mountain cleaved in half at the far end; a bountiful waterfall pouring off the edge of a cliff, its impact point disappearing into a cloud of mist; a colossal rock monolith, the trees at its base appearing as mere blades of grass tickling a gravestone. The features were enormous; a sculpture garden of the gods.

The name of the photograph arrived: *Tunnel View.*

Despite the stunning composition, the famous photo failed to convey the immensity of the scene in-person, especially the granite monolith. Its name popped into Jordan's head: *El Capitan.* The sides of the valley, to his acute eyes, were not a few hundred feet tall, but a few thousand, which meant the expanse of the monolith would be larger than the entire city of Saint Paul, its height ten times greater than its tallest building. Jordan stood on astonished feet, making these implausible calculations. Then he remembered what he was supposed to be doing.

Find the bindo.

Jordan flayed his hand, not sure what to look for. At once, a stream of reads rippled through his mind. He sorted them out, finding it was like eavesdropping on individual conversations in a crowded room. He sleuthed out seven freelight of roughly equal signal strength off to the southeast, including Sebastién.

A more distant group of signals snared Jordan's attention, coming in from the east. He aimed his deveiled hand toward them, holding it outstretched. A lifetime of memories flooded through his head. He couldn't count them all. There had to be hundreds. Moving right at him, coming fast.

"Shit…" Jordan staggered backward, toward the cover of the forest. Just then, another signal burst strong into his awareness.

It was right behind him.

It read like a soothing summer rain, bringing back a childhood memory: running outside just as a storm was breaking. With cool, wet grass under his bare feet, he dashed with arms outstretched, the final sheets of thinning rain hitting his skin. A soft thunder rumbled in the distance. Dark clouds parted, revoking a brief amnesty from the hot summer sun, making his cheeks campfire-warm again. Jordan snapped back to the present and started to turn around. An intuitive thought raced through him.

It was *her*.

As Jordan finished his turn, his deveiled hand facing forward, he saw Lila walking toward him. He knew her even at a distance; the geometry of her eyes, the shape of her face, and her long brown hair. He dropped his deveiled hand to his side and saw her gaze follow it. He couldn't decipher her emotions, only that there were a great many.

Her fingertips touched trees as she came closer, her arms performing small, graceful movements to maintain balance on uneven terrain. Every action was crystal clear, vivid. Jordan veiled his hand as she completed her final steps, stopping a few feet from him. She placed her palm against a tree, her forearm facing him.

She was real.

Jordan wanted to reach out and touch her, just to make sure. Something in her eyes suggested she wanted to do the same.

She was real.

Though he'd fantasized about the moment for years, he found his tongue locked. They just stared at each other, each recognizing the other's uncertainty, each about to speak, but deferring. They traded smiles on account of the verbal impasse. Then Lila upped the ante with a gentle laugh.

"I knew it was you," said Jordan, "but I don't know how." Her eyes were not gray. They were green. Beautiful and kind, not emoting the tragic sadness in his birth echo. She wore a gray Lumineers t-shirt, untucked and falling an inch past the waistline of her blue jeans. On her feet, earth-toned sandals. Quite casual, as though she'd just come from the beach.

She spoke at last: "I saw you come in minutes ago—"

An orange freelight rifled in from the forest and veiled midflight. A man flailed forward from the burst of light, as though trying to regain his balance after being thrown from a moving car. He crashed into a tree between them and fell backward onto the ground. After an earnest groan, he popped up to a standing position.

"I'm Bindo," said the man. "I trust Sebastién has told you about me. You're late. We need to go. *Now.*" An Indian accent to Jordan's ears. Bindo turned to Lila and nodded. "Lila, I should have expected you'd be here." He teetered back and forth in a dizzy manner, prompting Jordan to grab his elbow to stabilize him. Insulted, Bindo whipped free of Jordan's grasp. He went ram-rod straight and yanked his tweed jacket down tight. The outfit, fitting for a literature professor in academia, looked positively comical here in the woods.

Bindo turned to Jordan again. "Oh, right. Whatever your name is, meet Lila Harper." Bindo snatched Jordan's hand and pulled it to himself. He did the same with Lila, joining them in a handshake, nearly making them fall face-first into each other. "Lila, meet Lux Sanguinis returned."

"Jordan Wakefield," offered Jordan.

Lila blushed on account of the sudden proximity, while Bindo continued to assist with the mechanics of the handshake. "Okay, brilliant." Bindo released them. "Now, let's go. We have to get inside *now*." He deveiled, causing Jordan and Lila to release each other's hands and lean away.

Lila deveiled next, a deep green hue that resembled the color of the forest covering the valley. Jordan went last and followed them. Bindo felt like the first time Jordan tasted beer he snagged from his father's fridge as a teen. The three of them raced through the forest, halting at the edge of a cliff. A fast river flowed far below them, the rush of its waters competing with Bindo's voice.

"Stay close, but stay behind us. If we stop, you stop. If we—"

"Wait," said Lila. "We're going in under West Leaf— "

"Yes we are," snapped Bindo, grabbing the conversation back. "Everything's being watched. It's the only viable passage."

"How do you know?"

"Because I just came from there. It's the least bad option." Bindo flared, humming brightly. "We have to go. Now." He gave Jordan a sharp glance before shooting up into the air and then back toward the earth. He jammed into a crevice and disappeared, as though sucked down a drain. Jordan eyed the gap in the rocks, claustrophobia hitting him like a rash.

"It widens out after the mouth," said Lila, her expression still troubled by Bindo's words. "You'll lose your vision for a moment when you pass through. Imagine you're diving into a thimble."

"That's hard to imagine."

"Do it anyway." Lila nodded an encouraging glance. She shot up and repeated the maneuver, leaving Jordan alone.

Jordan glided to the crevice and tried to look inside. Though he saw nothing, he read Lila and Bindo down there. Ascending to a higher starting point, Jordan looked down, scrutinizing the fissure, feeling genuine doubt. The mass of freelight racing in from the east was almost on top of him.

"Like a bunch of damn rodents," he muttered to himself. Jordan plunged, headfirst, arms outstretched. His senses scrambled when he hit the gap. A second later, he was through, floating in a much wider passage. Lila and Bindo were hovering below, arms folded and waiting.

The hum of their three deveiled forms sang a dissonant chorus as they raced along the passage, diving great distances, then bending through sudden turns. Finally, horizontal movement became the dominant direction. The sound of a subterranean water flow entered Jordan's awareness.

A hazy blue light appeared in the distance, emitting a signal that read like kicking dry leaves on an autumn day. The blue blur took shape as they approached. Jordan realized the shapes were composed of vines, clinging to the walls of the passage, cultivated in a way that approximated strip lighting found in roadway tunnels. But the vines weren't translucent, as he expected of the deveiled form. They were solid and real, with blue light stuck to them like luminescent cobwebs. The light terminated in twinkling flares in the flowers or at the tips of leaves.

The vinelight reached toward Lila and Bindo as they passed. It ignored Jordan completely. The patterns mesmerized him, growing brighter and denser as they pressed on, enough to illuminate the lazy flow of water below them. The passage became generous, perhaps twenty feet wide, thirty tall. It terminated at a semi-circular, moss-covered wall with an immense round pool at the base.

Lila and Bindo came to a stop.

Threads of water trickled down the face of the wall from above, beading up on fluffy green tufts of moss. Thick nets of vines, intentionally nurtured on each side of the waterflow, climbed to somewhere far above. When Jordan reached Lila's side, he peered up into a round vertical passage, beyond which was more light, blinding in its intensity. It was like looking up from the bottom of the world's deepest well, one that was quite wide, but of such great length that its distant mouth looked like a tiny disc that could fit in the palm of one's hand. The vinelight was changing hue: it twinkled a deep purple-red now.

"I'll take a look." With a nervous expression in tow, Bindo shot up the well and disappeared through the opening.

"We'll have to move fast once we're up there." Lila stared incessantly up the shaft. "We need to get you in without anyone seeing you deveiled. Everyone is supposed to arrive through West Leaf. Bindo intends to avoid the formal gateway but join the incoming crowds arriving for the Trid."

"What's up there?"

"Home," replied Lila in a wistful tone.

The vinelight was shifting to orange now.

Bindo came sailing back down.

"We're clear to the drain," he said, eyeing Lila, ignoring Jordan. "The dimways are our best chance, but it's a bloody long way to Upper Grey and the vents in South Aria." Bindo blazed brighter, his facial expressions intense. "We're going to be seen."

"We'll blend in," said Lila, trying to reassure him. "There are hundreds arriving, as we speak."

"But they aren't arriving through the damned tunnels are they!" snapped Bindo. He spun to Jordan, training his index finger on him. "*You*. Follow us and veil if we do. And don't act like a bloody tourist. Got it?"

Jordan nodded, uncertainty rippling through him.

"Alright." Bindo's nervous eyes canted upward. "Let's get this over with."

The three of them raced skyward, past the falling water, past the illuminated vines. Past the mouth of the well.

PART TWO

ARBOR FLORUM

*The constraining principle is known as hoop stress in the
modern faintlight tongue. We pushed this rule to the limit
in Rome's Pantheon, which has stood for two thousand years.
What we've done in Arbor Florum will stand for two million.*

—Publius Crispus Fluximous

from "Engineering the Arbors: A Contemporary Review"
Aurora Transitus, 11849 ‡ February 19, 1978 Gregorian

18

THE GREY CITY

Jordan flew past the mouth of the well. For a split second, intense harvest-orange light blasted his vision. Trees and branches and leaves shot by, all wrapped in the same shimmering luminance as with the place below the well. Then he was past it all, floating in the open air far above a grove of glittering treetops, bisected by a wide gray-granite thoroughfare.

Lila and Bindo were no longer at his side.

Wonderment seized Jordan, sending his attention skyward. His eyes struggled to make sense of what he was witnessing: he was inside an immense circular tower, hundreds of feet across. Ringed in granite, its walls rose monumentally—perhaps a thousand feet. Cut into the tower walls, from bottom to top, were buildings; doorways, windows, and staircases, all crafted with extraordinary artistry; level after level, like a skyscraper turned inside out. Twinkling runs of vines clung to the perimeter of each door or window, draping the tower walls in a continuous luminescent mesh. The light was still changing, now to a rich yellow, the hue of the early morning sun.

Freelight of every hue drifted through the space above, conveying the mood of an aquarium. At the zenith of his gaze, a vast dome topped the tower, painted with frescoes like the Sistine Chapel, but too distant to discern with any clarity. The exhibition drowned Jordan with the force of a hurricane.

This was Crispin's world of disbelief.

Bindo flew in front of Jordan, cutting off the scene. "You bloody fool!" Blazing bright, he struck Jordan repetitively, the impacts spinning him, prodding him toward a massive gateway cut into the far tower wall. Jordan accelerated, but Bindo continued to jam him along. Twin waterfalls spilled from each side of the gateway. From beyond it, beamed an extraordinarily bright light. But Bindo's continuous assault denied Jordan a chance to catch more than a glimpse. Lila darted in front of them, a green streak racing toward one of the waterfalls. She disappeared into its mouth. Jordan followed, Bindo still railroading him from behind. They both passed through the spray of water.

Darkness now.

They were inside an enclosed aqueduct chamber, black except for their deveiled glow. Before Jordan had his bearings, Bindo struck him in the face with his bright orange hand. Red light spilled off, sizzling where it struck the water. Jordan veiled involuntarily, falling into the cold channel, smashing his knee against the rocky surface. His head thumped with a sudden headache. Coughing up spurts of mineralized water, Jordan struggled to his feet and limped out. Bindo hovered above him like judgment day, pointing a searing finger:

"If we stop, you stop! What the hell were you thinking?" Bindo flared and buzzed like a nuclear violin. "If you signed my death warrant—if anyone saw us together—"

"Stop it!" Lila flew in between. "We have to move. The worst of it is over."

"I highly doubt that," snarled Bindo.

"It's plan *B* now, the rooftops to Upper Grey." Lila drifted in a slow semi-circle, luring Bindo away from Jordan. "I'll spy ahead and tap you through it. Move on one, take cover on two."

"And what about three?" said Bindo, shouting. "Been nice knowing you, the interfectors are here?"

"Calm down. We can do this veiled. Nobody knows what he

looks like—even if they heard the rumors, nobody would believe he's already here." Lila flew to the side of the aqueduct chamber and paused, the sound of water passing by. She turned and cast Jordan a dead-on stare. "Don't do anything like that again."

Before either could respond, Lila disappeared through a crevice in the side wall. Bindo turned to Jordan, speaking in an irritated voice. "Once we're back out there, don't flay so much as a fingernail. Keep your head down."

Jordan deveiled and followed Bindo. They zipped through the crevice, darting down into the cover of more illuminated trees. They veiled. Jordan glanced about, but Bindo grabbed him by the hood and yanked him forward. They emerged onto a stone path constructed of wide slabs of granite, set perfectly edge to edge. With a discreetly flayed finger at his side, Bindo marched ahead, the pace making Jordan feel like he was being abandoned. He shoved his hands into his pockets and tried to match stride.

Jordan's eyes wandered again.

Above him ran what looked to be a grand church nave; more than a hundred feet wide, a continuous array of double-barrel vaults stretching as far as he could see. His line of sight was habitually obstructed by lazy branches of the iridescent forest, a perpetual canopy over the wandering pathway. To his left, where gaps allowed clear sight, ran the open archways supporting the aqueduct. Beyond that, beamed the bright light he'd seen before Bindo rammed him into the aqueduct chamber. In this brightspace, freelight whizzed by in both directions like commuters.

"Keep up, dammit," Bindo slowed, yanking Jordan along by his coat again.

"Crispin said I wouldn't believe this. How is this possible?"

"You know Crispin?" Bindo shot a distressed glance. He turned away and shook his head. He resumed, speaking in choppy sentences, interrupted by heavy breathing: "Listen, I am in Sebastién's debt—that's the only reason I'm doing this. I want nothing to do with your activism…I am *not* part of this—you *tell* them that if it comes to it."

Unable to comprehend, Jordan stumbled along, his footsteps

jacked with adrenaline as if he had springs for feet. Despite the heat of the moment, the air felt cool—cooler yet when Jordan's arm came near the illuminated leaves, as though the leaflight was stealing warmth from the air.

An opening in the tree cover gave Jordan a glimpse across the brightspace. On the other side ran an identical set of arches and matching aqueduct. Beyond that, a second forested nave. The brightspace ran parallel to the naves, connecting this so-called West Leaf to the source of the extraordinary illumination.

"To answer your question," said Bindo, still moving at a maddening pace, "*this* is all possible by the same rules of physics… the same principles of engineering that govern the rest of the world. Creating a functional ecosystem underground—*that* was the real miracle…and it's courtesy of the *Arborsolis*. A fascinating topic—my personal area of expertise, in fact…but not something we have time to discuss." Bindo huffed along, out of breath.

"This must have taken eternity," muttered Jordan.

"Nearly a thousand years. Stop gawking."

Jordan spotted a group of people on the path ahead, coming toward them. Above and beyond them floated Lila, signaling to Bindo, who jittered upon spotting the troupe. Lila's green silhouette zipped away, bending off to the left, out of sight.

"Head down, keep moving," snapped Bindo, veiling his finger and marching on.

As they reached the trio, fragments of conversation in a foreign tongue teased Jordan's ears. Bindo watched them obsessively and grew agitated, his hands tapping nervously at his sides as they drew closer. When they passed, Jordan caught a glimpse of their apparel: strange, long-tailed coats with gaudy buttons. One even had a top hat. Moments later, Bindo exhaled hard, as though he'd been holding his breath the whole time. He flayed his finger again.

The dazzling treelight was less yellow now; a nearly neutral daylight. Tiny particles of light hurried along this illuminative canvas, racing over branches and leaves, from one tree to the next, like air bubbles carried down a rapid stream.

Jordan's heart still hammered in his chest.

With declined chins they pressed on, taking Lila's leftward split in the path. Their course bent toward the aqueduct's arches. Jordan saw a bridge in the distance. They would cross the brightspace.

Jordan drew even with Bindo.

Bindo's dark eyes met his. "*How* could you know Crispin?"

"He discovered me. Didn't he tell you?"

"Bloody hell." Bindo puckered his mouth like he'd eaten a lemon. His pace quickened.

They were nearly at the crossing. The sides of the bridge showcased a run of stout pillars, lit pristine white by the brightspace. The temperature increased as they approached. On the far side, Lila was gesturing to Bindo; more people were coming. A lot more. Bindo panicked and jogged onto the bridge, abandoning Jordan.

Trying to maintain discretion, Jordan stared at the ground as he embarked on the bridge crossing. Curiosity pulled his chin left, sneaking a peek into the brightspace. It was a mistake. Vertigo snared him at once and he stumbled toward the pillared railing, grabbing it for support, coming to a stop halfway across the bridge.

His eyes dropped in free fall.

Hundreds of feet down ran a tree-lined thoroughfare teeming with people, stretching all the way back to West Leaf where they'd come in. To each side, ascending all the way to the aqueduct arches were the façades of granite buildings: storefronts and homes, articulate and immaculate, garnished by illuminated vines. It was a new-urbanist masterpiece of green-on-gray, infinite points of sunlight twinkling forth like the cosmos. To Jordan, the spectacle evoked Times Square from above but beckoned back to antiquity: no cars, no electric light, no machines. Feeling as though he would fall over the railing, Jordan stumbled backward. His whole body was sweaty, baked by the intense light of the brightspace.

The source of it was just behind him.

With the heat of June Texas cooking the back of his neck, Jordan begged himself not to look. Just move. Yet he knew a quick turn of the head would do it.

So he did.

Then he dropped his arms to his sides.

Then he just stared.

At the end of the thoroughfare—beyond the cityscape, beyond another grandiose gateway—rose an immense tree. A great sequoia, its trunk massive and immortal, its upper reaches wrapped in light as brilliant as the sun. Coronal flourishes swirled about it in slow cosmic pirouettes, moving like the robes of a biblical angel. Freelight glided past Jordan, moving toward the tree and becoming tiny motes of differential color against its radiance. The scene was an optical symphony, impossibly complex in its instrumentation, the whole piece taking place in largo.

Jordan just stood there with retinas ablaze. A tree of light at the heart of an underground city, a vibrant array of freelight floating in its keep. A moment so remarkable Jordan deemed it would be unnecessary to witness any other for the remainder of his life. If all went to darkness, he would have this. He trembled, nearly falling.

A hand grasped his fingertips.

It pulled at him, disengaging his trance. Jordan turned to find Lila, her eyes pleading with him. Motion and sound were still reaching him in lethargic time.

"Move…" Her voice came as a desperate whisper. "Please."

"New here?" asked a man walking past. Hearty laughter followed, which shattered Jordan's daze, sending his senses back to presto.

Jordan blinked to life. He moved, and Lila let go of his hand. They reached the other side and found an apoplectic Bindo. A minute later, all three were off the path. Bindo let loose, jabbing at Jordan's shoulder as he spoke:

"Someone saw him, I know it!"

"He was veiled. They don't know him," said Lila. "And we end up at that point anyway."

"Not with *me* involved." Bindo pointed his finger into Lila's face. "You don't want *him* discovered yet. You need time. You won't even make it to tonight before you're snared by the Kyzheres—who laughed at him on the bridge?" Bindo fired glances between the two of them.

"He's *Castellum*," said Lila.

"Oh perfect!" said Bindo, the veins on his neck flaring. "We'll be had an hour from now."

"Calm down. He's nobody."

"It only takes one to notice."

"They emptied Res Externa last night." Lila spoke in a slow, reassuring voice. "We know this. They're all a thousand miles east, watching the skies for red light. They aren't onto us."

"Not yet," said Bindo.

Lila tilted her head, as though that were answer enough.

Bindo stomped at the ground. Then he spoke in the least frantic voice Jordan heard in their short time together: "Okay, then. Let's finish this."

The three of them deveiled and slipped into an opening in the wall, ascending a narrow dark shaft. After a half-minute of flight, they glided across a horizontal passage and emerged into a dimly lit room. The space had a cozy feel, like a lounge, with shelves inset into the wall, sheltering a series of books. Glowing vines ran across the ceiling, sending soft light into the chamber. In the center of the space sat a polished bass violin perched on a stand.

"Where are we?" whispered Jordan.

"Albert's place," said Lila, no longer whispering. Bindo marched off down a hallway. "A friend of Sebastién. You need to stay here. Don't leave this room. We'll be back later." Lila held his gaze and studied his face with bountiful curiosity, which made Jordan recall their moment on the bluff.

"Even better, you should rest," said Bindo, returning with a fat book in his hands. "You have only one shot at this tonight. If you can't sleep, read." Bindo tossed the book onto a burgundy leather couch and marched up close to Jordan, over-enunciating his words as though speaking to a child: "Read the book. Or sleep. Stay in this room."

"I need to find Eli…to tell him I made it."

With mouth falling agape, Bindo shook his head. He stepped back, pulling his hand through his hair. Straightening his suit jacket with a double tug, he shoved his hands into its pockets. "I trust I have satisfied my debt—please tell Sebastién that. Best of luck to you all. You're going to need it." Bindo took two steps back, deveiled with a snap, and disappeared into the vent.

"I have to go too," said Lila. She paused, staring at him. No smile like on the bluff. Her expression was neutral, if not a touch grave. "I can't believe you're real."

"I was thinking the same." Jordan's thumbs found the belt loops of his jeans. "This is all so strange."

"We'll untangle it soon." With a burst of green light, she deveiled and glided above the couch. She tinkered with the vinelight at the ceiling, making it brighter; a reading light. "Stay here. We'll be back soon."

Like Bindo, she vanished into the vent.

Jordan's slight smile remained as he walked to the couch. He tipped his head to catch the book's title:

Regarding Freelight

by

Godfrey Brindle
83rd Edition

Jordan crept into the hallway where Bindo got the book, reckoning it to be as safe as the rest of the place. Reaching the end of the hall, he found a sitting room. Light emanated through closed curtains, tempting Jordan to take a peek. After some deliberation, he did. Grasping the edge of the curtain, he pulled it aside slowly, employing the caution of a bomb dismantler.

Far below was the tree, blinding coils of light orbiting it like planetary rings. Its radiance was neutral now, indistinguishable from daylight. It seemed to produce the sound of soft whispers, a phenomenon Jordan deemed analogous to the orchestral hum of his own deveiled form.

The tree marked the exact center of a vast round space. At the far outer edge of this circular garden ran two stone rings. The tops of the ring structures caught Jordan's attention: they were sealed in colored glass, similar to stained-glass windows in a church. Lit from inside, the two rings glowed through distinctly marked segments of differing color.

Beyond the rings, at the outer wall of the circular space, Jordan counted four immense gateways, separated at ninety-degree angles. Wide white staircases marched forth from each gateway toward the tree, terminating at the outer ring. Recalling Bindo's mention of West Leaf, Jordan speculated the gateways marked the cardinal points of the compass; four domed silos united by the largest in the center. If the world down there was city and community, the world up here was hearth and home. But Jordan couldn't decipher the meaning of the glowing rings.

A pair of blue freelight flew past the window. Jordan jerked back, almost falling. Not wanting to press his luck, he slinked back toward the room appointed for his sabbatical. On the way, a framed map in the hallway caught his eye. It depicted Yosemite Valley and within it—within El Capitan specifically—the five-united-circle pattern his mind had assembled from peeking beyond the curtain. A molecular depiction of a city: South Leaf planted in the heart of El Capitan, the others all north of it, each leaf connected by long avenues of unequal length—the brightspaces. The whole structure was rotated off-kilter to true north, turned an hour counterclockwise. The center dome—the one he had just peered into—was the largest by far. It was labeled on the map in elegant serif letters as *ARIA*.

Jordan returned to the study and went to the couch, its mere existence making him groggy. Picking up the book, he threw himself down and kicked off his shoes. The weight of the formidable tome amplified his mental fatigue, symptoms of a long journey and lack of sleep. He opened it to the first page and read the introduction, written in exquisite script:

Regarding Freelight

By decree of the 357th assembly of the Curia Prudentiarum, 23rd subcommittee on language, let it be known, henceforth, that the term Freelight be recognized as canonical and thus used in this and subsequent editions. All other variants, including the previously recognized "Timbrelumière," and the more archaic Latin terms of all variety—phrased in local dialects of New or Old Elysium—shall be considered deprecated.

Godfrey Brindle
Acting Magistrate
Fifth Circle, Prudentiarum
Placidus 14th, 11800

The cryptic words dragged Jordan closer to sleep. But he put up a fight. Flipping to the next page, he found a long list of chapters. Thumbing through a few pages, he scanned for the start of the actual text. Not finding it, he pinched a heap of them at random and settled on a paragraph under the heading *Lux Stellarum*:

Lux Stellarum, the final primary classification, is known as "the Influencer" and comprises two predominants: the namesake, Lux Stellarum, known in its cultural origins as Phos Phoenicia, and Lux Eros.

Stellarum's defining characteristic is its famous and unique variant on the writing capability, wherein the writer can violate and influence the emotional state of the reader in addition to transmission of the typical sensorium. This exploit can be conducted without the reader's immediate awareness, and the injected emotional stream can dictate a message that runs parallel with or completely contrary to said sensorium. From this, we derive the less polite and more colloquial "Seducir."

Jordan's mind failed to convert this into anything meaningful. The only invasive force he felt was sleep. He let it take him, tipping the book onto his chest. As he drifted out, he reflected on Bindo's words and his reaction to the mention of Crispin and Eli. Everything was off…he was involved in something else now, running with a different crowd, likely the ones nearer Eli's troubled talk of injustice at the heart of this world.

Sebastién had tricked him.

19

THE INCIDENTAL COWARD

As had become the routine, Jordan was prodded from sleep by the efforts of another. He groaned himself into a sitting position. The book on his chest fell to the floor, issuing a dense thump.

"That's as far as I got too," came a voice with a French accent.

Jordan blinked the weariness away. Sebastién was crouched in front of him, and had picked up the book. He weighed it in his hand and tossed it aside. The impact startled Jordan to full awareness.

"Was I supposed to actually read the thing?"

"Just enough to keep you out of trouble, and you've done admirably, having slept the entire day away." Sebastién got up and retrieved a wooden chair from the corner of the room. He set it down in front of Jordan with its back facing forward. Sebastién mounted it like a horse, his legs out to the sides. He crossed his arms over the top of the backrest and stared hard at Jordan. "Lila's down in West Leaf waiting for us," he said, exuding the same casual confidence from Jordan's loft, "but first we need to talk."

"You aren't Eli's associate are you?" said Jordan, launching a preemptive strike. "The one he mentioned in his message."

A grin slid across Sebastién's face. "No, I am not."

"Who are you and what do you want with me?" Jordan crossed his arms, his eyes wary, legs electric and ready to bolt.

"I am still Sebastién Saint-Vezina, and I still need your help."

"For what?"

"To free an innocent man. And catch a murderer, should you be game." Sebastién lowered his chin but kept his eyes on Jordan. "He's the man who killed your predecessor, and Lila's. And a woman named Helena too, who we intend to find tonight."

"Why do you need my help with that?"

"Because she's dead." Sebastién delivered the words so matter-of-fact, it caught Jordan off guard. "That means she's impossible for any of us to find. But not quite so impossible for you."

Jordan recalled the conversation in Crispin's library, where interest in this same talent had been expressed. "How did you find me?"

"As I said, I'm fast and I'm lucky."

"I'll need a better answer than that."

Sebastién's smile went flat. "Very well. I was in New Orleans when you made the news. I presumed you were the usual case of accidental self-discovery, but couldn't know for sure. What I did know was that *everyone* from our world would be looking for you, so I needed to get there first. And I did, fortunately." Sebastién drummed his fingers on the back of the chair. "But I had a problem, you see. There was no way to actually find you, unless you appeared again by your own volition—that special invisibility of yours. You have no signal, which meant my problem was everyone's problem. All we could do was watch and wait, hoping you'd reappear."

"You still didn't tell me how you found me—"

"I'm getting to that." Sebastién reduced his finger drumming to a light scratching. "It just so happened that the second person to arrive, just after I got there, was someone I knew to be close to Eli. He was of the same timbre, which means he was easy to detect. On top of it, unable to detect other freelight. In other words, he wasn't part of any official track-down team. And wouldn't you know it—he didn't camp out in the sky and wait. He never stopped moving from the moment he reached Saint Paul. He knew right where to go. So I tailed him, right to the Renslit Artists' Cooperative," said Sebastién, stressing each of the last three words. "I waited until he left, which was soon after he arrived. I wagered you'd flown the coop. I snooped about and once I found that grand portrait of Lila, I knew I had my man. Eli's pal returned a few times a day to check, and when he did, I'd hide out. When he'd leave, I'd return. He was so very predictable and wouldn't have known I was there unless he saw me with his own eyes."

"That's why you hurried me out of there last night. You knew he was coming back. You got lucky."

"I always do," Sebastién feigned modesty by surveying his fingernails. "The danger to your life was real, however. Neither Eli nor I were deceiving you on that point, and it's that particular tale I'd like to tell now. That is, unless you wish to hear more stories about me getting lucky—and I should warn you, I have a great many."

Jordan stood up and deveiled. Sebastién went tense, his attention anchored to Jordan's every move. Jordan hovered for a few seconds before he snapped back into physical form and sat down.

"Ah, you were merely hungry," said Sebastién. "And here I was, thinking you were about to flee."

"I still might."

"Now tell me, did Crispin and Eli give you a good last meal?"

"Steak dinner." Jordan could taste hints of it in his mouth. "They even asked me if I wanted to use the bathroom before they started waving guns in my face."

"How very considerate of them." Sebastién grinned and rubbed his chin against his knuckles.

Jordan leaned back into the couch and folded his arms. "I believe you had a story to tell, and then I'll decide if I'm sticking around."

"Oui oui." Sebastién adjusted the lapel on his suit jacket and settled into a more contemplative mood. "As I said, it's the story of your predecessor, and Lila's, and how they were murdered together. It was an act of revenge so reckless our world took it as a political statement. To this day, one hundred and twenty-eight years later, the murderer—an appellation used only in whispers and behind closed doors—remains free. The man it was pinned on remains in prison, right here in Arbor Florum, awaiting an investigation that will never happen." Sebastién averted his eyes and clenched his fists. "This man's imprisonment, I must confess, is my fault." Sebastién blinked a few times in silence. "My cowardice sealed his fate a long time ago. But now we have a chance to unseal it. To do this, I need your help."

Jordan uncrossed his arms and set his hands in his lap. The sharp features of Sebastién's face were still aimed away as if petrified by shame.

"In a hundred years they couldn't get this right?"

"It's not that they couldn't." Sebastién returned his attention to Jordan. "It's that they don't want to. It's all too…political. They wanted to forget about the whole thing, and for the most part they did. This falsely accused man would be vindicated someday, or so the conscience-driven Florumite would claim. That same type of person pretends it is justice enough that they managed to keep the accused here in the Grey City all these years, using clever legal maneuvers to bar him from being extradited away. In time, the issue faded, and people did what they do naturally. They forgot. But not everyone."

"This guy they pinned it on—"

"His name is Firas el-Sakar," interjected Sebastién.

"So…this fear guy, what was the evidence against him?"

"None whatsoever. Just accusations from a person of high station; an eye-witness set of claims glued together by political will."

"They sentenced him to prison forever?"

"Technically, he's not in prison. He's being detained while the investigation proceeds. But as I mentioned, that was a hundred and twenty-eight years ago."

"I'm not a lawyer or anything, but don't they have to let you go if there's no evidence? That's how it works where I'm from."

"And just like where you're from," said Sebastién, not skipping a beat, "people can be falsely accused and tossed away for eternity. They fall out of public awareness. This is especially so when the real perpetrator is prominent, and the accused is, shall we say, forgettable."

"In other words, it's as corrupt here as where I came from."

"In this particular case, yes, but some of us are trying to do something about it." Sebastién kept his blue eyes fixed on Jordan. "…and that includes Lila."

Jordan soured and shook his head, shifting his attention to the floor. "You're trying to use her as leverage."

"I am," said Sebastién softly, "but it doesn't make the facts false, nor the cause any less just. Lila needed no persuasion on being part of this—by all means, ask her yourself. But for now, understand this…"

Sebastién went silent until Jordan looked at him again.

"An innocent man has been sitting in a prison cell smaller than this room for over one hundred years, while the killer remains free. Nobody is willing to challenge this injustice. If not the successors of the murdered—who made your freelight existence possible—then who?"

Only now did Jordan realize how Crispin had avoided the history of his predecessor and Lila's with such surgical precision. "Why did he do it? The murderer, that is."

"In the case of your predecessor, it was revenge." Sebastién stood and started to walked about the room with hands behind his back. "In the case of Lila's, because she was his lover. In the case of Helena, to clean up a loose end. Firas, the accused, was yet another loose end, one they lost the opportunity to kill when I stumbled into the middle of it all. As to the murderer himself, executions were part of his official capacity. Not merely a duty in his case, but an exquisite pleasure. He was a Venator, which means *hunter* if you're versed in Latin."

"I'm not."

"Give it time," said Sebastién, looking at Jordan before passing behind the bass violin. "The story of the Venatorum is a sorry piece of freelight history, one we don't have time to get into now. I'll offer, in short, that before our world sought to disband the Venatorum, they were a necessary evil—one endorsed by all the arbors, though not quite with universal approval. As with all necessary evils, and especially ones given free rein to operate for more than three centuries, it became nothing *but* evil in the end."

"There's another place like this?"

"Yes, there are others, the one pivotal to this story being Arbor Castellum, over in New Elysium—Europe as you know it—but that's yet another story. In its stead, I'll ask you imagine a place like this, much bigger, but where the capacity for free thinking is tragically much smaller."

"And they murder people?" added Jordan.

"They do, though the Venatorum was a joint venture. There are many to blame. It was a grand plan to bring the freelight world underground once and for all. It underachieved in that goal but was spectacular in the realm of murderous zealotry. The latter was, in truth, the real goal, Once everyone realized that, it took decades of careful diplomacy to disband the Venatorum. It succeeded, except for a single rogue faction led by a man named Supernus Tacitus Kyzhere. The hunters became the hunted, and a lot of people died trying to bring this to a close."

"Let me guess. Supernus is the murderer."

"Yes," said Sebastién with a hiss, "and your predecessor was the one who hunted Supernus and his people down. Tit for tat, as the saying goes. The trials following their capture were conducted in corrupt courts, another feature of this joint venture. Because of this, Supernus remained free but his people went down. Supernus was, after all, the son of a king, and as you'll learn, Castellum worships its aristocracy. They live for it and when necessary, die for it. It is here I should mention that Supernus and the contemporary members of his entourage comprise the danger Eli was talking about."

"Where is this guy now?" asked Jordan. "Should I be looking over my shoulder?"

"They'd have killed you in Saint Paul if they could have, but once we take you public, it will be too risky, politically speaking. But before we do that, we want to make use of the upper hand while we have it. We want to put the murderer and his people on their heels. We want to free Firas. That's why we need to find Helena, and that's why we need you."

Jordan sank back into the couch, feeling a touch of relief that there was a plan to protect him. He looked around the room and imagined being confined here for more than a century. He couldn't fathom it.

"As to where Supernus is…" Sebastién glanced upward, "I'd venture to say he and his entourage have reached Saint Paul by now. They're circling the skies, hoping you'll appear. There's an official search party from Florum too, which is on its way. Their arrival will put an end to Supernus's plan. As to Eli's associate, I'd imagine he's been called back on a plane, lest he lead anyone to you by accident just as he did with me. But it's really meant to hide the fact that his people are involved in this too. I'm sure you've realized by now that Crispin's hunt for you broke a few rules in its own right. Though his interest in you is no secret to anyone here in the Grey City."

Aggravation burned through Jordan as the implications of his ill-fated flight continued to come into focus. "I have a feeling things would have been less complicated had I come in under his plan."

"Quite likely, but that option went up in flames when you crashed that rock concert like an utter fool, didn't it?"

Jordan glared at him.

Sebastién walked toward the center of the room, running his index finger along the stock of the bass violin. "I apologize for that. My tongue tends to run ahead of my manners at times."

Jordan released his stare.

"Allow me to finish the story and tell you where I come in." Sebastién walked over to a bookshelf. He examined its volumes as he spoke, running his finger up and down the spines. "The night it happened, I was out late, carousing in East Leaf. I was walking home, enjoying the fog of wine when I came across Supernus and his entourage. They had Firas surrounded. I was new to this world but had been around enough to know who they were." Sebastién rapped his palm against the bookcase as if trying to knock it over. "I saw it in Supernus's eyes immediately. He was trying to decide if I should be killed along with Firas." Sebastién pressed his forehead against the books. "But they never had to decide, because I decided for them. In the blink of an eye, I walked away. I pretended I hadn't seen any of them. I'm ashamed of it. In the parting moment, I saw the desperation in Firas's eyes. I thought for sure I'd hear him die, only later realizing they might come for me next. But they didn't."

Sebastién walked back to the chair and touched the top of it, but didn't sit down. His eyes drooped, weighed down by contemplation. "I couldn't sleep for what remained of that night. I decided I'd go to the Praetorium in the morning and tell them what I saw. By the time I got there, it was over. They hadn't killed Firas but had declared him a murderer; the murderer of your predecessor, Lila's, and Helena, who was Firas's lover and only real friend. The accusation was made by someone loyal to Castellum, someone who wasn't even there. He claimed he trailed Firas that night and saw him commit the murders and throw the bodies of all three into the Depths. Quite a feat, everyone thought, killing three people and dragging their bodies that far." Sebastién raised his eyebrows at the absurdity. "A carefully orchestrated series of witnesses placed Supernus in Arbor Castellum at the time. The political machinery of the Kyzheres took care of the rest. My later claims to the contrary fell on skeptical ears, and the Kyzheres worked to discredit me. I am, after all, a hedonist. This is not uncommon in our world, but I'm exceptional at it. All of it was made worse by the fact that Firas refused to fight for himself. He withdrew. He went silent."

Sebastién returned to the chair in front of Jordan and tapped his foot against one of its legs. "I can't blame him. He didn't withdraw from just me. It was everyone, even from those in Arbor Florum who had clout and came to his defense. Castellum has many enemies, which meant Firas had allies if he wanted them. Despite Firas's talent for pushing away would-be friends, he failed to get rid of me. I managed to force a friendship over the years, one where he grew to trust me, if only a little. We came up with a plan, one I vowed to help him enact; a penance for my failures as a human being. He demanded that I respect a single caveat. That we'd wait for something." Sebastién looked at Jordan, his affable smile returning. "That something was you."

Jordan shifted with unease.

"So, yes, I have deceived you, and I did it for my own selfish reasons. But they are just ones, and they are part of something bigger than myself, something that truly matters."

Jordan fell silent, letting his vision go out of focus as if to erase Sebastién from the scene and escape the decision.

"It is *we* that must do this," continued Sebastién. "For all the talk of standing against the Kyzheres, for all the rumors of hidden movements ready to make this right, nothing materializes—even after a century of injustice. You see, to get a man to look in the mirror and acknowledge his sin is a monumental affair. To get an entire civilization to do it is folly. But we don't need them to have a change of heart if we have you. Because with you, we can bypass the proverbial hearts and minds, and get testimony of the murder from Helena herself. We'll put it in front of the world, and they will be unable to ignore it. Firas *will* be free."

"And if I fail to find Helena?" asked Jordan.

Sebastién winced, his exhale flaring his nostrils. "If *we* fail at this, the injustice will stand. Firas will remain imprisoned until he loses the will to live. One day, not particularly long from now, he'll slip beyond those bars and make a symbolic escape. The interfectors that stand guard will strike him dead in the blink of an eye."

Jordan's head ached under the weight of the proposed responsibility. "Why doesn't Crispin want me involved in this?"

"He wants you to be a clean slate, politically speaking. Makes things easier for his purposes, his obsessive theories about the light. He is, quite simply, on the side of those who wish to turn away."

"But he found me," said Jordan. "I owe him everything for that."

"We only need to borrow you for a while. Besides, everyone knows how badly Crispin wants you—he and the Prudentiarum. A little dirt on your hands won't hurt anything."

"Can't we wait on this?"

"We cannot. We can't keep you hidden for long, and once it's known you're here, they'll snare up the valley and we'll never get a clean run at Helena. We have tonight only."

Jordan looked down at Sebastién's feet to avoid eye contact. "I'm sorry, I can't. I've screwed things up enough already."

Sebastién sighed and stepped closer. He dropped to his knees before Jordan, bowing his head.

"What the hell are you doing?" asked Jordan.

"I am begging you for help." Sebastién's eyes locked on Jordan again, his face devoid of charm. His eyes seemed to express a fatigue far beyond biological age. "I turned my back on an innocent man. For a hundred and twenty-eight years he's been condemned to unbearable isolation. For one hundred and twenty-eight years I've drowned my conscience in vice, trying to erase the memory of it. There were days I wished we were both dead—this was my darker half speaking. At times I felt it was all that was left of me." Sebastién folded his lower lip under his front teeth for a moment. "I need your help, Jordan Wakefield. I am asking you to *not* turn your back on me as I once did to him. I am asking you to make Firas free. I will be forever in your debt."

Jordan stood up, carrying Sebastién's attention with him. "Okay. I'll do it, but get off the damn floor." Jordan extended his hand. Sebastién grabbed it firm.

"Thank you." Sebastién rose to his feet and gave Jordan an extra squeeze before releasing. He walked to the bookshelf and grabbed a bookend, weighing it in his palm. As he returned, an orange light flared up from under his grasp. "One more thing. Could you deveil your hand and state your name to me?"

Jordan paused. Sebastién nodded him on.

"Jordan Wakefield," he said, flaying his hand bright red.

"Where are you from and where did you see your light—the red ghost, so to speak?"

"I was born in Ironwood, Michigan." Jordan recognized the writing process from Crispin's kitchen. "I saw it at a place called Lake of the Clouds. Why are we doing this?"

"To prove you existed." Sebastién pursed the side of his mouth. "In case you end up dead tonight. In case all of us do." Another flash of orange blinked out from his palm just before he returned the bookend to the shelf.

Jordan's stomach turned. He had no desire to probe the topic. "What if Firas gets cold feet again?"

"He won't."

"You're sure?"

"I'm positive." Sebastién stepped closer. "He trusts you."

"We've never even met."

"There are but two instances of Lux Sanguinis in the world. He's one. You're the other." Sebastién carried the chair back to the corner of the room. He turned and walked toward Jordan. "We hatched this plan long before you were even born. Yet over all those years, he's always referred to you in the same way: my brother."

20

FIRAS

Down, down, down. A return trip through the vents put Jordan and Sebastién in West Leaf again, but this time on a thin dark street, narrow to the point of claustrophobia. The buildings on each side rose a handful of stories, with façades and shops that anchored Jordan's thinking to Venice, Italy. Gone was the warm, morning-time ambiance. The scene glowed in sapphire blue now, proffered by sparse strings of vines running along the faces of buildings and their cornices. They found Lila loitering nearby, arms folded, leaning up against a tailor's shop. Its front window featured dresses mounted to hoops, vibrant scarves hanging behind.

They proceeded down the Euro-slim street.

"These are the dimways, where you were supposed to come in," said Sebastién, noticing Jordan's touristic eyes. "Dimways are streets that trickle away from the greys—a word on this: you'll hear much talk of greens and greys. The greens are the spaces under the dome, the greys are the avenues that connect them together. Thus, we are now traversing the dimways in West Grey on our way to West Leaf, which is a green. Got it?"

Sebastién's footfalls clacked sharp off the granite street as he moved ahead, leaving Jordan and Lila to walk side by side. Jordan's eyes scanned the storefront of a chair maker, its long window offering hand-crafted armchairs, stools, and chaise lounges every bit as opulent as in the faintlight world. A glance to the other side found Lila, who walked with hands at her sides. Her gait seemed apprehensive. Her enchanting smile from their meeting on the bluff was long gone.

"For the sake of the new guy, let's go over this," said Sebastién as they walked past a three-way split in the road. "Finding Helena will be like picking up a faint radio station in your head. Once you do, Lila takes over. She'll get the testimony. If we're lucky—and the whole enterprise depends on this—Helena will recount the moments before she died. This should lead to her remembering it was Supernus who did it—or ordered it—which should lead to her naming him outright. If we get that, we have proof that Supernus is the murderer. Then we can force the courts to free Firas."

"And send Supernus to prison in his place?" asked Jordan.

Sebastién bobbed his head side to side. "Not exactly."

Lila jumped in. "What he's really trying to say is those courts lack the courage to level accusations against the almighty Princeps Maximus of Arbor Castellum."

"Supernus is untouchable, Lila," said Sebastién, "you know it. But I admire your determination. If we get the testimony we *can* dismantle the charges against Firas and set him free, and that is victory enough."

"So you say," said Lila.

Jordan continued to gather scenes from the illuminated street like a curious infant. Though his sightseeing went out in many directions, it always returned to Lila, just long enough to appreciate her hair teased over the side of her cheek.

"You listening, Jordan?"

Jordan looked to Sebastién, who was looking over his shoulder at him.

"Yeah, tuning a radio station."

Sebastién pursed his lips and looked forward again. "The reason this works is because graylights never lie. Their thoughts are a bit disorganized, but they speak the unfiltered truth; the raw experience of the last moments of life. For that reason, it's considered valid evidence."

"Got it." On the sly, Jordan stole another look at Lila. She glanced at him in return. But when he smiled, she didn't return the gesture. Jordan looked away, only to find Sebastién glaring back at him with a cross expression.

Sebastién halted, causing Jordan and Lila to stop too. After twirling on his heel, an act that generated an abrasive grit-under-shoe rasp, he got in Jordan's face, a nose shy of uncomfortable proximity. "I can respect the novelty of this for you. But you need to focus, Casanova. You've been dreaming of dear Lila here your whole life and you've finally found her—I get it." Sebastién tilted his chin down, as though peering over glasses he wasn't wearing. "But tonight's not the night."

Jordan felt his face go flush. Though he wanted to listen to Sebastién, his eyes uncontrollably checked in on Lila. Not done lecturing, Sebastién grasped Jordan's chin and guided it back to center.

"When we're done with this," said Sebastién, "by all means, ask her on a date—ask her to the opera, in fact. See how well that goes. But get your head straight *now*. We have one shot at this, and it's been a century in the making." Sebastién turned around and resumed his walk.

Too mortified to look anywhere but at the back of Sebastién's head, Jordan followed. Despite the stern reprimand, his optimistic mind returned to the possibilities…*a date…the opera.*

"When a freelight dies violently," said Sebastién, returning to his instructor's cadence, "or more specifically, against their will, they end up trapped in a dream state until they are released. In this state, we refer to them as graylights. Mumblers. Sleepers. And a whole bunch of other words, but the faintlight term is the one everyone's familiar with: ghost."

"Who released our predecessors?" asked Jordan.

"Very good. You're paying attention." Sebastién tossed a satisfied look over his shoulder. "Your predecessors were wise, but even more than that, brave. They accepted they were about to die, which is *why* they didn't get trapped. Helena didn't accept it. Firas is certain of this. That's why we have to find her. Now, how a freelight knows they're about to die is one of the more interesting aspects of our physiology. I trust you're familiar with the concept of life flashing before your eyes?"

"Yes."

"But you never experienced it, did you? Not even when Crispin had that gun in your face, and you actually thought you were going to die."

Jordan reflected back to the parlor. "Yeah, you're right."

"That's because it doesn't become an active part of the freelight mind until after the first develing. It is, however, something both freelight and faintlight experience. It's when the soul is preparing to depart. But for freelight it's different in a profound way. It's more vivid, like a birth echo. For some, it can begin hours or even days before death. It can even happen if one believes truly they are about to die."

The dimway split, and Sebastién led them into a sharp left. In the distance, an intense blue light beamed across a larger avenue. Jordan posited that this was the so-called West Grey, the extraordinary street scene he saw from the bridge. His heart thumped faster, Sebastién's pace increased.

"We could have already been out there had Firas told us how to call her." Lila touched a filament of light that reached toward her from a drooping vine. The light flared upon her touch, turning warm yellow. When she broke contact, it snapped back and shifted to dim blue again.

"Firas has never been willing to share that," said Sebastién. "Not even with me. He wanted to see Sanguinis-returned first, face to face."

They reached the end of the dimway and turned right onto the much larger West Grey thoroughfare. The cosmic tree was to their backs now. Even at night, its warming effect was evident. They had emerged on West Grey just short of the grand gateway leading into West Leaf. Its immense presence made Jordan feel he was a species too small. A pair of freelight glided through the gateway in the air above them, the relative scale suggesting fireflies passing under a stone-arched bridge.

Jordan looked down the thoroughfare, beyond the gateway. The street cut straight through West Leaf's circular space. Wooded areas—the ones Jordan had flown above when emerging from the well—occupied each side of the avenue, shimmering midnight blue upon the residence-laden walls. At the terminating end of the thoroughfare rose a stately edifice, projecting out from the tower wall. It expressed the mood of a 17th-century chateau.

"That's the Carmen Vespere." Sebastién slowed his pace so that all three of them were walking even. "Latin for *Evening Song.*"

A grand staircase poured out from an even grander portico, merging into the street as if a natural part of it. The building's left and right wings provided stout accommodational bulk—three stories tall, capped with steep roofs. Yet the central part was an anomaly, rising dozens of floors, all the way to the top of the dome.

"This was once a magnificent place," said Lila, her voice melancholy. "An exquisite hotel for all travelers in the freelight world. Now it's the only sanctioned way in and out of Arbor Florum."

"Which is a polite way to say it's the heart of the police state that watches over us." Sebastién flicked his hand as though trying to dismiss that fact. "This is the Kyzheres' crown jewel, *Res Externa.*"

"Latin for..." said Jordan.

"External Affairs," said Sebastién with a smirk. "It had humble beginnings as an advisory bureau for freelight travelers in the faintlight world. Then, rather quickly, it became an imperial security apparatus."

"And it's also quite empty at the moment," added Lila. "Everyone's been ordered to Saint Paul to look for the red light in the sky."

"Nice job on that," said Sebastién, nudging Jordan.

Having crossed West Leaf, they ascended the Carmen's staircase, polished and smooth to the foot. They passed through an open door into a lobby with high ceilings, punctuated by fluted columns. The space was dimly lit, as if to prevent a showcase of its former glory.

Sebastién marched toward a brass hook stuck into one of the columns. A collection of leather satchels hung from it. He snatched the topmost one, a small pouch with a strap, and stuffed it into his pocket. With not a person in sight, they navigated hallways and staircases, arriving at a large desk with a very comfortable chair behind it. In that chair was a plump man in a dark maroon blazer decked with gold buttons. Head tilted back, hands crossed behind his neck, snoring as though it were an Olympic sport.

Sebastién cleared his throat. This failed to dent the man's herald of noise. Lifting a book up from his desk, Sebastién slammed it down. The impact sent out a sharp clap and the man jolted. He licked his lips but kept his eyes closed.

"Now why would you disturb me at this hour at my miserable post?" asked the man, eyes still shut, speaking in a droll, sadly musical manner. "Can't you see that I am sleeping?"

"I observed that for a good while, Mortimer."

"Ah, the esteemed Saint-Vezina. Shouldn't you be out imbibing somewhere? Luring women into your bed?"

"I'd like to see the prisoner."

"Which one?" His eyes were still shut, almost as if by protest.

"There is only one. Firas el-Sakar." Sebastién jammed his knee into the desk, causing Mortimer to purse his lips and open his eyes.

"That is right," said Mortimer leaning forward. "There is only one. Miss Lila Harper too, I see." Mortimer looked at Jordan. "…and stranger." His eyes narrowed, his haughty presence draining away fast. "It's a bit dark in here, Lila. Do you mind?" Without taking his eyes off Jordan, Mortimer stood up and pointed at a cluster of vines on the wall, emanating dim blue light.

Lila grunted a note of disapproval and flayed a glowing green hand. She put it to the vines and brought the illumination up fast, forcing everyone to squint.

A despondent voice called from beyond the desk, from deep in the throat of a dark hallway: "Brother…"

Down the hall, Jordan spied movement. A figure dressed in white rose to his feet and grasped what appeared to be prison bars. Blue light shone down on him from above, as though he were the sole performer in an intimate venue.

"Who are *you*?" asked Mortimer, stepping in front of Jordan.

"I'm Jordan Wake—"

"Don't give me your name, boy. *This* is what I mean." Mortimer flayed his hand purple.

Jordan looked to Sebastien, who nodded. Jordan deveiled his own hand, painting Mortimer's angry face an additional shade of red.

"So, it is true," he said, side-stepping to Sebastién, "all this talk of Lux Sanguinis returned; the red light in the Midwestern sky. Only one brief, reckless appearance and then nothing. And here he is, in Arbor Florum." Mortimer went on tiptoes to address Sebastién, the long tails of his coat flapping off his backside. "This is a remarkable circumstance."

Mortimer's pronunciation of Florum rhymed with *broom*, leaving Jordan to wonder if this man had been around as long as Crispin.

"Indeed," said Sebastién. "And as we said, we'd like to see the prisoner."

"He's not available." Mortimer's lips shuffled in aftershock.

"I am awake," called a voice gently from the hallway.

"All of you, wait here." Mortimer huffed. "I need to call on the recorder."

"Recording is Castellum law," said Sebastién, attempting to move around Mortimer. "Being able to visit the accused without restriction is Florum's. That's the agreement, as I'm sure you're aware."

Mortimer stepped into his path again. "It is against protocol."

"But it is not against the law." Sebastién glared back at him. "As you surely know, the interfectors can and will dispatch us should there be any real violations—"

"You know better than to use that *word* around me!" Mortimer leaned into Sebastién pushing him back. "You're being obtuse."

"As are you," said Sebastién, locking Mortimer deeper into the spat while Lila slipped by. "Allow me to amend my statement: Castellum's devout inhibitors shall dispatch us if there are any problems. Good, yes?"

Sebastién pushed past.

Jordan attempted to do the same and Mortimer caught him by the arm. Jordan shook free, leaving him trembling, unable to decide on what to do. Mortimer deveiled and flew out the way they'd come in.

Jordan joined Sebastién and Lila. Together they traversed the wide hallway, which deposited them into a very large ballroom, long out of use. Firas's circular cell was in the middle, its perimeter established by a series of iron bars that ran from floor to a very tall ceiling. The confinement space spanned twenty feet at best—generous for a holding cell, but less so, considering he'd been here for more than a century.

Firas's world inside the bars consisted of a meager bed, a small desk and chair, and a scattering of books and papers. A dense arrangement of illuminated vines hung down from the ceiling like a chandelier, casting dim light. To the side of the cell stood two stern-faced women, dressed in black robes. With rigid posture, they gazed straight ahead, expressing no particular interest in Firas nor the visitors. Something about their faces disturbed Jordan. They were observant, but somehow…dead.

"Greetings, brother," said Firas.

A nervous nod was the only response Jordan could muster. Firas conveyed a tired face, bags haunting the underside of his nearly black eyes. He looked to be in his fifties, of Middle-Eastern complexion, with black hair hanging in long mottled strands. Jordan's first appraisal was that of a madman rightly confined to this place. He arrested his crass judgment, reminding himself of the man's circumstances.

Firas flayed a single red finger and wagged it side to side, as though making the naughty gesture. Two bursts of yellow light cracked to life on each side of his prison, attached to the wrists of the stern-faced women, who sunk into fighting stances. The gaze of one locked onto Firas, the other onto the visitors. Jordan's muscles went tight, and Firas grinned old, yellowed teeth.

"Attentive watchers, my inhibitors," said Firas leaking a broken laugh. "No sudden moves, brother. But it is no matter." Under watch of his guards, Firas brought his deviled finger near one of the bars. A bright violet fire jumped out and hummed at his finger.

Jordan recalled Crispin's lesson of the teaspoon relic, and how contact forced one to veil. Firas's red finger blinked out. Seconds later, the yellow fire of the guards did too.

"All the time in the world and here we are with so little in which to act." Firas looked Jordan in the eye. His face, like his laugh, conveyed a strange misery.

"Firas, please." Sebastién struggled to maintain a charismatic tone. "You saw Mortimer flee. He's marshaling whoever they have left. They've recorded everything we've said over the years. They know where we're going to look. Tell us how to call on Helena. We need every second."

"But I never told you where to look." Firas conjured a crooked smile. "I told *them* where to look. I said she'd have a wide drift. I said she'd follow the river to the falls, to where she first laid eyes upon the valley. But this is not the truth."

Jordan took in the interfectors: both tall and thin like runway models, though they lacked photogenic faces. One was Asian, the other pale-European. Still finding their stares unsettling, Jordan examined their black robes. Long sleeves, cuffed with violet. A line— also violet—ran the vertical length of the ensemble, intersecting a symbol positioned just over the heart: an eagle with wings spread wide, its feet rendered as serpents.

"You've always suggested the wrong place," said Sebastién, recognizing a man who'd been playing a ruse. "You intend to keep them busy."

Firas hummed an affirmative note. "Do you remember Helena's tree? That lonely sapling of an elm she worried herself over? She looked after it as if it were a child."

"I remember it."

"I asked you to watch over it too, and tell me of its condition throughout the years, all under the guise that it reminded me of my faintlight home." Firas looked down at the floor, drifting in thought. "It's there you'll find her, and when you call on her, use her first name only. Ask her if she's found her teapot—that's the shibboleth." Firas moved his hands together and intertwined his fingers. "The porcelain one with the blue birds on it—ask her of it."

Jordan watched a nervous enthusiasm emerge in Sebastién.

"We'll find her," said Sebastién nodding and turning to leave. Jordan and Lila followed.

"Wait!" called Firas.

They all stopped and turned around.

"Lila, when you release Helena, I want you to tell her something."

"What is it, Firas?"

"I realize it's just our peculiar superstition…but when you bring her to peace, tell her I'm sorry for all of this." Firas lowered his chin, pressing his forehead against the bars. "Tell her I love her, that I always did."

Lila paused, her shoulders sinking a degree. "I will, Firas. I promise."

They walked away, but before they reached the hallway, a purple streak of light shot down it and into the ballroom. A pair of violent cracks issued from behind Jordan. Jets of yellow light flew past, meeting the purple one head-on. The impact caused another cracking sound, sending bursts of liquefied purple light from the impact.

"Jordan, Don't move!" shouted Lila, grabbing his arm.

Jordan saw a human form on its knees trembling. The man's face was pressed against the floor by one of the interfectors, who was veiled except for her hand, which burned bright. She clutched the back of the man's neck. The other remained deveiled, hovering above the three of them, watching for any sign of movement. The trembling man struggled to speak, his words mangled by fright:

"Don't take my foot! I'm Finley, the recorder." The man's chest heaved. "Don't take my foot for Christ's sake."

"Release!" called out Mortimer, running into the room.

Without emotion, the interfector released Finley and deveiled, flying back to her post. The other did the same. Finley sat up and watched the three of them pass by while Mortimer eyed them with a sneer.

"No sudden moves," said Sebastién to Finley. "You, of all people, should know that."

Jordan looked back over his shoulder to the disheveled man in white. His face, despite being obstructed by vertical lines of iron, had hope written all over it.

21

FINDING HELENA

With the satchel Sebastién stole slung across his deveiled shoulder, the three of them raced through drain tunnels like the ones Jordan used in his arrival. They emerged into the Florum valley and headed east on foot. Jordan kept a finger flayed at Lila's request, monitoring everything nearby. He only caught blips of pale-feel; the occasional faintlight tourist out for a midnight walk.

"Do I want to know about the foot-taking thing?" asked Jordan.

"Probably not," said Sebastién, swinging the satchel like a pendulum. "But I suppose you should. Interfector protocol is to knock you back into veiled form first. If you persist—if they consider you a threat—they slice off a foot. That ends the urge to misbehave quite promptly—oh, and they usually don't let you deveil and heal until a handler arrives to sort things out."

"Wonderful."

"So if you ever find an interfector moving on you," said Sebastién, "submit, freeze, don't move an inch. You can't defeat one. Though the pain is temporary, the mental trauma of amputation is forever."

"Been there before?"

Sebastién cast an inert glance at Jordan.

The three of them continued in relative silence, moving under tall trees and through thick meadows until Jordan sensed a group of freelight in the valley. Four of them, a few miles east. They were moving away, likely on foot with flayed hands, making detection easy.

"As expected," said Sebastién after Jordan notified him. "I've underestimated Firas. All those years he'd been selling a decoy location. He knew the recorders would capture it. He knew the Kyzheres would listen. Whoever Mortimer sends out is going to be pushing in the wrong direction."

"And almost all their people are over Saint Paul," said Lila. "Only a skeleton crew here, nobody with any tracking skill."

Jordan's head skipped to a less optimistic thought. "Is there a chance someone found Helena. As in years ago?"

"Impossible," said Lila, ducking a branch. "It's much more than a needle-in-a-haystack problem. It's like trying to find a needle that's moving through the hayfield itself. Graylights are territorial, at least. First we find her. Then we have to pull her out of her slumber—that's what the teapot-talk was about. It requires very intimate knowledge of a person, knowing how they think. We have a distinct advantage here. Firas was the only one who really knew Helena."

Though the valley was nearly empty now, they kept off the walking paths, maintaining a clandestine march through the forest. They passed a lodge, its windows sending an incandescent glow through the black thatch-work of tree branches. Soon, the steady flow of a waterfall called out to them, reaching their ears as the sound used to calm an infant. A soft eternal hush.

"Sunlight obscures graylight signals," said Sebastién, "so we do this at night. Even moonlight will hinder. Fortunately, the moon will be down in minutes."

Jordan found himself sweating, despite the cool night.

The path reached the edge of a wide meadow, and they stopped. Lila crouched, plucking flat rocks off the ground. She examined them under Jordan's red lanternship.

"Anyone else out there?" Sebastién wagged his chin toward the dark meadow.

"The same four." Jordan aimed his palm at them. "Long ways off."

"Amateur hour," said Sebastién nodding. "We'll go unnoticed until

Lila starts recording. Then we risk detection, but they should be too far off and too unskilled to pick her up. Do tell me if they start moving toward us, though. It's likely they'll eventually split up and search both directions."

Lila stood up, clutching a dull flat rock in the palm of her hand. She spit on it and rubbed it against her jeans until it was clean. She thumbed its edges, breaking away loose fragments.

"Listen." Sebastién leaned in close to Jordan. "Once we have Helena, step back and stay out of the way. Keep your hand flayed and track Mortimer's people."

"What's going to happen?"

"Summoning the dead is a lit fuse. It blows up in the end, just a matter of how badly. Conversing with a graylight is hazardous in the best of hands. Only Lux Luna can mediate properly. In hands like Lila's, it could be lethal."

"Thanks for the vote of confidence, Seb," said Lila.

"Well, you haven't actually done this, have you?"

Lila demurred. "Just second-hand study through reliquiae and the standard literature."

Sebastién shrugged. "Don't sweat it, you'll do grand. Well, I mean, don't—"

"Just be ready to cut me loose," said Lila.

"I'll be ready." Sebastién straightened his cuffs and turned his attention to the meadow. It was populated by the twisted black silhouettes of trees. "Ready to play twenty questions, everyone?"

Lila squeezed the rock and exhaled, her breath pushing past her teeth with a nervous whistle.

Shoving the tall grass aside, they entered the meadow.

"Firas described Helena as feeling quaint, like his mother weaving a blanket," said Sebastién. "We might get lucky on the way there, so flay your hand completely and brighten up. It increases sensitivity."

Jordan did so. He became concerned over Lila's movements: stiff with tension, lacking the grace he observed earlier. His weren't much better.

"Wait a moment." Sebastién reached across Jordan and stopped him. Lila halted too. "What do I feel like to you? My signal. I must know."

"A hand of poker at a party in high school."

"Of course—and did you win?"

"…Yes."

"Perfect." Sebastién withdrew his arm and began to walk again. "See, good echoes."

"Quite cavalier, considering what we're about to do," said Lila.

Sebastién shrugged. "Now, regarding Helena, let's go back to that radio analogy. Ignore the two of us and you'll be left with something that rides like dead air. You'll be looking for the slightest disturbance in that silence. Graylight interruptions are much fainter than a faintlight. Always signaling, but barely awake."

They continued along the meadow line, Sebastién scanning about. His gaze locked up, finding a lone tree looming far ahead. It was removed from the natural edge of the wood line. Thick limbs erupted from its stump, twisting and intertwining. Its branches split at sharp angles, some reaching to the ground like emaciated witch fingers.

"Helena's tree," said Sebastién, coming to a halt, adjusting the satchel on his shoulder. He delivered a supportive pat to Jordan and shoved him forward. "Showtime."

With rattled nerves, Jordan walked to the tree. Upon arrival, he raised his flayed palm as though greeting it. The tree's bark took on a red cast. He sorted out the signals: Sebastién and Lila were easy despite being veiled; Mortimer's people to the east, still hunting. They were far away, still moving upriver. A few faintlights called from the distance, barely detectable. He turned them all off like light switches and panned his hand over the tree's bark, lighting it soft red, trying to feel…something. After tripping over low-hanging limbs on the first pass, he spotted Sebastién waving in his direction.

Frustrated, Jordan ran to him. "What!"

"Check *near* the tree, don't check *on* the tree." Sebastién mimicked Jordan's technique. "She's not stuck to the damn thing."

"How the hell am I supposed to know?"

Sebastién rumpled his face and scrubbed his forehead with

his knuckles.

"Keep trying. You'll get it," said Lila.

As Jordan made his way back, he realized two of Mortimer's people had changed direction and were moving toward them. He decided not to waste more time telling Sebastién. He tried to focus. With red hand aloft, a world of empty regularity unfolded before him as he circled the tree in an ever-increasing orbit. Minutes passed, his pace quickened. He grew uncertain of his so-called talent, avoiding Sebastién's judgmental gaze every time his search circle went past.

A nervous sweat gathered on Jordan's brow. A sense of despair crept in. He was so far from the tree now, he'd soon walk straight into Sebastién and Lila. Mortimer's trackers continued to move in their direction. The decreasing proximity sent Jordan's twin directives of finding Helena and reporting on the lurkers into a collision. Jordan looked up at Sebastién and Lila. From across the meadow—just out of shouting distance—they stood side by side, arms crossed. They maintained game faces, but ones spider-webbed with cracks of doubt.

Jordan abandoned the search.

He ran toward them, setting off distressed glances. A stone's throw away—at the very moment Sebastién's lips began to form words—the image of a frosty windowsill flashed through Jordan's mind.

Then it was gone.

Jordan stopped dead in his tracks. He turned around as Sebastién continued to say something. Moving his hand across his body in a wide arc, Jordan scoured the void. It was the faintest of visions—a tiny spark of a scene, a weak anchor on the warm dark air. Jordan retraced his steps, raising his hand to eye level.

Sebastién was still speaking, but he ignored it.

Jordan found it again: a snow-dusted window at his uncle's house, New Year's Day; apple pie cooling on the stove while Jordan and his cousins kicked off wet clothes after a romp in the snow.

"I have her," said Jordan, calling across the meadow. "And two of Mortimer's people are moving toward us—"

"Don't lose her!" Lila swish-swished her way through the tall grass.

"I won't." Jordan fixed his eyes on a twig-thin slice of air in front of his hand, tracking it an inch at a time. "She's right here, just off my fingertips, drifting toward her tree."

Lila came in tight next to Jordan, raising her hand and flaying it. Green light burst across the meadow, giving its grass a vibrant, electric sheen. Jordan felt Helena's signal shift sideways instantly, trying to reach Lila's deveiled hand.

"Helena," whispered Lila softly, as though waking a child. "Helena, where is your teapot? The one with the blue birds on it."

Jordan felt the frosty window image pulse. "It's getting stronger."

Lila nodded a half-acknowledgment, not looking at him. Her throat tightened as she swallowed down an ocean of anxiety. "Helena, where is your teapot?" Another burst of green light flashed out from the palm of Lila's other hand—the one holding the stone. Tiny green flames tickled at its edges and then vanished. "Tell me, Helena," continued Lila in a wavering voice, "where is your teapot?"

The light from Lila's deveiled fingertips began to dance in breezy flickers, despite the calm night. It stretched away from her hand. Eager tongues of green fire nipped at something in the beyond. Then, the farthest-venturing tendril found its quarry. Its pin-point tip flared like a struck match. The green tongue of fire went a strange dark: its color burned away, leaving behind a black fire, laced in silver fringe. The black consumed the green, pulling in more tongues of Lila's light, causing her to gasp. Lila flayed her hand further, all the way to the elbow. The blackness continued to steal her light, rolling it up like a hungry spider capturing prey.

"You did it." Sebastién grabbed Jordan by the shoulders and pulled him away. "Now get back."

Jordan's eyes remained locked on Lila as a malignant black form grew into existence off her fingertips, elevated in the air above the field. Details erupted: a woman's face, arms, and slender fingers. Her body was garbed in a Victorian dress, the hemline rippling above her ankles. With eyes shut and chin low, she slept. From her chest to Lila's palm ran a thick, wavering rope; an umbilical cord of light that transitioned sharply from bright green to silver-black. Jordan and Sebastién stared with wonderment at this ethereal, sleeping Madonna.

Her eyes flicked open.

Jordan jolted, Sebastién thrust his hands out to his sides as though catching his balance. Lila cried a note of surprise, her arm trembling, sending ripples up the channel of green light that tethered her to the shrouded form. The woman's head began to move about slowly. She was looking, searching, becoming aware. Her eyes blinked repetitively, evicting remnants of a long sleep.

Lila spoke, her words coming out frantic: "Flumen thirty-seventh, eleven eight eighty-nine, Arbor Florum, valley proper, east meadow. I am Lila Harper finding Helena Phaedria declared murdered Dēfessus fifth eleven seven sixty-one."

Helena's head darted side to side, hunting for the voice.

"Helena, is that you?" said Lila, trying to wrestle her delivery into a more controlled pace.

"Yes," said Helena, her voice innocent as dew.

"Do you know what day it is, Helena?"

"Dēfessus fifth, eleven seven sixty-one." Tiny wisps of silver light flared at the corners of her mouth when she spoke.

"Do you know it in the faintlight calendar?"

"Let me think." Helena paused. "The sixth of August, Eighteen eighty-nine."

"Do you know where you are?"

"I'm in my home in Arbor Florum, of course." Helena tilted her head to the side. Her eyes narrowed. Her mouth dipped open. "No… wait. I'm outside, in the Florum valley."

"What are you doing in the valley?" asked Lila, shifting her weight from one foot to the other, looking ready to escape.

"Why can't I see you?" asked Helena, her voice curious, the soft curve of her eyebrows going flat. "I hear you, but I cannot see you." She craned her head as though trying to peek around an obstruction. Her hand reached outward. Lila's eyes followed it like an errant scalpel.

"Why did you come to the valley?" asked Lila.

Helena paused again. "I'm meeting Firas here. We're going to have tea. I brought something to eat too—Firas is always hungry, he can't redraft." A smile broke across her quaint features. One of her front teeth was more pronounced than the other, crowded and offset. "He's late, but it's of no consequence. I had to go back for my teapot, the one with the blue birds."

"Are you still waiting for Firas?"

Helena's smile held tight as she considered the question. Then it faded. "No…we already had tea. He—he was upset…" She looked around again, her brow compressed. "Who are you?"

"Sebastién," called out Jordan. "Mortimer's people are getting closer…"

Helena's attention whipped toward Jordan. A brief flash of hostility coursed through her face.

"Keep me posted," said Sebastién, his eyes not leaving Lila.

"Have you seen anyone else, Helena?" asked Lila. Her tone expressed a sense of urgency.

Helena paused, deep in thought. Movement resumed with a slow sinking of her chin. Her eyes blinked rapidly. "Yes, I did. There was someone else…there were others. They came after."

Jordan tried to gauge the pace of Mortimer's trackers. They hadn't seemed to have detected Lila yet.

"Listen to me." Sebastién moved in front of Jordan, blocking his view to Lila. His face was mired in darkness, Lila's green light throwing flashes around the sides. "Stay back, don't interfere. When Mortimer's people read us they're going to deveil and move fast— you'll feel the tap, just like on our flight into Florum. Tell me when it happens. Yell it out loud—make sure we hear it. But do *not* come closer." With that, Sebastién dropped the satchel at Jordan's feet and dashed to a spot just behind Lila.

"Who did you see? Helena, please," said Lila, her voice becoming desperate. The flow of light off her hand was accelerating. Illuminated threads raced into Helena's corporeal form faster and faster.

"I was afraid…" Helena's attention jumped to multiple places. "Why can't I see you?"

Helena snatched at the air like a pickpocket, causing Lila to stumble backward. Losing her balance, she fell to one knee, arresting the fall with the knuckles of her relic-recording hand. But she didn't lose the stone. As she got back to her feet, Helena drifted closer by an apparent elasticity in the light tether. Sebastién moved near Lila, carefully avoiding contact with her.

"Helena, who did you see?" asked Lila. "Please *tell* me."

"I don't understand," said Helena. "Why can't I see you? Why is everything…distant. Why is everything dark?"

Jordan felt the trackers deveil. They pulsed, as though transmitting Morse code. They started moving fast.

Jordan called out: "Sebastién, here they come, they're—"

"Who are you!" shrieked Helena. "What do you want with me?" Helena's hands snatched at Lila, her fingers stretching to unnatural lengths, trying to reach the green light. Helena nearly clasped Lila's fingers. Lila jumped back. As before, Helena's agitated form drifted closer.

"Helena, who did you see? *TELL* me." Erratic flashes pulsed through the light tether, accompanied by bursts of rash static and sharp cracking sounds. Helena's head began to twitch as though she were experiencing a seizure.

"You're losing her, Lila," shouted Sebastién. "Let her go—"

"—Helena who did you see!"

Helena ground her teeth, placed her hands over her ears. Her face warped hideously, stretching like Munch's painting *The Scream*.

"Helena, please…" Lila, with teeth clenched, moaned as though she were lifting something twice her weight. Her light brightened, erasing the static crackle. Helena's features snapped back to normal. Helena removed her hands from her ears. Her chest rose and fell as though breathing heavily.

"Helena…who did you see?"

She looked directly at Lila, her eyes blinking as if reaching the answer. She responded softly:

"I saw Firas."

"No…," said Lila, nearly crying the word. She swallowed and redoubled her efforts. "Helena, who came after—"

She began to destabilize again: harsh crackling sounds, distortions in her facial features. Jordan watched with horrified eyes. His terror compounded as twin pinpoints of purple light appeared far in the distance. Mortimer's trackers had arrived, burning bright, closing in…

"WHO ARE YOU!" bellowed Helena, sending long, shrill syllables across the meadow. She clawed at Lila, who jumped back, creating another elastic gap. The light tether reeled Helena in again.

"I'm cutting it!" said Sebastién develling with a crack, sending an orange glare across the field.

"Not YET—" yelled Lila over the cacophony of Helena's failing form.

Helena scanned wildly for Sebastién's voice.

Jordan's stomach turned. He struggled to respect Sebastién's mandate, wanting to help somehow.

"Helena!" said Lila, her face strained as she tried to regulate the light flow. Lila cried out, pain wrenching her expression. "HELENA!"

Helena stared a straight angry line to Lila's eyes.

Lila struggled to deliver the words. They came out at last, loud enough to carry across the meadow: "Helena, have you seen the light?"

The words tranquilized her instantly.

Helena's frantic movements stopped. Her face took on a reflective expression. For a moment she was frozen in place, a vaporous image floating in the air. She dropped her arms to her sides, her appearance growing peaceful, serene.

"Firas wants you to know that he's sorry"—Lila stole a pair of fast hard breaths—"and he loves you."

"He…he loves me?"

Mortimer's trackers grew bright. They raced toward the scene, their light projecting flashes of vivid purple to treetops and meadow grasses.

"He loves you…" said Lila.

A smile emerged on Helena's face as her features began to disintegrate, issuing into the air like the gray ash of burnt paper.

"Jordan, get the satchel," yelled Sebastién.

Jordan, shaking with adrenaline, snatched it off the ground and fumbled to open it. Lila twisted sideways and threw the relic-rock to Jordan, a burst of green light flashing off her palm the second it lost contact.

Jordan caught the stone and bagged it.

"Drop the satchel. Leave it!" shouted Sebastién growing bright. His orange fire took on a loud, violent roar. The grasses around him were consumed by frost and collapsed onto the ground. "Ditch them in the forest. Wait it out—"

"I'm losing her," shouted Lila, her breath visible in the sudden cold.

"—then get to the bluffs," finished Sebastién.

What had once been Helena now looked ghoulish. Beyond her, the purple trackers were close enough to look human. Racing, yearning to get to them…

Jordan deveiled and went bright.

"FLY!" shouted Sebastién.

Jordan remained transfixed, watching Lila. A wave of green light struggled to move across her arm, but Helena was starving the deveiling process of the power it needed.

A bright light erupted inside Helena, like a camera flash, leaving behind a pink seed of light. It started to float away.

Lila wailed loud as if in great pain.

What remained of Helena transformed: her arms, hands, and fingers became unnaturally long, moving like snakes. Her eyes dissolved, leaving black sockets that grew as large as the empty pit of her mouth. She clawed at the shimmering umbilical cord, trying to haul it in, her wicked fingers nearly reaching Lila's green palm.

Sebastién jetted to Lila, delivering the blow. His fiery orange hand cleaved the link, sending Lila backward onto the ground, spraying arcs of green light into the field. Strands of grass burst into flame where the green rain struck. Sebastién landed a second strike to Helena's chest. She turned bright silver, and her movements ceased entirely. She was silent and paralyzed.

Jordan could see the faces of the trackers.

With a piercing wail, Helena jolted to life again.

Sebastién pivoted away from the reaper-like Helena. His face turned to Jordan's line of sight; a split-second glance, commanding him to flee. Lila was already racing southward, a blurred streak of green across Jordan's vision. The trackers arrived like purple comets as reaper-Helena gathered herself. Jordan spun away, catching a glimpse of Sebastién scooping the satchel off the ground in midflight. Purple light filled Jordan's periphery as the violent bullwhip crack of Sebastién's departure sounded out. A purple hand reached to the side of Jordan's face.

It caught empty air.

Jordan shot forward with vengeance, crossing the meadow, streaking westward into the thick of the forest.

22

POSTMORTEM

Jordan had ditched his pursuer easier than expected. Still rattled by the experience, he crouched behind the base of a huge pine. He kept a finger flayed, waiting it out as his chaser raced around like a rabbit, eventually giving up and moving east to join his counterparts.

Jordan made his way west on foot.

After passing by the colossal front of El Capitan, a walk which consumed twenty minutes, Jordan read Lila in tiny bursts: a stealth, radar-like blip. It was enough for Jordan to determine her location above the valley on the bluff. Jordan deveiled, dimmed, and weaved his way through the remainder of the forest, over the river, and up the cliff face. He arrived so suddenly that Lila jumped to her feet. She huffed and stepped back, leaning against a tree for support while Jordan veiled.

"Sorry I took so long." Jordan flayed his hand so they could see each other clearly. "Are you alright?"

"I'm fine."

"And Sebastién?"

Lila shrugged under the soft crimson glow. "It's Sebastién."

"What happened back there?"

"I failed," said Lila tartly. "That's what happened."

"I didn't mean it like that." Jordan raised his deveiled hand, gesturing an apology. "I wasn't sure what I was seeing. Why did she calm down when you asked her if she'd seen the light?"

Lila took a long breath. "It's a phrase that we all learn, one so common it leaked into the faintlight world. It can mean a lot of things, but in this case, it's a way to tell someone they're already dead."

"And that's what set her free?"

"No, it's just a superstition. Summoning always ends with release—that pink light you saw. By saying it, we gave her a chance to accept it, which results in a peaceful moment." Lila crossed her arms and rubbed her elbows. "It also gives the summoner a better chance to break away—that's what Sebastién had to help me with. Otherwise, I'd be the next Helena."

"That thing is still out there though, isn't it?"

"It's diminished by now. Mortimer's trackers saw it, so they'll know we found Helena."

"Were they trying to kill us?"

"You possibly, though I doubt they'd have been given orders like that. They were trying to disrupt us or get the relic I recorded—not that it's going to do us much good anyway."

"Helena didn't name Supernus as her killer," said Jordan, feeling he'd grasped the critical detail. "She just remembers Firas—"

"Which means the chronology was off too, which never happens. It makes no sense. None of this will vindicate Firas, nor incriminate Supernus. We have nothing."

"We set Helena free."

"Yes," said Lila, reconsidering. "That we did."

They waited in silence for a moment.

"What do we do now?" asked Jordan.

Lila closed her eyes. With her back still pressed against the tree, she slid down its trunk, taking a seat at the base. "Now we go the political route. We put the injustice in everyone's face—every last person in Arbor Florum. We become the unapologetic conscience of the Grey City." Lila picked at a thick root next to her leg. "For the Kyzheres to claim that Firas murdered our predecessors implies that they *knew* our predecessors were dead. In other words, it was a subtle declaration that they *had* murdered our predecessors—a long-expected act of revenge. Firas is not loved, but our predecessors were loved dearly. Reminding people of them is the way to Florum's heart and its ire. We must force the powers that be to disqualify the accusations against Firas and set him free."

"Sebastién didn't mention this."

"He doesn't believe it will work."

"Do you?"

"We have no other choice." Lila pressed her hand to her forehead.

Jordan sat down in front of her, elbow on knee, his deveiled hand lighting the space between them. "Helena's relic gets us there?"

"No." Lila looked up from the ground and held his gaze. "You do. Quite literally. Your arrival deals the final blow to the claim that your predecessor—that *our* predecessors—could have ever been murdered here in Arbor Florum. The geography doesn't work, which makes the accusations against Firas absurd. At least to any reasonable mind."

Jordan stared past the ends of his glowing red fingertips, trying to piece together the chronology.

Lila continued: "You saw the light—your red unharbored timbre—somewhere in Upper Michigan, near the southern shore of Lake Superior. Near one of those old mining towns, right?"

"Yes," said Jordan, surprised by her accuracy. "How—"

"That's where both our predecessors died. So that's where I saw mine too."

"You're from there?" asked Jordan.

"No. Chicago. I was passing through on a sailboat with some bootleggers."

"You were a bootlegger?" asked Jordan, even more surprised.

She slipped an amused smile. "No, I had a friend who was involved with one. She wanted me to come with her. I thought it would be fun, a fashionable experience. Something like that." Lila paused, her attention dipping into the past. "I was so naïve. Turned out the bootlegger's friend was there to get rid of him and everyone else." Lila's stare went distant and her smile dissolved. "I saw the light the night before. We were camping on the beach and

I took a walk alone." Lila looked at her hand, and then to Jordan. "It saved my life."

"How did you discover it?" asked Jordan, waving his deveiled fingers. "This, I mean."

"At gunpoint."

"Sounds familiar…"

"It was right after the guy shot everyone else on board. I was the last. I'll never forget the look on his face when I deveiled out of sheer panic. He looked like he'd seen a ghost. I guess he really did."

Lila's attention drifted. The silent surroundings granted them both the luxury of needed introspection. Jordan broke the silence first, perhaps on account of having fewer ideas to sort through, perhaps because all his questions derived from a single calculus.

"I need to ask you something." Jordan shifted his weight, easing the discomfort of sitting on hard ground. Lila looked at him, one of her eyes obscured by hair. "All of this happened so fast. What I did over Saint Paul…it was stupid, I know. I was scared to death. Then Sebastién shows up and tricks me into going with him. I knew something was off, but he's so…" Jordan stirred the air with his hand, trying to summon a proper description.

"Chronically persuasive," offered Lila.

"Sure, let's go with that." Jordan lowered his hand. "He knew right when I began to doubt him and used the promise of you to get me onboard. He did it again before we met up in West Leaf tonight when I was demanding answers. I realize I'm going along with all this because of you…or the promise of you."

"He's chronically persuasive," said Lila again.

"What I want to know is that I'm doing the right thing. Sebastién said Crispin doesn't want me involved in this."

Lila went silent for a moment. "Crispin turned his back on Firas too, just like the rest. That's why it has to be us. Someone has to stand against the Kyzheres and help Firas."

"How many people does *us* include, exactly—who's leading this thing?"

"Sebastién," said Lila, her lips letting the word go reluctantly.

"There's only a few of us, but in time—"

"*Sebastién?*" asked Jordan, nearly leaping to his feet. "I thought there would be something more organized, something more official."

"He's at the heart of this, and so am I. Now you're involved too. It has to start with us, Jordan."

Jordan stared at the ground, watching an insect traverse the red-lit dirt like a rover on Mars. "If the geography argument is undeniable, why is it so hard to sell?"

"Because the Kyzheres are on the flip side of that coin." Lila rubbed her hands together for warmth. "Arbor Florum may be the crown jewel of the freelight world, but it's fastened to a chain held by the Kyzheres. Arbor Castellum is far more powerful than us. The Kyzheres control the interfectors, which means they control everything."

Silence again. They drifted in thought like monks.

Jordan reflected on the events that had carved through his life over recent weeks. Years of being taunted by the mysterious vision of Lila's eyes seemed a paltry concern compared to what was unfolding here. At that moment, Jordan felt the faintlight world shift away from him; a distinct movement, like a tremor in lands prone to earthquakes. He tried to conjure the scene of a normal life, an idea in itself that now seemed abnormal. He imagined himself in an office cubicle, typing away as the years rolled by, his hair drifting into gray. That life struck him as fantasy now.

"There's a proverb in our world," said Lila, emerging from her silence. She brushed her hair aside, allowing Jordan to see both her eyes, the centers of which reflected the red light of his flayed hand. "We live our lives somewhere between fate and free will. Never entirely one, nor the other, but a dance where the lead changes and the partners move like tides." Lila stood up and brushed dust off her jeans.

Jordan responded in kind, his eyes fixed on hers.

"I don't really understand what my birth echo tells us," said Lila, "despite being questioned about it relentlessly since the day I arrived." She stepped closer, the distance identical to what Jordan saw in his birth echo. But there were no tears here; just a countenance that issued conviction. "In it, I see you, and in yours, you see me. We feel connected in this way, long before we ever met—in my case, decades before you were even born. It's an implausible truth. But a truth nonetheless, and one impossibly tilted toward fate. But at *this* moment, we're running on free will. The future is ours to shape. I want Firas to find his freedom, but I wish to my last light that the world learn the truth about Supernus Kyzhere. That he is a murderer. He *must* be brought to justice."

Jordan measured her demeanor, observing a controlled intensity in her eyes. "If you're in, then I'm in."

Lila's face softened, expressing something deeper than mere gratitude. "Thank you," she said, smiling a touch. "Let's get back inside. I'm cold."

23

A DEBT UNPAID

Even during the daytime, Arbor Florum's dimways felt like a night scene on account of sparse illumination. Light trickled down from the winding vinelight as before, but twinkled a warm incandescent glow this time, not the nocturnal blue of night. Sebastién and Lila walked at Jordan's side, the former hashing out the plan of what they'd say to Firas.

"We have to bluff," said Sebastién, animated beyond his usual verve. "It is essential you understand this and *believe* it. The ruse needs to be written in our faces, because they'll be recording every visit to Firas. When we're talking to him, we're also talking to *them*. They know we found Helena, but…" Sebastién went silent. They passed a group of people loitering near a shop, the bystanders' mouths lipping porcelain cups, eyes lingering on them. The scent of warm bread floated past Jordan's nose as they moved out of an earshot.

"As I was saying," continued Sebastién, "they know we found Helena, but they don't know what we got out of her." Sebastién slipped toward whispers as they rounded a corner, the main thoroughfare ahead of them. "We have to tell Firas we have the testimony and do it with a perfect poker face. Even he shouldn't know the truth."

Sebastién continued to chatter strategy as they reached West Grey. They took a right toward West Leaf. Jordan and Lila remained attentive, small nods and eager eyes hanging on Sebastién's designs. The brisk pace brought them under the monumental gateway. But out of the periphery, came hints of change in the local atmosphere, an inversion of the dimway bustle. Lila noticed it first: the crowds on the avenue were standing still as though cemented in place. Long faces and idle hands, eyes blinking unease at the scene in West Leaf.

"Look!" said Lila, grabbing Sebastién's arm.

Jordan and Sebastién did.

In the distance, a group of yellow freelight hovered in formation in front of the Carmen Vespere: interfectors. Each shimmered like a radiant strand of sunlight, casting a blinding presence across West Leaf. They hovered in pairs to each side of the Carmen's grand staircase. Dead center, above that staircase, floated a single violet freelight, his vigilant gaze surveying West Leaf. In whole, the arrangement looked like a quintet of flames on an invisible candelabra.

"Is this because of us?" asked Jordan.

"Yes," Sebastién's shoulders sank and he pursed his lips, "this is because of us."

"Interfectors have never operated outside the Carmen before." Lila's attention jumped between Sebastién and the front of the hotel. "This is unprecedented—this is not legal."

"Yet there they are," said Sebastién dryly. "It's preemptive, no doubt. A way to put a scare into Arbor Florum. To get everyone talking and dissuade would-be sympathizers to our cause."

"Looks like it's working." Jordan studied the petrified bystanders and airborne freelight. All of them lingered, unwilling to move into West Leaf as though they'd reached the edge of an active battlefield.

Sebastién took a breath and resumed his confident stride, moving into the West Leaf thoroughfare. Jordan and Lila followed, the trio walking in silence most of the way.

"This could backfire," announced Sebastién. "Arbor Florum has been tormented by the Kyzheres for more than a century. People disappear and nobody talks about it. Should tyranny move into the open, things might boil over."

"Wishful thinking," said Lila.

"I can assure you I do not wish it." Sebastién straightened his suit jacket. "Okay, game faces. Time to rattle the cages."

As they reached the steps of the Carmen, Jordan stole a skyward glance at the interfectors, who in turn noted him with a dispassionate appraisal. Their violet handler, however, leaked a smile just before they passed underneath and into the Carmen's grand foyer.

Inside, the Carmen was a polar opposite to the night prior. It was brightly lit now, humming with bureaucratic fervor. People marched in bee-lines from one side to the other, disappearing into halls and offices. A woman in stilettos cracked her way across the foyer right up to them. She was wrapped in a dark brown suit with a cranberry blouse peeking out from underneath.

"Good afternoon." She had a combative voice. "On account of executive order four-thirteen, this division of Res Externa is closed to citizens of Arbor Florum." Her pronunciation of the word *citizens* carried a particularly contemptuous hiss.

"We are here to visit Firas el-Sakar," said Lila. "We have—"

"As I said: closed to all citizens of Arbor Florum."

Sebastién put a thumb to his chin and came up with a smirk a moment later. "Our colleague, Jordan Wakefield, is not a citizen of Arbor Florum. May he pass?" Sebastién stared her down, his smirk expanding like a fault line.

After a moment, the woman winced like she'd turned an ankle. "He may pass," she said, "but those who *are* citizens of Arbor Florum must leave, lest we remove you from the facility by force."

"Hardly necessary." Sebastién eyed the pair of interfectors who glided up from the back of the room. "We were just leaving." Sebastién gave Jordan a nod, yet seemed reluctant to part ways. Finally, he and Lila left, and the stiletto woman escorted Jordan through the halls.

Jordan recited the words *perfect poker face* in his head, trying to organize Sebastién's strategy. He decided to keep the exchange brief as possible. In minutes, he was in the hallway of the ballroom where a smug Mortimer sat at his desk eyeing him.

Jordan's footfalls echoed down the hall. Despite the vibrant lobby, the ballroom remained grim. It was barely brighter than the previous night, though this time Jordan had the opportunity to digest it in full: broken tables, chairs strewn across the floor, remnants pushed into the corners. A coat of dust hid the woodwork, interrupted only by footprints. Tattered curtains hung across windows as though to seal the place off from the outside world.

Firas sat on the floor with legs crossed, eating rice from a small bowl with a metal spoon. A different pair of guards stood next to the cylindrical cell. They observed Jordan with indifference in the usual interfector way. Firas stood upon Jordan's approach, his hands grasping the bars.

Finley, the recorder, perked up from the comfort of an ornate chair that looked as though it had been annexed during the hotel's functional days. He got to his feet and picked up a polished copper disc from a nearby desk. As he crossed the room toward them, a purple light flared around its edges and then flickered out.

"Flumen thirty-eighth, eleven eight eighty-nine," said Finley, who glanced sideways. Jordan turned to see he was looking at a luxuriant grandfather clock stationed at the back wall. It was a striking artifact, at odds with the rest of the ruined ballroom.

"…Two fifty-nine in the afternoon. I am Braer Finley, site recorder for Arbor Castellum, special jurisdiction, Arbor Florum, documenting the visitation of detainee Firas el-Sakar by…" Finley paused again and leveled an impatient stare at Jordan until he offered his name. "…by Jordan Wakefield, presumed, but unconfirmed, Lux Sanguinis; presumed, but unconfirmed, standing of revenant."

Firas peered at Jordan from beneath his locks of disheveled black hair, trying to decipher mood in advance of words. "Please sit," said Firas with the finesse of a maître d'. "You too, Braer. Please, join us."

Finley hesitated before sitting next to Jordan.

Jordan spoke first. "They barred Sebastién and Lila from coming in, a special order of some sort. But they let me through because I'm not a citizen. It was a loophole Sebastién figured out."

"How adept of him." Firas lifted a strand of hair away from his face. "I guess we'll be having a more intimate conversation. It's what I was hoping for anyway." The words were gentle, not rushed.

Jordan glanced down at the bowl of rice in Firas's cell. Soft light from the greenery above twinkled muted reflections off the spoon.

"I'm always hungry," said Firas, recognizing the path of Jordan's eyes. "You and I, we are unable to change—we cannot redraft, so we are stuck with ourselves as ourselves. Forever. For me, that means constant hunger, dreadful only a few hours after I take mortal form. My jailers, don't like for me to deveil on an hourly basis, so we've come to an agreement. I'm granted release from hunger's snare in the faintlight way. It's of the few compassions I've known here."

The grandfather clock struck three times, causing Jordan to look back at it. Despite the dust covering everything in the ballroom, the clock was quite clean.

"It's the fourth of its kind since I arrived over a century ago. The finest of them, beautifully made, rare in its craft. Observe the second hand. See how it sweeps instead of ticks—smooth and never-ending, like time itself."

"How did they get this stuff into Arbor Florum?" asked Jordan, trying to sound casual. Anxiety sprouted sweat across his forehead. He resisted the urge to wipe it away.

"They didn't." Firas seemed charmed at the inquisition. "We made it—all of it. The real question is how we got the materials in here." Firas gave Jordan a moment to consider it, as though testing him. "Re-drafters. Freelight who excel at the very thing that is impossible for you and me. They gather up armloads of the finest of what Elysium offers and make it part of themselves, just as you can produce that coat you're wearing over and over. They return and reveil—cycling back and forth from the deveiled state for hours, or days if necessary, producing mountains of the softest silks, the finest pelts of leather, the most refined bolts of fabric. From there it goes to the artisans in North Leaf. The limitation is always size—materials like wood, especially." Firas's words carried a touch of enthusiasm, as though he were living a former life, one prior to imprisonment. "Nothing longer than the tallest of us—though it's nothing that good join work can't solve. *That* was my trade before they locked me away, and I do miss it, brother."

Jordan glanced about the room, noting objects crafted in this fashion: curtains, chairs, tables, and even the ballroom floor.

"But we aren't here to discuss carpentry, are we?" Firas returned to a dire tone. "Tell me what happened last night, if you have no further questions."

Jordan hesitated, wondering if the sweat on his brow was visible to Finley's watching eye. "I have one more. But it's not about carpentry." Jordan tried to prepare himself for the bluff, scouring his memory for a meaningless question in the meantime.

"Please." Firas presented a ready face.

Jordan rubbed his hands down the length of his jeans. A question came to him: "How did you know it was me last night when I came in? That I was Lux Sanguinis before I deveiled my hand?"

Firas's face shuddered, betraying a glimmer of dismay. He hesitated and responded softly, turning his head away from Finley. "The same way you already knew Lila." His next words reached conversational volume again. "Now tell me, how did things unfold last night? You found my Helena, I presume? I see so few faces in here, but the ones I do see I know well. And today they appear quite rattled."

"We found her." Jordan lifted his chin to a confident height.

"And did Lila tell her what I asked?"

"She did and—"

"How did she look when released?" asked Firas.

"She was peaceful."

Firas nodded and turned away from Finley again. Jordan spotted tears welling in his eyes. Taking a deep breath, he wiped them away. "Perhaps she'll return to us one day," he whispered before subjecting his face to Finley again. "And the testimony, I presume it is hidden?"

"I don't know where. They thought it would be better I didn't."

"Wise…and did we get what we needed? Did Helena remember her final moments?"

Jordan's response came out as two monumental syllables, resulting in an echo: "She did."

Firas's eyes burrowed into him, his chin moving in tiny nods. When he spoke, the words cut Jordan like a knife: "You play bluffs poorly, brother."

Jordan's forehead wrinkled, baffled by Firas's failure to recognize the strategy.

"I realize that Sebastién and others are certain of their tactics—I know they mean well, but I am asking *you*, brother, to trust me over them." Firas spoke in a controlled tone. "I need to know if my Helena declared Supernus her killer. Do we have him?"

Jordan stared at Firas with an expression begging him not to press onward. He saw in return Firas's black, intense eyes.

Firas continued. "If we have him, the relic would have to be presented to the Praetorium. If that doesn't happen, it's only a matter of time before the Kyzheres know we are trying to play an empty hand. All they have to do is wait, and time is against us. So please brother, tell me. Do we have him?"

"No," said Jordan, the word dying on his lips.

Finley let loose a choppy exhale, underpinned by laughter.

"But we have a plan. The geography of our predecessors doesn't work. It refutes the accusations against you. We're going to get you free—"

"It's not enough, brother."

"—both Lila and I saw our light in the *same* place, far from Arbor Florum. It's absurd that—"

"*Brother*, it is not enough!" Firas's words went dark like his eyes. "Logic is not the problem. The politics are. If I am to be un-accused, *who* shall take my place as the accused? The Kyzheres hold sway over three of the five houses of Arbor Florum. The First Circle will not turn against them."

Jordan let his gaze fall to the floor.

"But I know what *will* force their hand," Firas's voice became comforting, "and once again, I will need your help—yours and yours alone. I need you to finish something. A dangerous thing. Dangerous for all but those of us who are invisible, which leaves you and me. Since I am in here, it shall have to be you out there who does this. If you are willing, that is."

Jordan looked up from the floor and found Firas's eyes, which were filled with a fledgling hope.

"But first I must tell my story." Firas drew a long breath. "It's one I've never shared until now, for reasons that will become clear in time." Firas looked to Finley. "Are you ready to record my tale, Braer?"

Jordan looked sidelong at the recorder, who didn't respond. He just stared at Firas like a statue.

Firas ran his fingers along the bars and began:

"Like Sebastién, my tale is also one of guilt and unfortunate timing, also a story of walking away. It takes place one hundred and twenty-eight years ago, when I had taken shelter in a dark arbor during my travels. One near the southern shore of what I understand in the faintlight tongue is called Lake Superior."

"That's where I'm from," offered Jordan.

"An amazing coincidence." Firas directed a droll glance at Finley. "On that night, I was the only one there. Dark arbors had gone out of fashion, even back then. They were places to hide, places for freelight to avoid other freelight, so naturally I preferred them. I had been sleeping but woke to the arrival of Raphael Foscari and Elisabeth Di Lorne. Raphael was your predecessor, Jordan. Elisabeth was Lila's. We saw each other from across the commons. They knew me as one to keep to myself." Firas placed a hand around one of the bars, and Jordan noticed his fingers. They were cracked and scarred. "I could see they were frightened. They whispered to each other and watched my every move. So I did what I believed they wanted me to do: I left. But when I got outside, I felt others immediately—Supernus and his people."

Out of the corner of his eye, Jordan saw Finley shuffling as though wanting to stand up. Jordan was certain he heard gritting teeth.

"So I fled. I knew the history. I knew they were dangerous, but none of it was my concern, or so I told myself all the way back to Arbor Florum." Firas's grasp of the prison bar slipped, his hand landing on his knee. "I arrived in Florum and met with my dearest Helena in the meadow, as we had planned weeks earlier. She knew something was troubling me, and when I told her, she became frightened—clearly understanding the implications. She begged me to tell the Praetorium. But I didn't want to. It had nothing to do with me. This too, I told myself. It was a belief of short duration."

Finley continued to twitch in an agitated manner.

"As it turned out, Supernus and his people saw me leave the dark arbor, or Raphael told them. It doesn't matter which." Firas pushed hair away from his face. "What matters is that I brought death upon my Helena. After we parted ways on foot, I decided I'd spend the night on the rim and wait to see if any of them would arrive in Florum. To my surprise, they were already there. I knew it the moment I deveiled."

Firas looked up at the ceiling, as though reenacting the moment. Jordan saw bloodshot eyes, perhaps from the tears earlier, or perhaps it was just the way they were.

"I realized they were headed for her. They must have seen us together and waited for me to leave. I had been too foolish to bare a finger and check that whole time." Firas's mouth contorted into a sorrowful shape. His eyebrows arched. He struggled to keep himself from weeping again. After a few moments, he resumed. "I couldn't get to her in time. I found her teapot in the grass, discarded out of fear. I saw Helena at the other side of the meadow, surrounded. And Then I saw *him*—I saw Supernus murder her with his own hand."

"LIAR!" shouted Finley, springing to his feet. He kicked the prison bars. Violent cracks came from both sides of Firas's cell, bright yellow illuminating the scene. Finley froze, recognizing his mistake.

Jordan squinted at the intensity of the interfectors' fire while Finley clenched his relic, the tendons in his forearm standing out. Firas didn't recoil but gazed at the ground with a sad countenance. The interfectors buzzed wickedly, their palms and wary eyes trained on Finley.

"How dare you?" grumbled Finley, kneeling and lowering his voice. "How dare you lay such accusations upon the great son of Liaidor Kyzhere?"

"Because they are true," said Firas.

Jordan remained still, Sebastién's talk of merciless amputations running through his head.

"As you can see," said Firas, "our impartial recorder struggles with his impartiality from time to time. Please, Braer, sit down. Chronicle the end of my story before the inhibitors dispatch us all to the light."

Finley huffed and glared down at Firas before returning to a sitting position. The guards veiled and returned to theirs. Jordan listened to Finley's fast breathing, his perturbed breath hitting the hair on Jordan's forearm.

"I cried out after they killed my Helena," said Firas, speaking with increased vigor. "They saw me, but I fled before Supernus could order them to give chase. I took the ancient way into the Grey City, past the Depths, knowing they'd be reluctant to pursue me there. But it was a foolish choice. When I emerged in East Leaf, Supernus and his people were already there." Firas ran his fingers along the length of the bars, examining them as if they were obstructions he'd just discovered. "It was only by Sebastien's fortunate timing that my life was spared. Though my heart broke when he walked away, I understood why he did it. It was just as I had done to your predecessors that very morning." A distorted grin formed on Firas's face. "You see, brother, cowardice is contagious."

Finley's heavy breathing continued.

"Supernus struggled with his plan being cut short. He wanted me dead, and I saw it in that resentful face of his. But he failed to see the mistake I'd made by coming in past the Depths. His aide did not. Instead of another covert murder, it was a public proclamation: they declared me the killer of Raphael, of Elisabeth, of my dear Helena. They claimed I threw the bodies into the Depths, a place no one would be willing to investigate. With your predecessor dead, and me locked away as the accused, the investigation was over before it would ever begin."

"I still don't understand." Jordan employed a gentle tone. "What did they claim as your motive?"

"They did not need one. The Kyzheres declared it so, and thus it was accepted as the truth. It was a small price for Arbor Florum to pay, to hide me away and pretend I was a murderer. In exchange for maintaining this lie, the Grey City remains free. But so does the real murderer, Supernus Tacitus Kyzhere."

Finley choked back spasms of rage.

Firas paid it no attention, his gaze wandering past Jordan to the clock. "It would have been perfect too, good for all eternity. Except your predecessor and Lila's defeated it by not getting trapped as graylights. They were brave. And this courage gives us a chance. Without it, you and Lila wouldn't be here today."

Jordan, though familiar with this part of the story through Sebastién, only now recognized the debt owed to his predecessor. Jordan knew little beyond the man's name, yet acknowledged his own existence had been made possible through Raphael's death. The threads between these events, and himself, Lila and Sebastién, and others long dead, took shape through Firas's words.

"There's something I've learned, after all this time." Firas's intensity dwindled. He spoke to Jordan like an old friend. "Justice is small. It's not derived from documents or constitutions or monuments—those are just symbols. Justice is a light shared between people, a candle passed from one person to the next, and it is readily extinguished."

Firas's words painted a portrait in Jordan's conscience: here was a man imprisoned longer than anyone in the faintlight world had been alive. Wars had been fought; nations had been born and split apart; new cultures, new ways of thinking; airplanes and satellites and the moon landing. Every bit of it had transpired while the human relic that was Firas el-Sakar had waited right here. Waiting for his brother.

Jordan grasped the prison bars. "Tell me what to do." The cold iron nipped at his palms. It made him want to let go, but he held tight.

Firas's mouth bent toward a smile. His eyes narrowed in a dark way. "Good. Then let us play a dangerous game, brother."

Jordan swallowed.

"At stake is my freedom and the very soul of Arbor Florum. Upon a fulcrum of injustice rests an entire civilization. Which way shall it tip? Toward the oppressors, or toward liberation?"

Jordan released the bars, settling his hands into his lap. His eyes slipped down. He rubbed warmth into his fingers, the activity striking him as alien, as though they were someone else's hands.

"Brother," said Firas, winning Jordan's attention back. "I am asking you to trust me. I place my fate in your hands and ask that you place yours in my words. As with the world you came from, they will judge with their eyes. They will see only the colors, but miss the shades of who we are. When they question my judgment—and I assure you they will—tell them that I put my faith in you *because* we are brothers. Tell them that it is *I* who sits in this cell, not them. Tell them it is my brother who will play the decisive part, not them."

Firas's eyes burned, his skin drawn taut across jaw and cheekbone. Though he whispered the next words, they issued with the conviction of a mountaintop declaration:

"In the end, all of them will doubt you. They will beg you to walk away. But you must hold fast, brother. With all your light, hold fast and make me free."

Jordan swallowed again, feeling the gravity of compounding expectations, ones that had already pulled him clear of Crispin's orbit and threatened to do the same of Lila and Sebastién. Yet Firas's eyes beseeched Jordan, no longer acknowledging the presence of Finley, nor the guards. It was just the two of them and the ring of bars that reduced Firas's life to the domain of a small circle.

"There is more I must tell you, but it is a conversation for well beyond tomorrow." Firas settled himself, his manner calm and reflective again. "Let me tell you what you must do today."

24

VOLUNTEER

Jordan zipped out of the vent and into Albert's lounge. He veiled in-flight, landing on his feet so close to the bass violin, he had to wave his arms to keep from falling on top of the defenseless instrument. Startled gasps reached him from every direction.

"And there he is." Sebastién flourished his hand from a sprawled out position on the sofa.

Jordan noticed some new faces in the room.

One of them moved quickly to the violin, placing his hand protectively on its stock. He was dark-skinned with a trimmed beard, flecked with gray, indicating someone in his fifties physical-ly-speaking. His dark sweater, thin scarf, and pressed pants made for a well-considered personal appearance. He offered his hand to Jordan, having decided the violin was no longer in danger. "My name is Albert Birchwine."

The man's handshake was firm and enduring. Jordan glanced at the other stranger who stood next to Lila. She was Asian, well-dressed with long black hair drawn into a ponytail. She looked him up and down, her arms folded tight against her body.

"That's Mio," said Sebastién.

She nodded to Jordan, keeping her arms crossed, making no effort at a proper introduction.

"We were about to go hunting for you," said Lila. "Figured you got lost. Did you explain it to Firas? The way we planned?"

Jordan hesitated and put his hands in his pockets.

"What *did* you say to him exactly?" asked Sebastién, sitting upright.

"I told him about last night."

"How much of last night?" asked Sebastién.

"Well…a bit more than we planned. Firas talked it out of me—but he has a right to know. He told me about Supernus and the murders, and how he ended up in there because nobody would search the Depths on his behalf."

"That's complicated, Jordan," said Sebastién.

"Well, it should be less so now."

"What do you mean?"

"I signed up."

"You did what?" Sebastién popped to his feet, his eyes as alarmed as his voice. Albert lurched sideways, knocking his violin off the stand, but catching it in time.

"He asked me to search the Depths and I said yes. He told me where to file the petition. So I did."

They all stared at him in stunned silence. It blowtorched Jordan's confidence.

"The Depths," repeated Jordan, "you know what I'm talking about, right? The place where Firas is accused of dumping the bodies. Too dangerous to search, but if you're invisible in the Lux Sanguinis sense, like Firas and me, it's not a problem. Since he's in prison, it's up to me." Jordan delivered his words with hand gestures that mimicked the explanation of a flowchart.

The faces in the room remained paralyzed.

"I go down there and prove the bodies aren't there," said Jordan meekly. "Firas goes free."

"But the bodies *are* down there, Jordan," said Albert, his voice losing its restraint. "It's a near certainty."

Jordan's arms fell limp to his sides.

"Firas actually asked you to do this?" said Mio, walking up to Jordan, inspecting him as though he were the village idiot.

"He did."

"He's desperate," said Lila, pushing in between Jordan and the exasperated Mio. Lila shot a look at Jordan. It reminded him of Bindo and the aqueduct all over again. Though no scolding words left Lila's mouth, her eyes said it all.

"He's been in prison for over a hundred years," said Sebastién. "It's a wonder he's sane at all. This explains a lot. It's why they tricked us this afternoon with that closure nonsense—and I was dumb enough to loophole Jordan right past it." Sebastién flopped back down on the couch, letting his heels thump to the floor. "They must have known Firas would ask for this. They had all the obstacles cleared, right down to the Investigative Council's door. They probably had this scripted out years ago."

"Shit," offered Lila in a one-word reflection.

"Jordan, there's another reason the Depths were never searched." Albert licked his lips and spoke in a professorial manner. "It isn't just the danger. It's that the Kyzheres hauled the bodies all the way here after the murders and threw them down there—"

"On top of Helena," added Mio.

"—so if anyone searches the place," continued Albert, "they prove the accusations against Firas true."

Jordan tented his fingers and scanned the room for supportive faces. "Shouldn't Firas have known this?"

"He sure as hell should have." Mio maintained her chronical-ly-folded arms. "You've got to be fucking kidding me." Mio stomped a half-circle around the room. "We've been dicing out ways to do this for years—for fucking decades—and golden boy drowns the plan in the well on day one? It doesn't matter if we win over Florum now. That investigation will end with Firas a convicted murderer. How the *fuck* couldn't Firas see this?"

"He's desperate," said Lila again, dragging out the words. "He's been stuck there for over a hundred years. He could slink past those bars at any time, but the 'fects would kill him immediately, *Jus Homicidium*."

"That's Castellum law," said Albert with disdain. "We don't practice such barbarism here."

"No, Albert," said Mio, "Lila has it right. Firas *was* to be extradited to Castellum. Our politicals had the courage to keep him here, but the Carmen follows Castellum law—it *is* Castellum in there. That was the arrangement."

"And it seems they've extended their domain into Arbor Florum too." Albert put his hand behind his neck and rubbed. "We all saw the interfectors in West Leaf today."

"What I am trying to say is that there's still doubt," said Lila. "We presume the Kyzheres smuggled the bodies into the Depths, but we don't know it for certain."

"Terrible fucking odds, Lila," said Mio. "Those bodies are down there."

"It's not a certainty—"

"You really think this is a good idea?"

"No, but in Firas's eyes, it's good enough, especially with the Helena plan failing."

"We might be able to fix this," said Albert. "But we need to feel it out with care. Everything will be snared up in bureaucracy."

"Probably too late already," muttered Mio.

Jordan sank into silence while they continued to debate his predicament. Every strategy was a variation on desertion, prompting Jordan to recall Firas's prediction. The whole affair was weaved with acts of abandonment; each person turning away from the one before. And now they were looking for a way for him to do the same.

"You know what *would* make this better?" said Sebastién, cutting into the acidic arguments.

They all looked to him.

"A party."

"You've got to be kidding," said Mio, marching up to Sebastién.

"Liwei would be charmed."

"Seriously?" snapped Mio. "You think this is a good idea?"

"I do…" Sebastién tapped his index finger against his upper lip while he thought. "We have to take Jordan public for his own safety. And if we intend to make a go at this, if we intend to push the politicals to take a new look at Firas, we'll have to do it *fast*. They'll ram Jordan's petition through the court quickly. If we can't stop it, we need to raise hell ahead of it. The best way to do that is to put Lux Sanguinis in front and center."

"Too aggressive." Mio stomped her heel into the floor.

"Interesting, hearing that from you." Sebastién smiled at her. "Liwei and Isabella have always been sympathetic to this, and their crowd will be natural allies."

"And it's the Trid," said Lila, circling the bass violin, moving toward Mio. "The whole world will be watching."

Mio crunched her arms tighter against her chest. "This should start with Census, not us. If we intend to rely on goodwill, we can't thumb our nose at the conventions."

"Census is Res Externa," said Albert, "hardly an ally."

"Its leadership doesn't represent the whole," said Mio.

"Still," said Sebastién, "I'd rather everyone see Jordan firsthand— even better, talk with him personally. If we're going to make noise in the street, it's going to carry more weight if everyone's already gossiping about Raphael's successor, Lux-Sanguinis returned."

Mio craned her gaze away, staring at a bookcase.

"Besides," said Sebastién, moving in front of Mio, "all the best Trid parties are tomorrow night. The rumors are already out there. It's time to make an appearance."

"I can think of a few ways this goes south," said Mio.

"Jordan signed on to be *Investigator Forensis*," said Sebastién. "It's already gone south. We need to wave that red hand of his around. We need everyone to see it. He's going to talk about Firas openly. We all will. And we'll do it without reservation."

Mio bit her lip so hard Jordan expected to see blood.

"Come on, Mi-mi." Sebastién smiled and put his hand on her shoulder. "Are you really going to make Jordan hide out, or can he have some fun?"

Mio shook free and turned away.

Sebastién approached Jordan, his smile still hanging out. He plucked at the cords of Jordan's hoodie. "We're going to have to do something about what you're wearing, of course."

25

SOIRÉE

In a dressing room adorned with tall mirrors and ivory drapes, Jordan changed into a formal suit Sebastién had borrowed on a favor. On seeing his reflection, he tried to imagine his way back to the faintlight world. But the bustle beyond the door returned his thoughts to Arbor Florum. They reinforced the unpleasant reality that his arrival was cause célèbre, a fault line running through the Grey City that had already been issuing quakes.

Jordan closed his eyes and pulled in a long breath. Letting it go, he turned, passed down the hall, and emerged into an opulent ballroom. Three things grabbed his attention within seconds. The first was the grand piano floating through the air. It came in over the veranda, orange light buzzing loud across its underside where a team of deveiled freelight guided it through the air. Sebastién, wearing a black tuxedo, was waving it into position like an airplane to the terminal.

The second thing Jordan noticed, opposite the piano's landing zone, was the two-story ice sculpture. A pair of dancers pressed against each other in a passionate tango. It was nestled in next to a curved staircase that stretched to a balcony above. The ice dancers were carved to perfection, right down to the creases in their apparel. The female's leg, which was twice the length of Jordan's body, jutted

195

out toward the center of the room, the tip of her shoe touching the floor. Her other leg was lifted into the air, knee pressed across the male dancer's hip, where his hand grasped it seductively. Jordan moved into the open to take in the rest. The female face was looking up at the taller male, their eyes locked, faces so close they nearly touched noses.

The third thing Jordan noticed brought about the greatest stir: Lila in a black evening dress. She was facing away from him, adjusting the illumination of flowered vines that were coiled about the columns supporting the balcony. Her graceful fingers teased forth light like a magician. Jordan's eyes followed her hands down to her arms, then to her waist, finally to the curve of her hips. The frantic events of his first day hadn't granted him time to appreciate her beauty. He did so now.

She turned and smiled at him.

Smiling back, Jordan felt his face go a touch flush. A woman was standing next to Lila, older but of similar physique. She struck Jordan as Spanish, wearing a curious grin on her face. Lila waved him over. Jordan adjusted his tie and fiddled with his suit coat on approach. More freelight flew into the ballroom from the veranda. Some veiled and were already dressed for the party. Others hauled in clothes on wooden hangers, pulled along with fingers which lit up like road flares where they made contact with the hooks.

"Jordan, this is Isabella," said Lila. "She's the lady of the house."

"Nice to meet you."

Isabella offered her hand, which Jordan grasped as though inviting her to dance.

"Likewise," said Isabella. "So is it true? You are Sanguinis returned?" She pinched her lips together and pumped her eyebrows, daring him to prove it.

"Seems so," said Jordan, lifting his right hand and flaying it down to his wrist. A burst of laughter escaped Isabella before she covered her mouth. Jordan saw heads turn toward him, followed by bursts of chatter and a lot of pointing.

"Well, the times are going to be interesting, aren't they?" said

Isabella, squeezing Lila's hand gently. "Are you an artist too, like all your predecessors?"

"I am."

"And how many portraits have you created of dear Lila?"

Jordan's smile diminished.

"Oh, come on. Do tell." Isabella continued to smirk and wait for an answer. Lila's expression signaled an equivalent intrigue.

"A few." Jordan fiddled with the buttons on his suit. "Though they were rather incomplete until recently."

"Of course—just a pair of pretty eyes." Isabella blinked her own. Then her delightful demeanor faded. Jordan realized she had made the connection between the flicker and the full birth echo. She regained her affable poise, a grin sliding back into place. "So tell me, how were you transitioned? Drowning—or a car crash? My husband Liwei is positively obsessed with the subject—but listen to me, I'm no better!"

Out of the corner of his eye, Jordan saw Lila's chin dip. After some dead air, Isabella jumped to another topic. "I saw you eyeing my sculpture a moment ago."

"It's spectacular." Jordan turned to admire it again.

As Lila and Isabella moved in next to him, rapid runs on the piano danced through the room; Sebastién's talent was far beyond hobbyist. Jordan spotted Mio, Albert, and someone he hadn't met, preparing to perform. They tuned instruments against the growing noise of the crowd, who waited with eager eyes as bottles of wine and champagne were being uncorked.

"Isabella and her husband create a sculpture like this every time," said Lila.

"My dear husband insists that the female dancer is modeled after me, but I've never looked that good, nor can I dance like *that*—you must meet him, my dear Liwei. I'll bring him right over." Isabella touched Lila on the forearm and smiled at Jordan. She traipsed off into the growing crowd.

"They do this every year?" asked Jordan.

"They do." Lila's fingers tapped to the rhythm of Albert's warm-up bass work. "The Triduum is the new year's celebration of the Isternian calendar. A three-day observance anchored on the summer solstice—four during leap years. Freelight travel here from all over."

Mio's singing voice, which Jordan found more pleasant than her profane conversational style, lit up the room. With it came Sebastién's piano, a saxophone, and a busy melody from Albert's bass. A man with a tray of drinks walked by. Lila took two, handing one to Jordan.

"Thanks."

"This in particular," said Lila, "is one of the most prominent parties."

They stood side by side and studied the ice sculpture for a while before Jordan spoke again. "How many buttons am I supposed to do on the suit?"

"Leave the bottom one undone," said Lila, taking his drink so he could adjust.

"Thanks," said Jordan, releasing the button. "Based on how well you're dressed, I thought you might be in the know."

"Freelight fashion follows faintlight—at least in Arbor Florum. I don't usually attend these things, except to set the atmosphere." Lila pointed to the base of the sculpture, where a nest of illuminated vines cast a warm light upward into the ice.

Jordan received his drink back and gazed at her. "You look beautiful, Lila." It was the first time he had addressed her by name. She smiled at him, her chin floating up a degree before she looked back to the sculpture.

On account of the smile, Jordan's tongue got loose. "Was thinking about something Sebastién said."

"Yeah?" responded Lila.

"Now that the Helena thing is over…maybe we could get coffee, or dinner." Jordan side-eyed her for a reaction. "Or whatever people do around here."

"Jordan…" Lila's smile faded, and her gaze went to the floor. "You're a young soul." Her hands moved as if to communicate more, but no words came out.

A young soul.

Jordan didn't know what it meant, but it seemed a polite way to call someone a fool. Given his actions of late, the accusation felt warranted.

A woman with a silver tray of drinks breezed past, cutting off their view of the ice sculpture for a moment. "Why does anyone work," asked Jordan, "if there's no need for money? Like that waitress?"

"Money," said Lila, "in the faintlight sense, doesn't work here, so we trade in time. An hour of yours for an hour of mine."

She was speaking with a renewed enthusiasm, clearly happy to be past the topic of dating. Jordan's mind was half-stuck on being called a young soul.

"Those waiters," said Lila, pointing to one with champagne flute in hand, "are interested in Liwei or Isabella for their skill as artisans. That's also why Sebastién's here as the entertainment instead of as a guest. At the end of the night, Liwei and Isabella will declare debts, recorded on metallum. Seb, the waiters, and whoever else will redeem those someday, or trade them away."

"What prevents cheaters?" asked Jordan.

"Reputation. We all live here together. We all remember. Your word is the most valuable thing you have."

Jordan's head nodded with the logic and the music. From there, the conversation drifted into talk of the Triduum, the parties, the travelers, and the events that would take place over the coming days. Jordan listened, charmed by Lila's way of conversation. In moments of enthusiasm, she'd enter into dashes of chatter, often on the topic of Arbor Florum's gardens. She used the modern, *rum*-pronunciation of Florum, which Jordan wagered was a way to differentiate the older freelight from the younger.

Sebastién's quartet played on, and the room filled in tight. The effects of drink softened Jordan's apprehensions about Firas, along with his pledge and whatever activism was underway. Though they didn't speak of these things, Jordan found his mind skipping to Firas, imagining him at that very moment, sitting in the darkness, waiting for what might be an unlikely freedom.

An hour in, tick-tock drips of water issued from the ice sculpture. The room had grown so lively they could barely hear the music. Isabella returned with a slender Asian man who wore a stylish light gray suit and a thin scarf draped over his shoulders. Like Isabella, his hair was thatched with gray. His eyes, however, radiated a sense of youth.

"So you are Jordan, Lux Sanguinis resurrected, an artist like all those before you," said the man, delivering his words with the inflection of a statement, not a question. "I am Liwei, host of this fine soirée—I should say co-host, though, as my dear Isabella is instrumental in putting it together, more so than me."

Jordan shook his hand, receiving a firmer grip than he expected.

"I trust you're enjoying the evening? I'm honored that Sebastién brought you. It's a momentous occasion, is it not, your return to us."

Once again the words struck Jordan as a declaration more than a question, leaving him uncertain if he should answer.

"Have you toured the Grey City?"

"Not yet." Jordan sipped his champagne. "Though what I've seen so far has been remarkable."

"Well then, allow me to give you a top-down tour. Please." Liwei gripped Jordan's elbow. "It would be my honor."

Lila mouthed the words *have fun* as they walked away.

Jordan followed Liwei across the crowded ballroom, out onto a spacious veranda. They leaned against a stone railing that ran the length of the residence. Jordan parked his forearms on it and looked over the edge. Despite his ability to fly, the great distance to the ground spun his faculties.

Liwei noticed Jordan's unsteady manner and chuckled. "Welcome to Arbor Florum, Mr. Wakefield."

"How far down is that?"

"Over twelve hundred feet to the floor of Aria, but less than a thousand to the upper reaches of the Arborsolis."

The massive tree shimmered deep blue below. The two stain-glassed rings running around the edge of the garden floor made Jordan feel like he was looking down into an enormous light fixture. His mind, as though working on the puzzle of the rings, had suddenly solved it:

"They're clocks…"

"Very good," said Liwei. "The inner one is for hours of the day, like any faintlight timepiece. The outer one is for days of the year, divided into nine seasons—what faintlights consider months. The colors on the inner mimic the hues of day and night. The outer represents the cyclical shifts that occur in the eye color of Lux Viridis, like Lila."

Jordan gazed out across Aria, entranced by the mesh of twinkling light that clung to its walls. The illuminated tapestry served as an enchanting backdrop to crowds of freelight gliding about, arriving at parties like this one.

"How is this possible?" asked Jordan. "I can't fathom it."

"Neither could I at first. Our esteemed founding father, Publius Crispus Fluximous proposed it many centuries ago. You must meet him; wonderful man—just wonderful. He's Roman—comes to us from the days of Hadrian, if you know your faintlight history."

A pang of guilt struck Jordan at the mention of Crispin's name. He noticed that Liwei was watching his reaction. Jordan said nothing. He wondered when he'd see Crispin again, or if he'd see him at all.

"Crispin was inspired," said Liwei, resuming the story, "by sites in my native land, ones I had carved long before we built this place. I thought in terms of caverns and caves. As you can see, he thought in terms far grander." Liwei leaned on the railing, while Jordan looked across to the other side. "All those years ago, he explained to me that it was a matter of calculation. He went on about it incessantly, for years; that it was possible. It would take centuries, he said, but it could be done. I'm embarrassed to say it was beyond my capacity to imagine. I couldn't believe it, but he had me with the idea—the lure, the possibility. I could *not* resist the challenge."

"You did all this?" asked Jordan. "How long did it take?"

"I didn't do all this," said Liwei, releasing a chuckle. "I'm an artisan, one of many, including Isabella. It took hundreds of us to do this, almost a thousand years in total. We started in ten-three-twenty-five, which, in the faintlight reckoning, was the year four-fifty-two. We broke ground while what remained of

Crispin's beloved Rome was failing. As to the how, just conceive it as any other building made of stone. But instead of building it block by block in the open air, we carved it out of one of the largest tracts of granite in the world."

Jordan looked around, noting how every wall, floor, and doorway featured the same white-and-black-speckled granite, cut along precise lines, smoothed to perfection.

"We started here at the top and worked our way down." Liwei turned his attention to the ceiling. "Believe it or not, my home—the very place we're standing—was once little more than a tunnel used for hauling debris out into the world above. It's all piled just outside, hidden by centuries of weather and rock slides. As we went deeper, we carved new tunnels and reduced the old ones to vents for air exchange. We couldn't harbor the tree until we reached the bottom, so we lived and worked in relative darkness for what felt like an eternity. It took just shy of one hundred and fifty years to carve Aria—the great, open space we're looking at now."

Jordan's eyes scoured the architecture, recognizing the very Roman feel to it. He felt as though he were standing in ancient Rome.

"Yet the entire project was almost abandoned." Liwei's hands patted the granite railing. "Cutters like myself grew weary. We failed to see Crispin's dream. To us, it was just an endless, dark chasm. Our doubts grew, so Crispin redoubled his efforts. He took us to Rome to show us its great works. But what we saw was a civilization in ruin." Liwei ran an index finger across his chin, his attention slipping into the past. "It was one of your predecessors who inspired us again. She painted murals of Crispin's vision, which looked much like what you see today. Those depictions stirred a longing in us. We could finally *see* Crispin's dream. It would be a place as beautiful as the world above, but one sheltered from its tribulations. It would be our home."

Jordan felt proud that art could mobilize such acts of creation. He was further intrigued that one of his predecessors was female. "What was her name?"

"Sophronia," said Liwei. "Her inspirationals are still housed in the Prudentiarum, on the way to the Firmament. Have you seen them?"

"No," said Jordan, releasing his grip on the stone ledge.

"By the time of Muhammed's conquest of Arabia, we had entered a period of ease we called the Long Rest. Our pace slowed, and we lived in the comfort of our single-silo garden with its underground sun. We fashioned our homes in these walls. We brought other freelight here to see the world we had made. Those who came never left."

Jordan let his vision slip out of focus. The myriad freelight in the air transformed from illuminated human beings into soft, pastel clouds, crossing the open space in unhurried fashion, like colored dandelion tufts on the wind.

"By the time of Charlemagne and the origins of France, we had embarked on the construction of West Leaf. During Chinghis Khan's conquest of Asia, we were finishing the last one, East Leaf. By the dawn of the fourteenth century, when the Republic of Venice had reached its zenith of power, the Grey City was as you see it today."

"How many of us live here?" asked Jordan, aware of his use of the collective word. He felt a sense of belonging.

"About ten thousand, but many more this time of year. You see that?" said Liwei, pointing at the surface of the vast dome over Aria. "We painted the other leafs, but never got to this one. Perhaps you're the man for the job."

Jordan surveyed the vast surface, wondering how many years, or decades, it would take to fill that colossal stone canvas; a personal mural with an expanse greater than a domed football stadium.

"It would take a lifetime," said Jordan.

"Fortunately, we have many of those." Liwei laughed and sipped his drink. But then his smile flattened. His gaze went straight ahead. Liwei's free hand slid across the top of the stone rail, as though pruning a layer of dust. "You haven't been transitioned, have you, Jordan?"

Caught off guard, Jordan stuttered a non-answer. He recalled the word from Eli's mouth the morning after, in Crispin's kitchen. *Transition.*

"Rumor has it you found Helena, but came up dry." Liwei's voice was solemn, his gaze even more distant. "I'm afraid to ask what you intend to do next."

Jordan recovered. "Make Arbor Florum acknowledge its cowardice in the face of my predecessor's murder. And Lila's, and Helena. We intend to make the Grey City remember Firas. He's innocent."

Liwei's face remained stern, his cheek taking on a green cast as a pair of freelight whizzed past.

"We intend to bring the real murderer to justice," said Jordan.

Liwei swallowed, gripping the railing as if it were a prized possession. He shifted his champagne flute to his other hand. "The sins at the heart of Arbor Florum are great ones. I cannot deny this. But this injustice binds our world, it preserves it. Listen to me, Jordan." Liwei grasped Jordan's wrist and pressed it against the railing. "Arbor Florum surrendered much to end its war with the Kyzheres. We married Arbor Castellum to bring about this peace—but make no mistake, they are the stronger partner. For all the grandeur that is before you, understand that Arbor Florum must be a submissive bride." Liwei's chin declined, a soft sigh escaping. "Your predecessor accepted that Supernus might come for him one day—that revenge would be a fruit of irresistible temptation. And so it was. We cannot bring him back. Understand that Firas is trapped; we cannot prove him innocent. All we can do is keep him from disappearing into Castellum. This stand you wish us to take—to accuse Supernus Kyzhere of murder—would be an act of war." Liwei released his grip on Jordan's wrist.

"The injustice against Firas is worth ignoring?" asked Jordan.

"If it means preserving the freedom of ten thousand others…then yes." Liwei tapped his glass, liberating bubbles that raced to the rim. "The Carmen has already been made a prison. I do not wish for the entirety of the Grey City to become one too."

"What if it was you in that prison cell?"

Liwei looked away. He turned back, only slightly, unable to look at Jordan. "But it's not me."

A century of cowardice hung in those words. Jordan clutched at the railing, his fingernails prying into the granite.

Liwei turned in full and grasped Jordan by the shoulder, conjuring an affable smile. "Thoughts for another day, in any case. Now let us go back inside. We're missing all the fun."

Jordan turned with him. Liwei's grasp conveyed the touch of a friend, taming his provocative disposition in a nearly magical way. Jordan decided to let it go for now. He looked across the veranda to the ballroom. When he spotted Lila, he went rigid.

She was in trouble.

Standing alone, she was looking down at the floor. In front of her loomed a man with a colossal frame, staring at her with a derisive leer, every mannerism transmitting hostility. All others near her were sidling away like spooked sheep.

Jordan slipped loose of Liwei's grasp and ran into the ballroom.

26

A TOAST

Trying to reach Lila, Jordan shoved his way through a jungle of shoulders and faces. He caught glimpses of her harasser through the melee: the man was wearing an exotic black suit, heavily patterned with a strange silver filigree. The attire looked ready to burst on account of his physique, which struck Jordan as that of an Olympic wrestler. He continued to expel words at Lila. She continued to look at the ground. The man toyed with his necklace, a trio of white shards hung from a bright silver chain. The music continued unabated, but nobody swayed, nobody smiled.

Jordan arrived next to Lila. She didn't notice him, but the man did. With an outstretched hand, he welcomed Jordan into the fold. He spoke in a loud voice that seemed intended for an audience larger than the three of them.

"And here he is, Lila. Your gallant rescuer." The man cast a carnivorous expression at Jordan.

Jordan met his intimidating gaze.

"I came to make a toast. Someone get him a drink." The man turned and spotted a waiter. Before the waiter could escape, the man moved, seizing him by the wrist. Flutes tumbled from the silver tray and shattered on the floor, drawing whispers from the crowd. Plucking up two surviving drinks, he returned to Jordan.

Lila remained catatonic, the music played on. All conversation had ceased now. The crowd had turned into somber statues; faces turned away from the epicenter of conflict like a museum exhibit depicting the horrors of war.

"Your drink," said the man, delivering the words as two sharp sounds. He held it out to Jordan.

Jordan accepted, not knowing what else to do.

"It seems," said the man stepping closer, "that Lila isn't going to introduce us." He raised his free hand toward Jordan, who met it in a reluctant handshake.

The grip crushed him. Refusing to acknowledge the pain, Jordan pinned his expression down. He reminded himself that any damage done could be fixed later by develing.

"I am Supernus Tacitus Kyzhere," said the man, ejecting each word with volcanic pride. "The Princeps Maximus of Arbor Castellum, eldest son of Liaidor Kyzhere, the Dominus Stellarum."

The word *murderer* flashed across Jordan's mind like a neon sign.

Supernus tilted his head. "And you are...*who?*"

Jordan took a breath to prevent his words from coming out as strangled as his hand. "Jordan Wakefield."

"Ah yes." Supernus grinned, giving Jordan a moment to take him in. His features radiated a fast-evolving set of emotions, held taut under pallid skin. Blond hair tied back, except for a lock that had escaped, hanging off the side of his face like an errant golden rope. His mannerisms, while precise, suggested a violence boiling beneath, one barely within the realm of his control. The most haunting aspect were his eyes: icy blue, predatory, and devoid of kindness.

"Jordan Wakefield..." Supernus said his name between flashes of his canine grin. "So is it true? Are you *thee*—Lux Sanguinis incarnate? Returned to us here under Elysium?" Supernus released his grip.

Jordan faltered, spilling a dash of champagne.

"Show me." Supernus fondled his white-stone necklace and waited.

The faces of party attendees began to appear over shoulders, spying on the altercation. They were careful to avoid the eyes of Supernus. The music had finally stopped, the ballroom mute except for the tapping sound of water bleeding off the ice sculpture. From the rear of the room, two men in black robes were walking up to Supernus. One was tall and of European descent. Deeply-set narrow eyes and a prominent chin. The other was shorter and athletically proportioned, also European. Both wore the same black robes as Firas's guards. Same eagle-with-serpentine-feet insignia, same dead eyes.

"Show me like this," said Supernus, retrieving Jordan's attention. Supernus flayed his hand to the wrist, sending forth a deep violet light.

With reluctance, Jordan flayed his own hand. A rash of mutterings erupted across the crowd. Supernus's signal felt like a child crying from middle-school days. Kicked in the stomach, his assailant circling with glee. Jordan pushed the memory aside and responded. "I know that trick, you don't need—"

"But do you know this one?"

A mental shift occurred with Supernus's words. It was swift, like the snap of a finger. Jordan's thought process inverted itself like a waterfall rejecting gravity and shooting upward. Jordan's judgment was all off—he knew it at once. A new one floated in like a sweet inebriation, more intoxicating than any wine: Supernus Kyzhere was a great man, a benevolent man, a man who deserved respect.

Jordan's eyes consumed Supernus in detail: his gloss black suit jacket had long tails in front and back that tapered to sharp points just past the knee. A spectacular series of curved lines, symbols, and flourishes—all sewn in silver thread—adorned the coat. Single-breasted, with a lone large button, an eagle with serpentine feet. It was a work of art; exotic and regal like the man who wore it. The crowd was not granting Supernus the respect he deserved, especially Lila. Jordan was certain of this, and it angered him.

"That drink," said Supernus, holding his violet hand aloft. Jordan's gaze drifted into his magnificent violet glow. "A moment ago you wanted to throw it in my face, didn't you?"

Jordan nodded.

"More fitting to throw it in your own, I suspect…"

Jordan stared into Supernus's righteous eyes before looking down into the slender champagne flute. He jerked it toward his face.

The liquor sent his vision blurry, stinging his eyes. It was a fair atonement. Bird-chirp astonishment erupted from the crowd, the sound striking Jordan as a further affront to the man who had rightly shown him the error of his ways.

"Stop!" called a female voice. An electrical jolt hit Jordan's hand, causing it to veil.

Jordan's mind snapped back. He saw Lila's fingers burning fierce green next to him. Jordan tried to parse what had transpired, but couldn't. After wiping his eyes, he saw that Supernus was already several paces away, interfectors at his side. The crowd parted before him, all eyes pinned to the floor. Supernus stopped and looked over his shoulder.

"I nearly forgot. I came to make a toast." Supernus turned in full, his cold blue eyes sweeping the room. He raised his glass. "*Saw-vee eh-koos*…and a grand Triduum to all. Especially you, Jordan Wakefield. It is a noble thing, your arrival. Just hours ago, Brave Jordan petitioned to be Investigator Forensis."

More chatter rolled through the crowd.

"At last," said Supernus raising his glass again, "we shall have resolution on this matter of Firas." Supernus took a single sip from his glass. He dropped it on the floor, its breakage sending a discordant music through the room. Supernus turned and walked away with his entourage, his parting words delivered in a voice loud enough for everyone to hear: "Poor child. Understands so little."

Jordan saw red. He felt it burn from toe tip to tongue. "I *do* understand you're a MURDERER!"

The crowd gasped.

Supernus spun and deviled with a sharp crack. His violet form shot across the room, leaving Jordan no time to react. Supernus veiled point blank and seized Jordan: one hand catching his throat, bending his head backward. The other grabbed a fistful of suit. He hoisted Jordan off his feet, bull-rushing him into the ice sculpture, cracking the back of his head off it.

Through blurred eyes and ears that rang metallic dog whistles, Jordan caught sight of people deviling. Two bursts of yellow light happened with it. Then came screams and shouts, as sunlight darted about the room, knocking freelight of every hue out of the air. Those still on their feet dropped hard to their knees, as if out of habit. Faces down, hands crossed behind their heads like prisoners of war. In seconds, the room was silent again outside of the wicked yellow hum of the interfectors.

Jordan grappled at Supernus's hands, trying to undo the grip with badly impaired motor skills. Nausea flushed through him. His vision wavered toward darkness. Supernus lowered Jordan, pulling his face close so that their cheeks pressed together.

"Hear me," whispered Supernus into his ear, his voice gentle as a monk. "You are a child. All of you, children. You fail to understand you've already lost. But you will know it soon enough."

Supernus let go.

Jordan fell like a ragdoll. On his knees, gasping for air, he planted a palm on the floor for balance. He tried to lift himself, but failed, collapsing face-first onto cold granite. The impact hit his jaw like a hammer. He raised his chin, struggling to see through blurred vision. Supernus was walking past Sebastién, who was pinned face-down on the floor with a yellow deveiled hand at the back of his neck. Jordan's vision rolled out again, leaving Liwei's warbling of blurry words the only sound in the world. When it returned, he saw Supernus deveil and fly away, his bodyguards following.

A female voice reached Jordan's ears: "You have to deveil."

It was Lila, crouching next to him, Isabella on the other side. They pulled him to unsteady feet, shouting to him again to deveil. Jordan moved free of their grasp, staying on his feet long enough to do it. Clarity returned like a cold shower.

Then came a tidal wave of anger.

Jordan veiled and stood still for a moment, the entire room watching him. He marched toward the veranda, hands petrified into fists. Suddenly, Lila was there blocking the way, her palm pressed to his chest.

"No," she said, her eyes pleading with him as they did on the bridge over West Grey.

Jordan breathed fury. Lila's hand remained firm. Glancing about with rapid, hawk-like movements, Jordan noticed he was in hoodie and jeans again. He'd vaporized the suit. His eyes went past Lila to Liwei and Isabella. They stood next to one another, wearing solemn faces like refugees in a foreign land.

Isabella's face, in particular, haunted Jordan. Her expression suggested she was observing someone very brave or very foolish. Jordan hoped it was not the latter.

27

SOMETHING THAT MATTERED

Jordan's anxiety spread like a rash while Lila was in the dressing room. Music and conversation had resumed but lacked their former verve. Though he was at the fringe of the ballroom, partygoers took turns gawking at him, failing to be discreet. He tried to keep his chin high but found it sinking to the floor. Sebastién shot glances from across the room. His face suggested he wanted to come over and commiserate, but his duty as the entertainment kept him behind the keys. The party needed all the help it could get.

"I'm ready," came Lila's voice. Jordan felt a soft tug at his jacket. He turned and found her in jeans and the Lumineers t-shirt again. They were both back to civilian clothes, out of place in high society.

After brushing off lackluster requests to stay, they thanked Isabella and Liwei. They wandered down the back hall, until the music blended into dull monotony. The only distinct sound remaining was the murmur of Albert's bass. Following Lila's lead, Jordan deveiled and followed her out a doorway and into the great open space of Aria.

At this hour, the world was painted dim deep blue by the Arborsolis, a nocturnal scene that struck Jordan as medieval castle-scape lit by moonlight. They descended toward the garden surrounding the great tree, crisscrossing paths with small groups of freelight moving on horizontal trajectories. The droves of freelight sent bursts of memories through Jordan's head, mixing his faintlight past with the events of the present. He shuttered it out, his mind plagued by the altercation with Supernus.

They reached the garden and veiled at the edge of the outer clock ring. The structure wasn't inset into the surface as it had seemed to Jordan. It rose into the air like an aqueduct, tall enough to reach beyond treetops. Illuminated vines climbed the support arches and disappeared inside.

As Jordan's curiosity subsided, he noticed Lila had established a solitary distance ahead of him, following a trail that led toward the outer ring. She walked in a morose manner, chin down, hand in the air with fingers deveiled. Blue light from the branches above stretched down and curled around her passing green fingers. The ritual must comfort her. He caught up, his mind dicing through questions he didn't want to ask. He did anyway, albeit in fragments.

"They just stood there…when Supernus was harassing you. No one did anything."

Lila turned her eyes to him. They looked tired.

"Why didn't they…" Jordan trailed off.

"Humility is the first virtue discarded when one approaches immortality," said Lila. "The second is courage. You see the same in the faintlight world, only there it happens on account of money. People risk nothing once they have everything. That's why Firas is forgotten, that's why Supernus acts with impunity. He's confident no one will challenge him—and he's right."

Jordan considered this as they walked. Lila continued to tease blue light from the trees. "When Supernus had me pinned, he said we've already lost."

Lila sighed. "He means that the bodies of our predecessors are down there. In the Depths."

"So it's rigged?"

"Probably. They pulled strings to get you and Firas alone, knowing he'd send you down that path. Who knows what mind-jobs they've done on him over the years." Lila tilted her head to the side. "Still, it doesn't make sense to warn us. It's possible it's a bluff, but—"

"Maybe Supernus just lost it. Seems he has something of a temper." Jordan tried to smooth the statement with a manufactured laugh.

Lila continued to walk in silence.

Jordan resumed. "I hate to even ask—"

"Then don't," said Lila. She gripped her left wrist and stared down at a steep angle, eliciting the appearance of a traveler weathering a hard rain.

Jordan looked away, regretting it now. The tree cover receded on the path ahead, revealing the grandeur of the Arborsolis, its girth wrapped in shimmering armored bark.

"How does that thing work?" asked Jordan, breaking the quiet. "When I get back, I think I'd like to buy one. Get rid of my light bulbs."

Lila laughed. A little. She released the grip on her wrist.

"Seriously," said Jordan, "Does it fly around?"

"Not exactly," said Lila, her smile nearly remaining. "It's Lux Olivae, which is the most adaptive of the timbres. The first known Arborsolis was an olive tree, hence the name. All the light in Arbor Florum—be it the vines, trees, or leaves, right down to what you witnessed in the drain passages—originates from the Arborsolis. Its light clings to organic surfaces, like having sunlight for skin. The Arborsolis was planted above ground over a thousand years ago. It was protected and nurtured for some time. Then it was brought down here and harbored."

Lila plucked at the edge of a nearby branch with her deveiled hand. The light issuing from it changed to a bright daytime white. "Those of my timbre can cultivate it, stretch it from one tree to another. Its hue shifts in accordance with the world above ground, echoing it. Bright in the day but faint like the moon and stars at night."

"Green freelight have green thumbs," said Jordan. "I can remember that."

"Don't go by what you see." Lila raised her deveiled fingers in the air. "There are a few dozen variants of Viridis, each unique in some way. That's more than any other predominant."

"Same, but different."

Lila nodded, the green light of her index finger flickering.

"That's why Firas considers me his brother, isn't it? I can't tell if it's genuine."

"Like timbres tend to associate as ethnicities do in the faintlight world. In your case, there are only the two of you."

They passed through a tract of sweet-smelling cherry trees, gaining a clear view to the inner clock ring. Like the outer, it was raised on a set of continuous arches, giving the appearance of an immense pedestal from which the even more immense Arborsolis grew.

They began to pass others on their walk, many Native American in ethnicity. Some greeted Lila by name, others proffering that word, *saw-vee*. These interactions lifted Lila's spirits. Jordan could see her heart called this place home, not the opulent world above.

"*Saw-vee*," said Jordan drawing Lila's attention. "Supernus used that word in his toast. Just before he brained me."

"It's an expression of good will, though he might not have meant it in that particular case." She tried to smile at her joke but seemed unable.

Stopping just past the inner clock ring, they took shelter under an oak tree with branches that drooped. Sitting on sections of thick, exposed roots, they faced each other. Distant in thought, their minds wandered. Jordan peered into Lila's green eyes. Her gaze was looking past him.

"Do you really see me in your birth echo?"

Her eyes ticked back to him. "At first it was hard to tell. I saw only the silhouette of a man looking at me. But now that you're here for real…" Lila gazed hard at Jordan. "I'm certain it's you."

The reaction made Jordan swallow hard. "In my vision you're crying. And your eyes are gray. Crispin explained that in yours, you see it through tears, so—"

"I don't cry," said Lila.

"I didn't mean it as an accusation."

"I know." Lila moved her palms down the length of her jeans. "If I don't cry, it will never happen—bending fate, or so the theory goes. Gray doesn't make sense either. Are you sure my eyes aren't light blue?"

"Crispin asked me the same thing." Jordan ran his hand across the root he was sitting on, finding it polished, likely from others who used it as a bench. "They're gray, I'm certain of it."

"Viridis eyes echo the season, like the Arborsolis does the colors of day and night—but with our eyes, it's green, brown, and blue—never gray. How much did Crispin explain?"

"I was running on no sleep, so it didn't stick. I get that our predecessors carried around these visions long before we existed—for thousands of years. It's hard to believe."

"Yet it seems to be true," said Lila.

"Are they still uncertain?"

"It became very unfashionable to talk about. It still is." Lila curled a tuft of grass around her finger. "It was all speculation in the beginning. That led to a lot of unfortunate incidents. That was the justification for bringing us underground." Lila drew her hands back to her abdomen, folding them. "My arrival was controversial. It was the first tangible proof the forward-looking theory could be correct. It was based on your predecessors' art. But since it was surface echo, it was only a pair of eyes. This left room for interpretation. They questioned me endlessly, trying to trigger my full echo. Once we had it, they sat me down with an artist. She composed an image of what I was seeing."

"My face."

"Yes. A close match too. Then the research was closed down, and the drawings hidden away. It was all deemed a sort of heresy, a dark art. But nearly a century later, here we are, living proof that what they know about echoes is wrong."

"What *do* the echoes mean?"

"Well…" Lila bit her lower lip as though wishing the conversation hadn't gone here. "They called them birth echoes until they studied people like us. Now they have another term: *death echoes*. They believe it's what we see before we die."

"What does *that* mean?" Jordan watched Lila shift uncomfortably.

"It means we die together in a dark place."

The hair on Jordan's arms stood up.

"The Prudentiarum is going to be all over you. Once you're transitioned, you'll…" Lila trailed off and paused, looking away. "They're going to have you confirm what you see in your echo. It's going to validate the forward-looking theory, which will…"

As if by reflex, Jordan's thoughts flew inward, rifling through the talk he had with Isabella and Liwei until he found the word:

Transition.

He recalled his conversation with Eli the morning after his first deveiling, where he'd heard a variation:

Transitionist.

He realized Lila was no longer speaking. She was looking at him with a desolate expression. Unease spread through Jordan, which fast metastasized into a terrible realization.

"I need to ask you something," said Jordan.

Lila folded her hands, pulling them in close.

"Isabella and Liwei and Eli all used that word, *transition*. Liwei asked about it when we were out on the balcony, just before Supernus. I didn't have time to understand it then. But I think I do now…"

Lila looked as though she'd become ill but kept Jordan's eye contact.

"It means I have to die, doesn't it? The faintlight world needs to think I'm dead because I can't go on living there if I don't age."

Lila closed her eyes and kept them shut for the duration of her response. "Yes, that's what it means."

Her words sunk deep to the pit of Jordan's stomach. His mind raced through the implications, his thoughts coming out in bursts. "My mother died when I was born—she died *because* I was born. It destroyed my father, I'm all he has left and now he'll have to believe I died tragically too?"

Lila nodded, her lower lip trembling.

"I told him I'd be home for his birthday"—Jordan's voice grew frantic—"and that's only weeks away. He thinks I'm in Saint Paul getting ready to move to San Francisco—"

I'm so sorry, Jordan. It's not fair…" Lila trailed off and pinned her eyes shut. "I'm so sorry."

"—and these transitionist people, they're going to kill me off?" Jordan stood up and shifted on his feet as if trying to decide which way to run. "Has this already happened?"

Lila shook her head. "No, there are protocols. You're not officially recognized, so it couldn't have happened yet. They don't even know who you are in the faintlight world, but—"

"I have to see my father again." Jordan pleaded as though she were the decider for the whole terrible affair. "I promised I'd be there."

"Signing on for Firas will lead to transition," said Lila. "But now that you're here, they won't let you go back."

"I have to go back!" A headache pounded its way into Jordan's awareness. Feeling dizzy, he sat down. "There's no way out?"

"There's one. But it's folly."

Jordan looked at her, waiting.

Lila peered at him through her spring green eyes. "You could run away. They wouldn't be able to find you, not easily. But if you are locked into searching the Depths, fleeing would mean dereliction and that means Jus Homicidium. It means they'll kill you when they catch you."

Jordan shook his head in slow disbelief. The desperation in Lila's face made him recall her words from the night they conjured Helena, her passionate plea for the indictment of Supernus. Jordan felt solidarity for the task now, having met the man. But corrosive doubt ate away at his activist aspirations, coercing him to accept that he'd attached himself to something with dangerous frontiers. With little more than a handful of blind, altruistic gestures, he'd backed himself into a corner.

He was trapped.

As fast as that assessment took hold, a thunderhead of guilt rebuked him. Firas had spent one hundred and twenty-eight years in conditions far worse. Firas knew true imprisonment, true sorrow. He knew nothing of it. And somehow Firas survived. He persisted against the bulwark of an injustice eternal. The reason came fluttering in to Jordan.

It was hope.

An unwavering belief that one day his so-called brother would arrive to undo what a century of cowardice had wrought. Jordan recalled Firas's delicate notion of justice: a candle passed between friends, its flame easily extinguished.

The candle was in his hands.

He was part of something that mattered now. It was up to him to make it right, but he didn't know how.

28

LESSONS

Cherry trees adorned both sides of the East Leaf thoroughfare. Stout trunks rose and sprouted dramatic branches that craned out over the street. Tributaries of illuminated leaves bathed the sharp granite world of Arbor Florum in soft afternoon light. Even above the rooftops of East Grey, wisp-slender limbs peeked over architectural edges, spilling daytime down the building faces. Though the trees exhibited the green of summer, Jordan tried to imagine them in spring, pink blossoms descending like a dawdling snow, carpeting the street in velvet charm.

It was a pleasant distraction, but too weak to overpower the other side of his mind, which was at war with the reality of transition. Jordan decided he'd return to the faintlight world to see his father— the rules be damned. He'd do it before his fake death. He'd make it happen somehow.

Then Sebastién's voice interrupted his thoughts. "You made one hell of a splash last night."

Jordan reflected on the altercation for the hundredth time, finding that the wolf-like presence of Supernus still haunted him. "That was the point, wasn't it?"

"It was." Sebastién moved in enthusiastic steps, circling Jordan. "You said out loud what few would dare think. You actually called

Supernus a murder. It came out like a cannonball—so *je ne sais quoi*. Brave Jordan, indeed—and word's spreading like fire. People are coming to our side. I must confess, I didn't think this would actually work."

"It was your goddamned idea!"

"It was, yes, but—"

"How many people?" asked Jordan, trying to salvage Sebastién's optimism. "Enough to plan-B Firas out of jail?"

Sebastién rumpled his face. "Definitely not that many."

"Well, how many are we talking?"

Sebastién balked and shrugged. "I'd say handfuls."

"Handfuls? That's fucking it?" Jordan walked in front of Sebastién's path, stopping him.

"Patience, my friend. Activism is an arduous venture." Sebastién clasped Jordan by the shoulder. "The first steps are difficult ones. You can see it in their eyes. They know exactly what you're going to say, and they don't like it one bit. They turn away before the words leave your mouth. But understand *why* they do it, Jordan. You speak the truth." Sebastién resumed his carefree gait.

Jordan paused and then chased him down. "How the hell are we supposed to get them on our side?"

Sebastién wavered. "We keep at it. We advocate without apology. We hope they come around in the end. Your predecessor Raphael was highly regarded. Your return will remind people of him."

Sebastién's long stride forced Jordan to take occasional jog-steps. "Are you sure Firas is wrong about the Depths?"

Sebastién flopped his head back, looking skyward for a moment. "Jordan, you have to let that go. Firas is desperate and made a bad move there. Keep in mind the Kyzheres have toyed with his head all these years. He's resilient—incredibly so—but they played him on that one."

At the midpoint along East Grey, the thoroughfare opened wide into a circular piazza, with a bridge far above, crossing perpendicular to the street. Identical in size and height to the one Jordan crossed in West Leaf the day he arrived. Beneath it, a crowd had gathered, arranged in a loose semi-circle in front of a raised platform. On that platform stood Albert, addressing them. The distance limited Jordan's intake of the speech, though he caught words like *Firas* and *Kyzhere* and *justice*, soon followed by *Raphael* and *Elisabeth*.

"You see?" said Sebastién, rapping Jordan on the back. "Albert's already at it. Jiro's doing the same in North Grey; Easton's in West— that's the most daring assignment—and someone's in South. I think."

Upon reaching the edge of the crowd, Jordan's optimism took a hit. It was the body language: grim mouths, folded arms, long deep breaths, heads shaking out negatives.

"Not seeing a lot of support here."

"Patience, patience." Sebastién corralled Jordan by the shoulder and pulled him wide of the gathering. "The midgrey crossings are for public discourse, and we'll be working them every single day. Words take time to dig in, but once past the surface, they're the best of ferrets."

"If you say so," said Jordan. The whole damn thing felt out of control. A series of longshots without agreement on where to aim.

"Let me bring you up to speed," said Sebastién, trading nods with a man in a top hat who walked past. "It's much as we expected— which is to say you're snared. We're still looking for a way out, but it's unlikely. We know Florum's politicals will be pressed to remain hands-off. The First Circle will tilt three-to-two on every decision, always in favor of the Kyzheres. In other words, they're going to let this ride. This whole thing's going to move really fast."

"Isn't there a mayor, or someone that could—"

"That *is* the First Circle," said Sebastién. "The heads of the five houses form a single executive body. Those five choose one among them to lead—the mayor as you call it—but that choice also went three-to-two in favor of the Kyzheres. Certain decisions can be challenged and put to a vote, but again, three-to-two."

"Do the houses have equal power?" Jordan knew he was grasping at straws.

"Officially, yes. In actuality no." Sebastién's head teetered in thought, his hands gesturing as though assisting the process. "Think of it this way: the librarians and gardeners are on our side. The bankers, the courts, and the police are not."

"Well, shit." Jordan's mind ground gears. "Can't someone do something?"

"Not really."

"Excuse me," barked a voice in front of them.

A heavy shoulder hit Jordan, spinning him around, knocking him off balance. Landing knees-first onto the unforgiving granite street, Jordan slapped his hands down to arrest his fall. He looked up. A few paces away stood the man who had railroaded him. Broad shoulders, fists barreled and pressed to his hips. When the man turned his head, Jordan knew it was no accident. A pair of dark eyes, sunk into a dark face stared back at him, fuming contempt. A latticework of scars decorated the man's cheek like an incomplete tic-tac-toe grid. He turned away and disappeared into the crowd.

"That's part of activism too. Don't mind it." Sebastién pulled Jordan to his feet and gave him an encouraging slap on the arm. "That's Raleigh. He runs a bit hot."

As they continued, the wide piazza constricted back to a thoroughfare. Jordan looked over his shoulder and caught Albert still at work, his patrician face trying to win the war of words against an unfriendly crowd.

"So where were we?" Sebastién peered up at the cherry trees for an answer. "Ah yes…our glorious leaders are going to sit this out, so it's up to us to get you trained before you go into the Depths."

"Trained for what?" asked Jordan, finding himself more aware of passersby, some cordial, others wearing faces that suggested a definite disdain.

"The fighting arts, for one. There's a whole house dedicated to that—*curia* as they're called. In this case, it's the Praetorium—the police. But because this whole thing's political, they won't come near you. The hope is that you go into the Depths without a lick of training."

"That makes no sense."

"Makes sense to those who don't want you to come back out."

Jordan scanned Sebastién with apprehension.

"Stay with me, Jordan. Technically speaking, you're invisible, so nothing's going to come after you down there. It's the other person that's going to be the problem."

"Hello, Sebastién," chimed an attractive woman strolling by. The light from the cherry trees glinted off her elegant diamond necklace.

Sebastién smiled and continued. "Since you can't write relics, all you have is your word, your verbal testimony. And that won't do, so they're going to send a recorder with you. It'll be someone appointed by the court, some poor fool from Castellum the Kyzheres won't mind losing—"

"If only a recorder can gather the proof," said Jordan, "what's the point of me being there at all?"

"You volunteered." Sebastién proffered a moment of silence; just crisp footsteps on granite. "If the bodies are down there, you could claim they weren't, hence the second party; the accuser's advocate. To put this another way, volunteering forces a real investigation—one that should have taken place a century ago."

"Isn't there a police-type person for this?" Jordan connected the dots before Sebastién even answered.

"There is. And two days ago you petitioned to become him." Sebastién perused a shop window decked out in suits and hats. "But to answer your question with more formality, yes there is someone for this sort of thing. Also part of the Praetorium, but the last person holding that post resigned after Firas's arrest. Nobody's offered to fill it since. Until you. That was Florum's way of fighting extradition. There's been every manner of legal game played to keep Firas in Arbor Florum."

Jordan tried to digest it, realizing how truly he'd been flying blind.

"I pledged to go down there myself a long time ago," said Sebastién, looking down at the street. "Firas talked me out of it."

"Because he thought the bodies were down there?"

"I'd have to imagine so. Though it was likely to save my life. My darker half was steering back in those days. I would have died had I done it."

It puzzled Jordan. "So why does he want me to go now?"

Sebastién shrugged. "Maybe Lila has it right. He's desperate. After a century, those tiny odds grew attractive. But I still think it's because the Kyzheres were able to plant a conspiratorial seed in his head."

Jordan grimaced. "So I'm learning to fight to protect myself from the recorder?"

"Not entirely." Sebastién tilted his head. "Well, I wouldn't turn my back on him, but the noughts are the real danger. Do you remember Helena, after we released her?"

"That black, reaper thing?"

"Oui, oui. The Depths are crawling with those. That's why nobody goes down there. Remnants of the lost tribe of Florum Antiquus—don't ask, we don't have time for it, and it's sketchy folklore anyway. Just know those things are down there. They'll be all over your search partner. It's going to make the recording impossible unless you fight them off."

"Savis, Sebastién," said a man walking in the opposite direction. He stopped and clasped Sebastién on the shoulder. "Good to see you."

Sebastién returned the gesture and smiled as the man walked away.

"Who was that?" asked Jordan.

"Who the hell knows?"

"Why does everyone keep looking at you?"

"I'm a socialite…"

"Like a celebrity?"

Sebastién choked a grin back into the corner of his mouth. "These aren't locals. They're foreigners, in town for the Trid. I'm a bit exotic to their eyes, especially to the ones from Castellum."

Jordan realized something as he scanned the crowd: though most were dressed in contemporary fashion—incredibly well-dressed, at that—a great many championed styles from more than a century ago, the defining characteristic being the tailcoat. "Why are half these people dressed like they came out of Oliver Twist?"

Sebastién smiled. "Ah yes, the longtails; Castellum's upper crust. They're frozen in time, fashionably speaking. Tragic, isn't it? Now where were we?"

Jordan sighed. "I need to protect the guy I'm going down there with, but not turn my back on him because he might kill me."

"Quite right, and a few more things. One…" Sebastién whipped his index finger out like a switchblade. "Noughts just absorb whatever you hit them with and come back for more. You're fighting fire with fire. You'll need to fend them off carefully, and escalate slowly. That's the first rule." Sebastién unfurled a second finger. "The other is that the Kyzheres are almost certainly hoping both of you end up killed by noughts. No return, no proof, no more Lux Sanguinis, except for Firas. That means no more volunteers, no more searches. Firas remains in jail forever. Checkmate."

"This all sounds like a terrible idea."

"It is." Sebastién placed his hand on Jordan's shoulder and jostled him. "But fear not, mon ami. You're only in danger if a nought latches onto you, but that won't happen unless you go around giving them hugs. Besides, when we're done with you, you'll be rightly schooled, be it noughts or Lux Stellarum's mind tricks." He pushed at Jordan's arm with a closed fist, causing him to veer off course.

"What if I die down there?" asked Jordan.

"Bad echo, saying that." Sebastién pursed his lips. "But if it comes to that—if your life's flashing before your eyes, you have to let go. Accept it. Make your peace, see the light. Don't get trapped like Helena."

Sebastién stopped to shake hands with a cheerful old woman. Jordan spotted Eli walking toward them. He was accompanied by two others, a thin man in a tailcoat and a woman with curly hair.

"There's Eli," said Jordan after Sebastién finished his pleasantries. Eli noticed them. His face rang surprise before it looked away.

"He saw you, too," said Sebastién.

"He ignored me." Jordan cast a whiplash glance back at Eli.

"That would be the sensible move. They tried to bring you in on the sly, and now they're covering their tracks. Besides, you're *involved*." Sebastién air-quoted the word. "But don't fret. Life is more interesting in our clutch. Livelier than being a research assistant to the scholarly hordes in the Prude."

They reached the end of East Grey, with the gateway to East Leaf proper just ahead. Jordan looked over his shoulder again. He watched Eli fade into the distance, wondering if Crispin's reaction would have been the same. His attention returned to find East Leaf much like West Leaf: a thoroughfare bisecting a wide circular grove—this one packed with cherry trees. The open space rose to improbable heights, but the far side didn't harbor an elegant hotel.

Instead, a massive pair of doors.

Sick-gray iron barriers, long out of use, the seams and hinges lumped with beaded metal as though welded shut. A thick set of chains were wrapped around the handles, reinforcing the point. Its medieval mood spoiled the immaculate white-gray of East Leaf.

"The gateway to the Depths," said Sebastién, his tone suddenly somber. "Sealed off just after Firas's arrest. But let's not dwell on it. That's not why we're here today." Sebastién put his palm to Jordan's back and steered him toward a building tattooed with intricate relief work. He ushered Jordan to a pair of doors with fancy brass handles. He yanked one open, and in they went.

"Sebastién," said a man stretched out on a chaise lounge, putting down a thick book. "I thought you'd be rehearsing in the Asterhaus— why Gorgamushka's?"

"I was looking for something cozy, Sam." Sebastién surveyed the space as if he were looking to buy the place.

"Of course." Sam got to his feet, brushing off his tweed coat. "Only, I don't think there's a piano here at present."

"No need. We'd like to use the old Gorg, nevertheless."

Sam stared at him and then looked Jordan over. "Of course, Sebastién, whatever you need." He scurried ahead, his dark gray suit jacket hugging his stout frame. After traversing a dark hallway, they arrived at another set of doors. Sam pulled them open and deveiled to a deep green—similar to Lila's hue. He flew off into the darkness, rising ever upward. Sam moved his hand about, and a bright light erupted from an enclosed metal cone. An organic spotlight. Sam flew about, bringing others like it to life. They were pointed at a performance stage surrounded by inclined rows of seats. A tall balcony ran the perimeter.

Sebastién deveiled and flew to the stage, veiling at its center. He tapped his feet, delighting himself with the echo. "Sam, we still have those curtains, yes?"

"Rolled up, stage right," yelled Sam, bringing lights up at the rear of the hall.

"Jordan, some help please?"

Jordan deveiled and flew to the stage. Out of his periphery, he saw Sam's eyes stick to him. After veiling, Jordan followed Sebastién backstage where they found a series of red-gold-patterned curtains rolled up like giant tamales. Heaving them over shoulders, they hauled them to the stage one by one.

With Sebastién marching in front, Jordan's mind sifted through events on the horizon, trying to find something to keep his spirits up. He found one. "You mentioned some kind of opera the other night…Do you think Lila—"

Sebastién launched his end of the curtain roll off his shoulder, the act nearly toppling Jordan. "You're really going to ask about this?"

"Yeah," said Jordan. "Everything's going to shit and I'm gonna die in the Depths, so why the hell not?" Jordan looked away from Sebastién. "I kinda asked her already anyway."

"And?" Sebastién raised an eyebrow.

"She called me a young soul."

Sebastién laughed. It was a true, hearty laugh, divorced from the problems at hand. It had Jordan clenching his jaw.

"My dear friend," said Sebastién, clasping his hands together apologetically, "you and Lila—and myself, for that matter—all have bodies around the same age. But to live for a century is a different matter. Time shapes you, changes you. Some things take a hundred years to learn."

"So I'm naïve?" Jordan put a hand on his hip.

"Most definitely," said Sebastién. He stared Jordan down for a few seconds and sighed. "It's called the Donum Novissimum—the Last Gift. It's an opera, it's a ballet. I'm the conductor, and it's four days from now. By all means, ask Lila if you must, but keep your head in reality." Sebastién turned and marched offstage.

In minutes they had unrolled the curtains and piled them on one side, forming a thick cushion. The other side remained bare wood. Sam had settled into the center of the ground-level seating and waited, his arms cast across the chair backs.

"This is where I'm going to learn to fight?" asked Jordan.

"Yes," said Sebastién. "Ready for the first lesson?"

"Yeah, why not?" Jordan stuffed his hands in his pockets.

"Deveil and position yourself over the curtains." Sebastién pointed at them. He deveiled in a snap, blazing bright.

Jordan did the same and glided to the appointed spot.

"There are two schools of this. The faintlight world absorbed both without understanding the origins. You'll know the names. The first is Yoga, the other is Kung Fu. We have different names here, but that's not important now." Sebastién glided closer with chin tipped low, his stare fixed on Jordan while fiery orange light coursed through his ghostly presence. "This first one is a bit unpleasant, so I'll get it out of the way. A friend of mine taught it to me this way, and now I teach it unto you." Sebastién bowed in mid-air. "It's called getting knocked out."

Sebastién's hand came at Jordan like musket fire, striking him in the chest, sending streams of red light spilling off in every direction. Jordan veiled and plummeted. He landed on the piled-up curtains. Pain thundered through his head and his vision went blurry. Though he had landed safely, he remained in deep disorientation.

Sam cackled in the distance. Sebastién's words reached Jordan as foggy syllables; a repetitive mantra: "Eee…ay-el. Eee-ay-el." The words arrived like a chant delivered through a drain pipe. Jordan deciphered it: Sebastién was telling him to deveil. Struggling to his feet, Jordan deveiled. Clarity returned in a flash, allowing him to catch the tail end of Sam's Vaudevillian laughter.

"You'd have liked that even less if I'd told you it was coming," said Sebastién. "That's lesson number one, Harsha's limit. When you get the light beat out of you, you get veiled against your will and earn a bad hangover."

"Bindo did that to me," said Jordan, recalling the aqueduct.

"I was unaware. Well, consider it a refresher course. If it were a real fight, you'd have been easy to finish off."

"I get it," said Jordan. "If I go down, deveil again as fast as possible."

"Yes, but it comes with restrictions. An already deveiled freelight can prevent another from deveiling again. This is called *choking*. It's like blowing out a fire with dynamite—we'll get to that, but first comes lesson number two."

Jordan darted backward, raising his hands in defense.

"Relax. Rule two is more a maxim than anything. It goes like this: fights are rarely fair. Between any competent participants, the more powerful timbre wins, and it doesn't take long."

"Meaning, I couldn't defeat you."

"Right again. If I were inexperienced like yourself, you'd land a few blows, but you'd still be destined to lose. Even bad strikes on my part would get you down to Harsha fast. Sanguinis *is* positioned pretty well on the pecking order, though. You can knock around most others."

"How about Supernus?"

Sebastién looked dismayed. "Technically, you could beat him. He is quite skilled as a fighter, despite being so ill-suited for it—he's Lux Stellarum, after all. The problem would be him getting into your head, like at Liwei's party." Sebastién became even more morose as he continued. "I want you to stop thinking like this, Jordan. Supernus is a son of a bitch, but the freelight who protect him are far worse. Interfectors."

"The yellow ones."

"Yes, the yellow ones." Sebastién reinforced it with a dire nod. "They maim and kill on command. They do it without hesitation— and we're not talking headaches here. They can strike so hard as to end you outright—right past Harsha and to the grave. Like a hammer to the head. They're more like machines than human beings, completely loyal to the Kyzheres."

"How did they pull that off?"

"That's a long story."

"Give me the short version."

Sebastién shook his head, orange flame-like wisps wavering off his hair. "There is no short version. What I'm trying to teach you is to respect the interfectors. A single one could dispatch both of us in seconds." Sebastién put his arms out to his sides. His deveiled form went bright, most of his features disappearing into agitated fire. An enthusiastic buzz rippled to life with the transformation. "The Finalis is tomorrow night, so you'll get a taste of this firsthand."

"Another party?" said Jordan, suddenly anxious.

"Sort of." Sebastién glided higher in the air.

"What then?"

"Hands up," said Sebastién, scuttling the question.

Jordan raised his burning red fists in front of his face like an underdog boxer, glancing down to make sure he was positioned over the curtains.

"Now draw in. Blaze like me." Sebastién waited for Jordan to brighten before he resumed instruction. "What I did on our previous and very short bout is known as breaking, striking, or pushing. Using brute force to weaken the adynatos to the reversion point. Take a swing at me."

Jordan hesitated. "Shouldn't you be over the curtains?"

"You couldn't break me if you tried." Sebastién grinned at him. "But you should. Try, that is."

Jordan, feeling a bit insulted or perhaps a bit empowered, darted forward and swung away at Sebastién, who deflected the assault with ease. Jordan delivered jabs with remarkable speed, far faster than was possible in human form. His strikes bled arcs of orange light from Sebastién, star trails that fell and sizzled into the stage below.

Jordan continued to pound away like a schoolyard bully, and Sebastién grew dimmer. Then, at the edge of victory, Sebastién caught Jordan's jab in his own hand as though it were a baseball. Holding on, Sebastién grew bright instantly, and Jordan's light drained out. A second later, Jordan was veiled again on the curtains, an epic headache pounding away. He lifted himself into a sitting position and winced, finding a bright, smiling Sebastién overhead.

"That's called draining, or pulling. It's the other way to get to Harsha. Defending against it is the real lesson here, because draining is the only thing noughts do—and you can't drain them back. All physical contact is a losing proposition. They can kill you directly in the deveiled form. Even if veiled—or if you're a faintlight—they'll reach right down your throat and that'll be the end of you. We have reliquiae documenting this and it's quite disturbing." Sebastién dimmed out, veiled, and dropped to the curtains, landing in a sitting position. "There is but one rule here: strike them and push them back. But do it without getting hitched into a drain. That's what was happening to Lila with Helena. Do you remember what I did after I cut her loose?"

"You stunned Helena," said Jordan.

"Correct. There is no Harsha with noughts, but an overload of force can immobilize them for a few seconds. When they come to, they'll be more charged than if you had just pushed them back. So it's a move of last resort."

"Understood," said Jordan, cracking his knuckles. As he prepared for more of Sebastién's tutelage, he filed away what he'd learned so far, assigning a special pride to the fact that his timbre was able to out-gun most others. That fact birthed a specific idea, despite Sebastién's warning.

He wanted a piece of Supernus Tacitus Kyzhere.

"Get up," said Sebastién. "Next lesson."

29

FIGHT NIGHT

North Leaf was long like a Kansas highway, the route to its midgrey crossing alone spanning a distance greater than East and West Grey combined. Jordan and Sebastién soared through the upper reaches of its brightspace like condors, the endless pattern of aqueduct archways sliding by on each side like frames on a film reel. The northern realm of Arbor Florum offered yet another botanical theme, this time pines and aspens. The light-wrapped leaves of the latter fluttered with the evening's golden glow, shimmering like constellations of tiny mirrors. The frequency of air travelers increased the entire way. All of them moved northward, through the gateway and into the communal round of North Leaf's dome.

Unlike the other leafs, North Grey kept going. The thoroughfare pierced the far wall, slimming to something like a subway tunnel, perhaps ten stories tall. Smaller passages branched off like tributaries. The lighting was sparse and the building fronts plain, suggesting offices that served utilitarian purposes.

The passage itself remained crowded, freelight all moving in the same direction: away from the center of Arbor Florum. The flock telegraphed an energetic spirit, skirmishing with one other, sending spurts of sparks about. Moving with the playful souls, but trying to avoid them, were teams carrying huge metal platters loaded with mugs, meats, cheeses, breads, and other culinary artifacts. This, Jordan noticed, had the desirable effect of keeping attention away from him. But whenever he came within an eyeshot, faces snapped toward his red light.

Deeper into the merriment, the main passage reached a vertical shaft. The kaleidoscopic array of freelight followed it down, descending as though they were candle-bearers going over a waterfall in the night. At the bottom, it emptied into an oval venue, reminding Jordan of the rehearsal hall where he and Sebastién had sparred. Only this one was far larger. Engineered like a sports stadium with abnormally steep seating arrangement, the interior's open space was shaped like a stout whiskey glass. Already packed to the hilt with patrons, Jordan followed Sebastién to an aisle midway up. After veiling, they sat down in nicked-up wooden chairs, bolted to the floor.

Their arrival caught the attention of a man to Sebastién's right. They dove into conversation, leaving Jordan to digest the scene. First came the tropical heat, already sticking his shirt to his skin. Down on the floor in the center was a stone platform, the size and shape of an ice hockey rink. A series of wooden statues surrounded the platform: human forms in fighting postures. In the center of the oval was a tree—but not a living one. It was constructed from pieces of finished wood, like a giant prop in a stage play. A great amount of empty space surrounded the platform, buffering it from the crowd.

"Centuries ago," said Sebastién, turning back to Jordan and waving his hand across the scene, "the fighting arts were primitive. As they were perfected, the contests had to be divided out by timbre, much like heavyweights and lightweights in faintlight boxing—these are the heavyweights, by the way. A lesser timbre cannot compete with a greater, so the best of the best is always Solis Meridianus. Interfectors, in other words. The class below this is Solis Vesperam—still interfectors, but not the elite. To the inattentive eye, they're subtle shades of yellow. But here, they're worlds apart."

"Don't trust my eyes, in other words," said Jordan over the din of the crowd. "Same, but different." The lesson was starting to stick.

"Right," said Sebastién before breaking away to another conversation. The man to Jordan's left leaned into him and began to yell louder than seemed necessary.

"You're new here, eh? I can tell 'cuz you're staring at everything like a damned child. I helped build this place, you know."

The man leaned closer as if needing physical support. Jordan turned his head enough to acknowledge him, but no further. He threw his arm around Jordan anyway, his pronouncements reeking of beer.

"The reason it's so hot down here, it's the thermal stems. I helped cut them, you know. I worked on the magma gates too." He took an aggressive gulp from a mug in his other hand. "Many years ago, way down there…" He made circles in the air with his drinking hand, losing a splash or two. "Most of that heat's for the Arborsolis, and the baths, but the rest of it's for this place; for those freelight who beat each other's lights out." The man managed to stabilize his bobbing head long enough to focus on Jordan's face. "Who the hell are you, anyway? Sebastién usually brings ladies to this—fun ones." His eyes widened at mention of the fairer sex. He released his one-arm embrace and reached across Jordan's lap toward Sebastién, who was still facing away. "Sess-cha-bash-tin," rumbled the man, clawing at him. "Is this your date this year? She's awful."

"Yes she is, Hartwig," said Sebastién, throwing his arm around Jordan. "This is Jordan Wakefield. Jordan, this is Hartwig, purveyor of the Taberna Meridiei, the finest pub in the Grey City."

"The finest pub," repeated Hartwig stoically, before burping with his mouth and eyes closed. Jordan leaned away, expecting beer and food to erupt into his lap. Hartwig composed himself and mustered a sincere face. "Nice to meet you, Wockfeld." He flayed his mug-less hand: a vibrant purple. "Whoa, don't wanna go any further. I'll ruin my breeniation…my inebriation. So what about you?"

Jordan flayed his own hand.

Hartwig's plump, mottled face lapsed into momentary sobriety. A moment later, he loosed a vigorous laugh. "Well, I'll be damned. Ha! We're all gonna be damned. Heard rumors of you—you're the last one, aren't you? I've seen the drawings…" He leaned close to Jordan. "The secret ones."

Jordan veiled his hand, not certain how to respond.

"The orators!" called a voice from behind, causing everyone to shift their attention to the airspace. A quartet of brown-orange freelight glided into position just above the center of the platform. They arranged themselves perpendicular to each other, each aimed at a compass point. When they spoke, their voices roared as though massively amplified.

"*AH-KOO-TAH!*" bellowed the orators in unison. "*AH-KOO-TAH!*"

The crowd settled as the echoes dissipated.

"WELCOME TO THE CAMPUS FINALIS OF THE FIVE HUNDRED AND SIXTY-FIFTH TRIDUUM AT ARBOR FLORUM."

Jordan, startled by the unexpected power of the voices, leaned back into his seat. The orators continued, citing results of previous bouts, their force making Jordan's ribcage rattle.

"Vox bronte," shouted Sebastién, reading Jordan's curiosity. "Thunder voice. We can all do it but not like Cuprum."

The orators' speech concluded with the announcement of the final combatants. Two people walked onto the stage; one in the loose, black garb of the interfector and the other in vibrant orange-yellow robes. Even from this distance, Jordan recognized the man in black as one of Supernus's personal guards.

A flurry of deveiled fingertips sprouted across the crowd. The spectacle captured Jordan's attention. It was the peace symbol: index and middle fingers held aloft in the shape of the letter *V*, waving slow, like a clock pendulum. En masse, it was hypnotic. Mostly pinks and purples from the opposite side. Greens, blues, and oranges from theirs.

Sebastién gave Jordan the tale of the tape. "The one on the left, you might recognize from Liwei's party. He's Supernus's primary, Konstantin. He was the one kneeling on my back. We want him to lose, of course. Jinhai is the other."

The two combatants sat down at opposite ends of the rectangular platform with legs crossed.

"Jinhai is Florum?" asked Jordan.

"No. Emeishan," said Sebastién. "But he's not Castellum, so he's ours for tonight. In reality, they're all interfectors, all servants of the Kyzheres, though it wasn't always this way."

The orators flew off, while a pair of burly men started to crank large metal wheels. Trap doors near the edges of the platform creaked open.

"Is Jinhai Kung Fu style?"

"They both are—and it's called fast body," said Sebastién. "Everyone learns long body too, but it's too difficult to use in combat. Only one person ever could. That was the Devikira."

"Could he beat either of these guys?"

"*She* could beat both at the same time. Her timbre is without equal. So fast and violent. Unnatural, as though the hand of God. She was unrivaled in the fighting arts, despite the fact she was a dancer. She trained the Venatorum centuries ago, not aware of what she was creating. Horrified at what she'd done, she went into exile, vowing to live as faintlight, devoutly veiled to the day death should take her."

Hot air rose from the open trap doors, evident by the way it distorted the background. It was like looking down a roadway on a blazing summer day. The two fighters stood and faced each other. They bowed from the waist. After deveiling yellow, they disappeared into the dark shafts. Jordan, without removing his eyes from the scene, wrestled his hoodie off and used it to wipe his face before dropping it at his feet. The crowd started chanting and stomping out a four-syllable word.

"What are they saying?" asked Jordan.

"Vi-tru-vi-an," yelled Sebastién, mimicking the crowd. "As in Da Vinci's famous drawing."

Before Jordan could ask why, the fighters shot up from the shafts and hovered stationary. Their forms were so bright that Jordan had to shield his eyes. Arcs of fire raced around each warrior in violent orbit, making them resemble the Vitruvian Man sketch. The supercharged light roared in a strange, half-animalistic, half-machine way; pitched like a racecar's engine pushed past the limit. The fighters turned away from Jordan's side of the arena and bowed to the other. Two men, in a spectator's box, stood and bowed in return.

"There's our pal," said Sebastién. "Castellum's esteemed ambassador to Arbor Florum."

Jordan spotted him even before Sebastién had finished his sentence: black suit with striking silver patterns on it, recognizable even from here.

Supernus.

After Supernus flayed his hand, he panned it about to the crowd. An Asian man standing next to him did the same, his light a harvest orange. They raised their hands high into the air. Applause erupted when the hands came down. The two combatants turned to face each other. Their Vitruvian arcs continued to roar like atomic weapons prepared to raze the world.

A sudden silence took the venue.

Then it began.

The fighters shot toward each other, meeting in the middle. A thundering report, accompanied by showers of liquefied light. The combatants speared at each other in furious sequence, the strikes impossible to follow. With each hit, yellow light rained down, kindling fires to life on the wooden props.

The duel defiled Jordan's ears. Flashes of light overloaded his vision, printing imagery like a strobe light in a manic nightclub; human postures frozen in time but changing radically from one flash to the next. At one moment, Jordan saw two birds of fire, gnashing at each other. At the next, two gladiators, fighting with arc-welder fury deep in the cosmos.

Jordan's heart raced, his body pumped adrenaline.

The fighters traded volleys at close range, then launched apart, angling about the venue, often straying near the crowd. The spectators ducked and covered when jets of burning light reached the gallery. When separated, each fighter would assume the Vitruvian pose—arms and legs outstretched until the fiery orbital rings regenerated, all of it happening in split-seconds.

Flurries of action, indecipherable to Jordan's inexperienced eyes, spurred factions in the crowd to their feet. Fists pumped in the open air, indicating someone had gained the upper hand, if only for a moment.

"Look at the tree," yelled Sebastién. He grabbed Jordan by the back of the neck and steered his attention to the stage. The top of the prop tree was on fire now. "If the contest is still going when it falls down, it's a draw. If it comes to that—and it probably will—they're going to unleash everything they've got. So when things start looking unstable, don't blink."

"What happens when the statues burn up?"

"They burn up," said Sebastién, his voice growing hoarse, trying to cut through the thunder of the combat. "They're just symbols."

"Of what?" Jordan watched the fighters dodge and parry to a position just in front of them, causing the crowd to stand and shield their eyes, ready to evade the aftermath.

"Of life…" shouted Sebastién. "Of death…creation and ruin. It's beautiful, is it not?"

Jordan smiled wide, intoxicated by the viscera.

The first of the wooden statues collapsed, and the tree was engulfed in flames. Jordan looked across the crowd: brilliant flashes of light painted sweaty faces like a war scene. Mouths were agape with rapture, eyes wide as though pinned open against their will. People rose to their feet, inspiring others to do the same. They stomped and kicked, sending an aboriginal drumbeat into the searing air while the combatants fought on, a contest set amongst pillars of smoke and waving fists.

When Sebastién stood and joined in, so did Jordan.

For a moment Jordan jettisoned the politics of it, acknowledging only the beauty of the fighting arts. But a moment later, Sebastién's words climbed back up like heartburn. They made Jordan recognize what the spectators had long forgotten or readily ignored: the interfectors were weaponized life, the most dangerous instruments in all of Elysium. Whoever controlled them controlled this world.

This wasn't a sporting event.

It was a reminder.

A large portion of the wooden tree fell to the platform—somehow both fighters saw it. They split apart, racing to opposite ends of the arena. They assumed the Vitruvian pose, transforming into radiant suns, human figurines at the center.

But they didn't charge.

They waited, studying each other, looking for the knockout. As at the open, the venue became impossibly silent. At last, they moved. They met in the center, the impact birthing a supernova. A deafening crack of thunder hit Jordan's chest like a boot heel. For an instant, the combatants were one. In the next, a human form had been birthed from their union, falling like a discarded marionette amidst streams of bleeding light.

It was Jinhai.

Half the crowd burst into ecstasy, the other half gasped. Jinhai deveiled before reaching the surface and glided away from the fallout. He drifted down to the platform, where he veiled and dropped to one knee.

The burning tree collapsed.

The crowd on the opposing side applauded and waved victory signs, a sea of purple and pink flares. Jordan's side echoed disappointment, but applauded nonetheless, spurring Jordan to join in. He harbored no discontent toward the victor. Then Supernus flew out next to him. He lifted Konstantin's fiery yellow hand in his own. They floated down to the platform together and veiled. The orators glided to the stage, glancing approvingly at the burning wreckage along the way. They arranged themselves just above Supernus and Konstantin. They waited. When Supernus spoke, the orators repeated his words, pounding them out to the crowd:

"KONSTANTIN IS YOUR VICTOR!"

The opposite side continued to wave peace fingers. Some on Jordan's side did the same, though with less enthusiasm.

"I RECALL ONE OF HIS VICTORIES HERE," continued the orators, echoing Supernus's words. "IT WAS ONE HUNDRED

AND TWENTY-EIGHT YEARS AGO."

"Uh, oh," said Sebastién.

The orators boomed on: "IN THE DAWN OF THE SAME YEAR, WE WERE ALL SADDENED BY THE LOSS OF RAPHAEL FOSCARI AND ELISABETH DI LORNE, BELOVED CITIZENS OF ARBOR FLORUM."

Unsettling chatter broke out.

"We should leave," said Sebastién, grabbing Jordan's arm.

Though over a hundred feet away, Jordan saw Supernus's eyes land on him, then look away as though it were nothing.

"THERE'S BEEN CONTROVERSY—THIS IS TRUE. BUT THE QUESTION WILL SOON BE PUT TO REST."

Supernus said something that drew the orators' attention. They all craned their heads around to him. Supernus flashed his grin and repeated his words. Facing the crowd again with a look of reluctance, the orators relayed the message: "LUX SANGUINIS, HAS RETURNED. BRAVE JORDAN WAKEFIELD HAS VOLUNTEERED TO SEARCH THE DEPTHS ON BEHALF OF THE ACCUSED, FIRAS EL-SAKAR."

Supernus stretched out his hand dramatically, pointing to Jordan. Frantic chatter discharged from the crowd as they tried to hone in on Supernus's target.

"Shit," said Sebastién, pulling at Jordan as though trying to save him from quicksand. "Come on."

Jordan shook free.

Supernus spoke again. The orators continued with diminished passion. "SHOW YOURSELF, HERO."

Jordan stepped to the precipice. He glared down at Supernus, who flayed a two-finger, purple-*V* salute, raising it in the air. Jordan deveiled, triggering a shock wave of surprise. He glided past the edge of the balcony, while Sebastién and Hartwig barked at him to get back. A crack sounded out behind Jordan, and a moment later, Sebastién was at his side.

"We should go."

"Not yet," said Jordan.

A wave of astonished voices circled the venue, birthed on a rumor that had been lurking in their midst. Jordan extended the back of his hand to Supernus. Instead of two fingers, he gave him one.

The middle.

He stared at Supernus through it as though it were a gun sight. Supernus bared his teeth. Angry taunts erupted from the other side of the arena, and a mass-deveiling ensued, making Jordan feel like he'd stepped out of a limousine into a wall of pink-purple paparazzi. Memories flitted through his head, followed by an equal number of mind-altering seductions, hammering at him from across the way. Jordan grew frightened. Then he realized the signals couldn't seize hold of him from there. Proximity mattered.

Jordan kept his red, one-finger salute trained on Supernus, who maintained his dark sneer. The rapid deveilings continued, the spectators on both sides edging their way into the smoky combat space in small moves, showing no sign of backing down.

Jordan took it all in.

It was a mood more volatile than grandstanding over a winner and loser. Something that had been simmering for a great long time had just boiled over, something far larger than his petty insult.

Jordan retracted his finger.

Two blazing yellow forms shot up into the air, Vitruvian coils erupting about them. Recognizing Konstantin and Jinhai, the riled crowds on both sides retreated, surrendering the airspace.

Jordan turned to Sebastién, who looked rattled.

"Good speech," said Sebastién, giving him a lackluster thumbs-up. "Now let's get the hell out of here."

30

TENSIONS RISING

The Grey City projected an uneasy temperament after the Finalis. With hands in his pockets, Jordan made his way toward the rehearsal hall alone. He recognized a lot of changes on the street. Posters had been tacked to trees and storefronts during the night. They put uncivil reminders in everyone's face. Some depicted the black silhouette of a man looking toward the ground, with the number "128" in thick block letters. Others featured the call to attention the orators used—"ACOUTAH!"—printed over the image of prison bars. Yet others stated "REMEMBER FIRAS?" or made less-than-subtle references to Raphael Foscari and Elisabeth Di Lorne.

A regular barrage of high-beam stares kept Jordan's chin aimed at the street. He ventured that the rash activism of the posters ran quite simpatico to his one-finger activism from last night. People were whispering in numbers, and even when alone.

The next change—striking in its scope and energy—was the gathering at East Leaf's midgrey crossing. Packed tight, nearly to the piazza's outer rim. The scene vibrated discontent. Bursts of counter-activism shot holes in Albert's proclamations. Jordan slinked to the back edge of the crowd, head down, hands still in his pockets. Watching pant legs and shoes move by, he weaved through the observers, who didn't notice him. Winding back around to the mouth of the thoroughfare on the other side, Jordan breathed relief. He was nearly clear of the mob.

Then he looked up.

A man was planted in his path. Arms rigid, hands crunched into fists, latticed scars across his cheek. It was the same man who toppled him here two days back—Raleigh was his name. To his side, a woman with jet black hair and equally distressed eyes. With two thick fingers, Raleigh jammed at Jordan's sternum like it was an elevator button.

"This is him!" shouted Raleigh, his voice challenging the street noise. "This is him!" He shoved Jordan backward. The act caught the attention of bystanders at the edge of the crowd, who turned toward the fledgling altercation. The woman standing with Raleigh jittered, her eyes jumping between Jordan and the side of Raleigh's face.

Jordan tried to side-step around them, but the duo moved faster, blocking his way again.

"Look at me!" said Raleigh.

His black eyes bored into Jordan. His feet shifted as if standing on hot coals. Jordan curled his hands into fists, recognizing it was going to get physical.

But as fast as Raleigh's face tightened, it went submissive. His chin dropped, his eyes fell to the street. The same reaction spread like wildfire through the crowd. Many knelt, raising hands overhead as Jordan had seen at Liwei's party.

A purple freelight glided by, just over their heads. Jordan looked up, catching a haughty expression on the face. A group of four interfectors moved with the man, a sharp hum issuing from their presence. The entire piazza went silent. They waited while the interfectors and their handler passed into the upper end of East Leaf, moving toward Aria.

"Do you see what you've done?" said Raleigh. His face registered touches of aggression again, but less than a moment ago. "Interfectors. In the streets of the Grey City. Because of that stunt you pulled last night—and you've petitioned to become Investigator Forensis? You intend to go into the Depths?"

Jordan unballed his fists while the public discourse rattled to life again. "Firas asked me."

Raleigh leveled an incredulous stare, one that radiated doubt more than anger. "Then he's as much a fool as you. You're gonna die if you go down there."

"Firas didn't kill my predecessor."

"I know that," snapped Raleigh, bringing his face to Jordan's point-blank. "Everyone knows that. But what is to be done? It's a trap, don't you get it?"

"We don't know that." Jordan knew it was a pitiful claim.

Raleigh grabbed a fistful of Jordan's shirt and pulled him close. "We do—it's a certainty." Raleigh let him go with a shove. "Raphael's death was a tragedy. I miss him dearly. You may have his light, but you are *not* him." Raleigh shoved Jordan again, causing him to stutter-step. "You are *not* him." Raleigh turned away, his partner casting one last wicked glance over her shoulder as they disappeared into the mob.

Jordan resumed his solitary walk, doubts over Firas's judgment battering the foundations of his confidence. A zip and a snap hit Jordan's ears; someone veiling behind him. Jordan spun around, fists wound tight again.

"That's a bit tense," said Lila.

"Sorry." Jordan deflated, his arms going lax. "Was just meeting some of my fans."

Lila hummed a sad solemn note and walked past him.

Jordan turned and followed her, drawing even. "I was wondering when I'd see you again."

"Heard you went to the Finalis last night…"

"Were you there?" Jordan hoped she wasn't.

"No, not my scene." Lila smirked. "Heard you flipped off Supernus, though."

Jordan winced. "It happens."

"Probably not to him."

"I wasn't sure on the meaning of the two-fingered thing, so I gave him one."

"Two implies solidarity. So your response was…honest."

Jordan watched a lady wearing a purple hat rip a protest poster from a storefront and throw it to the ground, denying gravity its job.

"How are we doing on the Firas front?" asked Jordan. "We seem to have everyone's attention."

"Not well. Now that everyone knows you signed on to the Depths, they see our efforts as misguided."

Jordan frowned. "I was only trying to do what Firas—"

"Let's not talk about it." Lila grasped Jordan's forearm and released.

Her touch raised his spirits. Side by side, they walked, the streets echoing their footsteps. A pair of green freelight were brightening up the light of the cherry trees running the thoroughfare. Jordan reflected on Lila calling him a young soul, and then on Sebastién's laughter over it. He *was* naïve—schoolboy-grade naïve. He needed to keep his head on straight. Sebastién was dealing in good advice.

Yet Lila did track him down moments ago. And here she was, walking by his side.

"Hey, Lila?" said Jordan.

She looked at him.

"I was wondering if—" Jordan's shoe tip caught an uneven edge in the street, causing him to stumble past her. He caught his balance and cursed. Turning around, he found Lila had halted and was pinning quizzical eyes on him.

Jordan hung a thumb in the pocket of his jeans. He felt terribly self-conscious, but pressed on: "If you're not doing anything in a couple days, could I take you to that space opera Sebastién mentioned?"

Lila smirked, then giggled. "You called it a space opera."

"Yep." Jordan scratched his ear. "Just realized that. There's this movie *Star Wars*, and people called it a space opera. Seems that's my association with that word."

"Charming." Lila's smirk evolved to a full smile. "I've seen it—and I'll think about it."

"You'll think about *Star Wars*?"

"No." Lila walked up to him. "I'll think about your invitation. You were asking me on a date, weren't you?"

"I was." Jordan thumbed his other pocket. "I mean, I know I'm a young soul and all. And you're…old."

"Well…it's a lot to consider." She began to circle him, taking slow, heel-to-toe steps. "I don't know much about you. I hear you get into trouble. All the time."

Jordan lifted his chin and grinned. He turned his head, meeting her green eyes before she walked behind him, out of view.

"What would people say—me being seen with you?"

Jordan turned his head the other way—enough to hear her voice, but not enough to oblige her tease with his full attention.

She moved in close behind him, clasping his shoulder. Leaning against him on tiptoes, she whispered in his ear: "I'll think about it."

Jordan turned and took in her serene expression.

"Later, space cowboy." Lila flayed her hand and flashed him green peace fingers. Breaking into a bright smile, she deveiled in full. Up into the air she went, past the midgrey crossing, past its roiling activism, off toward Aria where the Arborsolis shimmered bright.

"Looking forward to it," said Jordan to the empty air, watching her distant green twinkle pass through the gateway.

Jordan resumed his journey, finding his steps issued with vigor. Then came the imposing doors that marked entry to the Depths. Ignoring them, he turned to the rehearsal hall and went inside.

He spotted three people loitering near the end of the hallway in front of the auditorium doors. They began to clap and holler as he approached. The celebration ceased when the auditorium doors burst open, producing an angry Sebastién.

"You're late," said Sebastién. "We have work to do."

"We're here to help," said one member of the trio, a black-haired man in a leather jacket.

"We have trainers-de-jour inside, thank you very much." Sebastién pushed the man aside.

"At least let us keep guard."

"Fine." Sebastién grabbed Jordan by the shoulder.

"Aren't you going to introduce us?"

Sebastién sighed. "Jordan, the eager one that looks like a teenager is Wiley. The one who looks like his sister is Georgia, and the one who looks like he lost a knife fight is Lev."

"Knife," said Lev with the ambiance of a stoned surfer.

Jordan moved to shake hands, but Sebastién dragged him into the hall and shut the doors.

"Charter members of your fan club," said Sebastién, leading Jordan to the stage. "They're hecklers, dedicated to harassing all things Kyzhere, so they love you on principle. They flirted with helping Firas over the years, and he flirted back. But they don't have what it takes. They'll scatter the moment there's any real trouble."

Down by the stage, Jordan spotted an attractive woman with short, spiky black hair and pale skin sitting on the edge of the stage. Her jeans and sharp-featured face gave Jordan a punk-rock vibe. Next to her, a bald Japanese man with round, wire-frame glasses. They stood up upon Jordan's approach.

"Easton and Jiro," said Sebastién.

They raised and deveiled their hands. Easton's was slender and pink. Jiro's thick fingers burned bright orange.

"Easton, would you sit this one out, my dear?" Sebastién deveiled and took his customary position opposite the piled curtains. "Jordan, deveil. Jiro and I will mimic noughts. We'll start lazy, and come at you harder every time you push us back. Make your breaks clean and fast—but don't overdo it. Don't give us any more than necessary. Let's see how long you can last. I have rehearsal in an hour, so make this count."

Jordan deveiled and blazed red. He glided over the curtains and adopted a fighting stance like what he'd seen in the Finalis. His brief stroll with Lila had filled him with zest. But the dread of the Depths burned it away fast. He was one day closer to whatever secrets were or were not down there.

31

A CAPELLA

Hours later, after a vexing rehearsal at the Asterhaus, Sebastién marched through the Gorg's lobby with brisk steps. Spying Wiley, Georgia, and Lev still lurking at the auditorium doors, he bit his lip. Damn children. They were crouched in a tight cluster with eager ears pressed against the doors. From beyond them, Sebastién heard the muffled sound of passionate, awful singing.

"What's going on in there?" asked Sebastién.

Georgia and Lev jerked away from the doors like kids caught raiding a cookie jar. Wiley remained unabashedly in place.

"Singing," said Wiley. "It's really bad too."

"That can't be good," said Sebastién.

"Why not? It's a rehearsal hall, ain't it?"

"Funny. Now out of the way." He grabbed Wiley by the shoulder and shoved him aside. Sebastién went in and slammed the door. Jiro was gone. Easton was perched on the end of the stage holding up a single, deveiled finger. With her chin buried in the palm of her other hand, she wore the face of an exhausted schoolteacher. Jordan stood at the center of the stage, a blazing red hand held in front of his chest with pride. Staring wide-eyed into the distance, he sang with dreadful, off-key force: "WHOSE BROAD STRIPES AND BRIGHT STARS…"

"Not going well?" asked Sebastién.

Easton shook her head. Jordan continued to sing, causing Sebastién to furl his brow.

"Are you going to release him or what?"

"I want to *see* how he does on the high notes."

Jordan's chest expanded. He bellowed: "AND THE ROCKET'S RED GLARE…" The veins in his neck bulged against flushed skin. His voice ruptured into a fishtailing series of sounds like that of a wounded animal. "…THE BOMBS BURSTING IN AIR…"

"That's quite enough, isn't it?"

"Someone from Census stopped in today, Sebastién…"

Jordan's tortured melody continued.

"Who?"

"Don't know her," said Easton. "Does it make a difference?"

"Not really." Sebastién moved in front of Easton, her knees level with his chest. He put his hands on her legs, waiting for Jordan to finish his disturbing a capella.

"…AND THE HOME OF THE BRAVE?"

Jordan went silent, letting his deveiled hand drop. He remained rigid, still staring straight ahead as if awaiting instruction from a distant command center.

"And what did you tell Miss Census?" asked Sebastién.

"The truth. That he wasn't transitioned." Easton moved her knees under his gentle touch. "I doubt anyone's going to make a fuss about it. Supernus and his people will make it a non-issue. Full steam ahead. Choo-choo."

"What's your gut feel on this?"

"Same as everyone, I guess." Easton shrugged. "Those bodies are down there, and this all plays into the Kyzhere's hands."

"Every time I come to believe that, I find myself unsure." Sebastién looked up at Jordan's entranced state. "Why sell it so hard? If Supernus has us cornered, why not clear the roadblocks and make sure Jordan gets down there? Why goad him?"

"Supernus *isn't* goading him. He sees Jordan as the antagonist. He can't help himself," said Easton in a matter-of-fact way. "He can't tolerate the sight of anyone near Lila."

"I know. That's the best part of this."

"If you tuck your swagger away, you'll see it's going to be the worst part of this."

"To think the freelight world was once rid of that man," said Sebastién.

Easton gave him a sullen look. "But now he's back, and worse than ever."

Sebastién bit his lower lip. "Still…maybe they didn't pull it off. Maybe there's nothing down there."

"Is that what you want me to tell you?"

"No," said Sebastién releasing her legs, "I want to know what you really think."

"I think we're walking into a trap." Easton's pink finger glowed bright near her fair, freckled cheek. "I think we already lost. Nobody's going to push to reexamine Firas under the pretense that the predecessors' harboring doesn't jive. Not if they believe it all ends in the Depths when Jordan finds those bodies."

Sebastién whistled an uncertain note. "When I step back and look at this grand game of chess were playing against the Kyzheres, there are moments—brief as a shooting star—when I think we have it all wrong."

Easton cast him a look. "What do you mean?"

"We see it as a contest between *us* and the Kyzheres." Sebastién paused, his fingers drumming his pant leg. "But what if it isn't that? What if it's been Firas moving the pieces all along?"

Easton's expression took on doubt.

Sebastién shrugged. "Like I said, it's a fleeting thought. I suspect I'm getting desperate too. I also think you should release Jordan now. His mind's not occupied. He might be taking some of this in."

Easton's finger went out. Jordan at once shed his soldier stance. His face twisted up and he turned to the piled curtains and pounded on them like a mad butcher.

"Easy, killer," said Sebastién, "I can't resist Easton's charms either."

Jordan gave up on his assault and sat down, back pressed against the curtain pile.

"Remember: you have to recognize it first." Easton stood up and walked over. "The moment you feel a rapid change of mood or manner of thinking, know it's the con—catch it right away and cut it off. If you can recognize it, you can beat it."

"I *am* recognizing it," said Jordan, throwing his head back, "and then I wake up, realizing I've been a fucking puppet again."

"Let's call it a day and have drinks." Sebastién waved Jordan down from the stage. "You'll be staying at my place from now on. We need to move you around."

32

TWO PATHS

Sebastién Saint-Vezina lived in the upper reaches of Aria on its southern face. The view from the veranda reminded Jordan of Liwei's residence. Though Sebastién's wasn't nearly as grand, it did have a grand piano, which occupied the center of a large room. A generous open space surrounded the sleek ebony instrument, providing an abundant orbit for guests. Lining the outer rim were sofas and chairs, and walls boasting a meticulous selection of art.

From the moment Jordan arrived, he found himself wishing for something darker; a place as bleak as his mood. Sprawled across a white leather sofa, he stared at the ceiling and kicked his heel against the floor in a rhythmic, apathetic fashion.

"White or red?" called Sebastién from a room away. "Or perhaps something stiffer?"

"Don't care," said Jordan, staring into the flank of the piano, studying the distorted curves the vinelight painted across its glossy surface.

Sebastién emerged from the hall with a bottle of red. He placed it on a table between two plush chairs. "Glasses, we need glasses. I'll be right back."

Jordan closed his eyes. His mind raced down dark avenues. It appalled him that Firas, given more than a century to reflect, had failed to consider a scenario as predictable as rigging the scene of the crime. Jordan struggled to excuse it as the byproduct of circumstance; a flare of intoxicating hope brought on by his so-called brother's return. As much as he tried to make that fit, he came back to Sebastién's theory that the Kyzheres had shaped him to believe the Depths were not rigged. He hated the likely truth of it. He wanted to set it on fire.

The sound of someone veiling invaded Jordan's awareness. Then came faint conversation, followed by silence. Probably Easton. He dreaded the thought of her, having served as her mental plaything all day. Jordan closed his eyes and tried to collect himself. A space of silence unfolded that spanned a greater amount of time than he'd expected. He relished its comfort.

An intermittent tapping sound broke his meditations.

It was like a clock.

It reminded him of the night of the art show…

Jordan bolted upright to find Crispin entering the room, his cane tapping its way across smooth granite. He rounded the piano, carrying a pair of empty wine glasses with him, crisscrossed at the stems. A leather satchel hung from his shoulder. Jordan's lips parted preemptively, while his head started in on an apology. Crispin raised an eyebrow as though ready to receive one. His enigmatic face neither frowned nor smiled, shuttering Jordan's resolve to speak.

As Crispin hobbled past, he slid the satchel off his shoulder, depositing it on the sofa next to Jordan. A few cane-taps later, he was in a chair, sitting next to the bottle of wine, conveying the mood of a man at a wake.

He waited.

Jordan eyed the satchel.

"Open it," said Crispin.

Jordan picked it up and peered inside, finding a tarnished copper-green disc. Grabbing the satchel by its bottom, he up-ended it, shaking the object out onto the cushion.

Crispin jolted as if to try to catch it, but settled after seeing it land safely. "Mind that relic. It just might save your life."

With thoughts still elsewhere, Jordan flayed a nonchalant finger over it. Blue fire danced up toward his red light. It felt like building sandcastles in the late summer, age ten. It wasn't Crispin's.

"Who wrote this?" asked Jordan.

"My brother."

"Didn't know you had one."

"We never got around to it." Placing the wine glasses on the table, Crispin lifted the bottle and perused its label. "This is a fine vintage." He began to fill the first glass, the trickle intruding on an unpleasant, silent vigil. "I asked Sebastién to step out for the evening. I was hoping we could talk." With the second glass filled, he leaned forward to stand.

Jordan got up and retrieved it. After sitting back down, he stared into the burgundy liquid. "I suppose there's nothing to toast at this point."

"I'd have to agree."

After turning his glass by its stem a few times, Jordan belted out an apology. "I'm sorry about all of this, I really am. I don't know what the hell I'm doing." He placed the glass on the floor without taking a sip.

"Then why continue to do it?" Crispin's tone didn't exude anger, only despair.

"Which of my many mistakes are you referring to?"

Crispin's stern, Mount-Rushmore face remained.

Jordan continued, his eyes going to the wine glass instead of Crispin. "Saint Paul was all me. It was stupid to go flying, and I know that. But all the rest…" Jordan's heart begged for a reaction from Crispin, a hint of any sort that might suggest he was still a friend, or at least an ally. But nothing came. "The rest was me trying to do what I thought was right. I understand little of this place, but I know it's wrong to imprison an innocent man for a hundred years." Jordan paused and leaned forward, planting his elbows on his knees. "And before you ask like everyone else, I signed on for Firas because he asked me. It's the right thing to do…I once believed that anyway."

"I can accept your heart's in the right place."

"Doesn't that count for something?"

"If condemning him to that prison cell for eternity is something."

"What the hell am I supposed to do about it now?" Jordan dropped his head against the sofa's backrest and stared up at the ceiling. Embossed patterns flourished their way across the granite overhead. Jordan wanted to swirl away into them.

"Don't go through with it."

Jordan whipped his head back to level. "What?"

"Don't do it."

Crispin remained indifferent, not a trace of emotion.

Jordan stood up, knocking the glass over with his heel. Glancing down, he watched wine flow away like impatient blood. He punted the glass, spraying red-wet fragments across the room.

"How can this be!" He spun toward Crispin. "We're immortal. There should be no suffering, no want; we should be wise and just and honorable. It should all be perfect, but it's not. It's just as corrupt and broken as the place I came from." Jordan paced over to the piano, pressing his closed fist hard against its surface. "After I met you—the real you—I felt I had purpose for once in my life—and I felt it without knowing why you wanted me. I believed you represented something. Something better, something that mattered. You were enlightened, and when you spoke of this world of ours, I believed everyone else in it would be the same. I desperately wanted that. But they're not. They're selfish and afraid. They indulge and look away." Jordan burned an unmerciful stare into Crispin. "And now you're asking me to do the same?"

"I am," Crispin took a sip of wine, "but for different reasons."

"Have you ever talked to Firas? Do you know what this has done to him? He sits there, year after year." Jordan pitched himself back down on the sofa and slouched forward. "What difference would it have made if you tried to hide this? I would have found out."

"It didn't have to be like this."

"It did." The rebuttal came out sharp, wicked. "Sebastién would have come for me. Lila would have come for me. Firas would have called for my help, and I wouldn't have ignored any of them.

I wouldn't have turned my back on those who suffered for being near my predecessor."

"Look into that relic, Jordan."

Jordan glanced at it with disdain. He continued to unload: "Even if what Firas is asking me to do is a mistake, what matters is that he asked me. This injustice stands because each person turned away from the one before them—because they were afraid. They tried to convince themselves it had nothing to do with them and look what's come of it. LOOK what's come of it! I owe it to Firas and my predecessor to try to make this right. Can't you see that?"

Crispin remained unaffected, gesturing to the tarnished green disc on the sofa.

Fine.

Jordan picked it up. With a cross look on his face, he flayed his other hand and reached for the relic, hearing a songbird hum just before he fell into its dreamscape:

Jordan was someone else now.

He was standing and his knees ached. In his right hand he felt a flat object—the relic he'd grasped moments ago back in the real world. The smell was distinct: stale wet air, like a cave. But the scene was dark, cast in a deep blue that emanated from the deveiled hand of a man standing in front of his viewpoint. It was Crispin's hand. Crispin was standing a few feet away. Next to him was a stout man with thick jowls who shifted from one foot to the other as though trying to keep his feet warm. His footwork accelerated as a graylight began to materialize into existence off Crispin's flayed fingers. Like Helena, it emerged from a shroud of inexorable black, outlined in silver shimmering light.

Jordan spied a relic in Crispin's hand. Clutching it tight, Crispin spoke in a firm voice: "Colorum thirty-fifth, eleven seven seventy-two. Dark arbor, north Michigan by faintlight reckoning in the present era. I am Publius Crispus Fluximous, finding Raphael Foscari, Lux Sanguinis, declared murdered in Arbor Florum, Dēfessus fifth, eleven seven sixty-one."

The graylight's face took shape in silvered features. Expressive eyes and sharp facial lines, a slightly mischievous grin perched on his countenance. Looking side to side, he tried to interpret his surroundings as the rest of his body came into being. His outfit struck Jordan as pure Renaissance: a tight, priest-like collar, a track of buttons down the vest, flared at the bottom and at the sleeves. His pants bore a similar style.

"Who is there?" he asked in a cordial tone.

"A friend," said Crispin. "Can you tell me your name?"

"I am Raphael Foscari." He tipped his chin in a polite way before looking about. "Is that you, Firas?"

"I am not Firas. Could you tell me what year it is, Raphael?"

"Eleven seven sixty-one, of course."

"And the day, if you please?"

Raphael's eyes narrowed. "Dēfessus fourth…perhaps the fifth. I'm afraid I've lost track on account of our journey." His expression went flat. His hand flourished as if trying to remember something.

"Where are you now?"

"The narrow lake, just off the shore of Lake Superior."

"Are you traveling alone?"

"I'm with my dearest Elisabeth." Raphael beamed at the mention of her name, but then the proud corners of his mouth sunk. He checked over his shoulder. "You need to leave. We are in danger, I'm afraid, and I do not wish to draw you into it." Raphael reached toward Crispin, his hand moving as if clearing away spider webs.

Crispin stepped backward, Raphael drifted toward him.

The stout man raised his hand, but it remained veiled.

"Strange," said Raphael, "I cannot see you."

"Why are you in danger?" asked Crispin, speaking with exaggerated curiosity. Crispin drew in more light, his hand glowing brighter.

"Supernus and his interfectors are pursuing us." Raphael's mouth became grave. "We had to rest—Firas if that's you, for your own sake, leave."

"I am not Firas," said Crispin.

Raphael furled his brow, and his mouth dropped open a trace. He was thinking, and thinking some more.

"Why are they chasing you?"

Raphael's head jerked as if he were shooing a fly. This caused the stout man to shift on his feet again, his attention anchored to Raphael's dead spectral form.

"If they know you've seen me, they'll come for you too—they're going to kill us. You must stay safe, you must—"

"I promise to remain safe," said Crispin. His flayed hand dimmed, as though Raphael were drawing an unsustainable current. Raphael plucked at the air, causing Crispin and the stout man to back away.

The writer of Jordan's relic stepped back too, his body becoming very tense.

"Have you seen anyone else?" asked Crispin, brightening his hand, trying to stabilize their union.

Raphael considered the question. His plucking hand retracted, coming to a rest at his side. His chin drifted low as though he suddenly lacked the ambition to keep it level. "Supernus Kyzhere was here. His interfectors too…they killed us." Raphael's lip quivered. "I remember it now. Elisabeth and I married in Fiji. We made our way west. We saw the world. But after Lebanon…" Raphael swallowed. The taut qualities in his face slipped away, as if going out of focus.

"Why were you in Leb—" Crispin's light flashed and flared, the instability cutting the question short. Crispin winced and adjusted his light, pulses of blue running tandem with a series of staccato cracks. Crispin steadied it, throwing a sidelong nod to the stout man.

The man nodded back and began to breathe heavily.

Crispin exhaled, not daring to go longer. "Have you seen the light, Raphael?"

Raphael stared into the palm of Crispin's deveiled hand. He blinked in rapid succession. Closing his eyes, he became motionless like a statue. The blue light of Crispin's hand rushed into him.

"Savis ēchūs, my old friend," said Crispin.

A flash of light erupted from inside Raphael, followed by the release of a tiny pinpoint of red light, which floated off. The remnants of Raphael's form, shrouded in Crispin's blue light, flickered away peacefully and vanished.

"You did it, Crispin," said the stout man.

Crispin's light winked out and all went to darkness.

A second later, Jordan's mind came back.

Jordan opened his hand and gazed down at the disc, its presence striking him now as that of a sacred object. "Firas said my predecessor accepted death…but he didn't. He *was* trapped. It was you…it was you that released him."

"Yes, it was me," said Crispin almost whispering.

"All this time you kept it a secret?"

"Yes."

"Why didn't you tell anyone!" Jordan stood up as though hit by a cattle prod, clutching the relic hard. "It proves everything! It proves Firas was there, that he was in danger. Raphael names Supernus as the murderer—Sebastién said noughts don't lie—and both Lila and I harbored near that place, right where our predecessors died. Everything needed to clear Firas and indict Supernus is right here."

Crispin nodded, his eyes measuring Jordan.

Jordan realized his hand was trembling uncontrollably. With eyes locked to Crispin's enigmatic expression, he back-stepped to the sofa, placing the relic on it with care.

"We have to make this public. We have—"

"No," said Crispin. "I would never allow such a thing."

Jordan quaked, his ability to find words slipping away.

"We spent years trying to find your predecessor." Crispin's voice sounded barren now, cold in a way Jordan never experienced before. "We did it because there is something wrong with our understanding of the light, and we need your help to solve it. There's important research the Prudentiarum does—"

"How could it possibly be more important than this?" The moral pedestal Jordan had raised under Crispin was disintegrating. Jordan's blood boiled, sending his attention to the relic on the sofa.

He could grab it and flee.

He could bring it to the others. They'd make it public and end the injustice. Jordan sat down next to the relic. Crispin narrowed his eyes as though having already divined this plot.

"Allow me to continue." Crispin paused. He made no effort to get up and reclaim the relic. "After you left San Francisco, I traveled east and met with Liaidor Kyzhere, emperor of Arbor Castellum. I revealed to him the relic you saw me recording. I told him there is an identical, secondary testimony—my brother's, which is next to you on that sofa. I said that I had found Raphael's successor and that I would bring him into our world under my care as someone dedicated to our research. I vowed to keep him away from anything to do with the past. In return, Firas would be released without ceremony and Supernus would be reined in. All of this, however flawed, would drift away as bygones. This proposal was accepted...that is until you made yourself a news story. By that time, I was traveling to my brother. When I learned what had happened, I returned to Castellum and found the arrangement off the table, and Liaidor in doubt of my claim—that you were under my care."

Jordan sank back into the sofa, his hand moving away from the relic. When he spoke again it was with monumental regret. "You had it all figured out...and we fucked it up."

"Not just yet..."

Jordan's gaze snapped to Crispin.

"My brother is meeting with Liaidor Kyzhere in Arbor Castellum as we speak. He will pledge that I can get you to disengage from this; pledge that you will not escalate hostilities with Supernus. It is a pledge, most importantly, that what we are discussing right now will remain a secret, forever."

"You did this without asking me?"

"There was no time." Crispin leaned forward, resting the base of his wine glass on his knee. "I wagered you would listen to reason."

"Supernus, the murderer, goes free?"

"So does Firas. But this will not be the case should you go into the Depths."

"How can you be so sure? It might be a bluff; they're hoping we'll back down because they were never able to rig it in the first place."

"Do you really believe this?"

Jordan answered in fat silence.

"We combed that dark arbor for years. Though we found Raphael's graylight, there was something we didn't find: his body. Nor did we find Elisabeth's."

Jordan swallowed bitter reality. "There's no way to get to Supernus? You're telling me he's above the law?"

Crispin's face flashed anger. "You fail to understand what you're asking."

"Justice?" said Jordan, as if it was an absurd idea.

"This is as close as we'll get."

"This is *not* justice."

"It is an imperfect one—the same as in the faintlight world. But here, the Kyzheres, including Supernus, are deities in the eyes of Arbor Castellum—even to many here in Arbor Florum. They are gods, Jordan."

"So God should be excused for murder?"

"God, in the exact sense you're using that word, is *always* excused for murder." The tenor of Crispin's voice rose. "It is no different than in the faintlight world. If you shame God before his followers as you did at the Finalis, what do you think will happen?"

Jordan looked away, his mind retrieving the scene at the close of the contest, when the crowd had burst into a frenzy because of his middle-fingered insult to Supernus.

Crispin waited for Jordan's eyes to find him again. "Understand that Liaidor Kyzhere will not indict his son. But we still might free Firas."

Jordan shifted the debate inward, trying to determine if his acidic confrontations with Supernus had driven him beyond the point of reason. He returned, unable to abandon his position. "So this is the way of the world? One gathers fanatics, and that means he's entitled to trample over those who reject his beliefs?"

"To revive your earlier parallel, that's precisely how gods are made. Throughout the entirety of human history, this has been the case. It is an undeniable pattern, not a fluke occurrence. Assailing the icon of devotion will draw the same response here as it does in the faintlight world."

Jordan shook his head.

"You fail to understand what you're involved in. You're standing at the crossroads of a conflict that stretches back centuries. You came here and set fire to our civil accord. This world is held together by a fragile peace—"

"A peace built on depriving Firas his freedom!" Jordan clenched his fists hard, cracking knuckles. "I know enough to know that this is wrong."

"I brought you into our world to help us understand the light," said Crispin, his tone easing down from anger, "not to start a war."

"Start a war?" said Jordan with a cynical tone. "If Supernus is already presumed a murderer, what difference would it make to prove it outright?"

"To prove it would open Supernus to assassination. A single attempt on his life would unchain the wrath of Arbor Castellum." Crispin gripped his cane and leaned on it, causing its business end to groan off the floor. "That would be war."

Jordan searched Crispin's eyes. He saw no bluff.

"Our world is governed by interarboral law." Crispin rested the tip of his cane on his shoe. "Just as the faintlight world has international law, ours has the Interarborals. Just as international law is convoluted, so are the Interarborals. There is something known as the Black Lily Precedent. A perverse legal interpretation advanced by Castellum many years ago to justify the political assassination of one of Arbor Florum's diplomats. Since that day, there is an activism that seeks to employ Black Lily to return the favor, to kill Supernus—"

"There is no activism in Arbor Florum! We've tried, but they're all cowards—"

"There *is* activism," said Crispin regaining the conversation, "but it may not be in Arbor Florum. There is a counterfeit silence where real opposition *should* be." Crispin rapped his cane on the floor, gaining Jordan's full attention. "There is something out there, but it hasn't shown itself yet."

Jordan felt his chest expanding and contracting, roused by the words. The complexity of the variables took focus, only making him feel more trapped on a runaway train. "I can't walk away from Firas, even if it's a mistake." Jordan glanced at the broken glass fragments on the other side of the room. "Don't you understand? It's a trap and I fell for it."

"Yes, it is a trap. But there is a way. A second path. In three days, after the Triduum concludes, you'll appear in front of a tribunal—one here in Arbor Florum, but administered by Castellum. The hearing will conclude with your appointment to Investigator Forensis—the role responsible for searching the Depths. There is no way to avoid this outcome outside of fleeing and becoming a fugitive. If you do, it's only a matter of time before they find you and kill you. But there is a way out."

The words hit Jordan like a snake bite. He tried to repel the idea of abandoning Firas but was already imagining the act.

"The charges against Firas—that he murdered Helena, your predecessor, and Lila's—should make this a concern of Arbor Florum. Our side tried to keep it that way, but the intricate nature of the Interarborals, along with the political will of the Kyzheres, dragged it out of local jurisdiction and made it an interarboral affair. The basis for that transference was the fact that Raphael, your predecessor, had been appointed Forensis under the very same interarboral law."

The connection came to Jordan by way of Sebastién's story. "So he could hunt down Supernus and his Venatorum?"

"That is correct. Parandis Tyrtaphernes, who represents Arbor Florum, will make a series of legal maneuvers. She'll play a game of chess, a sequence designed to lose. Every step will be anticipated, except the last. In the final move, you'll be appointed Forensis by way of the Interarborals, not by Florum law. After that, you need only declare the following…"

Crispin remained silent until Jordan looked him in the eye. When Crispin spoke again, he did so with gravity: "I wish to seek asylum in Arbor Florum under Thiago's Rule."

"That's it?"

"That is it." Crispin pulled his cane in close. "Thiago's Rule is buried deep within the Interarborals. It establishes that the successor of one freelight may be considered the very same person as the predecessor in certain circumstances. This is one of them. All you have to do is invoke it, and Parandis will take care of the rest. The search will not proceed, and we'll have time to pursue more diplomatic paths."

The venom worked fast.

Jordan felt knots of mental tension unbinding, imagining the momentum of the whole affair arrested, stopped dead in its tracks. But still, ramming it all from behind was the guilt: he had made a promise to Firas. His brother. Jordan's mind leaped ahead: "Does this loophole get me out of being transitioned? Or have I already been killed off?"

"I have been able to delay it, but I cannot stop it."

Jordan recalled the evening on the breakwater, fishing with his father. It was the last peaceful moment he'd known. He wanted to undo it all; go back and reclaim that innocence. He wished he hadn't accepted Crispin's invitation out west and the big check that came with it.

The money.

His thinking lurched sideways yet again. He felt ill as Crispin's real intentions came into focus. "All that money you gave me…It wasn't for setting me up out west, was it?" He already saw the answer in Crispin's eyes. "It was for my father. It was for the tragedy of his son's death."

"Yes." Crispin made no attempt to evade. "It is an inadequate act, I concede, but a practical one. Your father would believe you died being successful at what you loved. It's the best gift we can provide, given the circumstances."

Jordan's chin dropped, his eyes slipping to the relic. Its appearance distorted as tears piled onto his lashes. Jordan drifted deeper and farther away. Time became frozen, like a delicate winter stream. For some time—he couldn't determine how long—the silence remained.

Then the moment thawed.

The sound of a cane tapped toward him. He saw Crispin take the relic and return it to the satchel. Jordan stared at him in a daze.

Crispin walked away with it.

He stopped just past the piano and looked over his shoulder. "I will send word of my brother's efforts. There is still a chance, so you *must* disengage from Supernus." Crispin repositioned his cane, preparing to pivot away. "If we fail, remember: Thiago's Rule."

Sadness stung Jordan as he listened to the cane's lethargic rhythm and watched Crispin leave the room. The tapping became ever softer, ever more distant. Then came the whisper of a gentle develing.

After that, there was nothing.

33

WHISPERS IN THE DARK

With his heart ailing in political malaise, Jordan stared at Sebastién's piano for some time after Crispin left, his eyes making meaningless trips across its flank. Sebastién never returned, which gave him restless feet. He deveiled and drifted his way to West Leaf. Reaching the Carmen, he went in on foot. The interfector troupe keeping guard outside and their handler didn't hinder him. He found Mortimer snoring at his desk, Finley near the brink of sleep. But the latter grumbled to his duty and started to record the visit. Firas looked surprised by Jordan's arrival, but quite pleased. With a pair of interfectors off to their sides, Jordan and Firas communed, occupying each other's minds, avoiding topics that pertained to the troubles at hand.

They talked ever onward, Firas sharing distant recollections of traveling to Venice in the 17th century, seeing the spring sea invade San Marco square; how the church and tower would cast perfect reflections off still waters. Jordan spoke of the vibrant hues of autumn's wash in his Midwestern hometown; the crisp sounds and drowsy smell of the woodlands. A world littered in red-yellows, marking the approach of seasonal slumber.

The deep of night grew deeper as they traded stories, their faces observant like that of the interfectors, but trafficking in goodwill and a mutual longing that this should all be taking place under different circumstances.

Quite late into their conversations, a genuine smile crept into Firas's face, the first Jordan had ever seen. Firas cocked his head to the side and wagged his chin toward Finley.

Jordan looked.

Finley was canted forward with eyes closed, chin down, mouth agape. He was asleep and about to snore. The metallum in his recording hand had slipped free. It rested on his lap, just beyond the reach of his fingers. Jordan looked back to Firas, finding his smile still intact. It was a gesture Jordan returned, their exchange suspended in time long enough to kindle a sense of brotherhood.

But Firas's smile went away.

Slowly he leaned forward, his hands grasping the prison bars with a delicate touch. Jordan, out of mimicry, leaned toward him. With their faces inches apart, Jordan saw a deep desperation in his eyes. When Firas spoke, it came out in whispers:

"Brother, do not forsake me, for I carry a great secret. But it is not yet time." Firas released the bars and leaned away, receding like a glacier. From the depths of his cell, silent and serene like the Buddha, Firas looked at Jordan as though looking through him, as if he wasn't even there.

Jordan, for his part, felt a sea change in his beliefs yet again.

PART THREE

A PRACTICAL PICASSO

We are destined to become but memories to one another,
echoes that cross ever-wider spaces until at last,
we are whispers lost on the wind.

—Sofia Lyridell

from "Lyridell Reflects on the Origins of Savis Echūs"
Nivōsus 40, 11743 ‡ January 9, 1872 Gregorian

34

DELIBERATIONS

The deveiled forms of Sebastién, Easton, and Lila darted about Jordan in the open air above the rehearsal hall stage. Though Jordan still relied on his eyes, he'd grown confident in using feel to track opponents beyond the range of sight. These capabilities allowed his mind to drift during mock combat, and this time it did so in epic fashion, landing him in a binary thought loop. He replayed his conversations with Crispin and Firas from the night prior, their words forging ying-yang allegiances in his head.

During a moment of gross inattention, Jordan found himself locked in a drain perpetrated by Sebastién and Lila. A moment later, he was flat on the curtains. A headache thumped away while the trio of trainers veiled in front of him. Jordan slipped off the pile and stood before the conclave of dissatisfied instructors. Lila and Easton granted him consideration by looking away, but Sebastién glared straight-on.

"Where's your head at?" snapped Sebastién. "This is going down in days, and you need to be a hell of a lot sharper than this." Easton seized Sebastién's animated hand, pulling it down. But he freed it with a snap of the wrist. "The search is a lost cause, Jordan. Nothing's going to shake the public up enough to care about us. We're not going to get an injunction, which means you're going to have to go through with this. Which means you have to survive the Depths—and where the hell were you last night?"

"I went to see Firas." Jordan maintained his composure.

Sebastién paused and chortled, not expecting that answer. "And here I thought Crispin dragged you straight off to the Prude. What did he have to say?"

"Crispin or Firas?"

"Both." Sebastién crossed his arms.

Jordan observed three sets of attentive eyes on him. "Firas and I talked about our lives before all this. We talked about everything *but* this." Jordan recalled Firas's haunted face at the end and his claim of a secret.

"And Crispin…," said Sebastién.

Jordan's mind switched tracks. "He told me about the Black Lily Precedent." He waited for a reaction from Sebastién but got nothing. "If Helena had worked out, Supernus would have become a target for murder. You failed to mention that."

"I failed to mention it because it's impossible." Sebastién rapped his shoe tip on the stage a few times. "Nobody can carry out Black Lily, Jordan. Nobody's going to get near Supernus with his fects around—think about what you saw at the Finalis. Helena's testimony was for the courts, for leverage, for political pressure; That was *always* what we were going after."

Lila entered the fray with a burst of agitation. "What about the others?"

"What others, Lila?" Sebastién's eyes flashed to her.

"Those who didn't have the luxury of being locked up like Firas." She stepped in front of Sebastién. "My predecessor, Jordan's predecessor, Helena, and how many others among the dead? When does Supernus pay for what he's done?"

"He doesn't!" Sebastién's nostrils flared as he towered over Lila. "He's beyond reach. Accept it."

While Sebastién and Lila cooled, Jordan's mind churned over Crispin's secret relic and its implications.

"What else did Crispin say?" asked Lila, looking to Jordan.

Three sets of owl eyes on him again. "The same as everyone else. That this is all a big mistake."

"Is there more?" asked Sebastién, walking a suspicious half-circle around him. "Or is that all you're going to tell us?"

"That's all I'm going to tell you."

Frustration rippled back into Sebastién, who tapped fingers against forearm as though repeating the question by telegraph.

"If I decide that's all I'm going to share, then that's it." Jordan fought to keep his tone in check. He struggled even harder to keep Crispin's secret from leaking out of his mouth.

"Fine," said Sebastién.

"You have to focus," said Easton, stepping forward as if to derail Sebastién's temper. "You need a lot of improvement before you go down there."

The vote of no-confidence shook Jordan. Treason ripped to the surface like an oil strike, and Jordan failed to cap it. "The thing is, there's a way out."

The rehearsal hall went church silent.

"There's a loophole." Jordan watched their eyes grow optimistic. "That's what Crispin came to tell me. I'll be appointed to the investigator role no matter what, but if I declare I'm seeking asylum under something called Thiago's Rule, it all comes to a stop."

"Well, I'll be damned." Sebastién's voice carried the same enthusiasm present in all their faces.

They looked happy. They meant to betray Firas, and it broke Jordan's heart.

Firas would never be free.

"If Flux knows it, it must be legit," continued Sebastién.

"There's someone who represents Florum," said Jordan. "She's named…Panda—something like that."

"Parandis." Easton traded a whiplash glance with Sebastién.

"Right." Jordan saw that all three of them were miles down Treason Street. "She'll go through the motions. Then it's up to me to play the asylum card."

"Then you have to do it." Lila pursed her lips after the words zipped out. "It's our best chance. I know it means we're letting Firas down, but it means we live to fight another day—it means *you* live, literally. We'll have more time to change minds—Firas would understand."

"I'm not so sure about that." Jordan felt it all coming up now. "There's something else, something Firas said…"

Keen eyes and silence again.

"Firas said he had a secret—but it wasn't the right time."

Winces and heads shaking *no*.

"Finley had fallen asleep," continued Jordan, "he let go of his relic, so it was a private moment."

"Jordan, listen to me." Sebastién came in close. "Firas is desperate. He spins fantasy. He removes himself from bad circumstances by imagining better ones. It preserves his sanity—and who can blame him? I'd do the same if it were me."

"He's still insisting I come see him, just before I go down there."

"Which makes this all the more reckless." Sebastién poked at Jordan's chest with his index finger. "Because now his fantasy has its claws in you too."

Jordan turned away and stared down at the battle-pocked curtains. Silence ate the auditorium again.

Fantasy.

The word carried Jordan back to his conversation with Maggie a lifetime ago. He recognized the common thread: fantasy carried him through much of his own life; fantasy didn't need the safe harbor of well-established facts—in fact, it thrived despite them. It was comprised of articles of faith, nurtured and kept alive by a confederacy of strangers in the best of cases, or by intense personal devotion in the worst. In this way, he could excuse Firas's indulgence. He understood the desire to forge an imaginary world beyond that prison cell.

A place where he was free.

Sebastién broke the silence. "If we have a way out, we have to take it."

"But *are* the bodies really down there?" Jordan turned and stared at Sebastién again, whose arms went to his sides defensively. "Do we know it? This happened over a hundred years ago."

"It's the Kyzheres," said Sebastién. "So, yes…"

"There was something in Firas's eyes; the way he said it—"

"Jordan!" shouted Sebastién, moving in point-blank. "We've been through this. Once the Depths is recorded and the bones collected, your search partner's going to try to fog you and leave you down there. You're going to have to beat the seduction and break for the exit. He'll have no choice but to follow you out to save his own life. That's the ONLY way you're coming out of there alive. But you haven't beaten Easton yet, let alone—"

"What if we're wrong about Firas?" Jordan caught Sebastién by the wrist when his hand came up out of frustration.

"ENOUGH!" Sebastién tore free of Jordan's grasp. The word bounced across the rehearsal hall. Sebastién snapped his suit coat sleeve straight and returned to within a nose of Jordan. "I already have Firas's life on my conscience. I'm not going to add your death to it too." Sebastién's cold blue eyes gave Jordan no room to negotiate. "We have a way out…"

Jordan ground his teeth.

"…and we're going to take it."

Sebastién and Jordan leveled stares like prize-fighters until Lila and Easton separated them.

As tempers faded, Jordan watched wild hope return to their eyes. They'd already decided. Silently, unanimously. They didn't believe he could survive the Depths. They didn't believe in Firas. Jordan backed away and sat down on the curtains.

The remnants of his anger congealed into a depressive ballast. As much as Jordan wanted to condemn them for deciding on the escape route, he found he couldn't. He was the one that brought it up. And he did it because he also doubted Firas. It stretched back to the night of Liwei's party and Supernus's claim that they had already lost.

Jordan stared at the stage, unable to meet their eyes. "How did it ever come to this? A whole civilization on its knees before the so-called gods of Arbor Castellum." Jordan batted a glance at Lila. "Crispin claimed they're seen this way. Is it true?"

"It's true," said Lila.

"Wouldn't the freelight immortality thing give people time to weed out such bullshit?"

"Do you find the human mind grows more open with age?" said Sebastién. "It adopts beliefs, and beliefs become petrified. Faintlights live just long enough to realize they've been duped into a great many things. By then there's little to do but ride it out—anything to avoid looking in the mirror. Anything to avoid accepting you've been made a pawn."

"That's faintlight. What about us?"

Sebastién took a breath. "With the Kyzheres and Arbor Castellum, it's a unique set of circumstances. Let me explain it like this: consider Easton's charm for a moment. Remember how she had you singing— badly, I might add?"

Jordan cringed at the memory but managed a nod.

"Now imagine that charm being practiced continuously throughout a civilization of thousands. Every citizen dutifully keeping the other in check, reaffirming the pathology that Liaidor Kyzhere and his five sons are deities. Imagine an incestuous, self-reinforcing river of fealty, one that originates from and flows back to Liaidor Kyzhere. *That* is how this bullshit is maintained."

Jordan's posture sank.

"This gives me an idea." Sebastién straightened his cuffs. "Since we've all had enough fighting for one day, and it's getting late, and it's New Year's Eve…"

Jordan immediately recalled Liwei's party and the Finalis.

"What do you have in mind?" Lila's tone seemed to indicate the same vein of concern. Easton also looked nervous.

"Fear not, it'll be the quietest place in all of Arbor Florum. Consider it a field trip. A history lesson. A story about an enigmatic man of low station named Liaidor Kyzhere and how he came to rule the freelight world."

35

THE DOMINUS STELLARUM

The four of them departed through the rehearsal hall's backstage, avoiding the celebrations in East Grey. Coasting above it all, they glided over rooftops with the aqueduct channels at their sides. Through the canopy of cherry trees, Jordan stole glimpses of the street scene below. Crowds snaked through it like Mardi Gras. When he spied Sebastién's face, he knew at once the Frenchman wanted to be down there.

They passed out of East Grey and into Aria, where the Arborsolis simmered deep blue above the timekeeping rings. Bending into North Grey, they maintained a high altitude, descending only upon reaching the end of North Leaf at the passage Jordan likened to a subway tunnel. Lower, close to the action now, jubilant faces and a sea of raised hands flitted by. The gatherings swayed to street music. Jordan caught the closing refrain of The Beatles' "Hey Jude" just before the crowd thinned. A sharp left turn later, they were beyond the merriment. Quiet again, gliding above a dim street lit like a Victorian London night.

Patterns of repeating architecture—spanning four stories—went by on both sides, suggesting the mouth of a large, *U*-shaped building. At its heart, a few hundred feet ahead, rose an immense colonnade. A series of large white pillars that reminded Jordan of the Roman Pantheon. Above them ran a façade with the words *CURIA PRUDENTIARUM* carved in bold letters. Sebastién led them above that regal letter-work, through an open archway, and into a large room. Jordan glimpsed a communal workspace, littered with desks and chairs. The room went dark when they veiled, the objects announcing themselves now only by way of black geometry.

"Your desk, Mr. Wakefield, would have been somewhere here had Crispin had his way." Sebastién traversed the office, humming Beethoven's *Ode to Joy*.

The three of them followed Sebastién, who moved through an archway that leaked blue light.

Sebastién spoke:

"It is said that Arbor Castellum was born the day Liaidor Kyzhere came to Arbor Florum in the faintlight year of nine-fifteen. Liaidor's eyes burned with envy upon witnessing the house Crispin had built. In those fires was forged the desire that one day he would have a place like it of his very own. Those who repeat this anecdote, however, do so in hindsight. At the time, no one recognized Liaidor's ambitions, nor imagined the schemes he would enact over the course of centuries."

After a series of turns, they entered a slender hall. On one side ran intricate, numbered doors, interspersed by paintings. On the other, a long balustrade, beyond which—and several floors down—ran a vast array of tables and chairs; a reading room bathed in dim blue from above. Sebastién marched onward, his pace matching the cadence of the story.

"At the outset, Liaidor realized he'd be king of an empty kingdom. For those in Arbor Florum had no particular want of a king, nor need of another Arbor Florum. Liaidor's own timbre, known as Lux Eros in those times, was small in number and scattered across medieval Europe. Arbor Florum already had its founding father—the esteemed Publius Crispus Fluximous—and that man's chronic disinterest in power only increased his station as its unofficial sovereign. Liaidor, on the other hand, was enticed by the possession of power, a vice he guarded carefully for centuries. Though talented in mind, tongue, and timbre, Liaidor knew he couldn't achieve the patrician stature of Flux and Florum's cofounders. He participated in Florum's politics nonetheless, a sharp, dedicated civil servant, gaining notoriety for two things."

Sebastién waved an orange deveiled finger in front of Jordan, winning his curiosity away from a painting of North Leaf's thoroughfare.

"The first was his civic vitality, which was unmatched. Always at work, always deep in thought. The second was his background story. It's here we should note—and Easton can regale you for hours in this matter—that Lux Eros—those of pink or purple light—define their identity through folklore."

Sebastién winked at Easton.

"Liaidor Kyzhere presented a most remarkable tale in this respect, one telegraphed by his very name: that he was the son of Julius Caesar. A bastard son, but his son nonetheless. Sired during the conquest of his mother's homeland of Britannia."

"Is it true?" asked Jordan, an attentive expression on his face.

"Nobody knows." Sebastién relayed an uneasy smile. "But everyone has that same reaction. It's quite memorable, yes? Regal, yet humble; both pitiable and powerful at the same time." Sebastién tugged his suit straight and continued. "So onward went Liaidor Kyzhere, the busy bee of the Grey City. Dedicated to his station, brilliant in political thought, and unselfish in his plan for the greater freelight world. Of course, it wasn't until much later they realized how terribly wrong they were on that last one."

A right turn, another hallway. This one loomed taller and wider. It stretched for such a great distance that Jordan felt he was gazing down a highway tunnel. A tiny square of intense blue light marked the endpoint. On both sides, spaced at generous intervals, ran works of art. The exhibit spanned the entire length of the hall, each piece lit from below by small tufts of greenery planted in bronze flowerboxes.

"What's down there?" asked Jordan, transfixed by the bright blue square of light.

"The Firmament," said Sebastién, "but this part is called Visirdaram's Hall." With palms extended like a curator, he turned a leisurely circle while walking. "The works of one of your predecessors, Sophronia, is just ahead. There's an interesting history attached to it. In the early years of building the Grey City, the artisans lost heart. The grand dig was almost abandoned but—"

"She brought the vision to life through her paintings and re-inspired the effort." Jordan spoke with absent-mindedness, mesmerized by the blue light at the end of the passage. "Liwei told me about this."

"Very good." Sebastién halted and pointed, compelling the others to stop. Off his indicating hand was a painting of Aria from an elevated position. In it, the Arborsolis cast a bright yellow light over a crowd milling about, dressed like citizens of Rome. Jordan studied the painting's earthly palette, which even the blue illumination couldn't suppress. It was dominated by yellows and browns—beautifully composed, but cracked by the relentless tick of time.

Sebastién stepped to the opposite side of the hall, directing Jordan's attention to an empty exhibit space. "Sophronia's most controversial work is right here."

"Not funny," said Easton.

"How so, my dear?"

"I don't get it." Jordan eyed the blank wall. "What was there?"

"A painting, of course." Sebastién crossed his arms. "A subject you've depicted yourself, Jordan. Though not exquisitely as what I saw back in your loft. They took it down around the time the term *death echo* was coined."

"It wasn't taken down," said Easton with the tone of a reprimand.

"How do you mean?" asked Sebastién.

"It was stolen," said Lila. She resumed walking, moving ahead of the three of them, toward the blue gateway.

"Well I'll be damned. Second time in one night," said Sebastién. "I didn't know."

"Before your time," said Easton.

They continued, Lila still several paces ahead. The vibrant blue at the end of the passage grew closer. It was a gateway to some strange beyond. Lila deveiled and glided away, passing through it. Then Easton. Sebastién deveiled and zipped ahead, pausing at the threshold. He looked back at Jordan and smiled. "Come see Elysium."

Jordan deveiled as Sebastién flew off to join the others. With curiosity in high gear, Jordan zipped after them and passed into the blue world.

It was a spherical space, hundreds of feet across—as wide as one of Florum's leafs, immense in a way that invited airplanes to glide loops in its keep. Jordan's eyes were drawn to the center of the sphere, where a dense knot of greenery was speckled with countless pinpoints of blue light. It was suspended in the exact center of the room, skewered in place by a stout granite column that ran from bottom to top, threadlike vinery curling around it. An elongated enclosure encircled this twinkling mass, its appearance curved and feminine in contour—a flower's stigma to Jordan's eyes.

Lila, a tiny green silhouette at this distance, was sailing to it. She landed on the stigma, its size making her appear as a minuscule green insect. A moment later, a stream of bright yellow raced up the vines wrapping the support column. Ribbons of light erupted from the stigma, as though it were being peeled open to reveal the sun. The radiance caused Jordan to turn away, toward the gateway where they'd come in. With the interior space now lit in daylight, he saw a familiar shape: the California coast. Jordan drifted back, watching California shrink into the embrace of the western United States.

The spherical room was an enormous globe, turned inside out. Jordan studied the vast canvas. Lila arrived at his side. The light she had dialed up illuminated a precise ovoid section of the world, to the left of California, across the Pacific Ocean, and into Asia.

"The cupola controls the light." Lila pointed past Jordan's open-mouth gaze. "It replicates the boundaries of sunlight on the earth at this very moment."

"Now, on with our story," said Sebastién, gliding in front of them and then off toward the California interior. Lila followed, with Easton already camped out at touching distance to the map surface. When

Jordan arrived he was astonished to discover the features were not merely painted, but modeled in three dimensions: the Florum valley a meandering trench the length of a human hand; the mountain range east of it a series of wrinkled contours, with a skull-shaped lake beyond that. The entire world had been replicated in this fashion.

Sebastién extended an orange-flare finger to a thumb-sized El Capitan. "This is home."

A golden pin was driven into the surface, securing an array of tight wires—greens, oranges, blues, and purples. They ran like harp strings in every direction. Most toward the north, east, and west. A sparse few ran south.

Sebastién continued: "How our timbres came into being is not well known—even today we have a limited understanding of it. What we knew at the time was that we numbered a few thousand. By the dawn of the eleventh century, we stumbled upon the power to split our timbre and create new unharbored light. Twining, as it came to be known."

Easton drifted toward Sebastién and turned her palm upward. Lazy pink light reached up from her hand like smoke leaving a chimney. The light intertwined with Sebastién's orange finger, giving the appearance of illuminated strands of fire dancing together. They pulled their hands free, and the filaments of light separated, each snapping back to its respective owner.

"We knew that Lux Naturalis could do this," said Sebastién. "That's how the Arborsolis was harbored, after all; a lesson that survived our ancient times, and fortunately so, or Arbor Florum would never have been possible. But it wasn't known that other timbres could do it. Once we did, our world grew." Sebastién coasted away, waving the rest of them on. The scope of the map widened until Jordan could see the upper half of North America.

"The Prudentiarum's research into the light deepened, and Crispin's attention shifted away from the affairs of Arbor Florum. During that time, Liaidor's influence grew. This had been happening at a glacial pace, mind you. It was the suspicious eyes of his peers—themselves enamored of power—that became troubled by his ambition. Liaidor began to preach a vision beyond Arbor Florum; a constellation of arbors established in faintlight ancestral homelands. He went so far as to propose that our life's duty may be to convert the entire faintlight world to freelight through twining. That someday, we would *all* live together in Elysium instead of beneath it."

"Controversial, to say the least," said Easton, zipping past Jordan as a pink flash.

Sebastién waved his hand in the air as though conducting music. "But it was all a ruse, you see. The controversy of meddling in the faintlight world camouflaged Liaidor's real goal." Sebastién pointed across the interior wall toward Western China, where a focused beam of light lit the continent. "It started in East Asia, much at Liaidor's encouragement. Emeishan was a site from our ancient history. A dark arbor, a cave system without an Arborsolis and, at the time, meager in size. Its transformation took place around the time of the Song Dynasty. Liaidor's sons emerged during this era, Supernus first among them. They took up residence in the Grey City like most others. With them came rumors that Lux Eros was growing astronomically."

Easton glided up. "Busy rabbits, we were. And the reason it went unnoticed was that our activities were confined to Europe, much by plan. As it proceeded, Liaidor began to refer to that part of the world as *New Elysium*. Detractors criticized our timbre's expansion as reckless—that we would soon outnumber the stars. Liaidor responded by embracing this critique as virtue. He cast off our traditional names and declared our timbres to be Lux Stellarum, himself the Dominus Stellarum—the Lord of the Starlight."

Sebastién flew a figure-eight around Jordan and Lila. "It was here, as you might imagine, that Liaidor's ambitions became quite clear. The attention of the freelight world was in Asia on Emeishan, yet the real story was taking place in Liaidor's so-called New Elysium." Sebastién moved toward continental Europe, which slumbered in an unlit portion of the globe. Jordan followed, watching the United

States pass by, including Upper Michigan. He spotted a tiny metallic pin near his hometown with an orange wire running through it.

"The dark arbor where our predecessors were killed," said Lila, gliding next to him. They flew together, crossing the massive mapscape in casual pursuit of Sebastién and Easton. Despite the ominous story unfolding, the scene before Jordan was surreal, intoxicating. It plucked his thinking clean away from its faintlight foundation. They were underground, yet traversing the heavens. They were caretakers of this world, its far-flung wardens. They were firebirds of a granite stellar sphere.

Moments later, they arrived next to Sebastién, who was looking at the sprawling shape of the European continent, where a great number of wires converged in the Alps.

Sebastién stared into the jagged lines of the mountains as if mining their histories. "Europe was embroiled in the crusades at this time. Its emerging aristocracies were littered with freelight masquerading as faintlight, manipulating their way into luxury. Sightings of ghosts and demons and angels, and every manner of ethereal being reached a fevered pitch, making it clear that one day, we'd be found out. The faintlights' wary eyes for the unnatural wouldn't vanish from the face of the earth until we did. These circumstances demanded a place like Arbor Castellum long before its name was uttered. When it was, there was little resistance. It was all a matter of practicality, set into urgent motion. And so, Liaidor would have his kingdom after all, its inhabitants destined to greatly outnumber the rest of the freelight world. Yet even this was not Liaidor's masterstroke. That was yet to come."

Jordan gazed at the map features, dumbfounded by the amount of effort this must have required. It was a testament to a different way of thinking. It reached far beyond the faintlight mind, which in itself was a weak engine, destined to operate in terms of a half-century at best—a mere lifetime. Here, such an interval could have been consumed on mere details of this globe. It was extraordinary, nearly immortal. Yet some part of Jordan warned him it was all not meant to last.

Sebastién's voice again. "Away from all the excitement, was that quiet, cerebral world of the Prudentiarum. Within its walls—the very ones around us—concerns about our place in the faintlight world continued to grow. They posited that there would come a time when freelight anonymity would be impossible. A painting could capture a face for eternity or centuries at least. It would make reentry into the faintlight world a risky proposition. The printing press, its books, and the expansion of literacy made intermingling even more tenuous. Maritime advancements increased interaction between nations and shrank the world, leading to the so-called discovery of the Americas.

"The Prudentiarum proposed an idea long ago to address this. A simple principle: bring the freelight world underground. Under the Prude's guidance, however, this remained mere principle; a toothless mandate, an exercise in wishful thinking. It was Liaidor and his loyalists who brought it to fruition. They were successful because they were willing to do what the philosophically gentle Prudes would not. They would employ force, lethal amounts of it if necessary. The plan was scandalous, but Liaidor wielded considerable power by then. So this too came to pass, and the groups of freelight granted this new authority were given a name."

The word floated out of Jordan's mouth: "Venatorum."

"Yes. Those predisposed toward the fighting arts. Lux Solis—inhibitors as they're called respectfully, interfectors to the rest of us. Most originated in Asia, and thus felt a loyalty to Liaidor. It was he, after all, who birthed the Eastern Arbor of Emeishan, making it a peer to Arbor Florum. This was, of course, all part of the plan, but what could be done now? These solidarities had been nurtured. They were ripe and ready for the plucking. Cooperation came readily. Lux Solis were gifted outright to the Venatorum. Through indoctrination, they were made interfectors. Despite their bodies being trained by one of their own, their minds were engineered by Lux Stellarum. Programmed to be loyal; instilled with an unapologetic, intoxicating sense of devotion."

"This is why they never speak, isn't it?" asked Jordan.

"Their minds have been polished away," said Sebastién. "Duty is all that remains. They act on a narrow set of directives, ones the

Kyzheres feed into them like a machine. Programmed by gods, and just as lethal. With that, it was complete. The interfectors had been made loyal to the Venatorum, and the Venatorum to Liaidor Kyzhere. In this way, Liaidor claimed the mantle of the Dominus Stellarum, his five sons at his side."

An understanding coalesced in Jordan's mind like black clouds climbing the horizon: the absurdities of Firas's imprisonment; Florum's pathological deference to Supernus; the ever-present interfectors and the snared political system. All of it painted a picture that Jordan had only prior seen by its edges. Even Crispin's secret diplomacy seemed folly now. There would be no negotiation with them. The Kyzheres were driven to possess the commons for their own. They'd mar the world with their jealousy, they'd push roadways into precious antiquity, trying to seize its heart.

"I told you how this story ends the day you came here." Sebastién's voice was far less enthusiastic now. "A necessary evil leads to an exclusive one. Quite predictably, it produces a counter-reaction. By the time the American Civil War was drawing to a close, we were trying to end one of our own. After years of diplomacy, the Venatorum were disbanded, the official termination observed on the day your predecessor and the Devikira brought Supernus down. The dénouement, two years later, was an act of revenge—the murder of your predecessor and Lila's."

Jordan felt neck-deep in a lethal thicket. "And Supernus has four siblings just like this?"

"Only three remain," said Sebastién.

"One less, at least," said Jordan.

"Unfortunately, he was the good one," said Sebastién. "Paris Kyzhere, the youngest. Easton is a descendant of his line."

Easton floated in close to Jordan. "He's in exile, according to the official story. The real one is that he's dead, murdered just after your predecessor, murdered by the same person." Easton's face glowed dismay under its pink light. "It was a practical assassination. Paris's numbers were too small, his arbor too sparsely populated. Supernus, on the other hand, had the largest lineage, and his arbor was never completed. It's dark to this day."

Lila interjected: "Supernus needed the space."

In a sad haze, Easton drifted away toward the Middle East. Jordan's eyes followed her. Curiosity carried his attention beyond her pink presence to the Black Sea. From its eastern shore, a massive array of metallic markers fanned outward in every direction. Wires ran to locations in the Middle East, Russia, Eastern Europe and Western Asia, as if marking the epicenter of an earthquake.

Jordan moved to get a better look. "What arbor is that?"

"It isn't one," said Lila, arriving at his side. "That's the garden. Where freelight history began, eleven thousand, eight hundred eighty-nine years ago."

"It's also the story told in the Donum Novissimum," said Sebastién gliding up to join them, "the opera tomorrow night. I suspect it's going to be a rather—"

"The opera!" shouted Jordan, collecting everyone's attention. He looked to Lila while his hands attempted to straighten his deviled clothes to no avail. Lila took on a deer-in-the-headlights expression, but it was too late for Jordan to turn back. "Do you want to go to the opera…together?"

The question lifted Easton clear out of her glum reflections, causing her to smirk. Sebastién trickled out laughter. All eyes went to Lila, who wore a restrained expression. But her eyes smiled at Jordan like the morning they met on the bluffs. "How can I say no to that?" she said.

Easton broke into a full grin.

"Splendid," said Sebastién looking Jordan over. "We *are* going to have to do something about what you're wearing, of course. But don't worry, I know a guy."

36

THE NETHER DOVE

The next night, Jordan sprinted down South Leaf trying to reach the opera house on time. Despite his hustle, the spectacle of the structure stopped him dead in his tracks. Set into the end-face of South Leaf, it featured paired columns, supporting arches of impossible detail, and exquisite tapestries painted vibrant blue by Arborsolis light. Jordan shook off the awe and ran again, bursting through the first set of doors he could find.

The grand lobby was nearly empty. A lone usher, startled by his arrival, looked him over with amusement before his expression slipped into something rather cold. He snapped at Jordan to follow without ever asking who he was. Straightening the tuxedo and wiping sweat from his wrists, Jordan trailed him, traversing long halls and elegant staircases, each expanse adorned with runs of petite purple flowers, emitting nighttime blue.

They came to a stop midway along a series of gold-trimmed doors. With his chin directed at the floor, the usher's eyes flicked up to Jordan, disapproval beaming out of them like twin lighthouses. "Miss Lila Harper awaits." The usher straightened his posture, his chin now high and haughty. He grasped the door handle but paused. "This Firas matter…you think this is a good idea?"

It was the last thing Jordan wanted to deal with tonight. He stepped closer, but the usher didn't open the door. Jordan met his gaze at close proximity. "Firas asked for my help. I gave him my word."

"And *this* makes it wise?" The usher raised his eyebrows. "Because of *you*, there is an interfector here tonight. In the Asterhaus." The words came off the man's tongue like venom. "In the name of security."

Jordan maintained the staring contest, while doubts circled his conscience like ravens. The usher finally relented and opened the door, letting him pass inside.

Lila was sitting in one of the two seats within the cozy loge box. With her back to him, she was poised and attentive, her eyes sweeping the auditorium. Her fingers poked at her hair, which was done up in an intricately woven bun. She turned quickly, and then back, the sequence suggesting she'd been repeating the pattern for some time. Realizing he was there, she whipped around again bearing a smile and rose to greet him.

She was wearing a deep blue dress that wrapped her figure aggressively, blooming outward at mid-thigh like an inverted flower. Her electric presence washed Jordan's troubles away; gone was the irritating usher, gone were the tribulations of Firas and the Depths, gone was Arbor Florum itself. They were in Europe now—Italy perhaps—on a date, flown in by private jet. The fantasy came alive. A fully plausible escape that Jordan embraced without hesitation.

"Spectacular…" said Jordan, breathing the word out.

"The opera house?" Lila glanced behind herself, "or the—"

"You," said Jordan, regaining his composure.

The word amplified her grin. Gone was the darkness that haunted her recent days. Jordan moved to his seat. He waited for her to sit before doing the same.

"Thank you." Lila resumed her sprightly poise, which suggested the same escapist trappings.

"Sorry I'm late. Sebastién's tailor is a bit meticulous. I had to make a run for it by the time he let me out. I forgot I was wearing this thing. I almost deviled and vaporized it, like at Liwei's."

"But you didn't," said Lila with reassurance. "For a moment I thought you were scared off by the fine arts."

"And I thought you might stand me up, me being such a young soul and all."

Lila held his gaze. "I guess you reminded me I once had a young soul too."

Jordan took the compliment to heart. He leaned back into his seat and crossed his arms behind his neck. "Well, I'm ready for this space opera. It's going to be in Latin, isn't it?"

"Well yes," Lila leaned toward him as if to impart a secret. "At the risk of breaking etiquette, I'll whisper you through it."

After they released each other's gaze, Jordan looked out into the Asterhaus, which further reinforced his European fantasy. An elegant venue wrapped in dark, warm woods, leaving not a trace of stone. Generous swoops of red tapestry with golden braids adorned the front of each viewing box. It was a cozy venue, smaller than what Jordan expected, but logical when considering it from a classical, pre-electric sense of design. The house lighting, as anticipated, consisted of illuminated foliage confined to metal cones like the rehearsal hall. Dim freelight hovered next to the installations, manning them like battlements.

On the other side of the house, toward the front of the stage, hovered a dim interfector, positioned in front of a loge box. His yellow light drew regular attention. Behind the interfector sat a man with a pink-flayed hand, talking to another well-dressed man, who Jordan took to be a Castellum dignitary of some sort.

Jordan frowned.

"Let's not let it ruin the night." Lila drew his chin away with a gentle finger. They smiled at each other while soft, polite conversation floated up from the crowd; an ambiance more cultured and congenial than at the Campus Finalis.

From the stage, the sound of a single violin rose against the genteel chatter. The rest of the orchestra joined it, the myriad instruments all calling out the same note, each adding character. The effect was beautiful, nudging Jordan to recall Eli's explanation of timbre. After the rich drone faded, an orange freelight zipped out far above the stage, drawing applause. Jordan recognized it as Sebastién, who flew in spirited loops, curling his fiery form through the air like a ribbon in the wind. Wide smiles and polite laughter followed Sebastién to the conductor's pulpit in the orchestra pit. He veiled. Soon after came another freelight, this one the shade of a sandy beach. He coasted to the front of the stage and grew bright. He addressed the crowd in vox:

"Florumites and friends, citizens and travelers," he said, his voice echoing pleasantly about the house. "Welcome to tonight's performance of the Donum Novissimum. We recognize our crossing into the new year—our eleven thousand eight hundred and ninetieth." He raised his palms, eliciting a wave of applause. "The Donum is the story of our journey from ancient past to near present. It is a story of making homes and losing them. It is a story of the light and a pursuing darkness. It begins with a tree and ends with a tree. It is…" The sandy-hued freelight bowed in midair to a wave of applause and, quite unexpectedly, changed color to a deep blue, "…the story of us."

"Whoa," said Jordan, his eyes following the now-blue freelight, who flew flourishes like Sebastién and departed stage left. Jordan was about to nudge Lila when she spoke preemptively:

"Lux Naturalis. They can mimic a hue, but not its talents."

The house lights went down, leaving a bedtime glow about the rim of the orchestra pit. Sebastién raised his arms, a white baton in hand. With elegant movement, he drew life from the orchestra, issuing a gentle melody that wandered over a pulse of deep strings. It moved at the pace of a lightly galloping horse. The curtains drew wide to reveal a painted background: a starlit night. The black silhouette of a tree was stationed at the center of the stage, a prop like at the Finalis, but far more detailed here.

As the higher strings and wind instruments joined in, streams of blue light trickled up from the base of the prop tree, wrapping its branches, making it look like a small Arborsolis. The body of the music and light of the tree grew to fullness together, the treelight illuminating the stage and pushing its glow into the audience. Jordan noticed that the effect was produced by the deveiled hands of a performer who hid behind it. Her fingers split into vibrant streamers, each flowing out to remarkable lengths, tracing the branches with intimate proximity to produce the illusion.

"The Garden," whispered Lila, leaning into Jordan. "The place on the shore of the Black Sea."

Jordan found himself distracted by her proximity. With faces forward, her whisperings brought their cheeks close together, brushing in a way that didn't seem accidental.

Deveiled vocalists arrived next, singing in vox. Their performance was perfectly attuned to the orchestra's force, neither drowning in it, nor surpassing it. Finally, came the dancers; some veiled and circling the prop-Arborsolis in dexterous frolic; others deveiled, stretching their bodies into long streams, gliding in a way that matched the mood of the song. At center stage was the lead, the one who had addressed the crowd. He was blue again and flew in nimble paths. Jordan tracked the faux-blue freelight while the enigmatic Latin verse of the vocalists unfolded in warm harmony. Pleasant melodies persisted for some time.

Then the orchestral temperament shifted.

A disconcerting theme arrived. With it, a figure garbed in a tattered black cloak at the far side of the stage. This person moved, one slow step at a time, toward the tree. Those in its path deveiled and fled, seeking refuge over the audience. From there they eyed the dark figure with dismay. Sebastién worked the orchestra into a fury as the invader arrived at the tree and reached out to touch it. The moment of contact coincided with a great crescendo of sound. The hall went dark and silent as if its story world had blown a circuit.

Applause roared up from the darkness. When the house lights returned, Jordan found Lila wrapped in joy. Her mood was contagious and sent the remainder of his concerns away like thin smoke. Her smiles persisted through the intermission and into the second act. It depicted a nomadic way of life. A slower pace now, the painted backdrop creeping by as if drawn through a lethargic printing press. An eastward journey, into India, into China.

Lila's discreet commentary brought new intimate collateral: bumped arms and legs. Spirited hands tapped with the orchestra's efforts, which led to fingers touching, and then hands intertwined. Their grasp would break, but always return over time. Though their eyes were on the performance, their hands continued to seek each other, each reunion finding greater confidence. Before the end of the act, a scene familiar to Jordan came into view. Yosemite Valley, much as he saw it the day he arrived.

Once the applause at the end of the second act subsided, Jordan's curiosity moved to the forefront. "Liwei told me they began building Arbor Florum in Roman times, that there were others before this."

"The Depths were the precursor to Arbor Florum, built thousands of years ago," Lila slid her hand across the balcony rail. "They were tracked down by the dark wanderer. All that's left are the noughts."

"Garden...I keep thinking of the garden of Eden when you use that word."

"Which is where that story came from, along with *Ee-dra-sill* in Norse mythology, the *ash-va-tha*, and others—all of them united by the tale of a mystical tree. Most things unnatural enough to be worthy of faintlight lore originated from ours. After the fall of the original garden, those who remained—or survived from what we can tell—migrated in every direction. They carried the story with them. It crept into local mythologies, becoming less recognizable over time."

The third act opened with renewed enthusiasm. A man in a toga moved about the stage with an armload of scrolls, dropping them, picking them up, chattering with excitement to one stage performer after another. Each conversation concluded with an expression of disbelief. During the performance, members of the audience cast glances to the back of the opera house, which steered Jordan's head in the same direction, trying to locate the target of their curiosity.

He found it at last, in a prominent loge box: Crispin.

Jordan recalled Liwei's conversation and realized he was witnessing Crispin's evangelization of the idea of Arbor Florum. The face of the real Crispin suggested he wasn't comfortable with this celebrity. Yet

Jordan couldn't know with any certainty; he might be mired in deep contemplation, marred by the politics of their conversation from two nights ago. By the time Jordan's eyes returned to the stage, the backdrop had changed to a scene from Aria, with a new tree, dark and center-stage. Freelight circled it as an elderly woman approached with great difficulty. Upon reaching the tree, she knelt at its base, her body trembling through the downward motion. She bowed her head and kissed a root, causing light to rush up its trunk and into its branches.

It was the birth of Arbor Florum.

The orchestra and vocalists reached greater elation. Freelight drifted toward the newly-lit Arborsolis, emerging from places all throughout the opera house—from loge boxes, from balconies. They were drawn to the tree. They gathered around it, moving as if locked in its orbit. Behind the celestial display, the background image scrolled to an Asian theme. Another dark silhouette of a tree, freelight buzzing around it in anticipation. A kiss delivered, another tree brought to life. The locale changed once again. The European middle ages, a castle-like setting, another tree, another crowd.

Then something in the music changed.

A note issued from the violins, one that didn't belong. Jordan's ears told him it was a mistake. But the offending note returned moments later. It thrived, evolving into a countering motif, a troubling melody hung in a minor key. It began to infect the musical tapestry. Freelight continued to glide with thick delight, casting gestures of exaltation to the old woman as she moved closer to the tree.

The musical contagion continued to spread.

It arrived in the vocalists next, beginning in the deep registers, then escalating to the tenors. Still, the aerial dancers swirled in confident, cheerful paths. By the time the old woman knelt, ready to deliver the kiss of light, the conquest of the song was complete, the entire orchestration rendered desolate. But a single soprano remained, loyal to the original melody, singing desperately for its survival. She reached the highest of notes, as though trying to escape into the heavens.

The kiss of light arrived.

Light flowed up into the tree, rousing it to bright, brilliant life. The freelight performers rejoiced while the voice of the lone soprano persisted, crying out one final, sustained note. When it ceased, the frail woman collapsed. The melancholy of the orchestra remained, plodding onward, murky and somber. The deveiled joined the veiled on stage. They gathered around the old woman's body. They touched her arms and cheek in disbelief. They knelt down together under the light of the newly harbored tree.

And they wept.

The sound of the morose orchestra faded with the house lights as the curtains drew shut. All went dark. A respectful silence ran its course before the crowd rose and started to applaud. Joy returned, and with it, shouts of *bravo, brava,* and *bravi.* It continued without fatigue, finding greater potency when the curtains parted to reveal the cast. As each performer stepped forward and bowed, Jordan's mind went to work on the finale. He made connections to Sebastién's story and looked at Lila. She leaned in to hear him.

"The Arborsolis was the gift—the last gift."

Lila nodded, responding over the applause: "There was only one human harborer of Lux Olivae. They didn't understand the limits of what she could give until that day."

The applause continued, while Jordan pieced more of it together. "That arbor, it was the murdered Kyzhere's wasn't it—Easton's..."

"Yes, Paris." Lila's face went somber. She stopped applauding, letting her hands fall to her sides.

"...that's why Supernus's arbor was never completed."

Lila nodded again, her joy fading fast.

Jordan saw the trajectory. He smiled at her. "Hands down, that was the best space opera I've ever seen."

Lila's smile came back.

She laughed and swayed toward him, their arms touching. Jordan caught her hand in his and pulled her in close. He leaned in, seeing her eyes go shut just before he closed his own. Exhilaration ripped through him with such force the whole world seemed to grow bright. Before their lips met, applause became a roar of mass panic.

Violent flashes of light, staccato cracks of thunder.

Jordan's eyes flew open. A swarm of lime-green freelight was assaulting the lone interfector just outside the dignitary's box. Like suicidal pilots, they attacked from every direction, jetting straight into the interfector's yellow-sun fury. The interfector moved like lightning, striking assailants dead in the air, their bodies falling to the stage like ragdolls. The opera performers fled under sprays of bleeding light; green and yellow spilling down in fiery streamers, igniting the curtains.

But there were too many. The interfector's light dulled and then flashed out. He fell to the stage dead, his body landing unceremoniously upon those he'd conquered only seconds ago.

Scores of attackers remained.

They arranged themselves in the air above the stage in a symmetric pattern, their light still coursing Vitruvian. From the back of the opera house, a solemn copper-hued freelight floated out to the space above the abandoned orchestra pit, taking refuge in the invaders' keep. She faced the crowd with fierce eyes, long hair scintillating like auburn fire. Far below her, Sebastién remained on the pulpit, arms at his sides, white baton clutched in his hand.

With the flick of the fierce-eyed woman's chin, a group of her protectors descended upon the Castellum loge box. They dragged the dignitary and his colleague to the front railing. With arms pulled wide as though being prepared for crucifixion, they were pressed down, necks to the railing, heads extending past its edge.

They shouted for mercy, but their cries were buried under the crowd's expression of horror. The impending execution tamed the audience to silence quickly. With the quarry subdued, the fierce-eyed woman returned her attention to the audience. Her protectors dimmed, their wicked Vitruvian drone dwindling into mere hum. When the fierce-eyed woman spoke at last, her voice came like thunder:

"COWARDS!" The word whipped through the hall in sharp echoes. "BEHOLD what your weakness has wrought. The Kyzheres rope tightens about Arbor Florum's neck while you revel. Your liberty, constricted over a great many years, is about to end."

One of the spotlights, which had been casting a steady beam to the stage, spun suddenly. Its stern light swept across the audience. It landed square on Jordan and Lila. Jordan squinted. Lila was still clutching his hand. He felt terror in its grasp.

"Behold, Lux Sanguinis returned…" The fierce-eyed woman's voice fell into a softer tone. "Behold Jordan James Wakefield, brother in light to the falsely accused, Firas el-Sakar. His untimely desperation has snared them both into the Kyzhere's trap."

Though the spotlight restricted Jordan's ability to render the crowd in anything other than black shapes, he could feel their eyes. Lila's frightened grip crushed his knuckles together like fused vertebrae.

"They called upon YOU, citizens of Arbor Florum, to aid them. To press the First Circle for reprieve. But you turned your back." The fierce-eyed woman went bright, thin Vitruvian coils erupting into orbit around her. "SHAME upon you!"

The spotlight swung away, panning slow across the audience. Jordan saw a universe of sinking chins, weighed down by festering consciences. The spotlight finished its sweep, arriving at the Castellum loge box. Its occupants were still being held face down upon the railing.

Silence again.

The fierce-eyed woman spoke. "Behold, at last, the mouthpiece of Liaidor Kyzhere. Stripped of his interfector, his fate falls readily to our hands. SEE this truth. SEE the fragile hold Castellum wields over the Grey City. SEE that it can be broken."

The dignitary twisted his head. His face craned up to the fierce-eyed woman, the whites of his eyes showing from the effort. Those restraining him continued to wait, emotionless as the interfector they had dispatched.

The fierce-eyed woman nodded.

A surge rippled through the crowd. But just as fast as it came, it fell to silence again. The dignitary struggled against his captors, his voice the lone sound now: "I meant no harm—I've never ordered anyone killed—or hurt…This is my DUTY! This is my—"

"RELEASE HIM!" called out the fierce-eyed woman.

The captors hauled the dignitary and his counterpart back from the rail, throwing them into sitting positions on the floor. The dignitary's hand trembled. He raised it to his face as if to confirm he was still alive.

"Your lives shall be spared," said the fierce-eyed woman. "Consider this a token of peace."

Lila released her death grip on Jordan. She moved close to him, the top of her head finding its way under his chin. He put his arms around her, trying to give refuge while the world kept its eyes fixed on the spectacle.

She spoke again, her words directed to the dignitary. "Go back to Arbor Castellum. Tell them what you have seen here. Tell them we demand all interfectors be released from their minds. Or we shall release them from their lives, as you have witnessed here. Tell them we too, number as great as the stars. Tell them we stand ready to trade our lives for theirs. When you speak to Liaidor Kyzhere and his criminal descendants, tell them…"

The fierce-eyed woman turned her gaze to the audience, her face expressing a terrifying resolve. She raised her arms, lifting everyone's attention as if by hypnotic force:

"WE ARE THE NETHER DOVE!"

Then she and her entourage drifted away, the procession happening under dead silence. After they departed, a great roar erupted from the audience while stagehands put out the fires. Castellum's dignitary was on his feet, clutching the railing for support. Jordan spotted Crispin, who surveyed the scene from on high, chin down, hands pressed solemnly to the top of his cane. Jordan recalled their private exchange, and the theory of an activism that hadn't yet shown itself.

Here it was.

The counterfeit silence broken, casualties littering the stage for all to see. It was no longer a contest of words.

It had moved into deeds.

37

INVESTIGATOR FORENSIS

The morning after the opera, the Grey City had transformed. Steady patrols of interfectors—flying in quartets, each with a Stellarum handler—crisscrossed Florum's leafs and greys, streets and skies. No longer constrained to the Carmen, they watched over all, their presence coaxing Florum's official police force into the background. Whether that was by political decree or by choice remained a mystery. The citizenry, agitated beyond measure, was forced to swallow it. The loss of limb or even life was real. All were treated as suspects, all were potential co-conspirators of the so-called Nether Dove, who had vanished as fast as they arrived.

"Word has it they came in through South Leaf," said Lila walking fast, Jordan and Sebastién at her side. "The old entrance, sealed off centuries ago. Its lobby was all that remained. But they managed to cut a new passage awfully quick. And without anyone taking notice."

The elegant façade of the Carmen rose in front of them as they marched under West Leaf's dome. A crowd was planted on the Carmen's grand staircase. They were there on account of Jordan's day in court. Jordan found himself involuntarily making fists.

"…even more remarkable was that they vanished without a trace," said Sebastién. "Rumor says not even the dead ones gave up leads. They're unknown, undocumented."

A pack of interfectors and their handler coasted over the treetops, cutting a path perpendicular to them.

"This is like martial law," said Jordan.

"This *is* martial law." Sebastién's eyes followed the interfector pack to the other side. "South Leaf has been sealed shut—even the drain tunnels are locked down now. Res Externa isn't allowing anyone in or out. We're trapped, and that *had* to be the goal of those Nether Dove people. To make conditions intolerable, to make everyone pick a side."

"Seems people are more pissed at us than the Kyzheres," said Jordan. He was close enough to take in the facial expressions of the mob occupying the staircase, and it didn't look good.

"Like all oppressions," said Sebastién, "the oppressors are the last to earn blame. It's those who challenge them that earn the wrath—strange, is it not?"

They reached the staircase and began their climb. The crowd went silent and parted to let them pass. All eyes on them, condescension roaring like a furnace.

It started with a spattering of snide accusations.

One sharp tongue begat another, and words quickly grew into more. Jordan took an earful. Then a barrage of shoves. Angry hands pulled the three of them away from each other. Regaining his balance after slipping down a step, Jordan twisted free and muscled his way toward Lila. A wild punch caught Sebastién's shoulder. Shouting broke out.

Then a flash of yellow lit the scene from above.

With it came the Vitruvian snarl only an interfector could make. This led to a reflexive panic. People pushed each other, then dropped to their knees, hands in the air. Some tumbled down the stairs. Lila snagged Jordan's arm in time, sparing him the same fate.

After it settled, faces dared to peek skyward. Jordan saw the forward interfector, her three companions close behind. Dead-eyed, but wide-awake. Above them hovered their Stellarum handler, his purple light coursing fast. Wearing an impossibly wide smile, he surveyed them. He shook his head, indulging in the moment.

The handler twitched his chin upward.

The crowd returned to its feet with caution. Before Jordan turned away, the handler looked him dead-on and winked.

Sebastién yanked Jordan around and pushed him toward the Carmen's doors. He whispered violently in Jordan's ear: "Did you see that? He fucking winked at you—best of friends. This is doomed, Jordan; you have to take Crispin's way out." Sebastién shoved him along for good measure.

Lila joined them, and they pushed into the lobby.

The sounds of hectic administration replaced the dissonance of the mob. Castellum personnel scuttled through the lobby, pretending not to notice them. But as they made their way to the courtroom, frequent corner-of-the-eye glances and a collision between a pair of bureaucrats gave them away.

They'd been waiting for this.

"Remember your magic words?" whispered Sebastién.

Jordan's head was still outside the Carmen. He pondered their fates had the interfectors not intervened. They had been saved by the enemy. Fragments of the event piled up in Jordan's landfill of a conscience, compelling him to accept the facts: first came the prisoner who time forgot, forced back into public awareness by his brother in red light, who arrived out of the blue. A middle finger, an opera, and a public execution later, civilization itself had come unglued.

And Jordan had everything to do with it.

It *was* his fault.

"Jordan?" said Lila as they hustled down a wide flight of stairs. She looked around, making sure they were alone. "Thiago's rule, remember?"

"What if we're wrong?" asked Jordan. "What if Firas picked up on something?"

Sebastién and Lila stopped in unison.

Jordan recognized the silence and halted a few steps below. He turned around. "What good am I if I don't keep my word? I'll be the man who betrayed his brother."

Sebastién blew out frustrated air. "He's not really your brother."

"But that's how everyone will see it." He started down the stairs again, forcing Sebastién and Lila to follow.

"You can't go through with this—take Crispin's out." Sebastién's machine-gun steps pattered past Jordan. He blocked the way at the bottom of the stairwell. "What the hell are you going to do in there?"

As Lila joined the blockade, another chorus of sharp steps rattled off the granite floors from across the way.

"Jordan Wakefield," called a raspy, female voice.

Upon gaining his attention, a woman with half-moon glasses completed her march, skirting around Lila and Sebastién. She shoved a note into Jordan's hand. He slid it into his pocket, drawing glances.

Jordan moved toward the court's outer doors.

Inside, the courtroom was much like Firas's prison; a study in the dreary. Poorly lit, with plain wooden tables arranged in two rows and a small aisle separating them. A tall woman, who struck Jordan as Persian, nodded at a chair on his approach. Probably Parandis, his appointed savior.

Jordan sat down.

Lila and Sebastién parked themselves a row behind.

Across the aisle loomed a larger group, all well dressed, taking up three rows. At the center of it was a bald man with a well-proportioned face, who sat with arms folded.

In the privacy of his lap, Jordan opened the envelope. It was sealed in blue wax, the image of a feathered pen embossed into it. He removed the letter and read:

Jordan:

As you can likely guess, negotiations with the Kyzheres are off. There was a secret vote by the First Circle last night to suspend this whole affair, but it failed. There is but one path now. Upon accepting the authority of Investigator Forensis, declare the following:

I wish to seek asylum in Arbor Florum under Thiago's

Rule.

—C

"Good advice," whispered Sebastién, his head over Jordan's shoulder. Jordan scowled, folded the letter, and crushed it into his pocket. He turned to Lila whose eyes blinked the same sentiment. Giving up, he turned around and crossed his arms.

Jordan was lost the moment the proceedings began.

The words came fast, and they were littered with Latin, though the parts in English were just as opaque. Jordan assembled the most studious face he could, trying to avoid an expression that would reveal he had no idea what the hell was going on.

"Once again, denied," barked the irritated Judge Vawsk. He glanced down from his elevated station before returning to the pile of paper under his bearded chin. "Mr. Wakefield's status as an undeclared citizen is *not* grounds to deny his petition to serve as Investigator Forensis. That authority *can* be granted through the Interarborals, by this very court. He is qualified. He has offered to serve by his own volition."

Parandis continued to make the case against it, firing off statements that only seemed to amuse Vawsk.

"The matter of Firas el-Sakar has gone on long enough." Vawsk scanned the courtroom as though fishing for something to fuel his waning interest. "A one-hundred-and-twenty-eight-year detainment on account of a failure to conduct a proper investigation is a farce of the greatest order, made worse by the fact that the barriers erected to hinder it were constructed by the very people demanding its resolution. To continue this—"

"Your honor," shot back Parandis in a voice loud enough to eclipse his, "it is further the position of Arbor Florum that the court consider the origins of the successors on grounds that these very origins contradict the known provincialism of unharbored timbre. That a successor could reemerge so far from here strains plausibility. That the second successor emerged from the same location is nearly impossible."

"As I'm sure counsel is aware, this court is not concerned with matters of probability. It is only concerned with the Interarborals. *That* body of law states that the release or trial of Firas el-Sakar is a matter subservient to the completion of the investigation. I see no grounds against proceeding."

Jordan looked away to the confident faces on Castellum's side. All self-assured, except one woman who maintained a rigid posture. Short blonde hair, bright blue eyes, uncommonly attractive.

A whack of the gavel stole Jordan's attention.

"To the matter of Lux Sanguinis's inadequacy as recorder, the court will appoint a surrogate." The judge looked to the Castellum side. "Are you prepared to offer an appointment?"

"Yes, your honor," said a gray-haired man next to the rigid blonde. The blond stood up. She was wearing a black blazer with long sharp tails, and tight black, equestrian-style pants.

"We ask the court appoint to Gretchen Poesthoffer, Lux Stellarum."

"Well I'll be damned," muttered Sebastién. "A woman."

"The investigation of the Depths in the matter of Firas el-Sakar is hereby granted," Judge Vawsk fired off his words with impatience, "to be performed in three days at the stroke of noon. To the matter of Jordan Wakefield, standing of revenant, I grant the power and title of Investigator Forensis under Interarboral sixty-eight, code fifteen, subsection twenty-eight, article one. Jordan Wakefield, please rise."

Jordan stood.

"Do you accept this appointment and the responsibility it carries?"

"I do." The disinterested look on Vawsk's face suggested he had no knowledge of the loophole. Jordan patted the fabric of his pocket, nearly feeling the words on Crispin's note. His mind raced through conversations with Firas, recalling his hopeful face the night they went looking for Helena. He recalled the story of Helena's demise, and that of Jordan's predecessor, and Lila's. He recalled Firas's intensity during that tale, every word of the tragedy spinning a declining orbit around the black gravity of his eyes, culminating in that final, prophetic declaration: *In the end, all of them will doubt you. They will beg you to walk away. But you must hold fast…*

Jordan's mind flashed ahead to Liwei's party, to the fierce altercations with Supernus, to his own desperate need for retaliation. All of it had spiraled out of control, but to Firas, it mattered not. There remained an unshakable confidence in his desire to stay the course. Jordan's mind arrived at the night they last talked. The midnight communion, pleasant until shaken by Firas's closing words, ones that hit Jordan now as if he were hearing them anew. As if Firas were right there with him: *Brother, do not forsake me, for I carry a great secret. But it is not yet time.*

A calm came over Jordan.

He felt the truth down to his toe-tips: the bodies weren't down there. The conventional wisdom was wrong and Firas knew it. All that remained was to prove it.

The motion of Judge Vawsk's gavel rising into the air pulled Jordan back to the courtroom. Before it hit the sounding block, Parandis yelled:

"The appointee is permitted to make a statement!"

Vawsk leaned forward and glared at Parandis. He rubbed the gavel against his beard and laughed. "Counsel should be aware that the appointee did not appear to be making one." He raised the gavel again and looked to Jordan. "Would he like to do so now?"

Jordan held Vawsk's eyes and answered. "No."

"Confirmed." The gavel cracked twice. "Adjourned." Vawsk got up and gathered his papers while chatter in the courtroom accelerated. When Jordan stood, Parandis moved in front of him, locking eyes. He looked away, only to find Sebastién and Lila wearing the same caustic expression.

On Castellum's side, the participants traded business smiles. But the accuser's advocate, Gretchen, remained rigid as a statue, rooted to the floor. When she looked at Jordan, he read her with perfect clarity:

She was terrified.

"Hey…" Sebastién moved in, waving his hand in front of Jordan's eyes. "What the hell are you doing?"

Jordan felt the pocket-lump that was Crispin's crumpled plea. He moved his fingers away from it as though it were toxic. "I'm doing what my brother asked of me."

38

BLOOD ON THE STREET

The dark worn floorboards of the Gorg creaked under rapid footsteps as Jordan and Sebastién traversed its hallway. Sebastién's demeanor, once an undeniable fount of enthusiasm, was polluted with anxiety. Jordan knew he was trying to control it—trying to protect his pupil's confidence—but his mouth failed to filter such concerns.

"You've got combat down," said Sebastién, "but not the con."

The mere thought of pink light triggered a Pavlovian response in Jordan. An instant paranoia, a sinking of his spirits that routinely carried his chin toward the floor.

"You've beaten it a few times but not reliably enough—you need to get it right, because you're going down there in *days*." Sebastién walked sideways next to Jordan, driving fist into palm as he preached. "At all times you *must* remain aware of it, like recognizing footsteps behind you, but refusing to acknowledge them."

"Will this Gretchen person be worse than Easton?" asked Jordan. "More powerful, that is?"

"I don't know." Sebastién abandoned his sideways gait. "Nobody knows. There's something very strange going on here. The Grey City's census records are impeccable—even for the other arbors. Yet this Gretchen Poesthoffer doesn't seem to exist." Upon reaching the Gorg's lobby, Sebastién turned and leaned against the outer doors, bringing Jordan to a stop. "We do, however, keep turning up the same rumor: she's one of Theron Kyzhere's wives."

"*One* of his wives?"

"Well, you know royalty, harems and all."

"Not really."

"Nevertheless, it's like she's never existed until now. So she's either as new as you—which is *highly* unlikely—or she's been hidden away all these years, quite literally." Sebastién kicked the Gorg's door open with his heel and turned. They marched into the Eden-bright of the thoroughfare, the intensity blinding them momentarily.

Sebastién caught Jordan's arm, trying to hold him back. Through squinted eyes, Jordan saw it: a mob, arranged in a semi-circle blockade. Shoulder to shoulder, a continuous silhouette of black paper-chain dolls.

For a moment a shared silence held everyone in check. Then voices and motion broke loose. Jordan turned to his blindside just as Raleigh arrived, mid-swing. His fist landed full on Jordan's cheek, sending his eye shut like a Venus flytrap and spinning him. Landing on one knee, Jordan threw his hand out for balance.

"DON'T LET THEM DEVEIL!"

Before Jordan could recover, Raleigh's foot caught him in the chest, breaking ribs. Jordan toppled forward, the cold street hitting his forehead. Sebastién, impaired by the same tactics, fell next to him. Jordan tried to breathe, the intake feeling like a drill press to the lung.

"Look at me!" said Raleigh, his voice unhinged.

Jordan extended his hand as a shield. He turned his face away, awaiting the next assault.

"Look what you've done—"

"Let him up, Raleigh," called another voice. "He gets the point."

"He doesn't!" Raleigh kicked Jordan's shoulder with his heel, landing him in a sitting position.

Jordan looked up at Raleigh through one eye. Raleigh's female counterpart stood behind him, her hand on his shoulder. Jordan couldn't tell if her grasp was meant to restrain or encourage him.

"He's a tool of the Kyzheres." Raleigh's breaths came and went in bursts. "He doesn't realize it. He's a traitor to Arbor Florum. A disgrace to his predecessor."

Jordan rose slowly, his hand hovering protectively in front of his ribs. Unable to stand erect, he looked at Raleigh from a hunchbacked posture. Sebastién moaned, tugging at Jordan's pant leg.

"This isn't…about me," said Jordan, pushing his words through a wall of agony, "It's about…Fir—"

"Don't speak to me of Firas! He cares *nothing* of us. He toys with Arbor Florum—he deserves what he got." Raleigh came closer. "You don't know what we've lost to the Kyzheres."

Jordan couldn't find words worth speaking. Nothing would suffice, but to go into the Depths and prove Firas right. Jordan waited, silently reciting a personal mantra, born of his freelight experience: all pain is but temporary.

Raleigh's jaw tightened as he cracked knuckles. "This is for Aberdeen and Julia, and Sazonov. For the Twelve, for the Soft Council. For those lost on Glass Pond, and for countless others—you know nothing of them!"

Jordan swallowed, unable to parse Raleigh's list. It came to him in imagined fragments, all of them ending tragically, like the life of his predecessor.

"Most of all, this is for Emilia." Raleigh drew his fist back.

Jordan forced himself into an upright position, looking Raleigh dead-on, accepting what was to come as punishment for his own selfish naivety, for his belief this only concerned Firas. Raleigh's swing unfurled, carrying with it the pent-up frustration of the Grey City.

Blinding yellow light flashed between them.

A spray of hot crimson liquid splattered Jordan's face, delivering a coppery taste. Raleigh's expression went to horror, his severed hand whipping spirals in front of him, casting a pinwheel of blood through the air. Raleigh fell, landing on his knees before his amputated hand hit the street. The roar of an interfector drowned his screams. The mob went to its knees. Faces down, hands in the air, submitting to the aurulent angel of death that blazed before them.

With stunned eyes, Raleigh rocked into a sitting position, watching blood shoot from the stump of his wrist. Eyes wide, chin bobbing as though experiencing a seizure. Jordan's eyes remained riveted to the spectacle. After three more interfectors arrived, Jordan realized he was the only one still standing.

"Good afternoon, Investigator," called a voice from above.

Jordan, still transfixed, watched Raleigh's woman scramble to him. Tears spilling forth as she wrapped her arms around him, her hands clutching Raleigh's wrist, unable to stop the bleeding.

"Let him heal!" said the woman. "PLEASE!"

"Investigator…" called the voice again, unhurried, unconcerned.

Jordan looked up, finding a purple freelight handler floating above the interfectors. A haughty face, chin perched high in the air. He reveled in the scene, ignoring the fading Raleigh.

Jordan began to kneel.

"Oh no." The handler glided quickly down to him. "That is for *them*. Remain on your feet, Investigator—reveil and fix those nasty wounds of yours." The handler swept his hand in a flourish, inviting Jordan to proceed.

Jordan deveiled, drawing the notice of the interfectors, but no combative response. Jordan veiled again, his body healed. He looked at Raleigh and then shouted to the handler. "Let him up! He's going to die!"

The handler shook his head, disappointed. "What is he to you, but your accoster? He assaulted the Investigator Forensis. We could put him to death right here if it would please you."

"No!" Jordan's stomach turned. "He's going to die if he doesn't deveil." His attention snapped to Raleigh, whose chin hung low. Fading fast, Raleigh started to tip toward the street. The woman cried out his name. She held him harder, trying to keep him awake, trying to keep him alive. The pool of blood had nearly reached Jordan's shoes, its surface reflecting interfector fire like sunlight off a black-horror lake.

Jordan shouted at the handler. "Let him up!"

The handler closed his eyes and shook his head, dissatisfied.

Jordan didn't know what to do.

Opening his eyes, the handler looked at Raleigh. "Very well. Inhibitors, relent."

The interfectors dimmed and backed off. The woman and others near her yanked Raleigh to his feet, one of them slipping on the blood and falling. Slapping his face, they tried to rouse him. They peppered his ears with the word *deveil.*

Raleigh's eyes rolled open and closed.

Then, a burst of green light flashed across Raleigh, and he was restored. He veiled and knelt again, not looking at Jordan, not looking at the interfectors. His accomplices did the same. Raleigh stared into the sea of his own blood, his eyes drawn to the horrific siren call of his severed hand. It rested palm up in the street of blood, the tip of its index finger bent toward the sky.

The handler glided behind Jordan. "I'd advise our esteemed Investigator and his associate to be wary of these streets. They are savage…" The handler waited while Jordan got Sebastién to his feet. "But fear not, Investigator. We have your back."

A dark malaise invaded every cell of Jordan's body while he watched the interfector troupe fly off. He felt the eyes of his assailants, rising from the street, finding him. He saw faces peering down from the buildings lining East Grey.

The whole world was watching.

And they'd seen the truth: the Kyzheres were protecting him. They wanted him untouched. They wanted him to go into the Depths. With head down and Sebastién hanging off his shoulder for support, Jordan walked away.

39

GRADUATION DAY

Jordan gazed down at the Gorg's stage. Lila was standing on it with her hands at her sides, facing away from him. From his deveiled viewpoint, ten feet above and another ten behind, she looked like a mourner standing at a gravesite at midnight, visible only by Jordan's red light.

"This is it," called Sebastién's distant voice.

Jordan pulled his eyes from Lila. He tracked deep to the rear of the auditorium where eight deveiled freelight floated high in the air. Eight opponents, eight stern faces trying to shore up doubts about him, about his choice to go into the Depths. He wasn't sure he believed it himself anymore. But he had to. He had made his choice.

Sebastién floated in the center. To his left, Easton, bright pink. To her side, Jiro rippling fiery-orange. Jordan's impromptu fan club of Wiley, Georgia, and Lev—all burning lime-green—hovered on the right side, while a purple deveiled Albert floated next to them. Rounding out the troupe at far left was a vibrant green Sam, the Gorg's faithful caretaker. Though differing in hue, their expressions were the same, anchored to the relentless gravity of tomorrow when Jordan would go into the Depths.

"We lack a true survey of what's down there," said Sebastién, his voxed words echoing about the Gorg. "Firas, your predecessor, and only a few others have been in the Depths. They confirm what older records assert. It's a giant cavern, about three hundred feet tall, two hundred wide. It's quite long, perhaps a quarter mile, with smaller passages equidistant along the way. The indictment claims that Firas was observed tossing the bodies in there, which means they'd have slid down the entry passage and dropped to the floor."

Jordan watched the glow of his mock opponents begin to dim. Without the aid of the house lights this time, the world drifted into a suffocating darkness. He glanced down to Lila, who was turning over a recorder's coin in her hand, still turned away.

"Now, keep in mind…" Sebastién pointed at his own outstretched hand. "While Gretchen is recording, the noughts will be drawn to her writing hand. Moths to a flame. You *must* keep them away without interrupting her work. Escalate slowly slowly slowly—*that* is the key. Remember, the noughts are dangerous if they latch on to you, but you're invisible to them. They can neither see nor feel you. There's a couple dozen of them from what the records state, but there's only eight of us. So it'll have to do."

Jordan felt the final instructions, as though they were being chiseled into his heart. It was painfully real now.

"We don't know how long it will take the noughts to wake and interfere," continued Sebastién. "You might complete the whole thing without having to do more than brush them aside. So we're going to make this a lot harder than it should have to be. Lila's going to record for ten minutes, which we understand is the Praetorium's model for how long this should take. If the bodies are not at your feet, the recorder will be expected to sweep a circle before calling it done. To simulate this, Lila's going to record and walk off the stage to the back of the hall. You need to protect her that entire time. Got it?"

"Yes," muttered Jordan, glancing at Lila again.

"I didn't hear you."

Jordan stared at Sebastién's orange glow, and shouted in vox: "I said, BRING IT!"

Eight nods, eight sets of uneasy eyes.

Lila's recording hand flared up and went out. She began to mouth numbers. Jordan watched the cloister of opponents drift in, their faces bearing no expression, no hint they were once his friends. They moved like the dead. When they arrived, Jordan began to tap, turn, and haul them away like mannequins. Lila walked about and paused, and walked some more, mouthing numbers. Her performance was so authentic it frightened Jordan.

The attackers returned faster and brighter.

Jordan accelerated in kind.

Lazy drifting became determined gliding, deveiled forms now rippling in the air as they moved. They stuck to Jordan, who had to escalate, breaking loose, punching them away, maintaining the perimeter around Lila with a controlled antagonism. Jordan blazed ever-brighter, hoarding the heat of the hall only to have it siphoned off. Faster and faster now, his strikes became reckless, sometimes missing his target on the first attempt. Between rapid loops, he spied Lila's breath fogging the air, nervous puffs of white on a winter day.

The contest accelerated.

He spun and pivoted and raced, trying to preserve Lila's world, hoping desperately that she'd start moving off stage at any moment. But she remained stationary. It wasn't time yet. The air howled with freelight movement. Jordan's confidence began to fail.

With rapid dashes and streaks of light, the sphere of Jordan's defense shrunk. He was losing the battle, unable to determine how many minutes had passed, how many remained. Finally, he saw Lila begin her exit. He'd made the ten-minute mark; closer to the end than the beginning. His heart leapt, and he redoubled his effort.

With icy breath and trembling hands pressed to her chest, Lila clutched her relic. Reaching the end of the stage, she descended to the floor. Jordan, operating in a fast, cyclical flurry, struggled to keep Lila at the center of his universe.

Reaching the limits, Jordan's motions became desperate. His opponents arrived in bright sweeps of light, reducing his efforts to jamming them only a few feet away with each encounter. Spurts of light hit Lila as she marched the aisle. She yelped at the tyranny of the fiery rain but never broke character.

Neither did the attackers.

It was real. Lila's life was in his hands.

Jordan's motions became automatic, like an athlete who erased all distractions, relying on instinct. He failed to distinguish between his self and others, capturing kaleidoscopic flashes of Lila's face from an impossible number of vantage points.

Yet it still wasn't enough, it was, it—

It was *over*.

Jordan emerged from his trance, realizing the enemies were no more. With applause sounding out, he spun to find his opponents transformed back into friends, veiled and standing on seats. He whipped back to Lila, who conjured a quaint smile, but quaked in the ferocious cold, her face bone-white, cheeks blotched red as though she'd been fished out of the ocean. Terrible burns covered her forearms, and her clothes were pocked with holes. She dropped the metallum onto the floor and deveiled.

"You did it," she said as she flew by, looking relieved.

While Sam zipped about like a hummingbird, bringing the house lights up, the others convened on-stage.

Jordan arrived in their midst, a proud, bright red apparition.

"Stay deveiled a moment," said Sebastién.

Jordan, smile still intact, felt Easton's siren-seduction kick on from behind. Then came her voice:

"Jordan, I want you to sing for me again."

Sebastién watched Jordan's grin fall flat. His eyes went distant, Easton's pink hand glowing behind. Jordan nodded and turned drunkenly toward Easton.

"Dammit," said Sebastién, jamming his heel into the stage.

Jordan raised his hand to his chest and sang: "Oh, say can you see…By the dawn's early light…"

"Cut him off," Sebastién snapped at Easton. "We'll have to train into the night. If he doesn't get this, he's screwed."

Easton pursed the corner of her mouth. "What if he—"

A flash of red light struck Easton's fiery pink hand, forcing it to veil. She shrieked, falling down as though bitten by a snake. From a sitting position, she gave Jordan an astonished smile.

"Nice try," said Jordan, veiling and landing on the stage with a polite thump. He reached out and caught Easton's hand, pulling her up.

"You did it." Easton slapped him on the shoulder. "Nice work, kid. I guess you graduate."

Smiles and congratulations went around, the compliments making Jordan feel like a winning prizefighter. He hoped this new-found confidence would last.

But when Jordan reached Lila, he saw her face drain out. Her attention had jumped to something behind him. The others went silent before Jordan had even turned around. When he did, he saw a tall woman standing in the middle of the auditorium.

Short blond hair, bright blue eyes. Gretchen Poesthoffer's voice shook like a winter branch. "The bodies are down there."

Silence.

"The bodies of your predecessors." Gretchen rushed onto the stage, moving straight to Jordan, grabbing him by the shoulders, shaking him. "Do you understand me?"

"How could you know this?" Sebastién pushed in, separating them.

"Because I was there." Gretchen's breathing raced, the house lights dashing across her cheek as she moved around Sebastién to face Jordan again. "I was there when we threw them into the Depths."

"Why would you tell us this?" asked Albert, moving in.

"I want out. Out of the Kyzheres, out of Castellum. They're going to kill me if Jordan comes out of there alive. They'll kill me even if he doesn't. They're afraid of me."

Albert took a breath before he spoke. "How is it you are involved in this to begin with?"

"I was made one of Theron Kyzhere's wives when I arrived in Castellum. I was trusting, loyal. That night, I was there to wash minds, should it have been necessary." Gretchen steadied her breathing and checked behind herself. "There is only one way out of this—the Nether Dove. They'll get me out, but it has to be Jordan too. They want him more than me."

Jordan felt his stomach tighten. His words burst out: "The Nether Dove are killers. They killed that interfector, they—"

"Releasing an interfector is an act of mercy!" Gretchen's eyes burned with fire. "They are trapped in their minds. I've *made* them—many of them. They live in misery."

Jordan took a step back.

"My orders are to seduce you and order you to attack the noughts once we have the evidence." Gretchen shook, tears in her eyes. "You must understand, no one can withstand my light."

"Nonsense," said Sebastién.

Gretchen whipped toward Sebastién. "Who's the strongest of you?"

"I am." Easton stepped forward and deveiled her hand. "Give it your worst, see if—"

Gretchen's hand flared deep violet, and Easton's words ceased. Her eyes glassed over instantly. Her mouth fell open into a dumb smile.

"Impossible…" whispered Albert.

Sebastién's hand flared and struck Gretchen, killing her light.

Easton recovered and blinked like she was transmitting Morse code. She looked at Gretchen with fear. "What *are* you?"

Gretchen scraped tears away with an unsteady hand. "They were troubled by it from the start, so they kept me hidden. In time we all learned the truth: my light is stronger than even Liaidor Kyzhere. That's why they want me dead—I'm telling the truth—put the liar's light to me." Gretchen flayed her hand again and everyone stepped back. She looked over her shoulder. "Hurry, I can't linger."

Sebastién nodded at Wiley. "Do it. She can't fog all three of you at the same time."

Wiley, Lev, and Georgia flayed their hands. Lime-green light painted the sharp features of Gretchen's face. Wiley spoke: "So…are the bodies down there?"

"Yes they are…" Gretchen swallowed. "We cast the long-dead bodies of Raphael Foscari, Elisabeth Di Lorne, and Helena Phaedria into the Depths one hundred and twenty-eight years ago."

The trio nodded an instant consensus. "She's telling the truth. No quavers, no attempt to haze—"

"My directives," continued Gretchen, "are to record evidence and trance Jordan Wakefield, Investigator Forensis, when we're done. I am to command him to attack the noughts until they are defeated. I am to claim he died trying to protect me. And then, once we leave Arbor Florum, they will kill me. That is why I am defecting. That is why I have pledged myself to the Nether Dove." Gretchen checked over her shoulder again. "I want OUT."

"She's telling the truth," said Georgia, drawing more nods from Lev and Wiley.

Gretchen looked to Lila. "Lila, your friend vouches for me. She remembers your blue shoes in Argentina."

"Darbi…" whispered Lila, her breathing accelerating.

"She'll meet with you tomorrow—they'll find you at Sebastién's through the vents. This is coming together fast. There will be little time." Gretchen looked to Jordan again. "It has to be both of us or my life is forfeit."

Jordan's response limped out. "I can't betray Firas…"

"You must," Gretchen approached him and locked eyes. "The Kyzheres toyed with his head all these years. They leaked and hinted that the Depths were clean. But it is a lie, constructed for these exact circumstances; that one day Raphael's predecessor would return; that Firas would convince him to go into the Depths; that I would end his life down there."

Jordan's body went numb, his hands hanging like ship anchors. Gretchen had already evacuated the stage. She ran up the aisle, pausing at the doors. She turned around. "We're all trapped in this. The Nether Dove is the only way out."

Before another word could be uttered, she was gone.

They all turned to Jordan, unable to conjure a single word. At last, Lila broke the silence. "We have to talk to Firas."

40

ULTIMATUM

Jordan crossed the Carmen's dim ballroom with reluctant steps. Firas spotted him from a cross-legged position on the floor. He cocked his head a few degrees to the side. The two interfector guards noticed Jordan as well, but maintained their indifference. Finley, caught off guard, leapt to his feet. He snatched a copper metallum from a nearby stack, sending the rest clattering to the floor. Glancing at the clock, he rattled off a preamble and intercepted Jordan at the prison bars.

"Firas…" Jordan struggled to make eye contact.

"I'm pleased to see you, brother." Firas stood up. His dark eyes flicked back and forth, scanning Jordan's face. "Our time is almost at hand. I hadn't expected to see you until tomorrow, just before you go in—you remember this, do you not? It is important."

Jordan held his tongue.

Firas tilted his head, his mouth opening a crack.

"Firas, this thing we are about to do…there are rumors." Jordan moved to touch the bars but stopped. "There are rumors as old as your imprisonment, rumors about what's in the Depths."

Firas licked his lips and shifted about. "You are afraid, brother."

Jordan paused, realizing he truly was. "Yes, I am afraid."

Firas grasped the bars and leaned his forehead against them.

"Brother, listen to me. I've been in the Depths, your predecessor had been in the Depths. There is no reason for *us* to fear that place."

Jordan wished for a way to explain Gretchen's bombshell revelation, but under Finley's eye it was impossible. "What if I'm not good enough? What if I can't go through with it?"

"You must, brother. *We* must proceed as planned." Firas spoke steady words, but his face betrayed a subterranean anger. Jordan watched him wrestle it into submission.

Firas closed his eyes and breathed it away.

Jordan watched the struggle, reflecting on Firas's century of isolation, his claim to a great secret, his need to breathe life into misguided fantasy to remain sane.

Firas opened his eyes. "*We* stay the course, brother."

"I understand." Jordan, having released those two words, turned away. "I have to get back now."

Jordan started to walk away.

Firas's voice became loud: "You see, brother, I can stay here no longer."

Jordan paused mid-step, turning the side of his face to Firas. "I understand."

"What would you *know* of it?" snapped Firas, his voice hostile. "You are snared into this too, as you must now realize. You are Investigator Forensis. Castellum's puppet court will not let you walk away. Indeed, the Nether Dove has guaranteed that nobody will walk away." Firas laughed, and it echoed.

"I'm not abandoning you." Jordan wondered how much his face had revealed, recalling how easily Firas spotted the Helena bluff.

"You gave me your word, brother."

"I did," Jordan started to walk again, "and I will keep it."

"Stop!" shouted Firas. The word crossed the ballroom like a gunshot. "It is *I* who have been sitting here for one hundred and twenty-eight years, not you—not anyone else! It is I who was made to suffer. It is *my* choice!"

Jordan kept walking, the mouth of the antechamber in sight.

"Brother!"

He was almost out, almost free…

"Then let us bring it to an end now!" bellowed Firas.

A sharp sound hit Jordan's ears, one he knew to be deveiling. He spun around to see Firas's hand flayed bright red. At that moment the interfector guards deveiled, exploding into bright yellow. The twin suns blinded him as Vitruvian arcs ripped into existence around them. Firas's breath pumped fog into the icy air as Finley scrambled away. The interfectors elevated above Firas to each side of his cell, hands drawn back, ready to strike.

"Stop!" shouted Jordan, running halfway back Firas.

Firas clutched the prison bar with his veiled hand. "If you are to betray me, brother, stay a moment longer. Witness my end. Let us spare everyone another day." Firas's face trembled. "I will come to thee, brother. This iron corral is but trivial." Firas moved his deveiled hand to the prison bars, which shimmered violet and rang out. Splinters of red and yellow light danced across Firas's face, glinting off his tears. "Ten feet? Five feet? Wager, dear brother, but do it fast!"

"No!" Jordan sprinted closer.

One of the interfectors spun around, his coronal wrath within striking distance. Jordan dropped to his knees, sliding to a stop. With hands in the air, he submitted, his eyes finding Firas.

Firas shouted at the interfector: "CALL UPON YOUR MASTER! Tell Supernus to come here and witness my death. Tell him my brother is afraid. Tell him my brother betrays. Tell him I am ready to go free at last. Tell him—"

"Stop!" shouted Jordan over Firas's harangue. "I'll do what you ask!"

Firas trembled and stared at Jordan.

Terrible seconds passed.

Firas finally veiled his hand. He continued to breathe heavy under the fierce light of the interfectors, whose radiance removed all contrast from the scene. Jordan saw in Firas's face the infinite weariness, the torment, the weak grip on reason. As that abysmal moment hung in the air, Jordan took in his contagious sentiment. He tasted the bitter pain of one hundred and twenty-eight years of injustice.

At last, the interfectors veiled.

The room went dark.

Jordan's eyes adjusted slowly, finding only black shapes at the onset. He heard Firas speak in a wavering voice:

"If I do not see you tomorrow when the clock strikes noon, I shall know you have betrayed. I will pass beyond these bars. I will be struck down, but I will have lived my final moment in freedom."

"I won't betray." Jordan's eyes continued to adjust, watching details of Firas's traumatized face emerge from the darkness.

"Then return to me tomorrow, brother. Just before the appointed hour." The voice of Firas withered into whispers. "There is one last thing you must know about me."

41

THE MERRY

At the end of the dimmest of dimways in North Leaf was the Taberna Meridiei. Its outer façade was welcoming, white, and wooden. Window frames and shutters decked in turquoise, a steep, faux-roofline jutting out from the stone. The pub's unapologetic Bavarian flare stood in stark contrast to the Grey City's classic sensibilities. The worn path to its door, however, suggested an enduring popularity.

But tonight it was closed to the public.

Though nicknamed *The Merry*, the spirit inside failed to live up to its namesake. At a large round table ran a ring of grim faces, the participants in Jordan's final training run, plus the ever-irritable Mio. Debate came and went like tides, the present phase being one of silent reflection. Hartwig orbited the group, doling out steins of dark beer. At a second table, Jordan and Lila sat next to one another, removed from the group. Dim vinelight presided over sullen spirits and a sea of nicked-up tables, the majority with chairs piled atop.

Dark walls, dark floors, dark thoughts.

"Firas will end his life tomorrow if Jordan doesn't go through with it," said Albert, his voice rising out of the silence. "He'll give up, he'll go mad—"

"He's already gone mad." Sebastién delivered the words while massaging his forehead with frustrated fingers. "He's unhinged. He believes exactly what the Kyzheres fed him all those years."

"You'd believe the same if it were you," said Easton, laying her fingers across the top of Sebastién's hand.

"Oui, oui. I would." Sebastién's gaze sunk but returned fast. "But what is the alternative? The Depths will incriminate Firas, not to mention, kill Jordan." Sebastién slammed his stein down on the last assertion, gathering everyone's attention. "He can't go down there."

Jordan knew the words were directed at him. But he kept his head down, catching Lila's sad, folded hands out of his periphery.

"But what of this Nether Dove?" asked Albert. "Have you bothered to consider *why* they want him? It's madness—"

Sebastién nodded. "I know it is—"

"—He'll be pulled into their war against the Kyzheres—"

"We're already in it." Sebastién's barreled fist pounded at the table. "War has already been declared. The Kyzheres aren't going to back down from this."

Faces tipped and turned. Responses erupted in half-thoughts; a congress of unconfident minds, uncertain about tomorrow. During a thin gap in the silence, Sebastién spoke, his tone waving a white flag. "This is the best we can hope for. Jordan remains alive, Gretchen remains alive."

"But Firas will die."

"That is his choice…" Sebastién closed his eyes as if something was stinging them. "When this goes down, we have to persuade him to hold fast. Convince him things could change. He's already waited over a hundred years—what's a few more?"

Subtle shrugs and acquiescent faces.

"So tomorrow," continued Sebastién, "Jordan's going to look Firas in the eye and listen to whatever last fantasy he wants to spin. Then he's going to flee."

Bodies shifted and furniture creaked as they turned toward him. Jordan surveyed their faces but avoided looking them in the eye. Though a table away, he became hyper-aware of himself, the sound of his own breath reaching him like he was in a wind tunnel. He felt his every movement being digested by collective scrutiny.

"Seems our brave hero has nothing to say," chimed Mio.

"Mio…," said Easton.

"Seriously," Mio turned toward Jordan in full, "at least concede that signing on to the Depths was a shitty idea…especially after you *knew* you had a fucking way out."

"Mio, stop it!" said Easton. "It doesn't—"

"—How do we know this thing even comes together! We're supposed to believe they're going to whisk him away under the nose of the Kyzheres *and* Arbor Florum's Praetorium?"

"You're not seeing it." Jiro grasped Mio's forearm, trying to turn her back around. "They *must* have defectors in the Praetorium. How else could they have done the opera? There must be collaborators. This is bigger than us."

"Yeah, and maybe Gretchen's sneaking around has already done them in." Mio gave them all a mocking shrug. "She might already be dead. Oh—and I wouldn't stick around the Carmen to explain this to Firas once the Kyzheres learn the jig is up, or we'll be writing your sorry epitaphs too—"

"The fucking cynicism with you!" Easton shoved her stein toward Mio, causing froth to jump the rim and splash onto her sleeve.

Mio glared at her and folded her arms. "You're all fucking mad!"

Four people spoke at once. Jordan didn't bother to sort it out. He faded it and turned his attention to Lila, who was barely listening. "What does the Nether Dove want with me?"

Lila frowned and cast Jordan an unhappy glance. "A lot of things…" She returned to staring at her folded hands. "An early warning system; detect them before they detect the people you're with. A spy, or a hunter, like your predecessor, when he and the Devikira tracked down Supernus. Or worse…"

Jordan waited on the last speculation.

Lila turned toward him. "I'll find a way out of Arbor Florum eventually—we all will. We'll find you or you'll find us." Her eyes reached through him, as though seeing far-flung events Jordan couldn't fathom. "Promise me you'll stay away from the front lines."

Jordan swallowed.

The debate table grew even louder. Jordan watched Wiley, Georgia, and Lev trade glances on a regular basis, like baby birds in a nest. Each seemed ready to speak but refrained, letting Albert and

Sebastién dominate the discussion.

"—and you're a fool to think this Nether Dove means peace—"

"Move over," barked Hartwig, returning to the table with a full pitcher and a stein adorned with images of stag antlers. He shoved in between Mio and Jiro.

"—the only visible resistance to the Kyzheres since—"

Jiro scooted over, which made Sebastién do the same, his chair bumping into Wiley's foot. Sebastién stopped speaking and glared at Wiley. "Aren't the three of you supposed to be keeping watch?"

"We are."

The debate stopped entirely.

"Then do it. Outside."

Wiley just smiled, tapping the floor with an energetic toe tip. Then his grin flattened. He hunched over toward Sebastién. "Supernus is here."

"Exactly," said Sebastién. "That's the sort of thing you clowns are supposed to be watching for."

"No—Supernus is really here, Sebastién. Right now."

Sebastién's side of the table turned in unison and watched Supernus walk in, bringing an insuppressible grin and swagger. The dead-faced Kristof and Konstantin walked at his side, hands crossed like monks, black robes hanging past their wrists.

"We're closed," said Hartwig, rising to his feet, stein in hand.

Sebastién pursed his lips.

"Of course you are." Supernus walked toward them with palms up like a preacher calling a congregation to rise. Konstantin and Kristof remained alert as eagles. "I only wish to speak with Mr. Wakefield."

"I said we're closed." Hartwig blocked the way.

With a pair of thick fingers planted on Hartwig's chest, Supernus pushed him aside.

"What is it you want?" asked Sebastién, arm slung over his chair's backrest, conveying a false confidence.

"Nothing from you, piano man." Supernus walked past. "I wish to congratulate the new Investigator Forensis." Supernus arrived at Jordan's table, placing his palms on its surface. He leaned forward toward Jordan. Lila looked down, pulling her hands into her lap like she'd touched a hot stove. Supernus leaned closer, causing his white-shard necklace to flop out. Jordan wanted to rip it loose and shove it down his throat.

"Then congratulate me," said Jordan. "And leave."

Supernus sneered at him, rotating his palms on the table's surface. "Such an unbecoming tone. I wanted to thank you, after all."

"I'll hand it over on a silver platter tomorrow, won't I?"

Supernus drummed his fingers. "What you'll hand over is the truth and a justice long overdue." Though he smiled at Jordan, his eyes transmitted a contrary message. "'Tis a shame, though, what happened today." Supernus stood upright, the necklace falling flat against his black shirt. "I heard it from Braer. Poor bird wants to fly, and all because his brother is afraid." Supernus started to toy with the shards on his necklace as if trying to draw Jordan's attention to it. "Word has it he wanted *me* to witness his departure from Elysium. I'll honor this request and pay him a visit tomorrow. Perhaps the opportunity will arise again—tell me, Mr. Wakefield, might you have cold feet?"

"Anything else?" Jordan glanced at the others. Tense, restrained faces, all watching him. Returning to Supernus, Jordan saw his false amiability eroding. Jordan pocketed this as a victory. It firmed his resolve to not let Supernus get the better of him.

"Lila," said Supernus, side-stepping so that he was looming over her now. "So quiet. What changed between us?"

Jordan clenched his teeth. Wait this fucking guy out.

"That's enough." Sebastién stood up, causing the others to emit chirps of panic. Interfector eyes darted to him.

"Konstantin," said Supernus without turning around, "if Saint-Vezina takes another step, cut off his hands and lay them upon the table."

Albert stood up and roared: "One does *NOT* speak like that in Arbor Florum!"

As though hitting a tripwire, Konstantin and Kristof deveiled with explosive force. Every person at Sebastién's table jumped to their feet, moving away as the interfectors rose, their light painting the pub daytime-bright.

"But I just did," said Supernus.

Nobody moved, nobody spoke.

Supernus relished the moment before speaking, "Konstantin, Kristof, hold." Then, to Lila again with an unnatural affection: "Look at me, my dear."

Lila's eyes maintained a death grip on the table. Supernus reached toward her slowly, tracing a single finger across her cheek. She jolted upon contact.

Jordan jumped to his feet, kicking his chair backward. Before it cleared, he had deviled, disintegrating its front legs. Supernus deviled in response before the chair remnants hit the floor. They both ascended, meeting face to face, fiery stares locked. The interfectors zipped to each side of Supernus. One spun toward the crowded table, the other remained facing Jordan.

"Hold," said Supernus through wicked laughter.

Sebastién's face pleaded with Jordan to stand down. Before he could contemplate it, Jordan felt Supernus's seduction bite him, its potency far beyond Easton's.

"And here we are again," said Supernus calmly, moving his violet hand through the air in a slow flourish. "Seems you've not learned your lesson, the one about respect." Supernus stretched his hand out to Jordan, palm facing the floor. Jordan's glossy eyes clung to it. "Seems I have to teach it again. I am patient, yet I am forgiving. Kiss my hand and all shall be forgotten."

"What is it you want?" asked Sebastién.

"Respect, as I said." Supernus watched and waited. Jordan drifted forward, dipping his chin reverently. Upon reaching the outstretched hand, Supernus elevated his head, his chin reaching a zenith of pride.

Suddenly Jordan blazed bright.

With serpent-like precision, Jordan's hand struck deep into Supernus's chest, blasting him back past the interfectors. Streams of violet light rained down on Sebastién's table. Supernus veiled, his physical form falling out of the light, crashing onto the table and obliterating the steins. Fragments of porcelain shot in every direction, followed by the chatter of ale raining to the floor.

It was a brief victory.

Yellow light hit Jordan's vision, and he was struck by lightning. Then he was on the floor, veiled with a jackhammer headache.

But he was still alive.

Someone was shouting to him.

Recalling Sebastién's first lesson, Jordan sprang to his feet. Stumbling, his field of vision went supernova as Konstantin arrived again. An inferno perched above him, body tipped horizontally so that those wide, dead eyes stared right into him. Plumes of yellow light raced around his body.

"NO!" called a chorus of voices.

Sebastién overpowered them all: "JORDAN DON'T MOVE!"

Jordan didn't listen. He leaked a toxic smile, watching a veiled Kristof help Supernus to his feet. He shouted above the din of Konstantin's fiery light: "Don't you see it? They won't hurt me. They've been ordered to protect me, to refrain from anything that would prevent me from going into the Depths." Jordan's chest heaved as though he'd been sprinting, while Konstantin's eyes remained fixed on him, absorbing every millisecond. "I am to be treated as one of them!"

"Konstantin, relent," said Supernus, on his feet again. His words came out slurred. Konstantin dimmed and backed away from Jordan as Supernus teetered closer, still being assisted by Kristof.

"That's called getting knocked out," said Jordan, his vision blurred by pain. "A friend of mine taught it to me that way…so now I teach it to you." Jordan managed a drunken bow on unsteady legs.

Supernus snarled and shoved Kristof aside. "You," he said, grabbing Jordan by the throat, "cannot do *that* to *me*."

Jordan broke Supernus's grip. "But I just did."

"Do you understand what I could do to you?" Supernus trembled, his muscles ready to leap out of his skin.

"Jus Homicidium?" returned Jordan.

Supernus closed his mouth. His face twitched.

"So say it!" shouted Jordan, his fists closed like tourniquets. "I fucking dare you!"

Supernus's nostrils flared like twin furnaces.

"But you won't because you need me for the final act," said Jordan. "We all know you're the murderer and you're going to get away with it."

Supernus's eyes drowned in malice.

"You won. We get it. Now fuck off."

Jordan watched Supernus's face go loose. Then an unexpected grin arrived. It caught Jordan off guard.

Though not as much as the uppercut that followed.

Jordan's line of sight went from Supernus to ceiling to floor, a broken jaw added to his interfector migraine. He willed himself to stand, somehow doing it. On shaking legs, he spit teeth onto the floor. Just like Crispin's parlor. He stood his ground while Supernus turned away. With the interfectors veiled and once again at his side, the trio walked out of the Taberna Meridiei without another word.

Jordan waited for them to depart before he deveiled to health. Pain-free again, he took in his colleagues. A semicircle of astonished countenances, none more joyed than Wiley, who wore the wide eyes of a child on Christmas Day.

"You're my hero," he said.

"This one's a keeper." Hartwig flayed his hand. He hovered it near his stein. His own purple light hummed back at him. He'd recorded the whole thing. Hartwig shrugged at Jordan. "If he killed you, at least we'd have proof this time."

"They would have killed every one of us, you fucking dolt!" said Mio, crying the words out.

"But they might not have checked my mug." Hartwig looked proud. He poured himself another.

The post-insurrection debate ramped up like a forest fire. Jordan turned away. Lila was still in her seat, face tilted down, hands folded in her lap. He went to her and touched her shoulder gently. She jerked, quavering syllables with the act. Her surprised eyes found Jordan, as though he'd appeared out of thin air. As though she hadn't observed a single thing since Supernus touched her.

42

Vigil Under Elysium

The last of the amber light coursed over the Arborsolis, signaling the end of day. Soon it would shift into fainter reds, then sink into purples before giving way to the placid winter-blue that would claim the Grey City until morning. Jordan realized that it was the last time he would witness this transformation. On a stone ledge halfway up the inner wall of Aria, they sat next to one another. Lila's legs dangled over the edge next to his. Both felt cool granite press against their backs. Both felt the weight of parting ways, Jordan's flight into the unknown. Lost in thought, they stared into the light of the great tree, removed from the world like two marionettes abandoned on a shelf.

For ten days Jordan had lived in this bright world with its dark history. Tricked and played and backed into a corner, he now reflected on the betrayal he would have to make.

It was impossible.

Firas would see through him, just as he did the day after Helena. Just as he did only hours ago, on the heels of Gretchen's revelation. Jordan blamed his weak poker face but found himself wondering if it was instead a particular talent of Firas, to see through the eyes of a stranger and pluck out secrets on the other side.

Firas had all the time in the world to practice it.

Jordan's gaze fell out of focus, causing the Arborsolis to slip into an array of soft, orange-red circles of light, the world reduced to a comforting bokeh. He imagined himself floating off into it, joining those indistinct colors, vanishing into them forever.

But his conscience wouldn't let him.

It threw him face-first into tomorrow, forcing him to speculate how it might go down. He wondered if Firas would call him out. If the interfectors would end both their lives right there. Or maybe Firas would let him go with silent acquiescence and a tear in his eye. Maybe he *would* pull it off. Maybe Sebastién would convince Firas to persevere. But if it was all in vain, Jordan wished for his brother's death to be instant, a deliverance by interfector fire as final as the sun.

It was the best he could hope for.

Jordan's mind reached further back, recalling his faintlight life. He saw Maggie's face on the night of his grand confession. He remembered announcing his aspirations to be part of something that mattered. And here he was now, wish in hand. Real circumstances with real consequences. He'd gotten dirt on his hands, and tomorrow it would be Firas's blood. The whole affair, born out of a wish to solve the mystery of a pair of eyes...

Lila.

She was right next to him, distant and withdrawn. Questions surfaced again and again, ones he didn't want to ask. But somehow he did this time.

"What does Supernus want with you?"

Lila's eyes narrowed at the sound of his voice. She blinked back to reality, crossing her hands at the wrists and leaning away. A moment later, she looked at him, but it was a struggle.

"He just wants me."

"Like..." Jordan fought to finish it. "A lover?"

"A possession. Something to own wholly, though he used the word bride." Lila looked away, her cheek capturing the plum-red light of the fading Arborsolis. "He was obsessed with me before I even existed."

Jordan connected the dots. "My predecessor's portrait of your eyes, in that hall. He stole it—that's what Easton meant."

Lila nodded. "It's incomprehensible. To fixate over a face—just the image of one's eyes. Proportions and distance between features render one person beautiful and another unsightly. We wrap these impulses in virtue, but they're deplorable. Our sight makes us blind. Supernus was blind in this way. I rejected him from the day he pursued me, but he was unwilling to accept it. In his mind, I was his." Lila curled her fingers into a fist. The tendons in her hand stood out, and her jaw went tight. "I wish he was dead."

At those words, Jordan found his own fist balled up, fingertips biting into his palm.

With effort, she undid the tension. "It's my darker half saying this—I realize it, I do." Lila continued, her face nearly turned away from him now. "That he murdered my predecessor made him feel entitled to me. He confessed it. Twice. The second time there was even metallum in my hand. He said he alone made my existence possible, and for that, I was his—"

"He confessed the murders to you?" Jordan nearly slipped off the ledge.

"Twice."

"Do you still have it—the metallum?"

"No," said Lila shaking her head in slow wide sweeps.

"Why?"

"You don't understand…please."

"Help me understand—what did he do to you?" Jordan touched her arm. "Tell me…why do you withdraw? Tell me how to reach you."

"You can't." She quivered, resisting the urge to twist free of his touch.

"I want to do one right thing, at least by you—"

"Then don't ask about this," said Lila.

Jordan let his fingers slip away. "I can imagine so many terrible things—"

"All of which I'd prefer to the truth."

Jordan let it go. Their sad gazes floated back to the ribbons of light circling the Arborsolis. It was purple now, the deep blues about to emerge. Before either found words again, a quartet of copper-colored freelight glided into the middle of Aria, arranging themselves at ninety-degree offsets.

"ACOUTAH! ACOUTAH!" They called in perfect harmony, their vox-voiced delivery carrying throughout the wide expanse of Aria. The citizenry began to emerge from their homes as a second call went out. They peeked through windows and leaned on balconies, their faces a study in misery. After the third call for attention, most of the citizens were visible.

They waited.

"LET IT BE KNOWN TO ALL IN ARBOR FLORUM," called the orators, "THAT TOMORROW, CARMINA THE FIFTH, ELEVEN EIGHT NINETY, AT HIGH NOON, THE DEPTHS SHALL BE UNSEALED BY ORDER THIRTEEN SEVEN-TY-FOUR..."

Jordan took in the citizens' expressions as the orators continued their proclamations. They ranged from contempt to aloof; no faces suggesting support. Their activism accomplished nothing. They had shoveled new coal onto an old fire and brought it back to life.

"AN INVESTIGATION SHALL BE CONDUCTED IN THE DEPTHS BY THE NEWLY APPOINTED INVESTIGATOR FORENSIS, JORDAN WAKEFIELD, LUX SANGUINIS..."

Jordan saw faces tighten at the mention of his name, two words that had become a verbal scourge even to his ears. A name irrevocably tied to the Kyzheres. The blame would fall to him.

"IN ACCORDANCE WITH THE INVESTIGATION, ALL CITIZENS ARE TO BE EVACUATED FROM EAST LEAF BY NINE O'CLOCK IN THE MORNING. THEY WILL BE BARRED FROM RETURN UNTIL A TIME DEEMED APPRO-PRIATE BY THE PRAETORIUM..."

An orange freelight raced into Aria

It bee-lined right at the orators.

It was Sebastién with Easton right behind him. The crowd resounded surprise upon seeing the impending collision. The orators, noticing it, aborted their announcements and broke away. They scattered, ceding the center to Sebastién and Easton.

Sebastién scanned Aria, stopping when he spotted them on the ledge. He flashed a fatalistic smile. Blazing bright, his features vanished into a flare of orange fire. His voice boomed forth like magnificent thunder:

"ACOUTAH!"

The word drew disconcerting looks from the citizens. Sebastién called for attention again as Easton's gaze went to the other side of Aria. Jordan followed it to the displaced quartet of orators, who had clustered together over the treetops near the West Leaf gateway. Next to them, floated a purple freelight and four interfectors.

"ACOUTAH!" called Sebastién a third time. The observers, their interest snared by the intrusion, pressed against their balustrades and craned their heads out the windows. All eyes on Sebastién, faces tightening even further into displeasure.

Jordan whipped his attention back to the cluster of displaced orators. They gestured madly to the interfectors' handler. To Jordan's relief, the handler seemed amused. With arms folded, he ignored the orators and watched Sebastién.

Sebastién strained his voice, his words clipping as they came out: "DO NOT FORGET WHAT HAPPENED HERE ONE HUNDRED TWENTY-EIGHT YEARS AGO. DO NOT FORGET WHAT THE KYZHERES HAVE DONE TO FIRAS. TO RAPHAEL FOSCARI. TO ELISABETH DI LORNE. TO *ALL* OF US!"

As the words filled Aria, more freelight came streaming in. Leading the way was Albert, with Wiley's troupe just behind. Then Hartwig and Jiro. Even Mio. Then dozens of others Jordan had never met. They flew in circular paths along the outer edge of Aria. They ascended, their trajectories evoking a scene of autumn leaves caught in a cyclonic wind.

Sebastién continued: "WHAT JORDAN WAKEFIELD DOES, HE DOES FOR HIS BROTHER. HE IS THE FIRST AMONG US TO NOT TURN AWAY. REMEMBER THIS."

Jordan felt a charge of pride. Watching his friends and unmet allies swirl about Aria, he found himself on his feet. Lila rose next to him, her hand clutching his far shoulder for balance. They stood together, chins high.

With his address complete, Sebastién dimmed, his features coming back into detail. With Easton at his side, he held out his hand. They both projected V-shaped salutes to Jordan. The others, who had now positioned themselves all about Aria, did the same. Albert, over the South Leaf gateway with bright purple fingers; Wiley, Georgia, and Lev, perched proud on someone's veranda, arms outstretched, lime-green fires burning bright; Jiro standing on the arch to North Leaf.

But as fast as Jordan's heart swelled, it constricted. He understood what they were really doing.

They were saying goodbye.

On the far side of Aria, the interfectors' handler was nearly hugging himself as though restraining laughter. Even the orators watched the scene with indifference and an air of pity. Jordan ignored them. He extended his hand and flayed his fingers, lifting his own rose-red salute high in the air. Lila did the same.

Jordan felt all of them.

A tidal wave of memories crashed into him, scenes from his faintlight life finding freelight association. They rooted deep into his heart, forging unity with all those who stood unafraid. Jordan felt the entirety of their lives, worn bare by the tyranny of the Kyzheres. Dealt a losing hand ages ago, they were now reliving this ancient defeat. And then, within the flood of those supportive reads, Jordan felt one he didn't expect: folding paper airplanes with his father.

It was Eli.

Jordan hunted him down, finding his faint blue salute deep within the recess of a dark window, hidden away from public view. Yet it was there.

It meant everything to Jordan.

The vast majority remained unmoved. They sneered and booed and spit. They turned away, disappearing back into their homes. Jordan's last sight of them was a crowded panorama of defeated faces.

That image drilled into Jordan's mind, breaking loose an idea from his conscience. In that moment, Firas's riddle revealed itself. Jordan understood his secret at last:

It was revenge.

Revenge for turning their backs on him. For one hundred and twenty-eight years, Firas had been locked away. Arbor Florum remained free as long as the citizenry protected the lie. Subjected only to soft coercion by the Kyzheres, it had now turned hard.

They were all Firas now.

Trapped under Elysium, stripped of their freedom. It was a game meticulously designed with Jordan as the star player, the unlikely arbiter of the end game. Firas had foreseen it all. The Depths and its inevitable trap. Their activism and its inevitable counter-reaction. His reckless altercations with Supernus and the tit-for-tat retaliation. Even the Nether Dove and the release of one hundred and twenty-eight years of angst. Every bit of it set in motion the day Firas asked his brother for aid. Every event orbited his nucleus of pure naivety.

And yet the game was incomplete. Only tomorrow would it be finished. At the stroke of noon, there'd be one final act of cowardice.

Jordan would leave them all behind.

43

ONE LAST THING

The next morning, with noon creeping ever closer, Jordan watched a band of orange freelight from Sebastién's sitting room. Stationed outside, off the veranda, they floated in formation with backs turned to him. A wall of closed curtains tried to maintain privacy, but their auburn glare pierced the linen barrier, glinting off vases, candelabras, and other ornamentry in his home.

Jordan started pacing again.

Firas had used him as an instrument of revenge. Jordan could barely fathom it. That the Depths *were* rigged was the only flaw in the ruse—yet the Kyzheres hadn't tricked Firas into believing it. It was Firas who tricked Jordan into believing it. The whole thing was diabolical, impossible. Yet it was done, a meticulous achievement a century in the making.

How it must taste to Firas at this very moment…

Perhaps this was the price. The way to force everyone to take Firas's side—to truly *feel* what he felt all those years. Firas had accomplished more than their feeble activism dreamt of. With the Grey City locked tight, the pressure would increase and eventually something would burst.

Jordan's pacing increased.

He'd have to face Firas soon. Lila had been gone for hours to her clandestine meeting with Darbi and the conspirators who would

347

facilitate the escape. No sign since. Perhaps it had fallen apart, perhaps she'd been caught. During the wait, Sebastién and Easton resigned themselves to the hind of the residence, granting Jordan peace during his final hours in Arbor Florum.

But Jordan found none.

Knots built in his stomach, then knots upon knots. Thoughts of all the things that could go wrong, followed by the sparse few that could go right. A realization hit him, halting his aimless march. His abandonment would trigger his transition. If he fled, they'd fabricate his death in the faintlight world and he'd never see his father again. To even attempt it would risk death. They'd no doubt watch for him there. He stared at the orange freelight outside again, wondering if—

"It's the Praetorium's show again," said Sebastién, suddenly next to him. His presence startled Jordan but failed to pry his attention loose. "The handlers, the interfectors—all of Castellum are standing down. Negotiated back into the Carmen on fears that things will spin out of hand. I suspect it's all part of a plan to get you a head start." Sebastién leaned close, also eyeing the four orange freelight outside. "Those praetors out there…no way to know if they're guarding us or part of it…Jordan?"

Jordan remained fixed on the orange light. Sebastién moved in front of him, blocking his view. With two fingers he flicked Jordan's chin like it was a light switch. Jordan's attention returned with irritation.

Sebastién folded his arms. "Listen: I want you to be careful. If anything seems off, if this goes south, flee. Ditch Gretchen if you have to—I don't trust her. Get away from Arbor Florum. Get to San Francisco—remember, they can only *see* you. They can't track you down. Change your look, hide out. Watch Les Rev—the newspaper. We'll find a way to communicate with you through it."

"And then what?" asked Jordan, his attention trying to sneak past Sebastién to the spectacle beyond the curtains.

"I don't know." They were the softest words Sebastién had ever spoken. "I'm sorry I got you into this. I misjudged everything—"

The rustle of a soft veiling in another room stole their attention.

They hurried to the lounge. On the other side of the piano, fresh out of the vent was Lila, Easton already up close to her. Sebastién checked over his shoulder to confirm no praetors had coasted in.

The four of them huddled like thieves.

"It's done…" Lila's face was ashen white, eyes distant, as though replaying the events of her secret meeting. "Darbi is part of this. A lot of people are part of this. It's bigger than we knew. After Firas you'll be brought to Hugo Frenatel in East Leaf. He's charged with unsealing the Depths. He's also the one who will get you and Gretchen out. Through South Leaf—same way the Nether Dove got in. The breach wasn't truly resealed." Lila stepped closer to Jordan as though to reduce his awareness to her alone. "I don't know where you'll be going. I'm certain you'll travel in the faintlight way, with Gretchen being so easy to track. You'll have only *minutes* before the Venators will be after you."

Jordan saw sadness flare in Lila's eyes. Together for only days, soon to be parted. Young soul, old soul. None of that mattered now. They were both lost souls, defeated souls. Jordan had seen it in all their eyes. Even Firas, despite the scheming, left Jordan harnessed in guilt.

"What about Firas?" asked Jordan. "The suicide pledge?"

"It's not on you." Sebastién grabbed Jordan's shoulder and turned him so they were looking square at each other. "He's not stupid. He'll listen to reason and stay in that cell."

"I'm not so sure."

"Then I'll knock him out myself before the fects—"

"You'll lose your feet."

"Wouldn't be the first time." Sebastién shook him by the shoulders as if trying to wake him. "Listen to me. You need to follow Hugo's instruction." Sebastién tried to find something else to say but came up dry. He walked away.

Jordan spent his final minutes alone, peeling back layers of anger. At its heart was a terrible truth: Supernus Kyzhere was going to win. The thought boiled in Jordan's throat.

Minutes later, the praetors came calling. Speaking in vox, they ordered the four of them to come out. Reconvening in the sitting room, Jordan and company parted the curtains and went out to the balcony. He stole a glance into Aria. With East Leaf evacuated, displaced citizens hovered in countless hordes over the Arborsolis. Thousands of them; not merely the exiled, but those from other leafs, and likely most of the Trid visitors, now forbidden to leave. They would all see how it would end. Their gazes habitually drifted to the East Leaf gateway. There, a wreath of praetors kept guard, floating in precise formation with busy, vigilant eyes.

Over Sebastién's balcony they went, drawing a chorus of jeers. They ignored it as they flew toward the West Leaf gateway with praetor escorts in front and behind. Then, down to West Grey where the Carmen rose above the treetops. An unruly crowd pulsed at its grand staircase. The four of them and the praetors veiled just short of it. They pushed through the crowd, the praetors clearing the way with tight lips and heated expressions. They remained outside after getting Jordan and the others in. The mob's clamor was downgraded to a dull rumble after the Carmen's front doors were shut.

Then a new source of harassment, a voice from across the foyer: "Sebastién Saint-Vezina…Easton Bray. You're under arrest for interfering with an interarboral proclamation the night of last, in Aria."

Sebastién leaked a grim smile. "Of course we are." He turned on his heels, facing Jordan as the footsteps of his arrestors chattered across the foyer. Sebastién placed his hands on Jordan's shoulders. Leaning forward, he bumped their foreheads together, his blue eyes eating Jordan's field of view. "Remember what I said. Be vigilant, do what you must. Survive."

With an uncertain smile, Sebastién was pulled away. They gathered Easton too. Over his shoulder, Sebastién volleyed his final words. "Lila, it has to be you to stay with Firas. Savis, my friends." Sebastién and Easton were escorted down a dark corridor.

Lila shut her eyes and struggled through a heavy breath.

Lacking the ambition to speak, Jordan and Lila walked the halls in silence. Arriving at the antechamber to the ballroom, they passed Mortimer who pretended to be busy at an empty desktop. When they entered, Jordan spied Finley's chair. It had been claimed by Supernus, whose broad back was to them. He perked up at the sound of their approach but didn't turn around. The evicted Finley sat on a stack of books nearby. Supernus's personal interfectors, Konstantin and Kristof stood to the sides of Firas's prison cell. Firas maintained the lowest station of all, sitting on the floor of his cell with legs folded like the Buddha. A half-eaten bowl of rice parked next to him, a spoon stuck unceremoniously in its center.

As Jordan drew closer, his confidence faltered. He looked away from Firas, pathologically dodging his eyes.

"A pleasure to see you, brother. Come, sit."

Jordan's gaze jumped about the room. He knew his avoidance was a dead giveaway, but couldn't seem to overcome it.

Look at him…

Supernus watched from his makeshift throne as they passed by. Finley stood and chattered a preamble, glancing at the grandfather clock, marking the time. He made his way toward Firas, relic in hand.

"Shouldn't the Investigator Forensis be down in East Leaf?" asked Supernus, rapping his knuckles on the armrest in a tick-tock way.

Jordan ignored it.

Lila moved off to the side, away from Supernus, away from the prison cell, away from the interfectors, leaving Jordan to complete the march to the man in white alone.

Jordan sat down in front of Firas, crossing his legs in kind.

Look at him, dammit.

Jordan's eyes found Firas's white robes at last. He couldn't seem to reach Firas's face…

"Closer, brother," said Firas. "Please."

Jordan moved forward, his knees nearly touching the prison bars. Finley repositioned himself as well; the three of them uncomfortably close, like spies prepared to exchange secrets.

At last, Jordan looked at Firas.

Firas studied him. Though his voice was calm as the afternoon, something about his eyes burned with urgency. They darted about in tiny bursts, digesting Jordan's every move.

"I'm here, brother," said Jordan.

Those two words froze Firas's busy eyes. For a moment divorced from time, they stared at each other like two photographs hung in the void.

Firas's eyes narrowed—just a touch. His lip quivered.

He knew.

He read clean through. He could see the betrayal like it was written in electric light. He was going to give them up. Jordan went tight, preparing to deveil.

But then, Firas's face conjured a smile.

"I'm sorry I ever doubted you, brother." Firas looked about the ballroom, his eyes running a long, slow arc across its ceiling. "It is strange…I've been here for all of eternity. But here we are at last, a resolution at hand. This is the end."

Jordan's throat locked like he was trying to swallow glue. In that instant, he realized he'd misread everything. He knew it at once. This *wasn't* revenge; Firas hadn't been trying to destabilize Arbor Florum. He had nothing to do with the Nether Dove. Firas was trafficking a different conspiracy. The one he'd been selling the whole time.

The secret was real.

It was ready to spring from his lips.

From beyond the ballroom, out by Mortimer, came a sharp snap; a freelight veiling. A muffled exchange of words, followed by footsteps. A confused expression lit Firas's face, one he secured quickly. Biting his lower lip, his eyes left Jordan for a brief moment.

Behind him, Supernus spoke: "What are you doing here?"

"Eyes on me, brother," whispered Firas, detaining Jordan's curiosity.

"I'm here to observe," responded a familiar voice. "We have the right to visit this facility at will."

It was Eli.

"Of all the people in the Prudentiarum, they send you?" asked Supernus, snickering. "Short on advocates, indeed."

"I am here on my own accord." Eli recited a preamble like Finley's, noting the time and location, that he was here to observe the prisoner during the search of the Depths. His voice betrayed terror beyond anything Jordan heard that fateful night in Crispin's parlor, even after the guns were out. Eli's arrival was unexpected. Firas's reaction told this truth.

Firas recovered. "Do you remember the story of Helena's end, dear brother?" Firas's eyes burned like fire again. "Do you remember the night I was arrested, at the edge of East Leaf? I snuck in through the passage leading past the Depths. The one they sealed off from the Grey City…the one they're about to unseal for you."

"Yes, I remember."

"Twenty minutes, Jordan…" said Lila.

The voices behind Jordan took their turn:

"*Why* are you here?" asked Supernus.

"I might ask the very same of you," said Eli. "As I said—"

Jordan heard new footsteps coming down the hall.

Firas went rigid. He closed his eyes and appeared to be swallowing air, not breathing it. Firas avoided looking at the new arrivals. The spat between Supernus and Eli got lost beneath a more hostile argument the new arrivals brought with them.

More familiar voices:

"Ask him, then! He's right there," shouted Wiley. "Konstantin won the Finalis the year you came to Arbor Florum."

"He lost," said Lev. "I remember it."

"What are *you* doing here?" demanded Supernus.

"Settling a bet," said Wiley, his voice quavering. "Who won the Finalis in eleven eight twenty-six—Konstantin, right?"

"Why don't you go ask him," said Supernus, scorn lacing his words. "He'll dispatch you and your foolish question."

Silence.

"I will," said Wiley.

Jordan heard two sets of footsteps come up behind him fast, then nearly break into a run.

Firas swallowed hard.

"Get near that cell and he's gonna torch you, idiot!" shouted Lev, breaking into a footrace with Wiley.

"Stop!" commanded Supernus.

It happened in a second: first a collision, then a scuffle erupting between Wiley and Lev. From the corner of his eye, Jordan saw Finley's head whip around.

It was all planned.

"Eyes on me, brother!" commanded Firas.

Wiley and Lev came tumbling down on top of Finley. Wiley's arm knocked the metallum out of his hand. Before it hit the ground, blinding flashes of yellow light exploded before Jordan's eyes, reducing the rest of the world to comparative darkness. Between the bright pair of interfectors was Firas, now a black silhouette. He remained stationary, unaffected by what was happening.

Wiley, Lev, and Finley—recognizing the rousing of the guards—scrambled across the floor, feet and hands clawing the ground for traction. The interfectors went past Jordan like lightning. Sounds of violence followed, set to a backdrop of Supernus's rebukes.

Jordan and Firas were alone.

"Deveil your hand, brother—do it now!" shouted Firas.

With his whole body shaking, Jordan flayed his hand and held his palm up to Firas.

Firas did the same.

A stream of familiar memories skipped across Jordan's mind—all originating from behind him.

"We are brothers," said Firas. "Do you understand?"

Jordan trembled, trying to ignore the chaos. "I understand."

"Look closer!"

Jordan saw it at once: Firas's hand was a different hue of red, the color of a traffic light, not rose red like his own. "I understand."

"Feel me, brother," said Firas. "Do you understand?"

Jordan heard Wiley beg for his life…he refocused, quickly sorting out the signals in the room, ignoring everyone behind him, ignoring the relic-infused prison bars. One signal remained: it felt like Jordan's first day of grade school, his father saying goodbye, prodding him toward his classroom.

It was a weak signal, fainter than any faintlight.

But it was real.

And it was coming from Firas.

Jordan felt blood drain from his face, sucked dry by Firas's secret. A three-word mantra hit Jordan like thunder; he had heard it in Crispin's kitchen, from Sebastién at the Finalis, from Lila that night under the Arborsolis:

Same, but different.

A split second later, Jordan had it: Firas could write.

Shouts and screams and Supernus demanding order…

"I understand," said Jordan, choking on the revelation.

"When they murdered my Helena," said Firas, "Do you remember what I found at the edge of the meadow?"

"Her teapot," whispered Jordan.

"Yes." Firas's voice grew strong. "We have him, brother. Everything to prove Supernus the killer is there. The Depths were the only place to hide it. Fifteenth hallway, left side, wrapped in my clothes." Firas clutched the white cloth of his robes. "We have him. Show the world what he is."

"I understand," said Jordan. The melee behind them ground to a halt, leaving only fierce interfector buzz.

"We shall see each other again, brother."

"I understand," said Jordan. "I'll be back in a few minutes."

Finley returned, stepping in between them, preventing Jordan from hearing Firas's final words. They were lost to eternity: "No, brother, you don't. I shall already be gone."

Finley raced through a new preamble, clutching fresh metallum. Jordan, his mind spinning in a daze, stood up just as Finley sat down. As he turned to Lila, he heard Supernus banishing Wiley and Lev, telling them if they weren't gone in seconds, he'd have their feet hanging around their necks.

They were still alive.

The interfectors flashed back into position on each side of Firas. They veiled and stood vigilant, like machines at the ready.

Jordan sorted his thoughts.

Lila next.

As he approached, her active eyes tried to decipher what had just happened. Hurried footsteps pounded out behind them; Wiley and Lev departing. Supernus returned to admonishing Eli, with Eli asserting his right to remain.

Be brave, Eli. Keep at it.

Jordan reached Lila. "Time to go."

Lila nodded, her mouth hanging open.

Jordan moved in and hugged Lila. Her hands spread across his back. Jordan pulled her close and whispered. "Change of plans. I'm going into the Depths."

Lila went rigid, her fingertips digging into his back.

Jordan continued his clandestine communication. "Firas can write. He has Helena's murder on the teapot and the teapot is in the Depths."

Lila tilted forward, her forehead pressing into his chest.

Jordan nearly burst beyond whispers. "We have Supernus."

She trembled. Jordan trembled.

Then he let go and stepped back.

"Be careful." Lila's eyes hung to his.

"As long as we're apart," said Jordan with all the confidence he could muster, "we can't die together in a dark place. Right?"

Lila tried to smile, but fell short. She just stared at him, eyes wide.

Jordan turned and started to walk away.

He looked back, trying to delay the separation, if only for another second. He saw a different Lila: one wrapped in fear, drowning in doubt. It was the Lila from his birth echo—only the tears were missing. Jordan's head came back around. During his next steps, he caught Eli's attention. He saw fear there too. In Supernus, Jordan observed a different fear. A confidence rent asunder. A man who, on some level, detected that the odds had shifted against him. But it was Lila's fear that halted Jordan in his tracks.

He turned around.

He marched back to Lila, her uncertain gaze following him the whole way. Face to face again, Jordan stepped in and kissed her. She surrendered to the act, strands of her hair spilling across her cheek and onto his. Her hand found the side of his face, and for a moment they were free. Free of Arbor Florum. Free for one eternal second.

Then it was over.

Jordan separated and flashed her a smile. "I'll be right back."

Before he turned away, he saw her transformed: he saw Lila from the day they met on the bluffs, bereft of words and grinning. Lila at the beginning of Liwei's party; Lila at the opera—stunning blue dress, hands intertwined throughout the third act. He fastened these memories to his heart, hoping they'd carry him through. On the way out, Jordan winked at Supernus, whose face twitched.

An impossible silence maintained itself behind him.

He deveiled in a snap, and moments later found Wiley, Lev, and Georgia in the foyer. Wiley looked like a wide-eyed corpse, while Lev snapped his fingers and tapped his heel as though nothing had happened. The praetor quartet near the front doors commiserated.

Wiley was hyperventilating. He grabbed a fistful of Jordan's hoodie and whispered angrily, "Whatever the hell Firas wanted with that, it better had been fucking worth it—I thought I was dead for sure, I was *begging* for it to only be my foot."

"It was neither," said Georgia.

"Your life didn't flash before your eyes, did it?" asked Lev.

"Fuck off." Wiley punched Lev's shoulder, causing him to spin and lose his balance.

The praetors started to walk over.

"Sorry to spring it on you." Georgia eyed the approaching praetors. "Firas didn't want anyone to know."

"What *was* that about?" asked Wiley.

"I'll tell you later," said Jordan. "I need you to do something while I'm down there."

"Wait—what?" said Wiley, reducing his voice to a tight whisper. "You're going down there?"

The three of them traded sharp glances.

"Name it," said Georgia, recovering first.

The praetors were nearly to them.

"Get everyone as close to East Leaf as possible. I'll need help when I come out of the Depths."

"Why? What the hell's down there?" asked Georgia.

"Proof that Supernus killed Helena."

"Time to go," announced one of the praetors behind Jordan, causing all four of them to bump heads. Not risking another word, Jordan turned and marched with the praetors to the front. He took a deep breath while they threw the doors open. The bright light of West Leaf and the anger of the mob flooded the lobby.

Jordan focused. Derailing the escape plan was next. Then the Depths, then the teapot.

Supernus Kyzhere is going down.

44

THE DEPTHS

The escape plan…Jordan tried to think of a way to stop it as he crossed West Leaf with his praetor escorts. Hugo would resist him, Gretchen would panic. They'd both want to kill him on the spot. In moments, Jordan reached the massive crowds in Aria. The praetors brightened and pulled in close on all sides to protect him. Everyone in Arbor Florum must have been here now. They fired taunts as Jordan weaved through the masses.

Focus…the escape plan.

They were less than a minute from East Leaf and Jordan continued to draw blanks. Even hinting at its existence would be a death sentence for Hugo and Gretchen and whoever else was involved. It would be treason, and the punishment would be delivered on the street, right in front of everyone. It was impossible to discern friend from foe. Were the praetors surrounding him on his side? He had no way to know.

But there had to be a window.

A moment when Hugo would make his move. It would happen fast, and when it did, Jordan would have to shut it down cold or delay it to death, pretending he hadn't the slightest idea what they were talking about. Jordan passed the praetor barricade at the East Leaf gateway. On the other side, was an empty, twinkling world. Nobody on the streets, nobody in the air. Only silent glittering treelight and exquisite architecture. In the distance, at the terminating end of East Leaf, Jordan saw shimmering threads of light falling to the ground where a team of freelight was cutting open the doors to the Depths.

After they passed the Gorg, Jordan spied two figures alone on the street in the middle of East Leaf proper. Even from here, he recognized Gretchen; her rigid posture, arms folded at perfect ninety-degree angles; her longtail-tight-black-pants appearance. She kept turning her head in sharp movements, sweeping the scene like a seditious beacon. She was electrified by fear, likely to give them all away.

And now Jordan would make it worse.

He couldn't explain a bit of it to her until they were alone, which likely meant the Depths. He'd have seconds to convince her, or she'd haze him straight to his grave as the Kyzheres had ordered. She'd preserve her life at the expense of his own. Jordan couldn't blame her.

The praetors led him down to the street and veiled in front of Hugo and Gretchen. The latter looked away while Jordan and Hugo sized each other up. Hugo was tall and gray-haired. Long-faced, with a narrow, sharp chin. A near-caricature of someone out of a revolutionary war story to Jordan's eyes. At his feet was a leather satchel.

Hugo exchanged words with the praetors, his German-tinted voice cordial, betraying no anxiety. His attention moved through the group, neither ignoring Jordan nor landing on him with any particular gravity. His demeanor was so business-like Jordan began to doubt the man was involved in conspiracy at all. This cooled Jordan a degree, raising his confidence of getting into the Depths without issue. Maybe the escape plan already fell through—that would explain Gretchen's unease; she realized they'd have to go through with it after all.

Good.

Behind Hugo, at the end of East Leaf, the team of cutters continued to work on the entrance to the Depths. Bright orange light flashed off the white streets as they cut into the seals that made the doors airtight. A lone hand blazed away at the huge chains wrapping the handles. Acrid smoke drifted into the air, while spurts of molten iron bled away from their industry.

"I'm going to call on Kerdavick," announced one of the praetors. "Twelve minutes…"

Hugo, still talking, nodded the praetors off.

They deveiled in a quartet of sharp snaps.

"Regarding the Depths," said Hugo, his voice competing with the hum and crackle of the torch crew. "The passage behind these doors runs for miles, from East Leaf all the way to Florum Valley." Hugo glanced at the praetors as they rose into the air behind Jordan. "The valley-end was sealed off just after Firas's arrest a century ago. The Florum end—the doors they're cutting open now—were constructed the following year. Within this passage, less than a mile from where we stand is a second set of doors, the actual entrance to the Depths. Those doors, though as old as Arbor Florum itself, were sealed shut only a few years after Firas. That's all that separates the Grey City from disaster, should the noughts get out." Hugo stepped closer, the gravity of his presence arresting Jordan's attention wholly. "We are unsealing every bit of it today. This poses a great risk to you, to me, to everyone in the Grey City."

The words delivered terminal doubt to the escape plan. It never existed, or it had already failed. He and Gretchen *were* going down there; a date in a deadly dark world. Though it was what Jordan wanted, he found himself frightened. The intoxication of Firas's revelation had worn off, leaving a cancerous terror.

But he had to do it…he had to get the teapot.

"Gretchen will capture the testimony. You will protect her," said Hugo. "The rest of us will keep guard at the inner doors. Nothing gets out of the Depths but the two of you."

Hugo's eyes went skyward again.

Then he stopped moving as if he were a wind-up toy that had run to its final click. When Hugo snapped to life again, he had cast aside his diplomatic demeanor like a convict's chains. "Jordan: listen to me. We have only minutes. They're waiting for us above South Leaf. First—" Hugo grabbed Jordan by the arm and swung him around, shoving him toward a path that led away from the thoroughfare.

Gretchen was already ahead of them.

"I'm not going," said Jordan, regaining his balance after a flurry of stumble-steps in Hugo's desired direction. "I have to—"

"—We *have* to be veiled before the Venators are looking for us. We have *minutes*. Barely enough time to—" Hugo shoved him down the path again. "MOVE, goddamnit!"

Jordan shoved him back.

Hugo recoiled, Gretchen shrieked.

"Jordan!" Hugo's face trembled with violence. "What are you doing? We have to—"

"I'm not running."

Hugo teetered like he'd taken a blow to the head.

"I'm going into the Depths," said Jordan.

"WHAT!" shouted Gretchen.

Hugo stared incredulously.

"We have Supernus." Jordan took a breath and sidestepped toward the thoroughfare. "You have to trust me."

Hugo moved fast, blocking him. Gretchen grabbed his arm and dug her heels in. Jordan elbowed Hugo and ripped free of Gretchen. He dashed back to the thoroughfare and shouted to them, "You have to trust me."

Jordan glanced at the doors. The cutters were occupied. They hadn't seen anything. Hugo and Gretchen remained frozen, shocked faces peering at him from the seclusion of a tree-canopied path.

Precious seconds went by.

A pair of praetors zipped in behind Jordan and snapped into human form. A third freelight, the hue of a bright afternoon, veiled right in front of him. Cocoa-toned skin with a frosty beard. A scar ran across his forehead like a fault line. This man and the praetors traced Jordan's line of sight, casting their gaze down the path of the aborted escape. The man with the scar narrowed his eyes, scrutinizing Hugo.

"Kerdavick," said Hugo, offering a diplomatic nod. He straightened himself and helped Gretchen forward. "She became ill, and we wished to avoid spoiling the street."

The two of them returned to the thoroughfare, Gretchen looking so distraught that Kerdavick seemed to accept Hugo's claim.

"This stays on schedule." Kerdavick turned toward the Depths. He crossed his hands behind his back and strolled ahead, admiring the hot chestnut glow about the rim of the nearly unsealed doors. The pair of praetors followed him. Hugo snatched the satchel off the street and moved in next to Jordan, his breath radiating fury. Gretchen walked on the other side. With a gap between the three of them and Kerdavick, Hugo fired words out of the side of his mouth:

"Trust you? You have no idea what you're doing or the damage you've done—can you even comprehend it? You're a fool, trained by fools."

Before Jordan could respond, the sound of clanging metal drew everyone's attention to the doors. The severing of the chain was complete. It uncoiled with vengeance, the links thudding in a pile on the street.

Kerdavick halted.

The freelight who'd cut the chain veiled and kicked at the horse-shoe-sized segment of glowing metal he had amputated. He spit on it for good measure, raising a violent sizzle. Satisfied, he joined his fellow cutters who stood off to the side, hands on hips.

They all looked at Hugo.

"Open it," he said, twirling two fingers in the air.

A struggle ensued between man and the four-story doors. Organic grunts issued from the men, mechanical dissonance from the doors. They came open wide, the light of the Arborsolis racing down the ancient passageway. It reminded Jordan of North Leaf's subway tunnel to the Prudentiarum. But it lacked adornment. It was nothing more than a tall, dark tunnel.

"Now, the Depths," said Hugo to his team.

"Seven minutes," added Kerdavick, who was the first to deveil and pass the threshold. Hugo and his team followed, with Jordan and Gretchen at the tail-end. They traversed the dark passage and veiled in front of the inner doors to the Depths. The light of East Leaf barely reached here, offering only faint illumination.

Hugo's team went to work on the secondary doors, which were smaller, perhaps ten feet tall and ten across, ancient and austere. Hugo turned his back on Kerdavick, facing Jordan and Gretchen.

Jordan trembled, unable to regain his confidence.

"As much as we'd prefer otherwise," said Hugo, glaring at Jordan, "we'll remain here during the investigation. We're going to close these doors while you're down there. We *cannot* risk anything getting out. Call to us in vox when you're on your way up, and we'll stun back any noughts following you." Hugo stepped close to Jordan, his eyes ready to emit fire. "I'd prefer that you refrain from stirring things up down there. Make it fast."

Jordan nodded.

"You'll have twenty minutes," said Kerdavick.

"What if we need more?" asked Jordan, already trying to envision the teapot's location, trying to calculate the extra time he'd need to get to it.

"You don't *get* more." Kerdavick bared his front teeth with a smile that tilted toward a sneer. "If you're not back in twenty, you're dead as far as I'm concerned. We seal it, and that's the end."

Kerdavick said nothing more, Hugo added nothing else.

It was impossible.

Within moments the unsealing was complete. The cutters veiled, and darkness swallowed the world again. Two hot orange rectangles awaited, the team looking to Hugo for the order.

"Gretchen first," said Hugo. "Minimal light."

Gretchen deveiled. A soft violet glow filled the passage.

Hugo threw the satchel at Jordan using more force than was necessary. He caught it, but Gretchen zipped in and snatched it away, refusing to look at him.

"Now you, Investigator," Hugo looked at Jordan, his throat attempting to swallow, but locking up.

Jordan deveiled and brightened to a soft hum. Under his red radiance, he saw an expression break through Hugo's façade. An acquiescence to his plan. Jordan wanted to appraise it as a glint of hope, but it looked more like an indication that it'd be the last time they ever saw each other.

Hugo spoke. "Open the doors."

Hugo's people pulled them open. The team stepped back, all of them eyeing the primeval blackness in silence.

"Investigator first," said Hugo, his back to Jordan. "Get to the bottom. Stay bright so Gretchen can maximize her freefall to you."

"Twenty minutes," said Kerdavick. "It's noon."

They waited on Jordan.

He glided to the entrance and stared into the carnivorous dark. He felt his courage drain away like blood from a mortal wound. Every prior test—from volunteering to be Firas's advocate, to his altercations with Supernus—were conflicts with other men. Human beings acting within predictable parameters. But this was a dalliance with something beyond humanity. Jordan tried to repel his fears, holding fast to Firas's revelation: they had Supernus. It was up to him now.

Jordan glided past the doors…

And into the Depths.

Down the entry shaft he went, descending at a steep angle. Jordan thought about Lila and their kiss. It was an electric moment—and it could happen again if he survived the day. He thought about his birth echo, commanding his mind to find faith in its claim: if they were to die together in a dark place, it would not be this one. If they were apart, they would live. It was as simple as that.

As long as he didn't bend fate…

Deeper and deeper, the passage became vertical, and from there Jordan made a quick shot down, a few hundred feet at least. At the bottom was an eternity of undisturbed dust. He hovered, looking up, watching and waiting for Gretchen.

He felt her, but he couldn't see her.

The faint glow from the entry point remained, a weak shaft of utopian light, calling all the way from Arbor Florum. Tiny specs of dust floated in its keep. A grinding sound roared out, and all went to darkness. Terror jetted through Jordan.

They'd betrayed him.

They'd locked him down here forever.

Then he felt something move; he felt *things* move. Dark, nearly-imperceptible things sprouting into awareness. *I'm invisible,* he pleaded with himself.

Invisible, invisible, invisible.

Still gazing skyward with religious desperation, Jordan spotted a dim violet light. He felt Gretchen's signal increase as she moved out of the shaft. She veiled and vanished, a faint pop reaching Jordan's ears a split-second later. Then a flash of violet, right above him. The deveiled Gretchen arrested the satchel's freefall. She darted the rest of the way to him, tossing the satchel on the ground.

She veiled again.

On foot now, she glared at him, walking in a slow, wide circle while he hovered stationary in the air above her. Rage burned across her face. Jordan's red light only made it look worse.

"What were you THINKING!"

Before Jordan could respond, her hand came up and flayed. Violet light blazed bright. It tore through Jordan's mind like wildfire, reducing his constitution to ash.

She was the Lady of the Violet Light.

He existed only to serve her. He *wanted* to serve her. There would be no secrets between them.

"Why have we come into the Depths?" demanded Gretchen.

"To get Helena's teapot."

"WHY!"

The Lady was angry. This upset Jordan. He had to explain: "Because it's a relic. On it, Firas recorded the murder of Helena by Supernus Kyzhere."

"Impossible!" The word echoed into the infinite black.

The Lady of the Violet Light continued to circle him. Jordan turned with her movement, his eyes not wanting to miss a single second. "Firas is not Lux Sanguinis…not like me. I can't write, but Firas can."

"Why do you believe this?"

"Firas proved it to me. There was a distraction—a trick that gave us time. He flayed and I felt him, I read him. He told me about the teapot and its secret. We can bring Supernus Kyzhere to justice."

A few seconds went by, tears welling in Gretchen's eyes.

The violet light went out.

Jordan blinked back to awareness. She was Gretchen again. She stared at him in disbelief, while Jordan, for his part, returned the gesture. He remembered every word he had said. He could still *feel* the devotion to her—the Lady of the Violet Light.

"I'm sorry. I had to know," said Gretchen. She shook her head and began to walk in a circle again. "I can't believe it."

Jordan, still weary-minded, stared ahead blankly.

"The Kyzheres are untouchable," said Gretchen. "They can't be brought to justice, even with evidence. You don't—"

Out of the corner of his eye, Jordan saw Gretchen stumble. She recovered. She screamed, causing Jordan to spin around in full. On the ground in front of her was a heap of bones. Three skeletons, broken and tangled with each other. The skull of one gazed right at them, its front teeth crooked.

It was Helena.

Jordan recognized her teeth from Lila's summoning. The other two had to be Raphael and Elisabeth. He gazed at the sad ruin of the predecessors, trying to imagine them in life. All that remained was off-white, tangled pieces. Lives discarded into the darkness on account of revenge.

Gretchen's breath raced. "We're going to die down here."

"No, we're not." Jordan tried to sound calm despite his sudden agreement with her. "You know about my birth echo, right?"

"Everyone does."

"Do you believe it?"

"I sure as hell want to." Gretchen scraped tears from her cheeks.

"Then you know that if Lila's not here, I won't die."

"What about me?" Gretchen's voice cracked an octave higher.

"I'll protect you." Jordan glided in close.

Gretchen sobbed. "Okay, I'll try to…" She trailed off.

She didn't believe him, but there was no time for more words. To Jordan's relief, she retrieved the satchel and pulled out the metallum stack, tossing them on the ground. With the most honor time allowed, she collected the skulls and bagged them.

Jordan remained close, hovering right above her. He eyeballed the space. His light was not bright enough to reveal walls, nor the ceiling above. He tried to spot the exit point, but could no longer find it.

They were already lost.

The noughts continued to stir.

Jordan didn't tell Gretchen the worst of it. Not merely to avoid swelling her fear, but because he only realized it now. It was going to be worse than anticipated—far worse. What had been said about the Depths was wrong. There weren't a few dozen noughts, as Sebastién had thought. There were hundreds of them. Jordan felt them waking up and venturing forth as if carried on a breeze. Strangely, they were all on one side of the Depths, a long distance from them, packed tightly together.

"I'm ready," said Gretchen, drawing Jordan's attention back. She snatched a metallum off the pile on the ground and nearly smiled at him.

In a flash, Jordan solved the mystery of the noughts. They were drawn to the only signal down here: the teapot. Like moths to a flame, it brought them together. Which meant they'd have to go through them to claim it.

Violet light flared around the metallum in Gretchen's hand. She spoke: "Carmina fifth, eleven eight—"

Ghostly gray fingertips reached into existence and seized Gretchen's recording hand. Shrieking, she dropped the relic and fell to the ground. The ghostly hand held onto her. It sprouted all the way down to a forearm.

Jordan chopped it loose, causing the gray appendage to erupt into a transparent human shape, curled into a fetal position. Garbed in what looked to be stone-age clothing, it floated in the air before them like an embryo in zero gravity. They stared at it, engrossed.

Its head began to twitch and move. Its black, empty eyes searched about, trying to interpret the womb of the Depths.

"Too much force," said Gretchen, her composure in tatters.

"I know." Jordan whisked the newborn nought away carefully, trying not to rouse its aggression. It pawed at him like a drunk. He returned to find Gretchen standing over the heap of bones with another metallum.

"Do it fast." Jordan felt the distant storm of noughts drifting toward them. "The teapot's going to be harder than I thought."

"What do you mean!"

"Just hurry, get it done! We have ten minutes before they shut us down here forever."

Violet light flashed from her palm again, and her voice ran like the wind: "Carmina fifth, eleven eight ninety. Arbor Florum, the Depths. I am Gretchen Poesthoffer, recording witness for the special investigation of the declared deaths of Raphael Foscari and Elisabeth Di Lorne, declared murdered, Dēfessus fifth, eleven seven sixty-one. This is my testimony on behalf of Investigator Forensis, Jordan Wakefield…"

45

—◆—

TEN MINUTES

Firas el-Sakar sat on the floor of his prison cell, its unforgiving, cold granite pressing up against his body. His knees ached, and his stomach yearned as it always did. Yet these eternal discomforts did not trouble him now. He reveled in elation: the clock was striking noon, delivering a sequence of sounds he long ago ignored. But today—*this day*—these sounds called to him like bells from paradise; a glorious song marking his brother's entrance into the Depths and very soon, the end of his imprisonment.

But then came the guilt.

His brother remained unaware of the danger to come. He wished he could have warned him—even hinted at it. But it could only work if he didn't know. Firas rubbed his hands together as if trying to remove remorse. He added to this act a creed, one he'd preached to himself on many occasions: his brother's birth echo would prove true. Jordan Wakefield would survive the Depths. Fate would protect him, as long as he didn't bend it.

The clocked stopped chiming.

Soon he would be free.

Free.

He would live the remainder of his life a fugitive, the target of the most fanatical Jus Homicidium the freelight world would ever know, and it would not be on account of his escape from this place.

It would be for the murder of Supernus Tacitus Kyzhere.

Revenge at last.

Supernus, within reach now. Supernus: pacing right before his eyes, unaware of what would soon befall him.

Firas steeled himself. He closed his eyes. He breathed deeply like a forest calling to it all that resided under the sun. Then he let it go in a long unwavering hush.

He opened his eyes.

His mind accelerated out of its meditative state. He latched his attention to the face of the clock, watching its slender hand glide past gilded numbers.

Ten minutes.

That was the opportune moment. Enough time to complete the work in the Depths but not enough to get the teapot and get out—his brother would need to be in the deepest part when the interfectors arrived.

The noughts should do the rest.

An eternity of planning, every bit of it conducted in the confines of his mind. He'd played out the sequence with such regularity that it sometimes felt as though it had actually taken place. A lifetime of imaginary trial runs.

The clock read two minutes past noon.

Jordan would be in the Depths now. The one certainty was they'd enter on time and move with haste.

Fear guaranteed precision.

Firas's eyes snapped to the long, dim hallway that separated his prison cell from the world beyond. He concentrated, raking his mind like a seafloor, attempting to stir its deepest memories. He pieced together his recollection of the world beyond the Carmen: he *saw* West Leaf and its thoroughfare; he saw the gateway to Aria; then the Arborsolis, blazing in its afternoon glory; he saw the Asterhaus; South Leaf and its high passage, and finally, the way out of Arbor Florum—rumor reached his ears that the ancient way remained open since the opera. His very freedom would depend on it. He saw, at last, the sun.

Free.

All of it possible, all within reach.

Mortimer flew in, drawing Supernus's attention. "They went in at noon, on schedule."

Supernus nodded without looking at him. Still pacing, Supernus's attention was bent so inward it resembled a trance. He waved Mortimer away with two fingers, emitting a single, uncaring note. Mortimer flew off.

Four minutes past.

Firas calmed himself. His face must reveal nothing. Glancing about, he cataloged the room: Lila, twenty-five paces to his right, behind him at four o'clock. The interfectors, just off to the sides of his cell. Konstantin, as always, perfectly composed…but Kristof's breathing was faster than usual. He was the lesser of the two. He was still roused by Wiley's performance—and what a performance it was. Finley, near Supernus. Mortimer, outside in the lobby. Eli Windali, twenty paces, eleven o'clock, watching and recording.

Eli's presence…it meant there was dissent in the Prudentiarum. That he was here now, capturing every moment, was divine.

Six minutes past.

Firas licked his lips. *My turn.* He drew his tongue across the cutting edge of his teeth. Then he intruded on the quiet: "The Princeps Maximus seems troubled." His words issued gently but grew strong. "This is what you call yourself, is it not?"

Supernus stopped pacing. He turned away.

"Did you really believe she could love you?" After releasing the words, Firas trickled cruel laughter.

Supernus's hand tightened into a fist.

"This troubles you too, I see…"

Firas glanced at the clock: seven minutes.

"She's with my brother," continued Firas. "My BROTHER!" The word bounced across the ballroom. "You saw it with your own eyes. It is as fate has shown. Yet you are surprised by this?"

Lila: five steps farther away.

Supernus turned to Firas, the longtails of his coat flapping. Wrath pumped beneath his taut skin, though he was trying desperately to maintain his composure.

Firas smiled at him and narrowed his eyes.

"My brother," he said again.

"Soon," said Supernus, his voice falsely restrained, littered with quavers, "the world will know the truth about you." Supernus stepped closer. "You are enamored with that clock. Are you so anxious to see what your so-called brother finds in the Depths?" Supernus stepped right up to Firas's cell, his eyes bearing down on him. "Or is it the antechamber behind me? Do you wish to fulfill yesterday's promise and fly away?"

Yes…thought Firas with such unguarded desire that for an instant he thought he'd said it out loud.

Supernus turned sidelong, extending his hand toward the hallway. "Go free, Firas el-Sakar. Let us see how far you get."

Firas gazed past Supernus's inviting hand but to the clock, not the antechamber.

Eight minutes.

"Coward." The word came out of Supernus sharp. But it was somehow frail. Supernus walked back toward Finley, sinking into contemplation again, keeping his back to Firas like it was a shield.

"Lila…" Firas's voice was soft again. "Lila?"

A few seconds passed.

"Firas…what is it?"

Lila was terrified, Firas could feel it.

"Do you believe in your birth echo?" Firas avoided looking at her. He drew his hand across his knee, watching his fingers bunch the cloth of his robes. "What I mean is this: would you govern your decisions by it? Do you truly *believe* it?"

Firas watched Eli's attention go to Lila. He too was trying to decipher the riddle, likely leagues ahead of Supernus.

"I used to doubt it." Lila paused. "But I can no longer refute it, however improbable it seems."

"This is good…and wise. You know what you must do to protect yourself and my brother. Or rather, you know what you must *not* do."

"Spare us your utterances!" snapped Supernus.

Nine minutes.

With Supernus still turned away, Firas risked a smile. It was brief, like the moment a bird spreads its wings to take flight. But Eli saw it, and his recording hand began to shake. He had grasped the edges of what was coming. Firas vowed to try to protect them both.

He would do his very best.

Firas bowed his head low. He felt his warm breath rebound, washing across his cheeks. He pulled the spoon from the bowl of rice and began to rub it against his robes. He made it pure, he made it clean.

He made it ready.

Firas looked at the clock for the very last time. A tragedy that such a beautiful instrument had been exiled to this terrible place.

Ten minutes.

Firas stood up, gathering the attention of everyone in the room. He wrapped one hand around a prison bar. The other clutched the spoon, its curved end pressed into his palm.

Supernus, at last, turned to face him.

"I wish to make a confession," announced Firas.

Supernus furrowed his brow. Eli: two steps closer, looking right at him. Finley, looking to Supernus for guidance, but getting none. Finley scrambled to find fresh metallum. Once he had one in hand, he recited a preamble.

Then Firas did the same, his voice crisp and benevolent, as though delivering the most important message of his life: "Carmina the fifth, eleven eight ninety, ten minutes post meridiem, Arbor Florum, the Carmen Vespere. I am Firas ibn Ja'lal el-Sakar. I stand here, where I have for the past one hundred and twenty-eight years, falsely accused of the murders of Raphael Foscari, Elisabeth Di Lorne, and"—Firas choked up—"my beloved Helena. This is my confession."

The eyes of Supernus burned like Nero's Rome.

Nobody moved.

"On the night of Dēfessus fifth, eleven seven sixty-one, I witnessed the murder of Helena Phaedria in Florum Valley Proper, in the east meadow. She was murdered by Supernus Tacitus Kyzhere, who stands before me; the Princeps Maximus, son of Liaidor Kyzhere, the so-called Dominus Stellarum."

Supernus's mouth trembled, his face going red. "How dare you accuse *me?*" With a caustic sneer, he marched to Firas's cell. His chin arrived in front of the bars, his mouth continuing its spate of tremors.

"Because it is true," Firas looked him in the eye, "and you know it. I saw you, and soon the whole world will see you."

Supernus clenched his fists, knuckles cracking like acorns underfoot.

"You believe me to be Lux Sanguinis, like my brother." Firas's voice carried through the ballroom. "But your eyes have deceived you. We are not the same."

"*This* is your confession?" asked Supernus.

"No…" Firas removed his hand from behind his back, holding the spoon before Supernus. "This is." Firas flung the spoon between the bars. It skipped across the floor, dinging like a bell, coming to a stop at Eli's feet.

Firas snarled with menace. "I *am* Lux-Sanguinis-not-quite. Unlike my brother, I *can* write. Do you remember the teapot in my hand when you murdered Helena? Because it remembers you."

Supernus's face rippled doubt. Firas watched it slice through a century of events, digging for evidence of a bluff. Supernus turned toward Eli just as he knelt down, lowering his non-recording hand to the spoon. Eli flayed a finger and red light shimmered up from the spoon, cooing gently.

"I can't believe it," said Eli veiling his finger. He picked up the spoon, his hand shaking so badly he could barely hold it.

Supernus whipped back around.

Firas clutched the prison bars with both hands now, as if needing them for support. "I saw you! I saw you murder her! My Helena!" He struck the prison bars with his fists, drawing blood. "I saw you!"

Supernus stumbled a few steps back, his eyes sinking to the floor. He remained silent while Firas seethed, tears streaming down his face.

"When my brother returns, the world will finally know your deed. The teapot will warrant Black Lily. The Nether Dove will come for you," Firas breathed through clenched teeth. "They will come for you and prune your interfectors one by one. This place will become YOUR TOMB!"

Supernus's mouth twitched. But then he settled. He looked back at Firas and closed his eyes in the gentle manner of a child going to sleep. His fists released and he went lax.

At that moment, Firas knew he played his hand perfectly.

And then Lila screwed it up.

With a violent snap, she deveiled and shot down the hallway.

"Lila, NO!" Firas watched her disappear.

Eli stumbled backward.

Supernus opened his eyes. His arm lashed out, knocking the metallum out of Finley's hand. Finley stumbled sideways, perplexed.

Firas backed away from the bars and prepared, marshaling his senses to acute station. It was going to happen.

Supernus's voice filled the ballroom. "Konstantin, Kristof: as acting agent of Liaidor Kyzhere, on behalf of Arbor Castellum, I declare Jus Homicidium on Jordan Wakefield and Gretchen Poesthoffer. Find them in the Depths." The interfectors clicked to life, their chins notching up at the sound of Supernus's voice.

"No…" Eli staggered backward into the chair.

Mortimer flew into the room and veiled behind Supernus, trying to make sense of the scene.

"No one in the Depths is to leave it," said Supernus. "Destroy the teapot and dispatch all who interfere."

"Jus Homicidium?" mumbled Finley.

"NEX!" roared Supernus.

The interfectors deveiled and raced out of the ballroom, gaining Vitruvian coils before they vanished.

"Finley, Mortimer," said Supernus. "We are evacuating. Everyone is to leave for Arbor Castellum immediately."

"Everyone?" asked Mortimer.

"EVERYONE!" bellowed Supernus. "The Upper Guard is to escort me personally—assemble them. Task the Lower Guard to the rest. Go NOW!"

With stunned countenances, they nodded, deveiled, and flew off while Supernus marched toward Eli. Still backed against the chair, Eli clutched the spoon in one hand, his own relic still recording in the other. He tried to escape as Supernus arrived but wasn't fast enough. Supernus's fist caught Eli hard in the mouth. Dazed, he fell, commanding his hands to hold onto the spoon and his relic. He felt the ground take him, his broken glasses falling away. He struggled into a sitting position and winced, a ribbon of blood leaking from his closed mouth. He looked up at Supernus, who stood over him like a god.

"I'll be taking that spoon, child."

Eli shifted his mouth about, testing the condition of his injured jaw.

"I don't suspect you're ready to die for it, are you?" said Supernus.

Eli spoke through the pain: "I won't have to…"

"Bravo, so rare to see courage from a Prude," said Supernus. "But do you really believe *you* could beat *me*?"

"No." Eli raised his shaking hand, pointing the spoon past Supernus. "But Firas can, and there's no longer anyone guarding him." Eli swallowed. "That was his plan all along."

The expression on Supernus's face imploded. A violent crack sounded out from behind him and brilliant red light blinded Eli's wide eyes. Supernus bellowed a battle cry and deveiled. He spun as Firas's ghostly form slid deftly between the prison bars like a serpent. Firas elevated and blazed, taking on an abrasive wail. Supernus tried to do the same, growing near-brilliant as Firas gained arcs of Vitruvian light.

Firas attacked, Supernus met him on the offensive.

Red and violet light danced across the derelict ruin of the Carmen Vespere's ballroom. Firas's light cut the air with bullwhip speed, striking Supernus, who spun and dodged and parried. He deflected Firas's blows with bright arms crossed over his head; an anvil surface already failing under the assault. Violet light rained down from the scourging, forcing Eli to scramble for cover. Supernus lost ground fast, resorting to desperate defensive measures. He tried to escape at the edges of the onslaught, only to be cut off every time. Pinned down, he was brutalized ever backward without mercy.

"WHY! WHY!" Firas shouted, issuing strikes to his besieged. "WHYYYYYY!"

With teeth bared, Supernus's mouth locked into a miserable arc. Backed up to the wall, he raised his dim arms overhead. With the final blow, Supernus veiled, landing on his heels, falling against the wall. He collapsed. From a sitting position, he moaned and flopped his head about, hands reaching about feebly, trying to fend off his assailant. Firas veiled in front of him with a crack that echoed harsh in Eli's ears. He flayed his hand and grabbed Supernus by the neck. Eli watched red light glint off tears that had already returned to Firas's face.

"My Helena…WHY!" Firas pinned Supernus's head to the wall.

Supernus struggled to speak, his eyes squinting, his words coming out lethargically. "Because…because my father asked it of me." Supernus craned his neck, trying to keep his head level. "And *that* is the only reason." With eyes tossing about under drowsy slits, Supernus bared his wolf grin, releasing deep notes of laughter.

Eli came closer, wiping blood from his mouth. "Firas—don't do it."

Firas breathed hard. "It could be over right now. There will be no greater opportunity—he must pay for my Helena."

"NO!" shouted Eli, stepping up to Firas, who eyed the relic still in Eli's hand. "It is assassination. It will be war."

"*Nothing* can stop that now!"

"Firas…," pleaded Eli. "This is your darker half."

With his red shimmering hand still about Supernus's neck, Firas snarled. He had only to veil it to disintegrate his throat. His enemy's life would pour out at his feet.

"This is not the way," said Eli. "Please."

Firas brightened his flayed hand. "Answer me, murderer. Is your life flashing before your eyes?"

"It is not." Supernus laughed, his eyes growing more aware.

"Then you'll live through *this*." Firas thrust his knee forward, ramming Supernus in the jaw, snapping his head against the wall. Supernus fell face first onto the floor unconscious, a pool of blood expanding about his mouth. Firas caught his reflection in the creeping blood before stepping away.

"The teapot," said Eli. "Is it true?"

"It is true."

Eli dropped his relic. It clattered off the floor. Eli shook his head. "It will destroy everything…the Nether Dove will—"

Supernus groaned and dragged his cheek across his blood. He collapsed into it again, his hand closing into a fist.

Firas roared: "I will be the cornerstone of a fraudulent peace no longer! Arbor Florum's cowardice wrought this, NOT what I have done here today."

Eli stepped back as though afraid.

Firas continued: "There's something wrong with all of this—can't you see it! Murdering the predecessors—it wasn't revenge. There were a hundred ways to do it and keep it a secret. There were a thousand better to make a political statement. You know the conspiracies. There's something else here!"

Eli's eyes sunk to the floor. He clutched the spoon, shaking his head. He spoke as if to no one at all. "To prove Supernus a murderer … it's war."

Supernus stirred again, his hand pulling in close to his face.

Firas had no more words.

He watched Eli—spoon still in hand—fetch his metallum off the floor and then dash to Finley's relics. Supernus drew his elbows in, positioning them for leverage to rise. His mouth leaked blood and indecipherable words.

Firas deveiled and blazed. A stark intoxication hit him.

He was leaving this place forever.

In moments, he was in West Leaf, finding it abandoned. He raced the length of the thoroughfare, staying low, rising only when the Arborsolis came into view. He went high, above its branches. Thousands of freelight were floating in Aria, not a single one noticing him.

All eyes aimed eastward. The East Leaf gateway had been abandoned. Beyond it, at the end of the thoroughfare, orange light spilled down to the street as a battle raged between Konstantin, Kristof, and scores of Arbor Florum's Praetorium.

Though vastly outnumbered, the interfector duo battered their opponents without mercy, driving them to the end of East Leaf where the doors to the Depths were still wide open. As Firas hoped, the praetors abandoned their duty upon recognizing certain defeat, refusing to retreat into the long passage. But Firas's hopes sank just as fast: behind the battle, he saw the tail-end of Lila's green light. She had skirted them and would reach the Depths in seconds.

"No," whispered Firas, watching the last of the praetors abandon the fight. In seconds it was over. Konstantin and Kristof had clear passage. They re-conjured their Vitruvian light and raced onward.

"Firas!" called a nearby voice.

"Firas! He's escaped," said another, "He's—"

Firas blazed and shot away toward South Leaf, no one daring to follow. Passing through the southern gateway, he flew down South Grey, columns and porticos and chiseled edifices racing by. All of it was as spectacular as he remembered. The euphoria of freedom pumped life back into the withered roots of his memory. He passed the far gateway where South Leaf opened wide. The Asterhaus below, a masterpiece of architecture—but only time for a glance. His attention went skyward, spotting the decorative portal near the rim of the dome: the high passage, the ancient way out.

Firas jetted to it. Inside, the world went dark. He saw light at the other end, then a face, animated by his approach. It turned and yelled to someone out of sight: "—Wakefield. I see him! Jordan's coming—"

Firas shot past the man and veiled in the middle of the room. It was a poorly lit lobby, darker than the Carmen, even longer out of use. Dusty, dilapidated, and filled with a group of six—no, eight. Their conspiratorial eyes tracked his every move. Firas backed himself against the wall.

"So the Nether Dove meant to steal my brother away," said Firas, taking cautious steps toward the exit side.

Three of the conspirators moved to block him. Though locked on Firas, their eyes checked repetitively to a man in a brown leather coat.

Firas waited.

"Where is Jordan Wakefield?" asked the coated man.

"My brother is in the Depths." Firas watched astonishment rip through the group. "Retrieving a teapot—"

"What nonsense is this?"

"—which has first-hand proof that Supernus murdered my Helena." The room went still, except for the fluttering of eyes. "I had him…I had Supernus. But I couldn't do it." Firas looked them over, trying to gauge intent.

A woman standing closest to the coated man spoke. "Firas, come with us."

Firas started to move again. Three of the group converged tight to block his path, hands reaching out diplomatically, encouraging him to halt.

"Come with us," said the woman again, her wild green eyes meeting his. "We could use you."

Firas shook his head. "For however long I may grace Elysium, I will never be used again. I will be free, and only free." He gave them a moment to weigh the declaration. He stepped forward. More joined the blockade. Heavy eyes and lowered chins reprimanded him for the attempt.

The coated man remained still.

"As you wish…" Firas tried to anticipate who would move first. If he could get into the escape passage, they could only chase in singular fashion, negating the group advantage.

"Sir?" said the woman, looking to the coated man.

Firas watched him from the corner of his eye.

"Let him go," he said.

The group hesitated.

"I said, let him go."

They disbanded.

Firas wasted no time. He deveiled and darted to the back of the chamber, toward the exit. Before leaving, he paused and spoke over his shoulder. "If you wish to fulfill Black Lily, my brother will have everything you need. Protect him when he comes out."

Firas didn't wait for a response.

He raced away, his red light shimmering off the walls of the narrowing passage, which constricted fast to a rocky crevice. It twisted and turned but straightened again, revealing light above, a spiraling sunburst where daytime was piercing the granite. It grew brighter and wider.

Free.

Firas extended his hands. His senses twisted as he hit the gap. He burst into the faintlight world and deveiled, landing on two feet. The noonday sun swallowed him. Dropping to his knees, Firas closed his eyes, letting his arms drop to his sides. His fingertips communed with the hot, dusty ground. Lifting his face skyward, he let the sun bathe him.

Firas wept.

Tears cut cool paths down his cheeks. He opened his eyes, letting sunlight sear his vision clean. In seconds, the valley rim came into focus; the split mountain in the distance; the eternal, cloudless summer sky; the scent of the trees. All that was once memory became real again. Tipping his head down, he lowered his lips to the earth and kissed it.

"I am sorry, brother. I could not remain." Tears segmented his vision. "If you make it out, I will be forever in your debt. I swear it with all my light."

Firas flayed his hand and lifted it to the sky. He read the heavens: far above, scores of interfectors and a vast flock of Lux Stellarum were moving east. In the midst of the exodus, Supernus Kyzhere.

Arbor Florum was free.

Firas deveiled and departed into the west.

46

TOGETHER IN A DARK PLACE

Minutes earlier, while Konstantin and Kristof waged war with the Praetorium in the heart of East Leaf, Jordan was slashing his way deeper into the Depths with a frightened Gretchen on his heels. Every altercation with a visible nought resulted in collisions with the ones that hadn't reached full awareness. They bloomed like lethal silver-black flowers, their mumbling voices multiplying. Jordan and Gretchen persisted, as though trying to reach the heart of a burning theater.

They'd already passed the tenth hallway, but the mission was falling apart fast. Gretchen's pleas to turn back ended at the fifth hall. She was silent now, her mouth pinned shut lest the noughts get down her throat and end her life. Flashes of gray arrived, ancient faces and bodies wrapped in tattered garbs. Jordan jammed them away recklessly, keeping track of Gretchen by the sound of her feet hammering off granite as she ran.

But Jordan's aggressive advance was compressing the noughts. They tangled with one another, more and more bursting to life as he snow-plowed them toward the fifteenth hall. Jordan felt a spark of Firas's first-day-of-school signal off to his left. He'd reached the teapot!

But Gretchen hadn't.

In a split second, Jordan decided it, yelling to her in vox as he drove the mass of noughts past the fifteenth hallway, "I feel the teapot, I'm going to get it—KEEP COMING!"

Jordan heard Gretchen howl something as he shot down the hallway, spotting a pile of gray cloth a dozen paces away. He veiled fast, then flayed his hand. Using its light, he scooped the bundle off the ground, finding the cloth so frail it disintegrated in his hands. A small rotund vessel emerged from the tattered nest: Helena's teapot. At close proximity, a lighter hue of red danced up from its spout, nipping at Jordan's flayed finger. The implications held him transfixed. Hot retribution pumped through his heart. He had Supernus. He had him, but now he had to get out.

They had to get out.

Jordan clutched the teapot to his chest like a football and sprinted. "Gretchen, I have it"—his heart hammered as he passed the mouth of the hall and turned—"Gretchen!"

He kept running, passing the fourteenth hall. His flayed hand wasn't bright enough to remove the dark veil of the Depths. Noughts flew by him, moaning and mumbling. They weren't interested in the teapot now. They were going for the strongest signal, which meant she was still alive.

"GRETCHEN!" called Jordan, still running. He blazed his hand bright, his red light reaching all the way to the twelfth hall.

She came into view, huddled on the ground in a fetal position, hands covering her mouth and nose, her eyes shut. Noughts whipped violently about her, lashing and grabbing, trying to drill in between her fingers like ferocious gray worms.

Jordan stopped dead.

Paralyzed, he watched the noughts assault her. Gretchen flashed her eyes open, a photographic instant of terror. Jordan panicked.

The teapot slipped free of his grasp.

Jordan snatched at empty air as it dropped. It reached the ground just as his fingers found it, popping it in the air. It fell again. He lunged at it with his flayed hand, veiling it in time to catch the teapot skin-to-porcelain, just short of ruin.

Jordan whipped off his jacket and wrapped the teapot, placing it on the ground. His lungs pumped like a steam engine. He deveiled and blazed.

"Get…th'm…off…me!" shouted Gretchen, while being pulled in zigzag paths across the ground.

Jordan flew to her and attacked, forging a sphere of safety.

"We have to get out of here now!" said Gretchen, on her feet again.

"The teapot!"

"No time!"

"Make time!" Jordan battled toward it, giving Gretchen no option but to follow. An ocean of noughts swirled about them. With each of his strikes, they grew brighter and brighter, their perpetual wailing reaching ever-louder pitches.

The teapot was within reach.

Gretchen grabbed the jacket-wrapped teapot and shoved it into the satchel as a trio of noughts hit her hard from behind. She twisted through the fall, landing on her back, protecting the satchel. Noughts tore at her again like a pack of wolves. With eyes pinned shut, face covered, she waited for rescue.

Jordan cleared them again, filling the cold air with wild lashings of red light—no finesse now, only raw intuition.

"Can't…deveil…or dead!" shouted Gretchen, scrambling to her feet. She staggered like a gunshot victim, satchel pressed to her chest with crossed forearms. "Keep them off me!"

As Jordan cut the darkness with crimson gleam, he tried to spot the way out. He didn't know which way they were facing. Everything was moving too fast. His own brightness had been eclipsed by the noughts. Stuck in a catastrophic feedback loop, he raced tight, fierce circles around Gretchen, spearing noughts point-blank, keeping her at the eye of the storm. Jordan saw tears erupt from her eyes. They glinted the red and white light of battle before leaping from her cheeks, blown away by the violence. She knew they were lost. Multiple collisions spun Jordan, disorienting him. Gretchen went down again, dragged across the ground, out of view.

Jordan fought toward the sound of her screams, slashing and thrusting until he found her. Curled up, she shielded her face with both hands.

The satchel was gone.

She flashed her eyes open, communicating the terrible truth: they were done for. It shattered Jordan's confidence. The noughts descended upon them from all sides, slamming into Jordan, crushing him against Gretchen, uniting them in their final moment.

Then it was over.

Jordan checked himself, his head spinning delirium.

He was still alive, deveiled and rippling dim red. His eyes scanned the scene, finding Gretchen nearby. She was alive too, looking up at him with a dazed expression.

The satchel was only a few feet away.

Their attention jumped to the far side of the Depths, where a river of gray light was racing. Before Jordan's eyes could interpret it, a familiar feel hit him: a soothing summer rain, a storm breaking, running on cool wet grass.

Lila.

She appeared in the distance, a tiny green firebird. She raced toward them and the noughts raced toward her. Jordan blazed and attempted to reach her in time.

He had no chance.

A crack rang out when Lila hit them, followed by a shower of green light. She was left perilously dim. For a moment, the noughts were stunned, as if a single entity. Each curled about in the air, bright, silent, and paralyzed. Then, a reverse chain-reaction: they returned to life, writhing, doubling back for Lila as she tried to blaze again.

Jordan accelerated with everything he had.

He felt Gretchen deveil far behind him.

Lila's face warped into despair as the noughts returned to her. But Jordan got there in time, slicing through the leading edge of the attack, giving her time to dodge and regain precious light.

Gretchen arrived with vehemence, slashing another column loose, while Jordan made a second cut on a return pass. They fought together, they fought in perfect harmony. But they came no closer to freedom. Once again, trapped at the edge of extinction with no choice other than to prolong existence, if only for another second. Jordan saw Lila trying to signal him, trying to communicate as their lease on life ran out. But he already knew her mind:

They were together in a dark place, as fate had shown.

This is where it would end.

The edge of their defense shrunk, their last moments an endeavor of red, green, and violet light, cycling faster and faster, but occupying a decreasing amount of space, like a failing solar system.

Then:

The world went bright as day, as though the thousands of feet of stone above them had been peeled away, allowing the sun to establish dominion deep inside the earth. Every detail of the Depths came alive in Jordan's spellbound eyes: its primitive architecture and ancient artistry; its vast common space and the array of hallways. Jordan spun to see two interfectors enter the Depths, burning with the fury of all creation.

The torrent of noughts flew to them, a wave of tattered black ravens bent on the Meridianus blaze. They collided with a thunderclap, the boom shaking rock loose from the ceiling. With the impact, a storm of golden light rained down. Against the brilliance, Jordan watched the charge of noughts torn apart, like a waterfall hitting stone. But before the thunder had even diminished, the stunned noughts—now shimmering bright white—regained their faculties. They resumed their assault on the interfectors.

Lila shouted in vox: "THEY'RE NOT HERE TO HELP US—"

Jordan's attention spun away from Lila—he couldn't help it. Konstantin and Kristof had brightened but failed to regain their Vitruvian aura. They were trapped, they would die in moments.

More of Lila's words: "...THEY'RE HERE TO KILL US."

Through the swarm of noughts, a fiery yellow tendril—a bullwhip of impossible length—ripped through the air, right at them. Jordan dodged as the fiery coil came within inches of his face.

Gretchen's voice called out in vox: "THE TEAPOT!"

The three of them raced deep into the Depths, the violence of the doomed interfectors thundering behind them. Gretchen was well ahead, diving down toward the floor. She veiled during flight, landing on her feet, skidding across the ground like an ice skater coming to a hard stop. She snagged the satchel's strap as she slid by. Sprinting back toward them, she whipped the satchel high in the air. She blasted back into violet light, ascended, and caught it in flight. She shot past Jordan and Lila before they could change course.

By the time they did, Gretchen was flying low in the distance, her violet light skirting the edge of war. Though striking with spectacular speed, the interfectors remained trapped, growing dimmer by the second. Lila followed Gretchen's path, and Jordan took up the rear. They slid past the howling nexus of silver-white light. They stopped short of the exit passage, Jordan well below Lila, Gretchen nearest to the way out.

Jordan turned around to watch.

They all did.

In their final moments, the interfectors took on unnatural forms. Like the iconic Hindu statues with many arms and legs, they battled the noughts with an array of fiery limbs—moving as though engaged in a violent ritualistic dance. Still, Kristof grew dim, drifting ever closer to Konstantin, who rationed strikes for his brother-in-arms.

"JORDAN!" called Gretchen from above.

Jordan's mind screamed at him to leave. Yet he remained. His heart turned; he felt pity for the interfectors. Seduced into service, programmed into suicidal devotion. Even now, Jordan could see Konstantin studying the scene, trying to find a way to complete his mission, to strike him dead.

"JORDAN"—Lila's voice this time—"THE DOORS!"

Kristof's light went out with a flash. His lifeless, physical body fell to the cavern floor.

The doors...The doors...

These words triggered Jordan's mind to begin an apocalyptic calculation. After Konstantin, the noughts would come for the next strongest signal: them. And the doors to the Depths were still open...

An explosion rang out, dragging Jordan's attention back to the spectacle, where Konstantin had delivered a massive stun. Many of the noughts rolled in petrified curls, yet it wasn't enough. Many remained unaffected. Jordan saw Konstantin's face. No trace of fear, no sadness. No desperation, nor want of rescue. Not a wisp of humanity remained.

He had died long ago.

Jordan spun away and raced skyward. Lila shot into the exit passage upon seeing him move. Gretchen was long gone. As Jordan accelerated, his calculation resumed, numbers firing through his head: the noughts would be on them in seconds, and then they'd reach East Leaf...

A thunder crack reached Jordan as he entered the mouth of the passage. All traces of yellow vanished from his periphery, marking the death of Konstantin. Lila's green light was far ahead. But below, Jordan felt the river of noughts take a new direction, pursuing the next strongest signal, which was her.

The calculation again: the noughts were moving fast, the doors would move slow. The long passage to East Leaf was their only chance...the outer doors had to be closed in time.

Jordan cleared the shaft to the Depths, shooting into the long passage. A glimpse of Hugo flashed by; dead on the ground, a pool of blood around his battered head. Three more lifeless praetors nearby. Jordan leveled out, racing toward East Leaf, the long passage framing the exit as a small rectangle of heavenly light.

The outer doors were still wide open.

No time no time no time.

They couldn't be closed in time.

Only seconds remained.

Jordan saw hundreds of people, just standing there in the streets. Gretchen and Lila hovered at the threshold, gesturing desperately. Reality constricted tight about Jordan's heart:

He'd killed them all.

The wail of the noughts erupted from behind and the passage lit up bright. Jordan imagined a geyser of apparitions, but didn't look.

A chain reaction began in East Leaf. Mass deveilings, bursts of light, the cracks reaching Jordan in delayed fashion like the chatter of distant machine-gun fire.

And then it happened:

Jordan's life started to flash before his eyes.

Vivid memories spilled into his field of vision, obscuring his view of the real world. Along with them, sounds and voices, tastes and smells. First came childhood; Christmas and other events long past; his father's steady hand teaching him to ride a bike; his first kiss; sliding his car into the ditch during winter. The visions came like a flood, but it *felt* as though he had all the time in the world to experience them.

Through gaps in the visions, Jordan saw the mass deveilings continue, a kaleidoscopic array of freelight jetting up and out of sight, a futile evacuation. The door to East Leaf drew closer. Lila alone was at the threshold waiting for him, her features nearly discernable now.

More visions bombarded Jordan:

The campsite where he'd seen the red ghost; fishing with his father on the pier; his loft in the city. He saw Maggie and his wall of sketches; the trip to San Francisco; the dinner with Crispin. He saw Sebastién's charismatic smile. He saw everything but Lila and her crying eyes— nothing resembling his birth echo. Then he knew why:

He was bending fate.

He was pulling free of the inevitable chain of events that would have him die in front of Lila's tearful eyes.

At last, the doors began to close.

But it was too late.

Guilt tore through Jordan. He traced its fault line. Firas for tricking him into this? Sebastién for bringing him to Arbor Florum? Crispin for finding him—for releasing his predecessor? Was it his own fault for trying to solve the mystery of the eyes in the first place? He raced back to childhood and the decision to see the stars on that fateful night. How could such an innocent act cascade into so much death?

He saw Lila's face now. Behind it, the bright utopia of East Leaf grew thinner as the iron doors crept shut.

It wouldn't be enough.

Their eyes locked.

Jordan knew Lila had made the same doomed calculation. In a flash, Jordan decided. It came to him with diamond-hard certainty, born out of his vow to Lila to do just one right thing. Its acceptance hurt more than anything he ever knew. He saw Lila's face break into anguish the moment she understood it. She screamed out his name as he turned in a desperate arc, rocketing back toward the Depths… back toward the noughts.

One final stun.

He'd buy them a few seconds and maybe it would be enough for the doors. He'd do it for her; for his friends; even for his enemies. It was for all of them; a penance for his foolish pride, for letting Arbor Florum down. It was the price of being part of something that mattered.

It was the price of one right thing.

Pulling away from East Leaf, he blazed brighter. He'd deliver one final strike, dead center in the sea of keening noughts. Then he'd join their ranks.

Jordan closed his eyes. Unexpectedly, the world went away, just as it would through faintlight eyes shut. The visions continued to flash to him nonetheless, and though they were happy ones—though they nudged him toward peace—they were not his heart's wish.

He conjured a final memory by force and made it stick. It took the form of a pair of eyes: warm green, beautiful, and looking back at him as if part of the real world. It was Lila from the morning they met in Florum valley. In her smile, a harbor of infinite possibility.

With that, he was ready.

Jordan opened his eyes just as the world went bright around him, far beyond the exterminating blaze of the noughts.

He was seeing the light.

It frightened him at first, arriving as a kaleidoscopic array—not pure white as he would have imagined. It lit the passage walls, catching up with him from behind with a roar. Greens and oranges and blues and purples, competing bands of color consuming him like a cocoon. Jordan pushed his red hand forward, preparing for impact, the horrifying faces of the noughts visible now…

The sea of multi-colored light flew past him: it was composed of hundreds of freelight, joined together, hand-in-hand, bodies intertwined like braids of fiery rope. They reached the noughts first, blasting them backward with tidal-wave force, stunning them into white silence.

As fast as this citizen militia had arrived, it retreated, punching and pulling Jordan toward East Leaf. By the time Jordan had his bearings, he was out. The doors groaned along, being closed by people on foot. Inside, the colony of noughts woke and thundered toward them again.

The doors were nearly shut when they arrived, but not quite. Silver-laced heads and torsos, arms and witchlike hands erupted through the gaps. The airborne freelight, still fused as a braided entity, met them, striking them back into the breach. Jordan whirled, following the path of the freelight rope. It stretched all the way into Aria, drawing its power from the Arborsolis directly, a blazing strand of humanized lightning. A civilization united, beating back extinction.

The doors banged shut, yet razor thin jets of white light continued to leak past the seams. Individual attackers broke from the common effort and battled the attempted escapees, while the leading tip of the freelight rope pressed to the seam, torching it shut in reckless fashion. The effort rendered violent flashes, burning light trails into Jordan's vision. Plumes of molten iron poured and slapped onto the street. Smaller groups of freelight worked near the torch edge, stealing heat from the faltering metal. Radiating it into the open air, they soothed the angry glow of the iron façade.

In moments, the Depths were sealed.

Nothing got out.

All that remained was the hysterical wail of the ancient dead, calling with such force that it made the iron doors hum.

Jordan veiled on the street, Lila at his side. Gretchen found them, cradling the satchel like it were an infant. Wiley, Lev, and Georgia, and a hoard of strangers gathered around them, at the ready.

The rest of the citizenry, reluctant to remove their gaze from the moaning doors, veiled and began to surround them. Shocked faces, angry faces, incredulous faces. As the scrutiny piled up, Jordan's guilt dragged his head down. No one spoke, but the fierce eyes of the citizenry screamed a single word at him:

Why?

47

AFTERMATH

Jordan stewed in the confines of yet another courtroom while the catastrophic events of the Depths continued to haunt him. The recollection of Hugo dead in the long passage ran on infinite loop: expired eyes staring up at the ceiling, his colleagues scattered nearby, the lot of them connected by archipelagos of blood. Jordan remained planted in his chair, head buried in hands. Parandis, who'd tried to engineer the loophole on Crispin's behalf last time around, was standing next to him. She waged an undiplomatic war of words with Castellum's lone representative: the man with the well-proportioned face who oversaw Jordan's appointment to Investigator Forensis. His name was Gaspero. He'd stayed behind to run damage control.

Overseeing the affair was another cantankerous judge. This one had the surname of Shay and wielded a fierce allegiance to the Grey City, his tone lacking all semblance of impartiality. The three parties volleyed words about the mahogany-skinned room, a venue that was otherwise empty, except for a short, barrel-chested man at the back. Despite the ferocity, the exchanges failed to keep Jordan's head in the room. His mind was conducting its own, private trial, already delivering verdicts.

For the death of Hugo Frenatel, honored praetor:

Guilty.

For the death of his colleagues:

Guilty.

For the near extermination of Arbor Florum:

Guilty guilty guilty.

Jordan pulled at his hair as if trying to uproot it.

Judge Shay's voice reached shouting volume: "You'll have to *excuse* the court's confusion on this point. It, like everyone else in Arbor Florum, is trying to comprehend why, and by what authority, Supernus Kyzhere, an *ambassador* from Arbor Castellum, instructed his inhibitors to execute Jordan Wakefield and Gretchen Poesthoffer—AND the entirety of Arbor Florum's Praetorium should they get in the way!" Shay puffed heavily at the finish-line of his diatribe.

Gaspero hoisted his posture. After a subtle pursing of the lips, he responded in a rumbly manner: "Supernus Tacitus Kyzhere, the Princeps Maximus of Arbor Castellum does, in fact, possess such authority, not as ambassador to Arbor Florum, but as high defender of the protectorate Arbor Castellum maintains in the Carmen Vespere—"

"And are we to understand that facility is now closed?"

Gaspero resumed in an equally snide tone. "The accused fled before the investigation was complete. Because he is a fugitive at large *and* under Jus Homicidium, we have elected to close our facility. That is, unless, you have word of the imminent return of Firas el-Sakar?"

"His teapot has returned…" Shay peered down at Gaspero with a fervent fire in his eyes. "We hear it speaks a *great* number of words."

Gaspero ignored the barb. "If the court wishes to understand Supernus Kyzhere's operational duties, it would be advised to file an inquiry with the appropriate body in Arbor Castellum. These events, though significant, are not relevant to this hearing. We are here to discuss the disposition of Jordan Wakefield, Investigator Forensis, are we not?"

Shay scowled.

Parandis waited for Shay's attention to return to her side of the courtroom. "It is the position of Arbor Florum that Jordan Wakefield, Lux Sanguinis, be instated as a member of the Prudentiarum."

Jordan recognized his cue and stood up, his chair issuing a grunt. His days of activism were over. Straight and narrow now; by the book.

"Castellum deems this acceptable." Gaspero exhaled, nodding through exhaustion. "With the following caveats. First, the order of Jus Homicidium upon Jordan Wakefield *will* remain in effect," Gaspero's eyes found Jordan directly, "but will *not* be enforced so long as he is acting in the capacity of the Prudentiarum. Second, an exception to this condition shall be made for a period of ten days from this appointment, a respectful allowance for transition. Finally, the appointee shall serve the Prudentiarum out of Arbor *Castellum*, where he is to report after transition." Gaspero turned to Jordan and Parandis with a diplomatic hand in the air. "I would ask this court to recognize that Arbor Castellum's generosity in these matters has been granted by the Dominus Stellarum himself."

"Noted." Shay grimaced imperceptibly and looked to Parandis. "Are these conditions acceptable to Arbor Florum?"

"They are," said Parandis.

"And the appointee accepts?"

"I do," said Jordan.

"The appointment has been made." Shay cracked his gavel. "Transition shall be complete within ten days. You shall be escorted to your faintlight domicile upon taking leave of this courtroom."

Jordan remained standing.

"Would the appointee like to make a statement?" asked Shay.

Gaspero's eyes narrowed.

"I would." Jordan felt Parandis's gaze bore through the side of his face. "I wish to seek asylum in Arbor Florum under Thiago's Rule."

"Granted." Shay cracked his gavel again.

Jordan spied a fracture in Gaspero's composure. His face went distant as he tried to exhume the obscure precedent.

"Allow me to clarify, should counsel for Castellum be unfamiliar"— Shay relished seeing Gaspero at a loss—"all terms agreed upon shall remain as stated, except asylum will allow the appointed to serve the Prudentiarum out of Arbor Florum, *not* Arbor Castellum."

Gaspero gave Jordan and Parandis sharp glances but not a further word. He whisked himself away, marching out of the courtroom before Shay could spit a farewell at him. Parandis also went mute, gathering her papers. She moved to the back of the courtroom as if engaged in a civilized footrace with Shay, who was proceeding to his chamber, his face crunched up as if he'd snorted a dash of pepper. The only person left was the stout man, who held the door open for Parandis, tossing it closed after she passed. He approached Jordan, bobbing side to side like a plumber with worn-out knees.

"I'm Plato," he said, dealing a fierce grip to Jordan. "Part of your transition team. I'll be taking you home."

"Plato, huh?" asked Jordan.

"Yeah, don't fucking ask—parents were fruitcakes. Had lofty visions for their baby boy." Plato slapped Jordan's shoulder and then dragged his fingers away as though using his hoodie as a napkin. They passed through the courtroom doors together. In the long, column-laden hall outside, people bustled about, engaged in conversation. A mob raced over upon spotting him. Jordan heard a mishmash of preambles.

"Lemurs," mumbled Plato, ambling out in front with his arm extended, ready to block them. Heads and bodies arrived, peering around Plato's bulk, their wide eyes fixed on Jordan. Faces perfectly still, eyes wide open as if time had frozen.

One of them finally spoke:

"What does the Investigator Forensis have to say for himself?" She skirted to the side of Plato, her doe eyes fastened to Jordan. "Was nearly killing everyone in the Grey City the virtuous endeavor you thought it'd be?"

Jordan's eyes slipped to the floor, spying a recording relic in her hand…freelight journalists. Fucking great. Jordan kept his eyes down, mouth shut as the floodgates opened. Questions blasted forth until a wall of praetors marched in next to Plato, assisting him with the blockade.

"He'll talk out front," barked Plato. "Now be gone, you rats."

Jordan watched the praetors herd them out. With the hall clear, he spotted Sebastién across the way. Arms folded, leaning into one of the fluted columns. Next to him was Easton, and next to her, a pensive Lila. Nobody smiled nor frowned exactly, but a silent sense of relief seemed to buoy them. Chins above water for the moment.

"Now listen up." Plato tapped Jordan's chest with pudgy fingers. "Here's where things stand: your pops thinks you were in San Francisco all this time. Your artsy friends think you were with the old man. They *all* believe you dropped your phone in a toilet, and that's why you've been out of touch—walk with me." Plato elbowed him along, marching in the direction of Sebastién and Lila. "The next part goes like this: your phone has been replaced and you told everyone about this through those telegraph-message things." Plato tangled his fingers together and wiggled them as a surrogate depiction of modern telecommunications. "Piece of cake, except for your nosy neighbor, Maggie—that woman has no sense of personal space."

"She's like that," offered Jordan, getting bumped sideways by Plato's lumbering steps.

"I wanted to punch her," said Plato, driving his fist into his palm, producing a bright smack, "but I didn't, so don't you worry. We'll go over the rest on the way back."

Jordan found this sneak preview of his alibis troubling, not to mention Plato himself.

"Hey kid, you ever been to Colorado?" Plato pinched Jordan's sleeve, slowing him down. "The Continental Divide?"

"No," said Jordan, lost on the conversational tangent.

"Top of the world; best place to take a big long fall." Plato hacked out laughter. "Ah that's funny, I'll explain later."

Jordan shook his head. "Were you in the mafia or something?"

Plato perked up. "I was, actually—not too good at it though. That's how I saw the light; a little help from a machine gun pointed my way." He imitated the incident with empty hands, bouncing them in Tommy-gun fashion. He peeled into laughter. "You should have seen the other guy's face when I burst." Plato slapped Jordan across the chest with the back of his hand, knocking him off balance.

Jordan stopped in front of Lila. Sebastién pushed away from the pillar, strolling forward.

"Can we have a moment?" asked Lila, looking Plato's way.

"Yeah, sure." Plato folded his arms and waited. A conspiratorial silence spurred him to sigh and walk to the other side of the hall.

Sebastién leveled his gaze on Jordan, admiration all over it. "I'll never doubt your intuition again."

"So you're an international criminal now?" asked Jordan.

"As much as any other day," said Sebastién, drawing a smirk from Easton. "Baseless charges. They wanted as few of us in the Carmen as possible. They were planning to move on Firas, but he moved on them first—quite a move too, the whole thing, really. Hell of a dance." Sebastién shed his cool-sly demeanor, giving Jordan a serene look. "Firas swallowed that injustice for a hundred and twenty-eight years—kept his secret all that time, waiting for you to arrive. Arbor Florum abandoned him, and they hated him in the end—they hated all of us. But Firas saved them. He rid the Grey City of the Kyzheres. He made us free."

"They're really gone?" said Jordan, feeling optimism.

"Between the Nether Dove and the teapot, Supernus panicked. He surrounded himself with his fects and fled."

"The Carmen is nearly empty," said Easton with the glimmer of a smile. "The muscle is gone. All that remains are the bureaucrats."

"Will it hold?"

Sebastién shrugged. "The teapot is what Firas claimed, and it's in sympathetic hands now—as are Eli's relics. Their existence hasn't been acknowledged openly, and that's an olive branch to Castellum; a way to keep them at bay, and the Nether Dove from pursuing Black Lily. They're still demanding the Kyzheres disarm, nonetheless."

"If they don't?" Jordan watched Sebastién's response closely.

"Well…" Sebastién crossed his hands behind his back. "It probably means war."

Jordan's optimism deflated. "Gretchen?"

"Gone," said Lila. "With the Nether Dove."

Plato whistled a broken, off-pitch melody. When they glanced at him, he tapped at his wrist as if a watch were there.

"We'll talk when you get back," said Sebastién. "Go see your pops."

Lila took him by the hand and pulled him away. Plato started to move toward them with his bobbling walk.

"This part's difficult," said Lila. "It would seem a good thing, to see everyone one last time." Lila paused, as though dipping into her own memories. "But it makes it harder because only *you* know it's the last time. I want to offer some advice…" Lila moved so that they were face to face. She took his hands gently. "Savor every moment of it. *See* everything, *hear* everything. Make good memories, because it's the last you'll have. We all become remembrances in the end—savis ēchūs, as the saying goes."

"What *is* that?" said Jordan.

Plato plodded up, planting himself next to them.

"A poem. I'll explain it when you get back." Just as Jordan was preparing a goodbye, she leaned forward and kissed him.

"Ah, Christ," said Plato, looking down, tapping his foot.

Lila broke away, leaving Jordan with a smile. "See you soon, space cowboy."

Jordan turned toward the front doors.

Plato hooked Jordan under the arm like a dance partner and spun him the other way. "Come on, Romeo. Backdoor. We're not gonna talk to the press."

48

A FOREIGN WORLD

Well after midnight, Jordan and Plato parted ways on the rooftop of the Renslit Artists' Cooperative. Plato had him recite the transition plan and after receiving a sterling account, told him he'd see him soon. He delivered a curt farewell and floated up into the night, a luminescent green fog with a gangster face. A few twists and turns later, Jordan peeked out of the vent into his loft. The cover was still propped up against the wall where Sebastién had left it, coated with a fine layer of dust. After gliding in and veiling with stealth, he tip-toed to the couch, trying to recall which were the creaky floorboards. His home was a foreign world now. Familiar sounds arrived but somehow seemed strange. The whirring of the refrigerator; a lone car passing by on the street below; the deep hum of the building's ventilation.

Jordan scanned his blank walls, studying the patchwork array of small squares where adhesives had pulled paint away. It was all that remained of his former shrine to Lila's eyes. The biggest absence—the undisputed altar of it all—was the masterpiece sketch of Lila. A thin gray dust line ran along the floor, the only evidence it ever existed. He didn't know if transitionists had hauled it off and destroyed it, or if Crispin rescued it first. Thoughts of the image—and by extension Lila and their parting kiss—sent a jolt through him, arresting his decline toward sleep.

Jordan checked the couch, finding his wallet, keys, and phone shoved deep under the cushion. He bounced the phone in his hand, the battery dead.

He plugged it in.

Jordan reflected on his return flight from Arbor Florum. Despite Plato's social ineptitude, the man's mind was nimble when it came to laying out the excuses he'd need to employ—*the lies*, as Jordan disdainfully called them. Plato drilled him on scenarios, replies, and rebuttals the whole way home, demanding Jordan play-act until the words came out as smooth as silk. By the time they'd landed, the lies had congealed into something that felt true.

Plato's script granted but one liberty: the parting words to those who'd need to hear them—within reason, of course. During the offload of rigid demands, Jordan detected a camouflaged compassion in Plato. He too had been here once; might have had to part ways with a wife or even a kid. The schedule, however, remained unassailable: just over a week from now, in the midnight hour, he'd need to be on Colorado Highway 82, heading west toward the Continental Divide. It was there they'd do the deed.

Then he'd be dead to the faintlight world.

Jordan tried to imagine what he'd say to his father—his birthday on the horizon, no less. With the clandestine specter of fake death at his heels, he realized he hadn't even figured out a birthday present.

Jordan kicked off his shoes and wandered to the door.

He flayed a finger, recognizing how greatly his skills had increased. He detected Maggie easily. After a moment of study, he determined she was sleeping. Back at the couch, he flicked on the table lamp. Packed boxes on the other side of the room called him over. Lifting a flap, he fished out two framed photographs.

The first was his father and him from his childhood. Standing on the breakwater with a fishing pole on Wakefield Rock, as his father deemed it. The other was a photograph of his mother and a younger version of his father. Their happy faces brought tears to Jordan's eyes. He could hardly reconcile the contemporary version of his father to the carefree one he saw in this photograph. He was unable—and quite unwilling—to imagine the next version, the one that came after this was all over. He decided to mail the photographs to Crispin's gallery in San Francisco. Maybe they'd find their way to him in Arbor Florum.

But first…

Jordan flipped on the light above his drafting table, his eyes sweeping the empty surface. He placed the photographs at the back edge, out of the way. Wandering to his storage closet, he returned with a portrait-sized vellum board. He fetched a tray of charcoal pencils. With an idea plucking at his heartstrings, he mounted the stool, flexed his fingers, and went to work on one last sketch.

49

DEPARTING SAINT PAUL

Jordan opened his door. Maggie came breezing past, spinning silly pirouettes in the middle of his big empty loft. She leaped onto the swing in a standing position, her feet leveraging the seat, coaxing it into motion.

"Weeeeeeee!" howled Maggie, peeling into giggles. "Whoa, this place sounds *so* empty…empty. *EMP-TY!*"

Jordan smiled, realizing how much he was going to miss her. His chin ping-ponged as he watched Maggie move in big arcs, tongue sticking out of the corner of her mouth like a child. She dismounted, two feet hitting the floor hard, producing a theater-stage thump. The swing waggled its aftereffects as she walked to him. She eyed the gift-wrapped canvas next to the small stack of boxes.

"What's in there?"

"Birthday present for my dad,"

"Oooh—a picture of Mystery Woman?"

"No…" Jordan's mind drifted to the image under the wrappings. "Something more…practical."

"Sold everything off, huh?" Maggie surveyed the empty space, her eyes halting where the giant portrait of Lila used to reside. "I'll miss your big lady picture…She was a dish."

Jordan's mind went back to Lila and their kiss. In days they'd be together again. More normal times ahead, or at least the abnormal normal he'd come to expect from the freelight world.

"I was here the day they came for it." Maggie grabbed Jordan's wrist. "Stubby short guy and a pair of goons. They wrapped it up so fast I honestly thought they were stealing it. The short guy said you'd mailed them your door key. Man, was he an asshole. I wanted to punch him."

Jordan's grin returned, and he choked back laughter.

"Hey," said Maggie, "I'm still pissed. You were too busy with the old man and drowning your phone in the shitter to bother with us, huh?"

Jordan erupted into laughter. It felt damn good.

"What is it?" said Maggie, pecking at him with playful jabs.

"It's funny."

"No it's not." Maggie stomped away a few steps, turned on him, and resumed the giggling. "Okay it is. But seriously, your dad got you for weeks, and I only got yesterday. You disappeared right when that ghost shit was gettin' good—HEY! Do you even know about that?"

Jordan held her gaze, suddenly nervous.

Never be evasive—Plato's rule number one when something bumps into the backstory.

Maggie rattled on: "The *Les Revenants* newspaper guy came forward claiming the whole thing was staged. Smoke and lights and special effects, shit like that. That guy was a total nutcase—French dude with way worse hair than mine." Maggie's hands waved flight paths over her head to illustrate. "The band denied it, of course—but it was brilliant. I wish I could come up with a scam like that."

Jordan felt his grin return. Freelight cover-up service, top notch.

"But I heard this other rumor..." Maggie took a step closer, brushing her hair away from her eyes so that she saw him without obstruction. She wasn't smiling now.

"Yeah...?" Jordan stuck his hands in his pockets, resisting the urge to look away.

The side of Maggie's mouth twitched. Then it came out: "You're the red ghost."

Jordan locked up.

Maggie's eyes remained fixed to his. They burrowed into him, monitoring every movement, peering through the very pores of his skin. "Steks claimed it the day after it all happened. Said you poofed into a ghost when he came to collect." Maggie simulated the event by pressing her hands together and bursting them apart. "Then you poofed back." Her hands were shaking.

She bit her lip and continued to stare.

Milliseconds of non-response leaked out; a pool of fuel for conspiratorial fires. Nothing in Plato's book of lies had anticipated this. Jordan felt his body turn to stone.

Fucking say something.

Jordan pressed his hands together as Maggie had done.

Maggie's gaze went to them.

"Poof," said Jordan, pulling them apart, causing Maggie to chirp a high-pitched note. Jordan looked his hands and arms over. "Did it work?"

"Oh, man." Maggie blushed. Her attention fell to Jordan's shoes. "I realize how stupid that sounds…I'm so sorry, I—"

"We're artists. We have social license to say shit like that, remember?" Jordan had his smile in place before her attention returned. "As for Steks…probably did too much of his own shit."

Maggie nodded. "He was never the same. He lost it and checked out of reality. He's on the streets."

"Sad…" Jordan waited it out.

Maggie pumped her shoulders. "So I guess this is goodbye?"

Jordan embraced her, pulling her close. He heard sniffles spouting up. He managed to restrain his own.

"You're making me cry, you asshole." She pulled away and wiped her cheeks with squeegee force. A big deep breath, then an exhale. "Uhhhg…look at me. It's San Francisco, not Shanghai. I'll fly out and see you soon. Okay, I gotta get to my shoot."

Maggie turned and walked to the door.

"Hey, Maggs?"

She turned, her hand already on the knob.

"Thanks for being there." Jordan studied her, burning her beautiful quirky presence into his memory forever. "Thanks for everything."

She smiled fondly, a lock of hair falling over her eye. She flashed a horizon-wide grin and disappeared from his doorway forever. A half-hour later, Jordan slapped his keys down on the kitchen counter and walked out of the Renslit Artists' Cooperative for the very last time.

50

——◆◆◆——

A GAME OF HORSE

Asphalt hummed beneath Jordan's wheels as Saint Paul slipped away forever. Interstate changed to state highway, then to thin rural road where the woodlands grew thick. For four hours, with the radio off and his hand hung over the steering wheel at the wrist, Jordan processed these transitions through a melancholy lens. Before he knew it, he was pulling into the driveway of his childhood home in Upper Michigan just as his father was pouring water into the grill to quell a batch of eager flames. He waved the smoke away with a spatula, smiling at Jordan through the haze.

"Hey, Dad," said Jordan, emerging from the car. "I see you're incinerating dinner."

"Had to hustle. You called me fifteen minutes out." His father walked over. "They'll still be medium, don't worry."

"Happy Birthday, Dad." Jordan embraced him, holding on for a few extra seconds. His father gave him a pair of reassuring pats on the back before returning to the grill. Jordan removed the gift-wrapped canvas from the back seat and walked it to the house, his father noticing it while landing steaks onto a pair of plates. Returning to his car, Jordan retrieved two sixers of beer, each adorned with a bow.

"Do I have to share?" said his father, unfolding a pair of lawn chairs at the driveway's edge.

413

"Depends on your shooting." Jordan set the beer down and took a seat.

"Was hoping you'd say that." His father passed him a plate. "Been working on some shots, you know."

Jordan took it. "Yeah?"

"See? Medium—told you," said his father, cutting in first. "Was thinking we'd go see the fireworks, like old times." He elbowed Jordan gently. "And then we could go to the breakwater and not catch fish."

His father's good spirits helped buttress his own. As they ate, Jordan let his gaze linger when his father spoke. He took in every word and absorbed every gesture, trying to memorialize the moments. Though his father's words tugged Jordan away from his freelight frame of mind, it was dinner that allowed his mental anchoring to truly slip back into the faintlight world, if only for a while. He hadn't eaten in weeks, always resolving the problem through deveiling. And though it was steak dinner yet again—and one that couldn't compare to Eli's five-star culinary skill—it was prepared by his father, wrapped in the nostalgia of a fine Midwestern evening.

That made it the best he ever had.

"I saw you sneak that gift in," said his father. "Is it a picture of a woman's eyes?"

"No, not that." Jordan felt an emotional crosswind when envisioning his final sketch. His smile slid. "Wait until after I leave. It's a bit sentimental and I know absorbing that in front of others is not your strong suit." Jordan's playfulness faded further with his utterance of that terrible word:

Leave.

"Oh, come on." His father shifted in his chair, causing its aluminum legs to scrape the driveway. "I'm not a barbarian. I've been to the museum, I've been to the opera."

"The opera? Really?"

"Yeah, before you were born. In Chicago." His father gazed off. "Your mother and I. She wanted Phantom of the Opera. I wanted to see the Packers whip the Bears—we almost moved there, you know.

Your mother was into the arts too. She dabbled—well, more than dabbled. She wasn't anywhere near your talent." His father drifted again for a moment as if seeing it. "But she was really good."

"I never knew any of this." Jordan set his empty plate down on the driveway and leaned back into his chair.

"We never talked about it." His father leaned back in mimicry. "I never knew how to get into that subject, so I tended not to."

"Why didn't you move?"

"Well, we tried for children for a long time. We decided that if it didn't happen soon, we'd try for a change of scenery instead. As fate had it, you were on the way. So we stayed."

His father sat in silence while Jordan contemplated the story, finding in that moment the same joy as in the wedding photograph over the mantle. "Have you ever thought about moving away? Getting remarried?"

"You worried about me becoming a cranky old man?"

"Kinda…"

His father let out a two-note, staccato laugh. "I'll be fine. I've got my leagues; softball and basketball and golf."

The words relieved Jordan, though he realized he wanted to believe them more than he really did. "Speaking of which…" Jordan did an over-hand, snap-of-the-wrist gesture toward the basketball hoop mounted over the garage.

"All right, kiddo," said his father, standing up. "Get the ball and a bottle opener. Let's see if you can hang with the old man."

"Going to have me doing hook shots from twenty feet out again? You lost a garage window on that masterpiece last time."

"That window was already cracked."

By the time they cleaned up, the sun was sinking auburn under the treetops. Jordan flipped on the outdoor lights. Clouds of tiny bugs were orbiting the bulbs by the time they started shooting.

His father settled into a lawn chair, wiggling side to side. "Okay… one-handed, beer in the other."

To the backdrop of Jordan's laughter, his father fired the ball. It rattled the backboard and danced on the rim before going in.

"Well, shit." Jordan took a tug of beer. "How long have you been practicing that?"

"All week," said his father getting out of the chair and gesturing Jordan to it like a doorman. "That's the first time it actually worked."

Unable to keep a straight face, Jordan sat and repeated the shot, the ball falling well short, smacking off the pavement.

"And that's *H*…" said his father, jogging to retrieve the ball with a grin.

The shootout continued, and they lost track of time in friendly competition. They swam through memories, some recent, others too distant for Jordan to recall. He merely took them in, trying to imagine himself as a child, performing the acts his father described between sips of beer and attempts at the hoop.

By the time the frogs and crickets joined in, the air had cooled and they were navigating topics of the recent past. Jordan avoided mentioning San Francisco and noticed his father did too. Only by nuance and indirection did they acknowledge the great distance that would soon separate them. Jordan felt a stone settle in the pit of his stomach knowing that distance would truly be infinite…and only he knew it was coming. Still, it was better than saying farewell from a hospital bed with tear-striped cheeks.

They were both alive. They were both happy.

"How long is it going to take you to drive out there?"

"A few days." Jordan dribbled the ball, then paused, pinning it to his hip with his palm. "I'm taking the scenic route once I get to Colorado. I want to see the mountains instead of whizzing by on the interstate."

And there it was.

Plato's script and the lies that came with it. Lies that protected their world. Lies that protected his father from going mad over the years, observing a son who never aged. Instead, it'd be a funeral without a body, a big bank account left behind as consolation.

Crispin's blood money.

Jordan despised every penny of it. Though he felt secure in the limited light being cast down by the garage lights, he was certain his face was betraying more than it should. He recalled Maggie's near discovery, wondering what would be done to her if she had found out. Jordan sucked it up and stuck to the plan.

His father took a shot and missed.

"Dad?" Jordan intercepted the rebound and set up near his car. "Can I ask you one of those meaning-of-life-type questions?"

"As long as you can accept a blue-collar-type answer." His father clapped a one-note salute when Jordan's shot snapped the net crisply. "What letter are we on?"

"Lost track." Jordan stepped aside for his father, who dribbled over and set his stance. The shot banged off the backboard but dropped in.

"How do you know when you're doing the right thing?" asked Jordan before rounding up the ball. He heard his Dad pry the cap off another bottle of beer.

"Having second thoughts about going out there?"

"No, I have to go." Jordan missed his shot. "I was asking in general. Do the right thing—we're always told this as if it's easy to figure out. But it's not. Sometimes the right thing turns out to be attached to a lot of stuff, much of it bad. The more you know, the more impossible it is to judge—maybe there isn't a right thing to begin with. There're just people who want things from you."

"Sort of like the cable company with all those packages?"

Jordan smirked. "You may have missed your calling as a stand-up comedian, Dad."

His father leaked a sly chuckle. He dribbled the ball and missed his next shot. The ball hit the driveway and thump-thumped off into the lawn, into the darkness. Jordan returned with it to find his father leaning against the car.

"Well, the easy answer is that you'll figure it out after you choose, but that's not the point, is it?" His father kicked at the car tire a few times. "The idea is to be able to figure it out before."

"Right." Jordan made a shot from just in front of the car.

"I didn't have a good sense of this until I was older," said his father, moving into position. "What I did learn is that it's *all* complex— every choice. It's all tied to more things than you recognize at the time. All you can really do is look at what's in front of your eyes. Consider the person that brings it to your door." His father made his shot. "The bad stuff seems to happen when your sense of right goes beyond what you know. Keep it familiar and local, I guess. Make smiles, and you probably have it mostly right."

His father retrieved the ball and tossed it back to Jordan.

"That's not too bad."

His father smirked and shrugged. "All in a day's work."

Jordan couldn't imagine the answer Crispin would have given to the question, only that it would be long and tempered with centuries of experience; wisdom extracted from lifetimes. For that reason, it would be beyond his ability to comprehend. He admired his father's simplicity of virtue—a heartfelt approach, not one anchored on cold, scientific calculation.

On the next shot, Jordan watched him close, observing a grace he'd never noticed before. His father struck him as a magnificent figure in the summer night, shooting hoops to the exaltation of crickets. He hiked his pants a notch after emerging from his shooting stance, a strong hand on his hip. He smiled at Jordan and winked.

That benevolent face had forever loved him.

He knew his father would be alright, despite what was to come. Jordan absorbed the scene with keen eyes, vowing to hold onto it forever. It was the nearest he'd get to closure, the best of what circumstance would allow. During their final days together, he'd savor every single second.

51

THE TRANSITIONIST

Jordan drove westward into the dark night, his car struggling to ascend into the mountains on Colorado Highway 82 toward the Continental Divide. He'd seen Plato for the second time that day only minutes ago, at a gas station in the mountain town of Twin Lakes. As with the first time, he said nothing. He just happened to be there, offering a nod of acknowledgment so brief it seemed more like a facial tick.

While switchbacks and thin air strained the engine, thoughts of transition imposed a similar stress to Jordan's mind. At the top of the climb was the end of his faintlight life, the event a mere joke to Plato; a piece of freelight bureaucracy. Jordan had made a habit of glancing out the passenger-side window—partially rolled down, by plan. He expected a freelight to zip through it at any moment, also by plan. But on account of the winding road, he abandoned his window check. He found it surreal to be concerned about crashing his car until he remembered that crashing it the right way really did matter.

Eyes on the road, two hands on the wheel.

Despite formidable temptation to call his father one last time, he'd honored Plato's fervent mandate: once he was on the road, it was over. No further contact. Just as he contemplated violating the rule once again, a flash of lime-green light shot through the open window. After a sharp crack and a gust of warm air, there was a man sitting in the passenger seat.

Jordan cast an expectant glance his way and waited.

"My name is David," said the man at last, speaking in an unhurried manner. "I hope I have the right car."

The joke kindled no humor in Jordan. In fact, there was something quite cold about its tone.

David leaned back, at ease, looking straight ahead.

"Jordan James Wakefield." David sounded out each word as if speaking at a commencement. "Your final moments are here. You are nearly free."

Jordan pulled his eyes from the road and looked David over: long, slender face, jet-black hair, and narrow eyes, blue—icy blue like Supernus. Weathered jeans and a leather biker jacket. Despite a gaunt physique, there was something ferocious about him. His face reminded Jordan of a gunfighter from the Western movies his father watched. But this wasn't the face of the hero. This was the guy who got shot in the end.

"Seems you are a man of few words. I am a man of many," said David, the leather of his jacket issuing sounds as he shifted. "You *do* understand what we are here to do?"

Jordan hesitated. "We're going to fake my death."

David breathed deeply. "There is a beautiful innocence in your voice." The car decelerated as Jordan turned to the next leg of the switchback. "And yes, I am here to kill you off, though I would like for *you* to kill you off. It is your life, after all. Something so precious should not be surrendered so readily, should it?"

"How did you know my middle name?" Jordan was irritated that *this* was the first question that tumbled out of his mouth.

"I am a transitionist." David twirled his fingers in the air like a magician. "I am freelight, but I live in the faintlight world most of the time and, as I'm sure you know, the faintlight world has become quite capable of finding anyone. You want to know how we tracked you down."

The answer flashed to Jordan. "My phone."

"Yes," said David with a tinge of joy on his voice. "Remarkable, isn't it, the world the faintlights have created up here?"

Jordan went silent again, beguiled by David's manner of speaking. Though there was little pause between words, his delivery was neither rushed nor tedious. It was seductive to the ear as Easton's pink light was to his mind.

Jordan hated it nonetheless.

"Once we get to the other side," said David, dragging two fingers across the dashboard and then fingering the dust free, "we'll be making a detour into the canyon."

Jordan's stomach tightened. He imagined the phone call his father would have to take, hoping this David would not be the one to make it.

"We'll also need a full set of your teeth."

Jordan squirmed in his seat. He could nearly feel David smiling at him. His words came out shaky, "You've got to be fucking kidding me."

"I am not." Restrained laughter rolled deep in David's chest. "Forensics are more rigorous than days of old. It will be nearly painless, though, thanks to faintlight ways. I'll only advise that you refrain from tonguing the empty sockets when you come to. Just deveil. Freelight magic heals the body, but not the horrors captured by the mind."

Jordan turned into the next switchback. The engine moaned, the night air whistled by, and David continued:

"I want to thank you."

"For what?" snapped Jordan. He wanted the conversation to end. He wanted his final faintlight minutes in peace.

"For ruining our plan to get you out of Arbor Florum." David turned so that he was looking at the side of Jordan's face. "Your plan, as it turns out, accomplished far more than we could have imagined. You have made Black Lily possible."

The confession petrified Jordan, his limbs going rigid as he made the connections. His hands clutched the steering wheel like a life raft, but he felt they'd slip loose at any moment.

"You see, Jordan James Wakefield"—David leaned closer, breathing the next words toward his ear—"I am the Nether Dove."

Jordan swallowed. "That was you? The opera? Gretchen? Hugo and the others. That was all—"

"Gretchen is one of us now."

"—and Firas, did he know?"

"Firas knew nothing."

"You…" Jordan shook his head incredulously. "You're the one behind this?"

"No," said David. Laughter followed. It was rhythmic, almost musical. "You misunderstand the words. They constitute a pledge, a sacred vow. To declare it is to submit one's self to the Nether Dove's namesake. We are many—more than you could possibly imagine. The opera was but our fingertip. We have remained silent for a great long time—hidden, as our name implies. But we shall hide no longer."

Jordan fired off his rebuttal. "The Nether Dove fails its namesake if it claims to represent peace. The dove is a lie!"

"It is only your understanding that fails. We acknowledge the dove's innocent white wings because they spread wide over the blackened ruin of what once was. Without ruin, it is just another bird. Understand: there can be no peace until the house of Kyzhere is reduced to ash."

Jordan's stomach turned, self-contempt pumping up to the top of his throat. He had failed to heed Crispin's warning. He had failed to see beyond his ego, to grasp the bigger picture. But it was right in front of him now.

He *had* started a war.

"We will bring about the demise of Arbor Castellum." David nearly whispered his next words: "…and you will help us do this."

"No." Jordan shook his head, turning away as though trying to remove David from his periphery. His hands slipped off the wheel. He snatched hold of it again. "I want nothing to do with this."

"Until the day you do." David's tone became tender, almost

fatherly. "You see, I too have a birth echo—a special one, just like yours. In mine, I see *you*, Jordan James Wakefield. I know you by your face, just as I see you at this very moment. I know the place we are in, and if we are in *that* place, it means you are one of us."

Jordan trembled. His mind raced, barricading every avenue of thought that might lead to solidarity with David and the Nether Dove. He retreated into himself and crushed his mind's eye shut. Yet through a narrow slit in his mental bunker, he spied the tyrannical violet light of the Kyzheres, a glow from the distant fog of the future.

No.

Jordan redoubled his efforts, blasting the thoughts away. He replaced them with scenes from the Prudentiarum: its tranquil library, its spellbinding map room. Wise minds, important research. *This* was his home now. Crispin and Eli and the others there—they were his friends. The Kyzheres *and* the Nether Dove were enemies in equal measure. Jordan's anger-jacked hands struggled to wrangle the steering wheel as the road turned again. They were above the tree line now, only shrubs and tufts of grass here.

"In time you will accept this." David flayed a finger and hung it out the window. He waved it as if beckoning someone closer. "But now, Jordan James Wakefield, it is time to die."

Jordan exhaled. His jaw clenched hard as if being wired shut. His hands ached from strangling the steering wheel.

"The Continental Divide is at the top. After that, the road goes down. When it turns, we'll be going too fast. We deveil, and gravity will do the rest."

Jordan spotted headlights in the rearview mirror. "There's a car behind us."

"Part of the team, part of the plan. Open your window."

Jordan complied. He felt cold night air rush in. The road leveled out. An empty parking lot approached on the left. "Are you sure we'll get through the guardrails?"

"Already weakened. Faster."

Jordan accelerated reluctantly, listening to his car lament, imagining it as a living being forced into joint suicide.

"Won't it be suspicious—" Jordan swallowed "—if there was no effort to stop?" At that moment a flash of green light zipped away from the underside of his car.

David smiled. "Try your brakes if you wish."

Jordan stomped on the pedal. It sunk to the floor without resistance. No effect.

"Won't there need to be a body?"

"Do you really want to know how we do this?"

Jordan started to imagine David robbing a grave, but stopped himself. Before he could conjure another excuse, his phone buzzed in the cup holder, lighting up the car. Startled, he looked down at it:

Dad (Home)

Jordan's heart found a deeper place to call bottom. His hand moved to the phone, his last connection to the faintlight world.

"No," said David, seizing him by the wrist, forcing his hand back to the steering wheel.

The buzz ceased and the phone glow blinked out. Silence now, just tires humming over midnight blacktop. A sign marking the Continental Divide whizzed by.

"Faster…" David leaned forward in his seat with enthusiasm as if waiting for a movie to begin. "Deveil when I say."

The car sound hummed to higher, more desperate notes. His phone buzzed and lit up again:

Missed Call and Voicemail

David took the phone and put it in the front pocket of his jacket. It was as good as gone. "Faster."

Anger tunneled through Jordan's body, erupting in his foot. He stomped the accelerator. With the downslope aiding them, the car roared to eighty, then ninety. He saw where the road twisted sharp to the right, the metal guardrail shining like a monstrous grin.

David shouted over the din: "Ten…nine…eight…"

Jordan felt cheated. He shook with nihilistic rage. He scoured his mind for its darkest thoughts: he saw David unable to deveil and relished the terror on his face as the two of them plunged to their real deaths. He conjured Supernus's cruel face and saw him on his knees, begging for his life. He saw the whole world choke under black skies.

"…two…one…DEVEIL!"

Green light exploded next to Jordan. The point-blank deveiling sent his right ear ringing. But Jordan didn't deveil. He cranked the steering wheel hard. His body slammed against the driver-side door. His faintlight possessions—pencils, papers, books, and clothes—took flight throughout the cabin. The car screamed sideways, issuing a horrific wail as the tires were sheared apart by the road.

"DEVEIL!" shouted David, floating next to him. "NOW!"

The guardrail arrived like the blade of an enormous knife. It was ripped from the earth upon impact. The car flipped out into the open air. David's green form was sucked out the window. For a photographic instant, Jordan's possessions floated before him as if he was in outer space. Then, the spiraling plunge. Through the windshield, Jordan saw the distant canyon floor race toward him under the twirling path of headlights. The freefall torched his rage away. He imagined a new image—a *good* one: Lila on the bluff, the day they met. She was smiling at him. With that, his constitution flipped.

Jordan deveiled.

The car's cabin blasted bright red. Jordan found the open window and shot through it. The car plunged into the darkness. Seconds later, a thundering crash called out, echoing as though the canyon had a heartbeat.

Jordan watched flames flicker to life on the underbelly of his car, which looked like a mere toy from this height. David flew in next to him while three lime-green freelight flew down the cliff's edge, surrounding the wreck. They blazed bright and torched the car, kindling the meager fire into an inferno. Jordan's eyes remained fixed to his faintlight funeral pyre.

"Plato will take you back to Arbor Florum." David flashed a series of hand signals to his colleagues. When he spoke again, it was as if to the whole canyon: "Do not dismay, Jordan James Wakefield. You are free."

52

A Practical Picasso

Steven Isaac Wakefield sat in his living room clutching his phone with a quaking hand. Exhaling, he put it down and stepped over the pile of torn gift wrap at his feet. He gazed at his wedding picture over the fireplace. He went to it and ran an unsteady finger across the top of the frame, wiping away an eternity of dust. He lifted it off the wall and put it aside.

With the care of a museum curator, he picked up the framed sketch his son Jordan had created, holding it by the sides to prevent his fingerprints from defiling the glass. He hung it over the mantle. Moving away in small, slow steps, he took in the extraordinary scene it depicted. Alternating bursts of joy and sadness shot through him as he revered the image. It looked like a photograph.

Yet it wasn't.

Nor could it have been.

That a pencil could recreate a sunset over Lake Superior was remarkable. It was a scene so dependent on color, yet rendered dramatically here in black and white. Yet this was the least of what tugged at his heart. The sunset was only background, as were the boulders of the breakwater—the same ones where he and Jordan went fishing only days ago.

His eyes moved to the center of the picture. This caused his lower lip to tremble and tears to spring anew. Sitting on a large boulder—his special rock—was Jordan. He was smiling and looking straight ahead, beaming with a confidence only a father could instill. Behind Jordan was an image of himself, standing and smiling with his right hand resting on his son's shoulder. His other hand was not visible. It was blocked by the elegant form of his wife, Valerie, whose face was turned to the side, as in their wedding photo. She gazed affectionately at her husband. Her left hand rested on Jordan's other shoulder. Neither he nor his wife had youthful faces here, as in the wedding photo, but they had the same glow. All three of them had it.

They were together, impossibly and beautifully.

He sat down, exhausted from navigating a sea of deep emotion. He picked up the birthday card and read it for the second time:

Dear Dad,

There's so little I understand of this world. I don't think things ever work out the way we want them to. We all have paths to follow. On some we go willingly. With others we're pushed along.

We live every day of our lives in the constant grip of the real. In it, life becomes routine. We become numb and drift on. But in the realm of the unreal, we awaken. We only experience these places briefly before we're pulled back again. And we can't reach them by the kinds of bridges engineers build. We reach them through art.

Consider this my practical Picasso, to use your words. I hope that it may keep us together when we are apart. Know that you are the brightest light in my life. Know that you mean more to me than I could ever express in words. Happy Birthday, and keep working on the hoops.

Love Always,

Jordan

His eyes went to the new portrait over the mantle again. His heart swam in the glow of his happy family. Through the tears, he smiled and picked up the phone. He dialed his son again, who was on his way to California. He let it ring and ring and ring, hoping Jordan would answer. If he did, he'd tell him he loved him.

53

SAVIS ECHŪS

Up on the bluffs where they first met, Jordan and Lila waited for the sun to rise over Florum valley. With legs pulled in close, she sat with her back against a tree. Jordan was directly in front of her, on his back, his head propped against her shins. His tired eyes browsed the scene's shadowed shapes. Starting with Half Dome at the far end, then taking in the cliffs and ridges, then the waterfall. And finally, the granite monolith the faintlight world knew as El Capitan—the monumental rock that harbored a monumental secret. His eyelids sank toward sleep, weighted down by his long flight from Colorado.

"You still awake up there?" asked Lila.

"Sort of…" Jordan stretched his legs and folded his hands on his chest, trying to stave off exhaustion. Bands of orange and yellow light haloed Half Dome, the sun about to make its appearance. "Keep me awake. Tell me a freelight folktale."

"We actually have those. They'll put you to sleep. How about this instead?" Lila began moving her knees side to side as though dancing the Charleston.

Jordan's smiled, his head bobbing back and forth. "That makes me want to roll away."

Lila laughed and stopped her legs. "A story, huh? How about the one about the guy who came to this very spot and met a girl. They went off on grand adventures together."

"Sounds promising," said Jordan. "What was the girl like?"

"She was pretty fine."

"And the guy?" Jordan craned his head so that he was peeking around Lila's knee.

"He got into lots of trouble. All the time."

Jordan glanced back wearing a grin. The horizon grew brighter, the changes now noticeable in the forest on the valley floor. "Do they fall in love or what?"

Lila's knees resumed the Charleston.

"You doing that on purpose?"

She laughed. "I am now."

Jordan's mind jumped to their conversation outside the courtroom. "How 'bout that Savis Echūs thing… before Plato hauled me off. I believe you owe me a poem…"

"It's in Latin—"

"Of course it is."

"—but it's been translated. Savis ēchūs means *kind echoes*. It's about parting ways."

Jordan stretched his legs. "All right, lay it on me."

"It was inspired by this very view," continued Lila. "Quite serendipitous on the timing too."

"I'll look that word up later."

"Okay, okay." Lila laughed again, the tones pleasant. Her voice settled into a graceful rhythm and Jordan listened, his eyes closed for the duration:

> *Go forth in the quiet hours,*
> *before the first rays of the sun can find you.*
> *Bare your feet and walk among the grasses.*
> *Feel the earth between your toes and let it feel you.*
> *For one day, my steps shall carry no weight,*
> *and my voice shall issue no sound.*

Be not dismayed that this day has come.
Do not surrender tears in my absence,
for I have not departed to some faraway land.
I am still here with you in Elysium.
You have but to find me.

Look for me in the places we wandered.
Feel me in the soft summer winds.
Hear me in the voices of those who knew me.
See me in the cheer of their bright eyes
and in their smiles when they speak of me.
Everything that I ever was, is now an echo,
and one day, it shall be the same for you.

We are said to be vessels of remembrance,
echoes ready to be lost on the wind.
If we are but echoes,
let us make them kind echoes.

Lila's voice ceased, yet the words continued to warm Jordan. He reached behind, grasping her fingertips as the sunrise breached the horizon. Sharp bright beams fanned across the valley, illuminating the trees. The sunlight, so radiant in its arrival, cut stars across Jordan's vision, causing him to squint.

Jordan found solace: though he'd never talk to his father again, he could hold fast to the fact they were still part of the same world.

It was something.

While Jordan worked through the reconfiguration of his young soul, he looked out over the valley, its features painted by bold morning light. Despite this grandeur, his mind fell into the troubles of the recent past, allowing a flood of concerns to rush back: the future of the freelight world; his part in it; Crispin's words, David's words; the death-order on his life; Firas's flight; the treachery of the Kyzheres and the ambitions of the Nether Dove.

He tried to push these things away. At first, they resisted him, behaving as though immortal in their sway. But they thawed, failing like icicles against the march of an indefatigable spring. Jordan released himself from the yoke of the past, recognizing only the present—his heartbeat and Lila's, moving ever onward together, beat by beat, sharing this tiny space in Elysium.

With this cadence running strong, Jordan felt something new. It arrived like a flock of birds on the horizon, moving over calm waters toward new land almost within sight. He surrendered to this feeling, letting it lift him up on its frail, determined wings. He knew they would eventually fail, and his heart would have to fall back to Elysium. But for the moment they sustained him and he knew what it meant with certainty.

He was free.

A monumental thank you to my ever-supportive wife for grinding though draft after draft, for finding the holes, for keeping my chin up. (Long live the coffee machine.)

Thank you to Esther Porter for the edit.

Thank you to S.L. Perrin, Helen B., Tracy D., the Chanhassen Author Collective, family, friends, and countless others who provided feedback in person and online.

Thank you to Cristelle Bilodeau for sketching "The Eyes" into existence for the "Have You Seen This Person?" campaign.

Jon Aspen was born and raised in a small ski town in Upper Michigan. Growing up with a busy mind and busy feet, he split his formative years between books and the outdoors. He currently resides in Minneapolis, Minnesota.

https://jonaspen.com

Jordan Wakefield and the Freelight world will return...

www.ingramcontent.com/pod-product-compliance
Lightning Source LLC
Chambersburg PA
CBHW050605170726
48283CB00001B/107